THE BOOKSELLER'S NOTEBOOKS

THE
BOOKSELLER'S
NOTEBOOKS

by Jalal Barjas

translated by Paul G. Starkey

Interlink Books

An imprint of Interlink Publishing Group, Inc.
Northampton, Massachusetts

*To all my readers who found a place for
my words in their hearts.* —JB

First published in 2023 by

Interlink Books
An imprint of Interlink Publishing Group, Inc.
46 Crosby Street
Northampton, Massachusetts 01060
www.interlinkbooks.com

Library of Congress Cataloging-in-Publication Data available
ISBN 978-1-62371-820-6

This translation was supported by a grant from the International Prize for Arabic Fiction

10 9 8 7 6 5 4 3 2 1

Printed and bound in the United States of America

PART 1

"My conscience chases me; it is the one that follows me, catches me, and judges me; and when a human falls into the grip of his conscience then there is no way out."

—Victor Hugo

1
Ibrahim

(A Voice Inside Me)

I was loaded with sadness, like a piece of sponge saturated with water, when a man of about seventy looked in my face as he paid me the money for a book he had purchased. "The more silent you are, the sadder you become," he said, before going off, leaning on his stick, and disappearing in the downtown crowd.

After all those years, here I am, remembering what that man said, and writing, in spite of my conviction that writing will not let me escape my predicament, or fill the dark hole that has molded itself to me in an obscure way, but rather cover it up, to enjoy a peace that, if it happens, will make me smile in the face of any pain, no matter how great. If only you could imagine how happy I am with this notebook, with the clear white paper and these pens, the most recent gift in my strange life, which a woman gave me. When I saw her for the first time, I felt lightning descending in the sky of my soul. I swear that when I felt it, I realized that love had a hand able to snatch to safety a drowning man who was breathing his last in the salty sea of this life. But did I live or die? That question stayed suspended in front of my eyes from that year on, as I saw how strangeness had deserted everything in this world and had come to attach itself to me, like metal particles piling up on my magnetic pole.

I am a solitary man, with no road but the one that takes me from my house in Jabal al-Jawfa to downtown, to the bookseller's kiosk I used to own. Solitary in a way I don't know whether or not you will understand, in a city so full of noise. I bothered with no one, and no one thought about me, except for a woman who lived next-door, though I didn't know where she had come from or what her background was. I never saw her leave her apartment on the second floor of an old building that faces my home. I only saw her a few times on the balcony, and all one could see of her face was two eyes behind her niqab while she was hanging out the washing. On one occasion she threw me a scrap of paper and pointed to it. I picked it up, and there were a few words written on it: "Come to my place after midnight, I want you for something important!"

But I didn't go. I wasn't curious to know what she wanted from me; nor did I have any desire for sex, though like other men I thought of the possibility that she might be inviting me to her bed. That doesn't mean I am a saint, but I am content with a procedure that I know is both negative and repulsive. As soon as my body utters its cries, I lie on my bed and conjure up a woman I have fallen in love with from a story, like the Gypsy Esmerelda the day she danced at the clowns' party in *The Hunchback of Notre Dame*. When I see her opening the door of the room, preceded by her penetrating perfume, the fires hidden inside me awaken. Then she circles around with her colored dress, and I see her smooth body and soft behind. She dances as if she is taming bees at the mouth of a rose in her soul; then she strips and lies down beside me, and we sink into a pleasure that inflames our bodies, until we start up like a goat who has received a bullet on the brow, then shuddered and surrendered to silence and nothingness.

I remembered my neighbor as I lay down that afternoon, gazing at a fine layer of paint on the room's damp, rotting ceiling. It was seesawing from the effect of the November breeze, the month that had just started, and was about to fall. I imagined the moment when it would fall and wondered what shape it would take; I wondered what the outcome would be, since things don't fall at random—an idea that changed the course of history when the apple fell on the head of Newton. The day they told me my mother had died, I heard a voice whisper in my ear, "She has fallen." I turned around but found only my father crying silently. It was the same voice that had started to whisper to me when we left our first house thirty-five years ago—in 1980, to be precise. I could have told any of my family about it, but who would have believed me? The day my mother died, I reckoned she had died with no prior warning, for I didn't know that cancer was ravaging her body. In the last few years of her life, as our situation deteriorated, she sat at a wooden table selling herbs that only the poor in the country would eat. She had deteriorated and become as dreadful as the streets and lanes, dreadful as the shape of the houses in Jabal al-Jawfa. She hid her stomachache, and whenever it got too bad she would drink boiled *mirmiyya*, and lead us to imagine it had left her, until the neighbors came and carried her away unconscious. One of them said she had vomited up a thick liquid the color of coffee. The doctor in the al-Bashir hospital said that this was a sign of stomach cancer, and she died during the first operation. My brother 'Ahid suffered a nervous attack, during which he attacked the doctors and smashed everything he laid eyes on while I stood silently beside my father, unable to shed a single tear: a harsh sorrow, inseparable from my preoccupation with the voice whispering in my ear that she had fallen.

Some years later, my brother 'Ahid disappeared after shouting in my father's face, "I won't be a copy of you!" That first day, my father believed that he would come back, when we found his telephone switched off, but after the passing of the second day, we began to feel anxious, for none of his friends knew anything about him. On the third day, my father made an announcement about his disappearance, and some days later I received a message that he had traveled to Turkey and was going to tear up his passport and move on as a Syrian refugee. The last letter I received from him before we

lost touch was full of pain and suffering. He explained how he felt
to be out of work in a quarter where no one paid any attention to
him, a quarter where he smoked hashish with some down-and-outs
until he lost the ability to dream. My father said nothing as he read
the letter but spent half the night beating his hands on his chest
until he went into his room and I heard his voice sobbing, full of
pain. After some years, my father left the house, and I found he had
left his antidepressants in the trash can. He also left me a note, in
which he had written: "I have found a job, which gives me a day off
every week. I will spend that with you." I reread what he had written
several times in astonishment, without reaching any conclusion to
justify his sudden disappearance. He came back after a week and
told me he had been in the north, where he had been appointed to
a post in the Center for Strategic Studies and that he would only be
able to come back home for a single day. A month went by, during
which he visited me four times, and then he disappeared. After
searching for him for a long while, I informed the police that he had
disappeared. Then I gave up, possibly in response to a hidden wish
for him to vanish from my sight, despite my great love for him. This
all appeared to me in my dreams, for dreams are a reflection of what
is hidden in our secret wells, which others may not know. But he
came back after seven months. I was greeted by his smell as I was
about to go through the door, then I heard his cough and hurried
to look for him. His mind was wandering, and nothing about him
moved except for the trail of smoke from his cigarette. His face
looked extremely tired, and his eyes seemed to want to talk. He said
nothing when I reproached him for his absence, except for a single
short sentence: "We'll talk later!" I went to bed early, seeking refuge
in sleep, as if I were fleeing from some nightmare. As I dozed off, I
felt the hair of his beard on my chin kissing me and I woke up. "I
heard you dreaming," he said, then left and I went back to sleep. In
the moments of hovering between sleeping and waking, I heard a

commotion in the kitchen. I got up and found that he had fastened a rope to the ceiling of the room, wrapped it around his neck, and stood on the chair. It was one of the most difficult moments of my life. I saw the short distance between the kitchen door and the chair as equaling the distance of my life from birth to that moment. All the words stuck in my throat, and everything changed to a terrifying darkness, made complete by his falling and the sight of his body suspended in the air. From that day, I have been wrapped in a silence like the one that surrounds me now on every side. Alone, like a crippled cat, I care for nothing, on a mountain with small houses and narrow streets designed by a drunken architect. The people here are tired: marginalized in the face of mountains where business towers, villas, and malls have begun to appear, and the sky at night is loud with games of fire that hint at pleasures we have not tasted. I see the world through two windows: the first supplied to me by the large number of books I have read in the Bookseller's Kiosk when it became my property after my father's death; the second the internet, at which, as the days have gone by, I have become so experienced that I can hack any account. A parallel world to the one we live in, it will one day become our only world, in which we are transformed into digital beings, driven like sheep in a pasture by the hands of owners unknown to us.

I adjusted the pillow in preparation for sleep, still staring at the ceiling. There were muddled sounds coming from outside: the voice of a woman cursing her child for not helping her with the housework and cursing the internet for stealing people even from themselves; another voice, the voice of a man humming a song telling of love, with some other voices I could hear coming from other houses, accompanied by a smell of fried garlic and the stink of trash cans. Drowsiness began to make the voices seem more distant, and the outline of the ceiling of the room gradually receded until I shut my eyes. A moment of pleasure only someone like me who has not slept for days can savor. But the moment was shattered when the layer of paint fell on my face and I started up, any desire to sleep completely gone. I got up and headed for the kitchen past the sitting room, where books had piled up—some in cardboard boxes, some secured with thick string, and others scattered here and there. A chaotic collection of books from the Bookseller's Kiosk set up by my father at the end of the sidewalk on King Hussein Street in 1981, which I had moved indoors some weeks ago after receiving a communication from Amman security telling me in no uncertain terms that I must quit the kiosk, as the sidewalks were due to be widened. They promised I would be compensated with another place one day, but I no longer had a job to live on.

I drank a glass of water, went back to bed with heavy steps, and lay down. On a small table near me was Dostoevsky's *The Idiot*. I had read this novel several times but kept going back to it, like several novels whose characters had remained in my memory so much that I started to imitate their heroes. I do not know the reason for this hobby, or how I perfected it in this strange way. I was once asked by the schoolteacher, who'd already asked most of his pupils the same question, "What's your hobby, Ibrahim, you *Sahi*?" This was an allusion to my reluctance to speak and my frequent inattention. One of the students shouted hurriedly, "He's an excellent mimic."

The schoolmaster had the same name as my father, Jadallah, but they were completely different. Jadallah was usually glowering; when he laughed, it was a sickly laugh followed by an intense anger. He once stopped me from going to the restroom when my stomach was being torn apart by gripes, so I soiled myself. From that day I harbored an intense hatred toward him. He approached me with his narrow eyes and told me, in a disturbingly hoarse voice, "Come on then, imitate me!" I didn't, because I should never be able to imitate someone I don't like, but I proceeded to imitate the Arabic teacher. I shut my eyes, imagining him in my mind and relaxing my face muscles, then twisted them until they took on the same shape as the teacher's face, and I started to speak in the same tone and walk with the same rhythm as he did when he talked with great affection about al-Mutanabbi. It is a talent for which I have no explanation; I do not know how it is that my face and movements can take on a different shape and become like those of the person I am imitating. It is something my family were disturbed about, but then, as time went by, they accepted it, despite it being very odd.

I moved, and the sound of the bed broke the harshness of the silence and the story of *The Idiot* between my hands. I had read two pages of it but found no desire to continue. I picked up my mobile phone, which had only a few numbers on it, such as that of my brother 'Ahid, though whenever I felt like phoning him I got a female voice informing me that the number was out of use. There was also the number of a café I used to call to order a coffee or sandwich when I worked in the Bookseller's Kiosk, as well as some of the kiosk customer numbers that I couldn't remember. I pressed the Facebook icon, which led me to its blue screen, where I had previously logged in under the name of Diogenes. I only occasionally posted some extracts of books I like, and I didn't spend long on it. I thought of writing about what had happened to the kiosk, when it had been demolished like a pile of thorns on a narrow lane, but as usual I gave up the idea and contented myself with reading some of what users had boldly written—which made me happy, but also made me face the pain of my fear of writing a single line complaining about what had happened. I threw the mobile to one side and lay down on the bed, looking at the ceiling and staring at the place with the coat of paint. Some new voices came to me from outside, the loudest being 'Abd al-Basit 'Abd al-Samad's voice reciting the sura of Joseph. Suddenly a movement stirred in my belly, and I saw it gradually swell until it became like the belly of a woman in her ninth month. I leaped up in terror, turning around in the room as my hands tried to touch it. I didn't understand what was happening, or why my belly was exploding. I took off my clothes and hurried toward the woman, terrified, to see whether what I was seeing was a dream or reality. How could this be happening? What was happening? I rubbed my eyes to check what I was seeing, then rushed to the tap and sprinkled my face more than once with a handful of water, but with no success. I was faced with a reality appearing in my stomach. Terrified, I ran toward the door of the house, tripped over the books, and fell, then stumbled once again. I crawled until I grabbed the door handle and heard the voice that had surprised me on the day my mother died. This time it was strong and clear: "What will you say to them if you go out, Ibrahim? I will disappear as soon as you go through this door. I told you some time ago when I found you disobeying what I said. 'I shall have to do what you haven't done yourself, you coward!'"

So terrified was I that I went out and stood in front of the door, panting, not realizing that I was naked until I noticed my neighbor on the balcony. As soon as she saw me, she put her hand over her eyes and quickly went back inside, her shoulders shaking with laughter. As I went back to the mirror and looked at my belly in astonishment, I could hear her mocking laughter. Scarcely able to breathe, and with a voice quavering despite my lack of conviction at what I was doing, I asked, "Who are you?"

"I am the one who will release you from your pains. Don't underestimate me. If I step on the earth, buildings will collapse before my footstep and dust will rise!"

"I don't understand. Who are you?"

I repeated my question several times, as a woman might who had been startled by a thief entering a house in the middle of the night, but I received no reply. I quickly dressed and ran toward the door, but the voice returned to dissuade me from going out and emphasized that anything I did would be of no use. I collected myself as best as I could, ran out into the street in a confused way, hailed a taxi that almost collided with me, then quickly jumped in. Despite my difficulty in speaking, I managed to ask the driver to take me to the al-Bashir Hospital.

"Are you OK?" asked the driver in alarm, before turning down the volume on a recorder that was playing a fast-rhythm popular song. Then, when he found that I didn't reply, he speeded up, using his horn to warn the crowd of pedestrians who were crossing the narrow road and the vehicles in front of him until we reached the hospital. As soon as I got out of the taxi, my belly swelled again, and the laughing, threatening voice returned, then disappeared as I crossed the door of the emergency room. I sat down on a bed to await my turn amid the hundreds of patients whose patience had been exhausted by the waiting time. I was shaking badly, hardly able to control the movements of my body, when I desperately approached a doctor who walked past me after examining a patient lying on a bed beside me. "What's the matter with you?" he asked quickly after putting his hand on my brow. When I didn't respond, he repeated his question.

"Tell me, what's wrong with you?"

I summoned up all my powers of speech for just a word or two word and replied, "My belly."

"Is it painful?"

"No."

Surprised and uncertain what was wrong with me, the doctor sat on the edge of the bed. He told me to calm down and held my trembling hand as I started to tell him what had happened. As he listened, his face registered surprise mingled with a smile, which appeared and disappeared from time to time. They did a test that day to see if I had been taking drugs, and when they didn't find anything of that sort, they took an X-ray of my stomach, which the doctor examined. Then he looked at me with an odd expression on his face, which scared me even more.

2
Leila

(Crossing to an Unknown Shore)

One step forward will make the orphanage fade into the background and a new life will draw closer—a life about which I know nothing, except what my imagination has constructed from conversations with brothers and sisters I lived with for eighteen years. One step toward a world with no family or relatives in it. They gave me two hundred dinars and an identity card with borrowed father's and mother's names on it, then showed me a house where girls who had been previous residents of the orphanage lived. Then they told me to leave now. Just like that!

I didn't look back, to avoid crying again, since even a place like that, where I had seen painful days, was too much for me. A hidden hand was grasping my shoulder, pulling me back toward the orphanage. I cried then, out of sadness at leaving those I loved, anger at those who had hurt me, and fear of what I was going to. As soon as I left the street where the orphanage is situated I heard a taxi hoot. I waved down the driver and it stopped and I got in. I gave him a piece of paper on which they had written the address. The driver was humming the words of a song coming from the tape recorder, smoking furiously, and looking at me in the rearview mirror.

"Are you one of the girls from the orphanage?" he asked, his eyes smiling mischievously. Then, when he didn't receive a reply, he turned his body to the right and craned his neck toward me.

"I'll take you wherever you want, then wait for you, so we can go out together!"

I secretly wondered whether something was written on my brow saying that I was an orphan with no family. Something pressed on my stomach and I felt close to vomiting. I remembered a night when the supervisor had harassed me. I had just come out of the shower and was standing in front of the mirror to dry my hair. I saw her behind me. Her breathing was getting faster, and there was the same look in her eyes I had noticed when she spied on me in bed, in the toilet, in the shower, and wherever I might be. She came closer and touched me. I hadn't noticed that she had closed the door to the small hallway attached to the shower behind her. Her words were like an unintelligible whisper as she touched my body and told me of her desires. Half a shout came out of my mouth as she stifled the other half with her strong hand. "If you struggle, I'll make the anger of the world come down on your head!" she said sharply, as she pushed me toward the shower. Then she violated me. Yes, she violated me. It is terrible how the feeling of degradation pursues you, however hard you try to forget it!

I woke to the movement of the taxi and the squeal of its tires as the driver almost knocked down a pedestrian. He told me he had lost his concentration as he thought of me. He said it with a dirty, frightening, painful expression on his face. I don't know why I didn't ask him to stop so I could take another taxi. I kept silent until he stretched his hand out and touched my thigh. When I cried out in terror and started to shake, he increased his speed and started to curse everyone and everything. He stopped in front of a building and pointed to the address that I'd asked to go to, then cursed me: "Will you sell your honor to me, you bitch?"

I got out of the taxi without looking at him, his words ringing in my ears. I could hardly climb the stairs to knock on the door. I was short of breath and everything about me was shaking. No one answered, so I stayed there until evening, my eyes fixed on the apartment door as if waiting for someone to suddenly open it.

It was a long time, full of fear and sorrow, and a feeling like one of loss.

I heard steps coming from the stairwell. It was Asma. Her face seemed tired and she looked thin. She was surprised to find me with my head on my knees, looking at her with worn-out eyes. She wept bitterly when she saw me; it was two years since she left the orphanage. We went inside to a small apartment with no furniture except some foam mattresses and a few covers and kitchen utensils. She told me she worked in a restaurant from morning to night for two hundred dinars a month. She was frustrated, tired, and devoid of even a grain of hope; she told me that if she had stayed in that house, she would have killed herself. When I asked her about Majida, she told me she would come soon, then pointed to a room with the door closed: "She's there!" It was a few minutes past nine when Majida emerged from the room, and I was shocked by what I saw.

3
Ibrahim

(An Obvious Crime)

The doctor's words were ringing in my ears as I walked back from the hospital to Jabal al-Jawfa, despite the tiredness that I had been suffering from for some days: "You need to consult a psychiatrist." My stomach wasn't swollen, and the voice hadn't returned to me, but I was suffering from anxiety, sharp as a blade with nothing standing in its way. I needed my father more than at any time previously that day. I was afraid; I just wanted to take refuge in his lap and cry—something I had never done even once in my life so far. He had never once hugged me or even touched my head, as fathers do, despite the fact that he had a lot of virtues that I could observe from a distance, like someone sitting in a dark corner watching someone else. It wasn't cruelty; it was, and still is, something obscure to me, which became worse after we moved to Amman, when I was forced to leave the village. I still remember the night of his return. It was one night during the summer of 1980 when there was a commotion in our house, a night when the only thing to be seen in my village was a faint light from a few lamps. There were no sounds to break the silence, except for the barking of frightened dogs. I was in bed with my brother 'Ahid, and my mother was telling us the story of The Ghoul and Nus Nseis for the thousandth time. We heard a knock on the door and somebody said, "Jadallah's back." My mother quickly jumped up and my father's face appeared. He had let his beard grow and his smile had deserted him. The light that we usually saw on his brow had gone out. I stood with 'Ahid

looking at my father as my mother embraced him, sunk in tears. I
will never forget my father's miserable expression as he looked at
us languidly over her shoulder. His face was tired as he embraced
us, and there was something new in it, like a crack in a mirror. He
fought back the tears as if he didn't want to show the weakness that
had come over him. As soon as those who knew of his return had
left, he started to check that the doors and windows were shut and
no one could hear him. He behaved in an oddly cautious manner;
he sat down near us, looked around him, and said in a quiet voice,
"From now on, you must trust no one."

We didn't understand what he was saying or what he was warning us about. All we had heard was that he had been imprisoned for
political reasons. He warned us about everyone and urged us not to
speak about anything in front of any of them. He was so scared and
lacking in confidence that whenever he dozed off he would wake
up terrified and turn around before going back to sleep, while my
mother would wake to see the face of a man quite unlike that of the
husband who had left her for three years. I never saw him in bed in
the morning. I stood at the door and found him sitting under the
intertwined cypress trees in front of the house, looking absently into
space without moving, more miserable than any man could bear. My
mother prepared breakfast and we sat eating in silence, stealing fur-
tive glances at him as he absentmindedly chewed his food. His eyes
were distracted, like the eyes of a child about to cry. He ate a little
and lit a cigarette with trembling hands, then drew a straight line in
the earth with another at right angles to it and said sadly, "We'll go to
Amman; there will be less to fear in the crowd."

My mother protested: "How can we leave the village? You've
been in prison and that's all there is to it!"

"I can't go back on what I've decided. And I can't give you the
choice between staying here or coming with me. We will all leave
this village."

I had to say no immediately but I couldn't. I was sorry for him and saw that something significant must have happened to him apart from his imprisonment, and I didn't understand what that might do to a man. My father was like the glass container my mother had inherited from my grandmother and which she had once found smashed without knowing who had done it. So all I did was give in to my tears. As the truck drew away, 'Ahid and I clung to the sides of the trunk, sitting on the furniture from our house as the village gradually rushed into the distance until it could no longer be seen. Then I sank my head into 'Ahid's lap and wept.

———

My neighbor looked at me strangely as I was about to enter the house, as though wondering what had made me go out naked that day and what could have come over someone like me—an amiable man living alone, seen by no one in the quarter except for a few people going out in the early morning or coming back in the evening. The night mounted an attack, pouring through the streets of Amman and then up its mountains; the rhythm of the day was extinguished and another rhythm took its place, sad and boring and painful. I sat on a sofa in the hall, clearing a space for myself among the books piled up there. My stomach was its normal shape and there was no sound coming from it. From outside, I could hear the voice of Umm Kulthoum singing "The night is long," as well as the mewing of a small cat that seemed to be close by—two sounds that did not disperse the heavy silence of the house, which was increased by the dreary ticking of the hands of the wall clock. A house with no family left in it but me, and a picture hanging on the wall showing me, 'Ahid, and our parents on a spring day in the village, smiling at the lens of a Polaroid instant camera that a relative working in Saudi Arabia had brought us. I examined the ceiling of the room. There was no coat of paint to fall again, despite the dampness and mold.

"Mold is the walls' cry for help. Look after the house, to avoid disaster!"

I was startled by the voice and stood up, but it disappeared. I wandered around the house in terror and when I had calmed down I went back to my place, wondering, "How could my father leave me like that?" I said it as if I were talking to someone on the roof, imagining that he would come down to me. How could he go to a fate that led me to this harsh wasteland? What did he hear me repeating in my sleep before he left the house? He was sitting in the hall in a patch of March sunlight that had made its way through the windowpane, with a container of coffee in front of him. As soon as he finished one cup, he would pour himself another while the smoke from his cigarette would go straight upward and then dissipate with every cough he took. He would read with great concentration about *Hayy Ibn Yaqzan*, the spectacles on the end of his nose like two windows peering out at some obscure event. I looked at him as I prepared lunch on Friday as food smells wafted from the houses of Jabal al-Jawfa. He let the book fall from his hand, relaxed his frame on the chair, and propped his neck on his intertwined hands. Then he looked at the philosophy certificate hanging on the wall and became distracted, as though the certificate was a window through which a hand had stretched and snatched him back to his past. He didn't take any antidepressants that day. He slept on the sofa after we had taken lunch, so I threw a blanket over him, lay down on my bed, and went to sleep. When I woke just before sunset, he had gone, leaving his glasses on the book.

———

I woke at six in the morning, the time I had for thirty years usually left Jabal al-Jawfa for downtown, a biological alarm clock I had not been able to destroy so I could sleep longer, like people out of work, and out of life like me. Yesterday I dreamed I was in an okra field in the village before they were swallowed up by a concrete monstrosity. I was crucified on one of the wooden scarecrows that the farmers would put up in the fields to scare off the birds, but they landed on my head—black birds, but not crows, strange creatures with curved beaks and eyes that laughed wickedly as they painlessly pecked my eyes and nose.

The morning din overtook me after I had turned on the TV and gone into the restroom, so I washed quickly and got dressed. But when I saw the books piled up in the sitting room, I remembered I had no work to go to. How could my memory let me down so dreadfully, when I had spent minutes reminding myself before going to sleep that I had become a prisoner of these walls? I collapsed on the sofa like an electric appliance that has run out of power. My stomach had swelled up again and the voice returned, but this time it returned with a rattle, as if like me it had gone to sleep tired. "You forgot that several weeks have gone by with no work. You should have skipped down to the kiosk so that they couldn't take it away and told them 'no.' If I'd been in your place, they wouldn't have dared come near me, for they wouldn't have been able to resist my blazing halo."

I ran away from him, pursued by his laughter, like a hornet pursuing someone to sting them, but how can you run away from something you are carrying inside you? I stopped and turned around; sometimes I heard him guffawing, and other times whispering threats to me. Then I ran back like a madman. There was nowhere in the house I hadn't hidden. When I became worn out, I crouched in the corner of my father's bedroom and started to listen to him:

"You should have killed the people responsible for your present predicament, beginning from the time of the village and ending with the time of the city. A lot of people hurt you, and their

voices still stick in the hair in your ears, but you were too much of
a coward to do that. So I will kill them cruelly. You don't know the
meaning of this word. You don't know that you can become cruel;
cruelty is the opposite of love, and the loving hand that gives a
warm touch can turn into a hand to cut off a head. The difficulty is
always just in the start of what we do."

I was hearing several voices: my father's voice, telling me
to go to Amman, then telling us to be cautious; the sound of
the kiosk collapsing; the sound of the hands of the wall clock
confirming my loneliness; the voice of *ustadh* Jadallah refusing
to let me go to the restroom, and the sound of my groaning with
embarrassment as I nearly soiled my clothes; the noise of women
lamenting around a shrouded corpse, the voice of my mother
selling herbs in the quarter, the voice of an official peering from
the TV screen to tell people to tighten their belts over their
stomachs. The distance between me and the strange voice had
grown smaller. I thought about what he had just said, then I
shook my head as if I were leaving an incorrect thought behind.
My head sagged between my knees until the voice disappeared,
leaving behind a ringing in my ears and a headache. I checked
my mobile and there was a message from a number not in my
directory: "I saw what happened in the kitchen." I went into
the kitchen, examined the window, and found that it faced my
neighbor's window. I realized it was impossible to see into the
kitchen except through her window, for the wall was high and the
windows of the other buildings didn't face our house. So this was
my neighbor's number, and it seemed as if she had witnessed my
father's suicide. But what did she want with this message?

The air seemed to be draining from the house, leaving behind a stifling feeling. I saw the newsreader smiling as I passed
through the lounge, the TV screen carrying a news bulletin in
which there was nothing to make anyone happy. I turned toward

the window and took several deep breaths, then sighed as if I had been tied to a peg at the bottom of the sea then suddenly escaped. Amman and the sun were just announcing the start of a new day, as they arranged the affairs of a crowd of people on their way to work amid the scream of car horns and the scraping of wheels against one another. On the horizon, flocks of pigeons hovered playfully, as if they were not going back to their nests. I saw my neighbor Anisa, a woman in her late sixties, by the side of the garbage. She was collecting loaves of bread, putting them in a bag, and then looking around her. I pulled the curtain but left a small gap I could watch through. She tore open another garbage bag and picked out some tomatoes from it, then opened another bag and selected some food. She looked around her, her face full of sorrow, and burst into tears before wiping her eyes on her sleeve. As I went out, the image of my mother appeared before my eyes, with her never-ending grief. At the corner of the building I met Anisa, who was walking slowly, feeling pains in her joints. There was a look of defeat in her eyes as she found me looking at what she was carrying.

"This is the only solution I have left, my boy," she said, taking a seat on a brick beside the wall. "The Social Development Director refused my application for a monthly salary on the basis that my son works in Amman security. I told him several debts had built up and he had only a few dinars left from his monthly salary, not enough to support me and his elderly father."

She lowered her head as she looked at some ants making their way toward a hole to deposit some of the food they had carried off. She smiled like a child catching a glimpse of something unfamiliar, then burst into tears, defeated, pained, and full of confusion. She wiped away her tears with one hand while with the other she pressed her knee. "The official agreed to give someone a salary that day, despite his not needing it."

She looked at me with bloodshot eyes. "This world is unfair, my boy. When we were younger, we didn't expect that it would be like that. I ask God Almighty for mercy!"

She dried her cheeks and got up, feeling her pain. She looked at me and pointed to the east. "His name was 'Imad al-Ahmar. I heard that he had a relative in this neighborhood. So I went to him to ask him to mediate, but it was no use."

The voice seemed to be pushing me after Anisa had left, so I sat down in her place. It came close to my face in anger: "What can you say now? Cast your memory back, bookseller, to Aristotle's idea of Justice, which he saw as an individual's relations with institutions, and to his Virtue, which he saw as the relations of individuals with each other. You will find that there is no Justice or Virtue in what has happened to this lady."

"But this is individual behavior!"

"The individual is a part of the whole."

I imagined him putting his hands on me. "One tomato may corrupt a whole boxful, Ibrahim."

I felt the air empty from my lungs and got up, wanting to go back home, but the voice came again, stopping me in my tracks: "I am no longer pushing you into any position, because I have taken up my own position."

"What do you want me to do, you evil man?"

"My good man, if Justice and Virtue are absent from an individual, then he must be uprooted, to preserve the rest of the tomatoes," he said, before disappearing.

I didn't go back home but took a service taxi downtown. A plump, large chested woman with wide, made-up eyes joined me. She gave off a penetrating smell, besides the smell of gum, which made odd noises as she chewed it with a strange persistence. I tried to keep a distance between my body and hers, but I couldn't. Her body was warm and soft, and mine was cold, with only enough flesh on it to cover my bones. I heard a whisper in my ear. I hadn't expected to be bothered by the voice as the taxi struggled through the crowds to the center of town.

"You've never been aroused by a woman in your life, even when one of them has been bursting with desire beside you like now. You're like someone living on a planet whose men have been castrated. But everything will change, I promise you."

The taxi spat me out, and I found myself standing on a sidewalk in the center of town like a drop in an ocean. A stream of humanity poured out and overflowed; posh cars passed by from time to time, some passengers viewing it just as an opportunity to see something popular and new to them to break the harshness of their routine. The newspaper seller who had been calling out the headlines ever since he came to the city passed close by me.

"Read all about the great corruption operation!" he shouted.

I bought the paper and put it under my arm, and the voice shouted, "You won't find the truth in the papers. The truth is in the street where you spent a whole lifetime but never got to know it well!"

The newspaper seller's voice disappeared in the midst of mingled voices. I stood in the middle of the sidewalk like an electricity pylon as bodies collided with me, and I swayed, sometimes to the left, sometimes to the right. From inside me came the sound of that unknown thing, bursting with anger: "It seems you enjoy playing the part of the victim!"

I could see the store that had taken the place of the Bookseller's Kiosk, and a great lump leaped to my throat. I imagined everything as it had been: books piled one on top of the other inside, while those on display outside looked like old women fortune tellers. Old books with flimsy yellow paper; new books whose paper smelled somehow virginal. The only thing I was certain of was that my passion for them would be renewed every time I opened the kiosk door, called the café, and ordered a cup of coffee. I put the newspapers in their place and then took the books out and arranged them around the outside of the kiosk. I would run my fingers over several books as if contemplating what I had read in them, then the coffee would come and I would sit to drink it and read the paper. I'd open my mobile and surf through Facebook and a few websites, then choose a book and pass through its door—a journey that nothing stopped me pursuing, except for the customers with whom I conversed briefly about the price of a book and sometimes a brief summary of it. I had learned over the years how to sum up a book in a couple of lines, which usually encouraged customers to buy the book. The kiosk gave me a modest sum to live on, but things had changed. Everything had changed—the country, the people, even the weather. The world was close to digitalizing everything, even people, to ensure that a small number of people we couldn't see could make everyone tread a single path they had mapped out for us. Only a few writers, researchers, and readers who still saw a book as a door leading to the truth now came to the kiosk. When they removed it, I read that some social media users had protested, but after a week no one talked about what had happened anymore. It was like the memory of a fish.

I walked downtown for several hours, staring into the faces, as if to look for a face that would explain to me what had happened to me since I woke up and started to ask myself questions about God, faraway stars, trees, and death. I once asked my mother, as I looked at a pomegranate tree that had suddenly dried out, "Why is there no fruit on the tree anymore?"

"It's died."

"Will they bury it like that woman?"

As I said it, I recalled the first time I had seen a dead body in the village. I was playing in the courtyard of the house when suddenly my mother rushed to a house not far from ours and I went after her. I saw women dressed in black screaming and scattering earth on their heads, and I saw a woman who had ripped her dress so that her breasts were exposed. My mother went into a room in the house and I followed her. I saw women standing around a table with a naked woman lying on it. They were sprinkling water over her. A woman noticed I was there, led me out of the room by the hand, and shut the door. I couldn't find my mother, I had lost her in the crowd of women who were lamenting and repeating words I didn't understand. Some masked men came in and carried away something wrapped in white cloth. I only found out that the woman was in it when I followed them and saw someone uncover her face and rest her on her right side. I went back home that day and sat in a corner of the dark room, crying without knowing why.

I sat on a bench in Hashemite Square, looking at the passers-by: tourists and Arabs, some hurrying, some dawdling, others quite expressionless. A thin woman in her forties, whose tiredness was apparent in her face despite her makeup, came up to me and stared at me with eyes that feigned an attractive smile. She sat down near me and took off her shoes, pressed a toe on her right foot, and moaned in a mock flirtatious way, "Ayee!" Then she tried to seduce me, saying, "Do you want to have some fun?"

I didn't immediately realize she was talking to me until she pressed her wrist on my belly. "You—can't you hear me?"

"Are you talking to me?"

Her teeth were yellow, and I could see that some of them were broken while others had been taken out.

"Yes, I'm talking to you. Would you like a bit of fun for ten dinars?"

"I don't understand."

She quickly put her shoes on, stood up, and walked away quickly, swearing at me. I opened the newspaper and flicked through the pages. I read an ad for a psychiatric clinic in Shmeisani.

I folded the paper up and thought to myself, "Shmeisani? I've lived in this city all my life and I am still a stranger there!"

———

I gave the paper to the driver and pointed to the address I wanted to go to. He was a man of almost seventy with a cigarette between his lips, the smoke from which rose through the white hairs of his moustache, coating it in yellow. He looked at the address through his thick spectacles, then looked at me as if he were looking for traces of psychiatric illness in my face. He set off, listening to a radio station that was broadcasting quick news clips: "Deaths among demonstrators in Beirut. Several dead in Baghdad following a clash between security forces and demonstrators. The Zionist entity is building a number of settlements. The government decides to raise the price of fuel."

The driver lit another cigarette, muttering in a croaky voice as he leaned over the steering wheel and looked ahead with almost excessive concentration. "It looks like we won't have enough mental hospitals if things go on as they are!"

The taxi carried on fighting the crowds until it left downtown. Suddenly, we were in a different world. Everything was different, as though two places had been forcibly stuck together. The streets were clean and the buildings were grand. Many of them were built of stone. The faces of the pedestrians were calm, the cars were posh, and the restaurants high quality, with neat glass facades. Everything was radically different from the other half of Amman; even the trees were green rather than dingy.

I got out of the taxi and looked at the newspaper to check the number of the building with the psychiatric clinic in it. I found myself on the seventh floor of the clinic, where the first thing to strike me was the sound of a flute coming from an invisible recorder. Then I noticed a girl sitting behind a counter. Her hair hung down over her shoulders and she had a nice smile on her face. What made her look even prettier was her mouth, which she painted with a light red lipstick. She welcomed me and took down my personal details. "So now you have a file, Mister Ibrahim," she said, smiling. "Please, have a seat in the waiting room until your turn comes to see the doctor."

As she said it, she pointed to some chairs. In one of them, a man was staring at the ceiling and smiling as a woman beside him held his hand. I chose a seat opposite the man, where the sound of the flute wrapped me in something approaching calm—a calm shattered by the sound of the "thing," whose coarse laugh emerged from inside me like thorns piercing my veins:

"Can't you see what a fool you looked as you walked a part of this city for the first time? Convincing yourself, because of the delusion that books had piled up in your head, that what you were feeling was not class envy? Books that had taught you how to stay poor and isolated, while life went on in a different way outside your dirty kiosk and your home on the point of collapse."

I distracted myself from him by looking at pictures and photographs hanging on the walls, but he went on with his provocative harangue: "You came here so the doctor could give you some peace from me, but his drugs won't help you at all—because you can't put the bullet back in its place after it has left the rifle."

I tried to ignore him by opening Facebook on my mobile to look for "'Imad al-Ahmar," then put the phone to one side and wondered, "What do you want with this man?" Spurred on by an obscure desire, however, I went back to his page and found that he had put a picture of himself on it in which he looked like an arrogant man, sitting at his office desk in the Directorate of Social Development with the kind of smile you see among people who are constantly demonstrating that their arrival at the seat did not come easily. His hair was combed extremely carefully; he had an international brand of watch on his wrist, a gold ring on his finger, and he wore a smart suit like a minister's. But behind his face another character was lurking. When I looked at the list of his friends and a number of comments on what he had written, he seemed like a man with a lot of female connections. There were comments that betrayed secret correspondence as well as symbols, faces, and allusions that gave away the man's passion and constant appetite for women. There were many imaginary women's names, and more than one presumed friendship with a number of officials.

The movement and noise of the voice returned, so I concentrated on the sound of the flute, trying to let it infiltrate my soul. The cool air from the conditioner wafted over me like the sunset breeze I had left behind there in my village. The voice stopped for a second, then shouted at me, "I'm not as weak as you—you should remember that!"

The voice of the girl reached me, gently informing me that it was my turn, so I knocked on the door and went in. I was expecting to be consulting an elderly doctor, but I found someone in their forties, who got up and greeted me from a distance, pointed to a chair, invited me to sit down, then linked his hands over his chest and said calmly, "Tell me, Mr. Ibrahim, what's the matter with you?"

I gave a deep sigh and looked out a window. After some hesitation, as I tried to put that laughter out of my mind, I said, "I want you to help me commit a crime of murder."

The doctor looked surprised. "Sorry?" he said, a little tensely.

"Yes, that is how I want you to help me."

He walked over to his desk, then turned toward me angrily. "Your face worried me from the start."

I looked at a piece of wood with his name carved on it: "Dr. Yusuf al-Sammak." Then I noticed his hands were shaking as he rearranged some things scattered over his desk, his extreme care reflecting the inner turmoil he was suffering from. "You would take my request seriously if you considered either Freud's views on the personal subconscious or Jung's on the collective subconscious. Both of them would lead you to reflect on what I have said."

The doctor seemed angry. He got up and paced between the table and the door for a few moments. He then came over to me and sat down, breathing erratically. "Are you presenting me with some information you've read in a newspaper or heard from someone?"

"This doubtful questioning is exactly what destroyed a close connection like that between Freud and Jung. I'm not making a presentation, I'm illuminating the way for you to know me. Didn't Jung think that the soul is made up of a number of separate parts which are also at the same time complementary?"

The doctor's face still seemed angry. "I don't believe in Jung," he said. "I'm a Freudian."

"Even Freud wouldn't deny the legitimacy of what brought me to you."

I don't know what induced me to say things like this, and I was amazed at myself when I prolonged the conversation by saying, "We're not a coastal nation, for me to speculate which city al-Sammak's family comes from."

He gritted his teeth, and his eyes became bloodshot with anger. "My dear man, have you come to make friends with me or for me to treat you? And do you think I'm a foreigner?"

"I didn't mean that. I'm someone that doesn't believe in origins or roots. But your name caught my attention, that's all."

Adopting a bogus appearance of calm, the doctor gave me a look with a faint smile in it. "OK," he said, "tell me more about what you want."

"There is a criminal inside me I want to kill, and there's no one better able than a psychiatrist to draw up a plan for such a patent crime."

The doctor was listening seriously to what I was saying, so I continued. "You must believe me, this criminal is real and not something I am imagining. I remember when he began to take shape in me. It happened the night we left the village and found ourselves after midnight in a city we didn't know anything about. We reached the house my father had rented, where my mother had hastily brought a bed for us and where everyone slept except for myself and my father. I watched him through a hole in the bedcover with his back resting on the wall, smoking one cigarette after the other until I found him crying silently for the first time. That night I was taken by surprise by something throbbing in my stomach, followed by a faint, incomprehensible whisper. As time went on, this throbbing worsened. I could find no logical explanation that would have helped me if I had complained to someone at the time, so trained myself to ignore it. The whisper and the throbbing grew worse. I could feel it worsen as I read the newspaper, looked in people's faces, or followed the news on the TV screen, until I heard his voice for the first time. It happened one day when I had a cold and had closed the kiosk and gone back home. When I arrived back in our neighborhood, I saw my mother sitting beside a platform selling herbs. Her face looked tired and she seemed a little on the thin side. When I surprised her by standing in front of her, she was pressing her hand on her stomach, so she feigned a smile that concealed a lot of pain. I asked her to go back home but she refused.

I lay on my bed with a bad stomachache and heard a sound like the groaning of a child, accompanied by a movement in my stomach. I got up from the bed in terror but in only a few minutes the sound had disappeared and the movement stopped, so I imagined I had been dreaming, despite the whisper that had followed it in previous years. But yesterday my stomach swelled up and I heard his clear, terrifying voice, hinting at crimes that might occur and blaming me for my weakness.

The doctor asked me a number of questions about my child-hood and youth, as well as my present age. He asked me how I spent my time and about my habits and way of life. He asked me a number of questions, and I gave him a number of replies. Then he got up, walked around, returned to his desk, and wrote something on a piece of paper. Then he looked at me and said, "I thought at first that you were suffering from a split personality, but now I think differently. Your condition is not incurable, as it seems you are suffering from depression. All you need to do is to change your routine. I've prescribed a number of medicines for you in this note. You need to consult me again a month from now so we can add some behavioral therapy to this medicine.

"Is that all I am suffering from?"

The doctor started to fiddle with his pen as his eyes looked around the room involuntarily.

"Yes, that's all there is to it. If a man told you he was pregnant, would you believe him?"

"Before what happened to me, I would have laughed at him, but after seeing what I have seen, I'd believe him. I've seen my belly swell up, doctor, I've seen it with my own eyes, and don't say to me 'let me see it,' because it only happens when I'm alone."

The doctor laughed and patted my shoulder, his face becoming more relaxed. "I certainly won't ask you to do that."

"Do you really not believe in principles or roots?" he asked, before I could reach the door to go out.

"No, I don't believe in them."

"Then how—since you believe in Jung—does a collective subconsciousness form?"

"Does a collective unconsciousness form simply from our coming together under the banner of a coherent social group?"

"Of course not," replied the doctor, who then asked me for my phone number.

I looked at my face in the mirrors that lined the elevator walls, and the strange, mad look on it stuck in my mind as I threw the doctor's prescription in the trash can near the door of the building. I stood on the sidewalk on Thaqafa Street looking at the cafés. Through the windows I could see men and women drinking coffee and smoking, their lips moving in a way that suggested short conversations.

I had never been inside a café before. My father thought of them as environments for collecting conversations and that there were people there who recorded everything that was said, noting down even the movements and appearance of a person sitting on his own. My father died, but I still feel him inside me like one of those genies I often wished would come out of the darkness on my way back from the kiosk and drag me into their bewitching world. I crossed the road, pushed open the door of one of the cafés, and went in. A strange, gentle song hit my ears as I stood by the door, not knowing what to do, and I heard a gentle female voice welcoming me. As I turned around, I found it belonged to a waitress wearing a short black skirt and a white shirt so tight that the buttons could not be fastened. She showed me to a table and handed me a booklet showing the drinks and light snacks served in the café. I would have liked to try one, but the names were strange to me, and I made do with a cup of coffee. I looked around shyly, examining the café; a man was reading a book and sipping from a glass; two girls were exchanging whispers and gossip and watching something on a small computer screen; a girl and a boy were exchanging whispers. I watched them like a hungry child gazing at food through a restaurant window, then turned my face away when my eyes caught the girl's eyes. The coffee the waitress put on the table had a piece of chocolate in it and tasted like something I had never heard before. How could I have believed my father was afraid of everything so much that

I became a copy of him—a frightened, unstable copy that saw everything as suspicious, and so lost myself?

I went back to Facebook, to 'Imad al-Ahmad's page. What he had written there consisted of quotes from other pages, and comments of his friends containing a lot of flattery pandering to his vanity. His pictures suggested a person striving for something. I saw a video clip of someone at a wedding party shouting "Greetings, 'Imad Bey" through a microphone. Then the camera moved to show his face, which looked pleased with what had been said. 'Imad al-Ahmar appeared on a number of important people's pages, to flatter them with weak and obvious comments. It seemed he was the sort of individual who is corrupt to the tenth degree. There was an invitation card to dinner in his house, including his website. I clicked on the link. So you live in the suburb of al-Rashid, 'Imad! I flicked through most of his pictures, one of which indicated he used to live in Jabal al-Jawfa. So you moved to a new house! How does that happen to an employee whose monthly salary cannot be more than 500 dinars? In a few years, all his circumstances had changed: smart clothes, a new car, and a new house where he lived alone. His information column made clear that he was divorced. I put the phone to one side and looked around again. Suddenly, I heard a sound like the abrupt movement of a fetus in its ninth month: "'Imad al-Ahmad is uglier than you think, you poor man! Your efforts to understand what is around you are pathetic."

Having said that, he started talking in a rapid, irritating way, as if he wanted to hem me in. My limbs went stiff and I started to sweat. My mouth went dry, and I grabbed for the glass of water but it slipped from my hand and splintered loudly enough for the café customers to hear. I left, not knowing that I was about to embark on an act of madness.

4
Ibrahim

(Office Number 4)

The walls of the damp staircase leading up to the police station on the second floor were gray and the paintwork was peeling. I was assailed by such a strange smell that I could scarcely walk forward, and as I hesitated I thought of going back. Immediately in front of the metal doorway, which was painted black, I stopped to put my hand on the top of my abdomen, feeling suddenly sick and possibly about to vomit. But all that disappeared when I thought harder about what I was coming for and the possibilities of escape. I went through the door and found myself in a hall with several people in it: one being led away by a policeman, some carrying papers, and others sitting with the marks of a long wait on some faces and expressions I didn't understand on others. There was a large ceiling fan rotating lazily, with dead flies stuck to it. I stepped toward the policeman who was sitting at a reception table and in a confused and quavering voice told him that I wished to make a complaint.

"What sort of complaint?" he asked, scrutinizing my face carefully, then repeated his question when I said nothing. "Are you making a complaint against someone for an assault, for example?"

"A terrorist plot."

The policeman suddenly leaped up and stared at me, his eyes turning in their sockets as my tongue attempted unsuccessfully to dampen my dry lips. I heard him repeat the same words: "A terrorist plot?"

He asked for my ID and hastily wrote down my details, then had a quick telephone conversation before pointing to an office whose door was labeled No. 4.

"Get in there quickly."

I wished he had told me to leave, for any reason he thought fit, but that didn't happen. I walked quickly toward the office door, which had been left open. I saw two desks with computers on them. Behind one sat an officer with two stars on his shoulders, looking at the computer screen, while behind the other sat an officer who was writing carefully on a piece of paper. I knocked on the door hesitantly but no one replied. I tried again to gain their attention, and this time the officer looked at me after taking his eyes from the computer screen. He scrutinized me carefully. "Come in," he said in a serious voice. "What can I do for you?"

"I have a complaint," I replied, trying to suppress the tremor in my voice.

The officer went back to looking at the computer screen. "An assault?" he asked.

"No, sir."

He took off his glasses and looked at my face, then took a cigarette and lit it. A plume of smoke rolled up into the air.

"What then?"

"I want to report a serious criminal, who may perhaps be harming the country."

The officer jumped up as though a fire had started under him, walked toward the door and shut it, pretending to be calm while the other policeman looked at me in shock. The officer told me to sit down, sat down himself in front of me, and then said in a whisper, with the concentration of someone trying to get a child to tell tales about someone, "OK, so tell me."

I looked around for a suitable sentence to begin with. "I will tell you, but I want you to listen, however long I go on for."

The officer bit his lip and said "OK," as if trying to overcome his impatience.

I again tried to prepare the ground for what I had to say, my hands flapping in the air as if describing something. "Sir, it's natural that you should find what I'm going to say strange, and I don't blame you if you laugh at what you hear from me, but it is the truth, the real truth, sir. My name is Ibrahim Jadallah, nicknamed Ibrahim the bookseller. I have come to tell you that I am extremely disturbed by the actions of an unknown person. He may be doing something to harm the country and its citizens with his evil intentions. That is why I have come here. He has an attitude that has frightened me in more than one situation."

The officer's face showed signs of impatience. "Where is this unknown person?" he asked.

After a moment of silence interrupted by the voices of the crowd in the reception hall and what sounded like the orders of a policeman forcing a prisoner to walk, I said, "Inside me."

When the officer smacked his lips in surprise, I reminded him of my request and he reluctantly allowed me to continue.

"I am a simple man. I used to work in a simple bookseller's kiosk on the sidewalk at the start of King Hussein Street. Every day, people would stand in front of the books and magazines I had on display. A few of them would make a purchase. I would only say a few words to anyone, and I hardly made enough from my job for rent and food. I had no pleasure in life except for reading. I had no family, relatives, or friends in this city. But this pleasure finished when I was informed I had to leave the site because, according to them, the road was going to be diverted. I went back to them more than once in an attempt to keep the kiosk but I failed. As soon as I had left the place, I found a larger store built in a more modern style occupying the same site. But it wasn't a bookstore—it was for selling mobile phones. I was told that it belonged to an influential man whose photo I would often see in the papers. On that day, sir, this criminal went mad. It was as though I was pregnant, like a woman with a fetus moving in her belly, pregnant with a dangerous creature that moved at moments when he was angry with her."

The officer interrupted me with a laugh. "And what does this fetus say to you?"

"Sir, he's bigger than a fetus. He's the size of a wild beast, with the same temperament."

"What does he say to you?" he asked angrily.

"He urges me to kill people. He even asks me to mutilate the corpses."

"Like the influential person, of course."

"Yes, sir, like the influential person. But faced with my refusal to do what he said, he started to threaten me that he would one day do what I hadn't done."

I stopped speaking for a little as the officer and policeman stared at me.

"Believe me, sir, what I'm telling you is not a delusion, I really can feel him moving at certain moments. At the station door, he told me they wouldn't believe me. I wish I had taken a picture of my belly so as not to appear a liar in your eyes. He is a dangerous criminal, who has an amazing ability to draw up plans for the crimes he is harboring, to such an extent that I have no appetite for sleep except when he himself sleeps, at erratic times. Save me from this criminal."

The officer and policeman laughed to themselves, the silence only being broken by guffaws escaping their lips from time to time. I raised my eyes and looked at them. The officer was shaking one leg, which he had placed nervously on top of the other and looking carefully into my eyes. "That's it. I've wasted enough time with you and your stories. I thought you might have something important to tell us. Now get up and leave, and don't come back here again.

If everyone listened to the voices in their head what he was thinking about like you do, the police stations would be full of people
complaining."

I was almost back down the station stairs when I saw the
shape of my belly change and I heard the same old voice.

"Didn't I tell you they wouldn't believe you? Even if you went
back I would hide, and this time perhaps they would arrest you."

I started to stumble and had to stop myself so as not to fall.

"Even if no one believes me, I will not surrender to you."

"You believe in me, but your fear drives you to jump away from
the truth. Some people are proud of the way they hover, because
they haven't been able to stand in the face of what is going on in
front of them."

His voice continued to pursue me until I disappeared in the
crowd, his words still ringing in my ears.

"A moment will come when you will listen to me and throw
away all your rotten defenses."

5
Ibrahim

(A Final Attempt)

I got out of the bus at the top of the street leading to my house. As I passed by the mosque, the imam was checking the water taps and closing the doors. I said hello to him and went on my way. But then I went back to him. He gave me a smile with the happy look that was typical of the local residents, then shook my hand and sat down on the edge of a low wall by the mosque door and scrutinized my face with wide eyes.

"I can see you're not yourself, my son."

I sat down beside him, head in hands, and told him everything. The sheikh was astonished by what I said, but he gave an even happier smile.

"And what does this creature lurking inside you intend to do?"

"Lots of things. He whispered to me that I should find a way to put on an explosive belt and blow myself up somewhere where they pay no attention to the poor."

The sheikh's smile gave way to a deep sorrow. "No religion will allow you to do what you are thinking of, my child," he said.

"No, it is he who is thinking of it, not me."

The sheikh recited a number of verses from the Qur'an that day before heading off down the street leaning on his stick and muttering. I followed him until I reached my house. As I threw myself on the sofa, the sound of the hands of the clock hanging on the wall near the picture of the family reached my ears. When we first moved into this house, I was surprised that my father dictated the conditions of our new life to us: no contact with the neighbors, no conversations in school that would reveal anything about his personality or way of thinking—even the volume of the TV had to be kept low, especially during news broadcasts. 'Ahid paid no attention to what he said, and my mother only listened to him out of politeness. She made friends with the neighbors as if she hadn't heard him at all. He knew how seriously I took his words, but I don't know whether it was really conviction or obedience imposed by my love for him. Before his arrest, he was known in the village as "al-Khatib Jadallah" because he was the first teacher there. He ran a school composed of two rooms and attended by ten boys and five girls. People used to turn to him in their disputes and consult him on managing their affairs or on any matter that they didn't understand. He visited every house without exception, and sometimes people even consulted him on matters involving illness and medicine. But after his arrest, everything changed.

———

The clock was showing twelve midnight when I woke up drenched in sweat, foaming at the mouth from a terrifying dream. It was one of those nightmares that had begun to pursue me since I had become a total recluse following the death of my father. The ticking of the hands of the wall clock turned into hammers hitting my head; the sound of the drops of water from the tap became the noise of constant explosions, and the silence sounded like the roar of bombs. I opened the door and stood outside the house. My breathing was tight. I continued to gulp at the air until most of the terror had gone. At my neighbor's window opposite from me, someone was watching me from behind the curtain. What did this woman want from me? What was her object in following me and her strange notes? I ignored it and went back inside. The nightmare was still affecting me, like a thorn that had stuck to the clothes of someone who had lost his way and gone through a field of parched grass. What road was I supposed to take to escape from all this blackness surrounding me?

I picked up a notebook in which I usually wrote down my nightmares and started to write down what I had seen. I knew that I was doing the same thing a doctor does when extracting a bullet from the body of a dead man. I was persuading myself to forget, though I was sure some of what had happened to us would become like seed time for harmful plants. All that happens in the moment of crossing is that we stop the water from reaching them. But what can someone like me do, whose inner winters are many and do not wait for the seasons?

The clamor in the quarter gradually receded, and I could hear from outside only the sounds of car horns coming from downtown. There was a new message from the same unknown number: "Yes, I saw what happened in the kitchen." The language of the message was both a confirmation and a prophecy of my inner questionings. I quickly got up and looked from the kitchen window to my neighbor's window, which was lit up. I could see her outline looking toward me from behind the curtain. What did she want? The question made me feel even more tired. I went to the bathroom and relaxed my body under the hot water tap in the hope of feeling more relaxed, which would help me to sleep. I looked at my body in the bathroom mirror as if seeing it for the first time. It was a taut body, with no flabby belly on it, and no lack of proportion in the ratio of height to breadth. A clear skin, unmarred by any hint of blemishes or signs of old wounds. I checked it over, starting with my hair and ending with the soles of my feet, as if I were a teenager who had only just become acquainted with the ins and outs of their body. I went closer to the mirror to look at my face. White streaks had started to appear in my black hair and wrinkles could be seen below my eyes. I touched them as well, as though I had just woken from a useless life—a life that seemed like a nightmare I had lived as an unchanging reality. I poured a glass of milk and took it with me to my bed. Out of loneliness, pain emerges, like plumes of smoke rising in a summer morning's sky. Creatures sleeping inside us peep out from their bottles, like the voice of that unknown creature that shattered my need for sleep and reminded me of the several things that lay behind his anger. Roused by his voice, I leaped from the bed to the kitchen and the restroom. I closed my ears, but there was no escaping his voice, which drowned out my own. "What do you want me to do?" I asked, like someone surrendering to his executioner.

"This question of yours is a real step toward the beginning of the road." I heard his breathing become stronger as he became happier. "It's impossible for two partners to succeed in their aims without trust."

"I won't do it, you have your road and I have another."

"Don't forget that the two roads lead to the same place."

I walked nervously to the mirror and looked at my reflection. "I said I wouldn't do it."

"Idiot, you only see what you want to see. Do you believe the world moves on as you have seen it in real life, on the TV screen, and in your cursed books? Life is more complicated than you imagine: blood is shed; there is a lot of deception and liquidation in numerous forms that only a few know about. You, and people like you, see politicians smiling behind the microphones, spouting gross lies about the homeland and collective security, and you believe them."

I got up and walked about the room while his voice rang out, producing a dreadful din. "I want to 'hang the bells' through you. If we do this, the bells will begin to multiply until they fill the space."*

---

*   The reference to the bells relates to an initiative to take action. It comes from an Arab saying (Who will hang the bell?), which is normally used during times of

My hands began to beat the air in anger. "What bells are you talking about, you wretched man?" I thought he had reached the limits of his anger, as his voice sometimes rattled and at other times grew clearer.

"The world is now in a state of extreme confusion. Those people who previously called for justice failed, because they were more paternalistic than was necessary. Those who shaped the world in a free fashion created new playboys, who started wars and appropriated everything. And people are dying between the two halves of a global millstone."

I thought he had left when he fell silent, but he started to talk again with a calm charged with a lot of anger. "You are one of those people who are ground by the millstone, a millstone decorated in an attractive color but terrifying in its cruelty."

As he moved away from my belly and settled in my head, his voice became clearer. "You have to confess that you hated your father despite your great love for him. You hated his fatherhood, and you hate those who secretly move people on strings and shout lots of slogans about freedom and promised opportunities. We will hang the bell between the two; it's the bell of counter-cruelty."

As he started dictating his plans to me, I could hardly listen to him. I tried to escape everywhere in the apartment, but he was like a tick clinging to my body. He lit a fire in me, planting knives that demolished my bed. I could find no solution but to plant a knife in my belly and be free of him.

---

troubles. So when the voice that speaks to Ibrahim tells him "I want to hang the bell through you," he's saying "I want to effect change through you." The voice is urging Ibrahim to protest injustice in all its forms. He later continues by saying to Ibrahim "If we do this then the bells will multiply to fill the entire space," meaning once you start the protest, the number of protesters will increase and become a large force. Ibrahim responds by saying "What bells are you talking about you idiot?" meaning that the idea of initiating a protest that would lead to real change is ludicrous.

"The knife won't help you at all."

I ran to the kitchen and searched for the knife in confusion. As I heard him threatening to move to my head, I was seized with anger. I tried to think of a way to smash my head, so I climbed the staircase, panting and trying not to listen to him. But his voice was too loud for me to ignore, and it came with a provocative calm.

"If you do it, I will move to a place in your body that won't come in contact with the ground directly."

"I will commit suicide by drowning."

I walked down the stairs without hearing his voice and sat on the sofa trying to quench my anger. "It will be a beautiful death, especially if you do it in the sea. You've spent your life looking at pictures of water on the pages of newspapers but haven't once escaped from your isolation and gone to it. It will be an easy suicide, you coward, especially as you can't swim."

He was silent for a moment, then gave a mocking laugh and said, "But remember that the only people to drown in the Dead Sea are those who don't know the secret of the water."

A Nightmare

Lying on my bed, pretending to sleep, I saw him out of the corner of my eye, walking lazily to the kitchen. My heart raced and the adrenaline spread greedily through my body. I was surprised by a feeling of pleasure mingled with anger as wild shouts surrounded me. Millions of images sped through my brain. I clearly heard my first, painful shouts when I was born. I crept out of bed, the veins on my hands prominent as they seized the knife. There were cries, pleas for help, angry words, sobs, laughter, and shouting, all following me. I stood at the kitchen door and saw him standing on the chair, one end of the rope fastened to the ceiling, the other wrapped around his neck. He was breathing calmly. Then he threw a searching glance into the void as he prepared to throw his body from on the chair. The knife fell from my hand as I moved toward him. He noticed me and thought of going back. My vision became confused and I heard a mix of voices. I took a step back, then a step forward, overcome by tears, sobbing wildly as I kicked the chair. My father fell, and I too fell in a faint.

PART 2

"If a knife is too sharp, it will wound its scabbard."
—African proverb

1
Leila

(Running Away)

Nothing changed. I thought it would be better after my first step outside the orphanage, but I found myself a prisoner with two frustrated girls: Asma, worn out by long working hours and exhausted by her struggles with a boss who thought she should open her legs at the first lustful look on his part, since she had come from the orphanage and had no family; and Majida, who had quickly submitted and turned into a whore who spent her nights in nightclubs. But nothing changed. I just stood at the window, looking fearfully at the street, exactly as I used to do in the orphanage whose painful memories still pursued me even while I was asleep. Asma went to work in the morning, and when I woke up Majida would have gone to sleep drunk, smelling of something that I later discovered was wine. She collapsed from exhaustion more than would seem possible for a girl in her twenties like her to bear—so tired out that she prattled in her sleep, gritted her teeth, and from time to time emitted a groan that often prompted me to go into her room and wake her up—at which point she would give me the look of someone who understands nothing and go back to sleep. God, what a miserable, tormented girl she was! When she woke up she would act with a feigned nonchalance as though nothing bothered her. She would immediately become distracted, as the expression on her face changed to the sad face of a girl who could not last long in a world we hadn't known was like this.

Two weeks after I had come to that house, Asma was defeated by the persistent harassment of the restaurant owner. When she refused him, the man made a lot of the fact that she was illegitimate. "You have to reward me for accepting you to work with me," he told her. He cursed her a lot before dismissing her from her job. She came back crying that day. I was cleaning the house, getting ready to prepare lunch, which was my contribution to living free with two girls who could barely cover the rent of the house and cost of food. Her face was almost black and her mouth was dry when she came in and sat down silently, not responding to my questions as to why she was in such a state. I realized that something must have happened to her, so I left her to calm down. As I started to forget about her, her voice came to me from inside. She had burst into tears. I hurried toward her and embraced her as she continued to cry until her eyes reddened and she lost her energy, so overcome with sadness that I thought she might throw herself from the balcony. I had seen her turn toward it more than once. It was just past one o'clock in the afternoon when she threw herself on her mattress and went to sleep until nine in the evening. She stayed awake before coming in to shower, and I heard her singing a song that sounded like crying.

Majida was getting ready to go out and sat smoking and watching TV. Asma emerged from the restroom and went into Majida's room. She shut herself in for a few minutes before coming out wearing one of Majida's dresses, which exposed half of her breasts and most of her thighs. She walked toward her, her high-heeled shoes clicking, with a piece of gum in her mouth that she pretended to chew. Taking a cigarette from Majida's pack, she lit it and blew out the smoke mock-flirtatiously. "From tonight on," she said, "I'm going with you, Majida!"

From that day, Asma worked as a prostitute, returning just before dawn and sleeping until evening. Two days later, she told

me, "I'll give you a wage for cleaning the house and buying what we
need then preparing the food." What could I do but accept what
two girls who longed to leave the orphanage had become? So I
became a servant, going out to the market twice a week and coming
back quickly, spending most of my time watching TV. I was fairly
content, but things changed. Asma and Majida stopped going to
the nightclub and instead started to receive men at home. They
would go into the room, spend half an hour there and then leave.
At first I didn't ask about what was going on; perhaps this was an
attempt on my part to keep a place to shelter me. One day, Asma
came and sat beside me, then bowed her head into my lap and cried
bitterly for some minutes before falling silent. "What do these men
who go inside do?" I asked her.

She raised her head and looked at me angrily. "Are you stupid?"
she cried, bursting into tears again.

I knew that two innocent girls had become prostitutes, for I
could hear the men bellowing inside when they were drunk, and I
would feel a pain in my stomach and a need to vomit, with a violent
hatred of my body. One day, three men came. One took Asma inside,
another took Majida into the kitchen, and the third looked at me,
walked toward me, and took off his clothes. He had fierce eyes and
a walk like one of those strange beings I had seen in the sci-fi films.
All possibilities of escape disappeared during those harsh moments,
as I heard Asma and Majida's fake moans of pleasure mingled with
the filthy words of those lecherous men. I screamed for Asma as he
came closer, but no one answered me. I don't know how I was able
to leap up at that moment, open the door, and flee as I felt his hands
grazing my back. I ran terrified into the street, and when I finally
turned around there was nobody behind me.

I was afraid of every man who looked at me, and I walked
unsteadily like I was drunk. I was constantly afraid that someone
might attack me, even while I was asleep in Asma and Majida's

house; they didn't resist for long. We are all the victims of desire. I walked on, not knowing where I was going. The important thing for me was to escape. But I began to experience a new fear in my heart: my body was a sign that could direct many men who are like that man. I stopped in front of a ladies' hairdresser looking at my appearance in the window. I checked my pockets but I only had fifty dinars left from the money they'd given me. The only thing I could do was to disguise my feminine features, so I went in and asked for a man's haircut, then went out and bought some men's clothes, which I put on and walked about the streets. I had to disguise myself from the fear inside me. One of the hardest things for a woman is to take on a man's way of walking and his movements, even the way he looks at his surroundings. She does that to save her femininity from destruction. As soon as I saw a man coming toward me as I walked along the sidewalk, I would move out of his way. I saw people looking at me and said to myself, "I obviously haven't perfected the part yet!" I stopped walking for a bit and started to look at how men walked and comported themselves. Then I went on, repeating insistently, "You are a man, you are a man!" I had to do that so as not to feel the pain that had come over me when the supervisor assaulted me, when the taxi driver harassed me, and when that man tried to throw himself on me in Asma and Majida's house.

I didn't think where I was going at the time. I said to myself that I would just carry on walking, but I was terrified when I saw the sun disappear behind the buildings as the city prepared itself for the night. I didn't know what lay in store for me. How could a young, pretty girl like me go on with her heart full of fear of men and of the world, on her first night outside of the walls that hide her?

When I looked at the windows of the houses, I would construct a daydream in which I saw my mother waving at me; I would look cautiously in some men's faces in the hope that one of them

might become fond of me and embrace me, and banish all that fear
from me. I remember a phrase of a poet I had read in a magazine:
"How hard it is for someone to be like a branch stripped from a
tree! How hard for those branches to live when they are torn from
their mothers by force. Some die, some become strong trees, hiding
their orphan state within them as they weep!"

I was lost and on the point of returning to the orphanage.
But how could I do that when I was no longer a child for it to
take in? I remembered that Asma had told me about a deserted
house that sheltered a number of people who had been residents
of the orphanage. It was near a street that led off the Third Circle
to downtown. Some people there were unemployed, some had
become beggars, and some had become thieves. Asma told me that
night that they had been punished by everyone because they were
illegitimate. As I tried to mimic the voice of a man, I asked a youth
who was standing under a bus shelter if there was a bus that would
take me there. He gave me an odd look and replied, "A bus will be
here in a few minutes."

It was only a few minutes before the bus arrived. I got on, sat
down, and looked straight ahead without turning around. After a
few minutes I glanced around quickly. The passengers had silent
faces: some were tired, some were fiddling with their phones, and
some were gossiping to one another. Though I couldn't see anyone
smiling, I thought life outside the orphanage must be nice, though
frightening for someone like me who didn't know anyone and was
looking for people who were forgotten like she was. I remembered
what Majida had said: "They threw us out into a world where if
you don't have a family or tribe, you remain an outcast and have no
value whatever you do."

The driver announced that the bus was approaching the Third
Circle and I got off. As I landed on the street, I said to myself, "Leila,
you must remember that you are wearing a young man's clothes.

You need to walk carefully and behave like a man!" I examined a long wall that ran along the street. There was a small opening in it that I just managed to squeeze through. It led me down a winding alley full of dirt and excrement and smelling of shit and urine to an old house. I stood at the door and knocked but no one replied. I was about to go back when I saw the worn metal door, but I saw someone looking through an opening, so I hurried toward the door and shouted, "I'm Leila!"

The person continued to look at me with surprise until the door opened and a girl's tired face looked out. I looked at her and I realized it was Salam. How was all this happening to us? Salam was among the residents of the orphanage most eager to leave it. She would describe the life outside as if she had lived there for many years. She built all her stories on fleeting scenes she had witnessed one time when she went to the hospital, and a few times they took us on an excursion outside Amman.

Salam embraced me at the door and then totally collapsed to the ground, sobbing as she cursed people and governments and her parents, who had been the cause of all this. She grabbed my foot and started to shout, "If I ever find out who my parents are, I will kill them. I swear I will!"

I followed Salam inside and was assailed by smells of damp and decay as well as other horrid odors. The house was dark and near collapse. We stayed there until evening, when most of the other residents arrived: Nur, Ra'id, Adi. They were worn out and miserable. That didn't happen to us in the orphanage. They clustered around some peppers and ate before each of them found a corner and went to sleep.

"How come all we had left was this deserted house?" I thought to myself. They had all gone to sleep, despite the cold. Some slept on worn-out mattresses and some slept on the floor, with tattered blankets over their bodies. I spent two days in that house with no food, and all I had left was twenty dinars at the most. I had to find a way to work, so I bought some paper handkerchiefs to sell to car drivers, not realizing that a strange surprise awaited me that would change everything.

2
Ibrahim

(A Watery Grave)

I didn't sleep last night. Despite that, I felt extraordinarily awake as soon as the bus set out from Amman to Aqaba. With a jelly-like consciousness, neither sad nor joyful, a man going to throw himself into the arms of death, I wondered whether it could be so easy. The road to Paradise was Paradise and on the road to death it would be death, but what would happen to me? It looked as if I was an employee going to his work to offer his resignation and get rid of this stress. I got up and walked up to the driver, who looked at me in the mirror.

"Do you want something?"

"I want to get off the bus."

Before he could carry out my request, though, I went back to my seat, having indicated to him that I was canceling my request. I leaned my head back on the seat rest and shut my eyes. I felt almost sleepy, as if I was recalling the barking of a dog in the jet-black village night. I saw a pale moon with black clouds passing in front of it, and I heard in the whistling of the wind a woman's cry for help that no one answered. I saw myself as two people, one of them a feeble shadow climbing up the body of a giant until it reached his mouth, then climbing up ropes until he reached a room with people in it, and countries and a sky in which there were many secrets: wishes, tumbles, crying and laughter, and a box from which I was assailed by a mixture of songs and crying as soon as I opened it. I woke and looked around me. The man sitting beside me was staring at me. "You were moaning; it seems you were dreaming."

I didn't say anything but simply listened to the voice that came in a whisper with a terrible echo as if coming from an empty well.

My phone rang. It was a text message from Dr. Yusuf al-Sammak.

"Dear Ibrahim, your talking about roots prompted me to write this message. I am thinking aloud with you: Can I live without belonging to a big family at a time when everyone is hurrying to groups like this? I know that there is an acquired belonging, and a natural belonging, and another that is formed of some sort of group, and I know that that can become a sort of joke so long as we belong to our minds. I studied in the oldest university in America and have enough money to last me until old age but I feel that I lack something. In America, people make their own way after eighteen. All that concerns them is to be free in everything. They respect only the law, but free themselves from their mothers and fathers and live their lives completely unfettered. All the years I spent there, I searched within myself for the secret of my longing to belong, which no one I live with would confess to. Thinking about something like that was like plunging into a whirlpool. No one I had read would acknowledge it: not Jung, Freud, Adler, Alport, not most of those who have dug deep into the human soul and its strange moods. Yes, that is what I longed for, but unlike you I felt—even when I am among people—that I am hollow inside. During my last year of study I decided to consult a psychologist and tell him what was disturbing me. But after knocking on his clinic door, I retreated, not because I was an outstanding psychology student, but because part of our Arab life would be impossible for him to understand."

What would induce a doctor to talk to his patient so frankly? Had I provoked him? It was something that puzzled me, but I couldn't find the energy to reply to his message. There was no longer any reason to do anything, for I had taken a decision that would cancel everything. Was I going to end an inner torment that I had been treating for years with books—I think—or was I going to support the legacy of those books? It was more trivial than a coward would suppose. All right, I would throw my body into the water; a few moments of pain, after which the white would disappear, to be followed by eternal rest. I imagine it as an endless orgasm. The sea salt and the fish would eat the wrapping of the soul, which would have escaped from its cage a few moments after plunging into the depths, and that would be the end.

On my Facebook page, I wrote, "When the surface of the paint falls away, I will know the truth," but I decided not to post it and contented myself with flicking through the pages. 'Imad al-Ahmar had posted a picture on his page, above which he had written, "God save this country!" I turned my phone off and started to look out the bus window as if I were a tourist visiting the country. I was leaving Amman for the first time since I had taken up residence there and making my way along the long road to Aqaba. I had often seen ads for it in the pages of newspapers and magazines and on TV screens, but I had never been there. My father was afraid to let me out of his sight. He had a strange fear and nervousness that I might be exposed to some incident that would take me away from him. How did my father get like this? What hole had he fallen into, to return stripped of how he had been at a time full of dreams? A month after we had settled in Amman, he went as a teacher to a school in Jabal al-Jawfa, where 'Ahid and I were pupils. He spent the whole time in silence, speaking only to the pupils. In the breaks between classes, he would sit on the edge of a wall in the schoolyard, staring into space. After the end of work, he would go to the kiosk to resume his silence. He went on like this until he retired a year before I left the school. He had organized himself to set up a book kiosk, which he called The Bookseller's Kiosk. The customers got used to his silence;

he would only speak about the price of books or their availability. He would take me along during school holidays and teach me about the books and their prices until he was certain I had gained enough experience. I passed the Secondary School Certificate with a weak grade, so he ordered me to work with him; yes, he ordered me.

I didn't disobey him in anything; in fact, I obeyed him in everything, great and small. But he wasn't content with my blind obedience. I could see the sorrow in his eyes as I carried out everything he said, as if he were remembering the years he had spent as a courageous rebel, doing whatever he liked. As I grew up and understood what it meant for a child to obey their father, I realized that my brother 'Ahid, despite his great love for my father, was not persuaded by his fears and unease at everything around him. He wasn't persuaded that so many people were informers, or that everything was so frightening.

My father never stopped preaching caution about everything that disturbed him. I remember the first time he started to dictate to me openly what I needed to do as we sat near the heater one winter's night. He had finished reading a book about the killing of the Iraqi communists in 1978 in Saddam's era. He was telling me about them when he suddenly realized that he should not be embarking on a conversation like that. He folded over a page of the book and sighed, then said in a tone that combined sorrow with an order, "Ibrahim, my son, you must learn to keep silent. How do you know, for example, that the grocer isn't passing information to the security services? Grocers gossip a lot; they get information from youths your age. Haven't you noticed how the laundry workers spy on the houses, picking up every word, and recording them in their daily reports? Even old women are to be feared; they indulge in casual conversations when they are sitting: "My son said so and so; my wife met someone; my brother went to that place." Some of them relay the conversations after their sessions have broken up. How do you know that someone's son or someone else isn't an informer or a member of the security services? Don't trust anyone, not your friend, not your colleague, not your brother, not your girlfriend—even avoid the whores in the streets!'

"I'm not interested in politics and I don't speak about it!"

He came closer and stared at me. "Everything in this world is politics, and everything is loaded against you! And you will reap the consequences without being aware of it!"

As the days passed, I got used to my father's way of thinking and turned into a recluse. He warned me about the kiosk customers and asked me not to talk to any of them about any book or its contents if he was away, and not to enter into any side discussions. He even warned me not to read certain books, whether they be fiction or books on politics, philosophy, or religion. He thought that if I had to read them I should do it at home. This was the one area in which I disobeyed my father. I read secretly and found a world that was different from the one I lived in, like a hand sweeping ash from a mirror. After his death, I started to read openly, which left me feeling like a blind man who has grown used to being led and shown the way by someone who has then disappeared.

I saw a sign pointing to Madaba. As we approached the bridge leading there, I was on the point of changing direction, leaving the bus and boarding another to go to our first house in the village. But I heard the mysterious voice laughing at me and threatening me. The game was up, and I was faced with just one choice, namely suicide, to avoid any undesirable consequences. The bus was heading south through yellow desert areas that stretched to the horizon. The further south we traveled, the hotter it became, even though winter was approaching. The wind was shaking desert plants and dry thorns there on the yellow ground, and the paper and plastic bags hanging on them made it feel even wilder. I leaned my head on the seat back looking at the village houses, which seemed to be using the road to protect themselves from the harshness of nature. Small houses in dark colors that in summer suffered the unrelenting heat of the sun, while in winter the cold dripped, showing no mercy to anything.

I was thinking about the sort of death I would embark on. "Since I cannot swim, I will inquire about the deepest place along the shore and throw myself into it. No, I will look for myself, to avoid arousing any suspicions about my question that would make my mission fail. I will choose the best time, early morning, when there will be no one on the beach who could come to rescue me. If that happened, I'd be grabbed by the unknown man who weighs on me like a deadly virus. I will resist sleep tonight because I know that he will try to invade my bed, and when morning comes I will surprise him while he is asleep."

The bus reached the outskirts of Aqaba in the afternoon. The sea appeared calm, and the sun was shining on it as small boats hurried in all directions, leaving behind white foam. I was overcome with a sense of regret at seeing it for the first time. The city on the edge of the sea appeared like a smile on the face of a woman in love. Palm trees rose from the ground toward the sky, and kites trembled in the clear blue sky as seagulls dived toward the water like boys scrambling for a ball at halftime.

It was only a few minutes before the bus stopped in the town center at the end of the long journey. The passengers took their bags and departed, all except for me, for how could a person who has come to commit suicide carry a bag containing his clothes and personal belongings? All I carried was a leather wallet with my ID, a picture of me with my mother and my brother 'Ahid, my mobile phone, and 2000 dinars, which was all I had saved. The driver turned around to look at me, surprised that I was still on the bus, and then told me that we had reached the end of the journey. I left to look for the way to the sea, though it was a long time until morning, when my life would end. As I crossed the road to reach the opposite sidewalk, I ran into a smart car with loud dance music coming from it that almost crushed me. I turned back and dropped to the ground, my heart racing with fear. I heard the voice of the unknown man, laughing. "How can a man who has chosen to die of his own free will be afraid of the chance of death? The car might have caught you unawares and ended the links between us!"

"If that happened, you would leave my body and take up residence in another body!"

He laughed sarcastically. "If you knew me, you wouldn't say that!"

I went on my way, the smile of a sad, frightened man on my face, which left me as the street took me to another one and introduced me to a delightfully chaotic crowd. I could see myself in the shop windows, a body heading for a single destination—death— while at the same time being pursued by a feeling that what I was embarking on was a mistake. I was surprised by an overwhelming feeling of hunger, which I found strange. How could I be wanting food when in a few hours I would be throwing myself into the sea?

Once again, I heard the voice of the unknown man. "Since you are going to end your life, live this day as you have to."

"I should certainly indulge myself before I destroy myself," I thought. I chose a posh restaurant, and as I stood at the door I could hear the sound of gentle music alternating with the clatter of spoons and knives on plates. The waiter looked at me and, scrutinizing my appearance, gave me a warning: "The food is expensive here."

"Don't worry, I'll pay whatever you ask." I replied, as I let my gaze wander through the broad glass window.

I chose a table looking out over the sea and consulted the menu. A waiter took my order and went away giving me an uneasy look. The gusts of air from the air conditioning gave me a little energy and banished the remnants of a day that had been full of

the midday heat. I saw men in smart clothes sitting at tables and
women in summer dresses that exposed their brazen femininity.
There was a table with three men and two women sitting at it,
drinking something that I later learned was white wine and eating
food that I could not identify. The man at the head of the table was
speaking a little tensely about some instances of corruption that
had rocked the country recently. He blamed various organizations
and thought serious measures needed to be taken to avoid a crisis.
He spoke about the middle class and its disappearance, and the importance of what might happen in respect of that. He said nothing
for a little, then looked toward the woman opposite him and said,
"We need someone like the Italian judge Antonio Di Pietro."

The man reminded me of the influential guy for whom the
kiosks had been cleared from downtown when there was no need
for it. I opened his Facebook page and flicked through it again. *Iyad
Nabil works as an important political official, and is fearful about the
homeland.* His page indicated that he owns a large medical supplies company, a medicine factory, and a number of international
agencies. He had a lot of photos and videos about his charitable
initiatives, and in most of the photos he was holding a rosary. In
two pictures of him, one in his office and the other in his home,
there were panels engraved with verses from the Holy Qur'an. The
waitress brought the food, put it in front of me, and went off to
the table with the three men and two women. I remembered what
my father had said to me one day: "Don't trust people with loud
voices. They are usually hiding a different reality behind them." I
ate my food greedily, as if I were trying to extend the part of my
life that had passed me by, before I ended it with a step that would
relieve me both of my father's legacy—which had chained me to a
painful fear and seclusion—and of the extremist who lived inside
me. The place was suffused with the scent of men's and women's
perfumes, and this gave me a sudden pleasure that made me turn

right around, as a new sort of peace flowed through my body. I heard the voice of my resident extremist: "You can only enjoy the power of the perfume. You can only look at these people and listen to their voices. You have stifled your own voice and the voices of those like you. You have come from an old hunger, while they are grounded in their ill-gotten wealth. What if you had a revolver and aimed it at them now? What would happen if the world was freed from some of those who made a path out of your shoulders?"

I felt threads being tied around my body, dragging me toward the unknown being. It was a strange kind of submission, like the advice of a murderer pointing his revolver at my head while at the same time talking to me from a region loaded with mercy. I submitted to it unconsciously then realized the importance of it. The spoon fell from my hand to the ground, creating a disturbance that made more than one person aware of my presence. I ate my food, resisting his voice nearby, as if he were sitting on my shoulder at one moment and opposite me on the table at another.

"Any step you take in the right direction will lead to new bells!"

"Your 'right' springs from a sick corner!"

I felt him grasping my hand as I brought the spoon to my mouth.

"You fool, do you believe that the world is going in the right direction? People are sick of what they have created for themselves. They start wars, they invent diseases, they kill off some voices and bear others aloft."

"I will not be defeated before you!"

I woke up to the waiter holding me and shaking me as I stood between my table and another one nearby, and he propelled me out of the restaurant. People looked at me as I paid for my meal. Back on the street, the heat from the blazing sun consumed everything. I began to feel exhausted as I crossed from one sidewalk to the other, like a wanderer searching for something he has lost. As I thought about how I could rest from the burden of the journey and the heat of the sun, I wondered, "What's the point of going to rest when you are aiming for eternity? What's the point of running way from a speeding car for fear it may run you over?"

Then I heard him telling me off. "Are you stupid? Going to death requires exceptional elegance. Look at your appearance: your clothes are old, you've got an old-fashioned classic haircut, and your face looks dumb rather than sad."

I crossed over to a barbershop on the opposite side of the street and told the barber, "I'm to be a bridegroom this evening; you must make me look good!" I found my face in the mirror gradually changing: a new hairstyle, hair combed in an attractive way, skin smooth and vital after the barber had spent some time treating it with creams and detergents. I looked in the mirror as I was leaving and saw a face that was free of the stupidity I had long grown bored of. I went into a clothes store near the barbershop and wandered among all sorts of shirts and trousers, bought new clothes and shoes, and put them on in the store itself. I tossed my old clothes in a trash can as if throwing away old times, and I became a new person. After the sun had begun to turn toward the seashore and it had cooled down, I walked along the street. People were coming out to walk in the streets and lanes.

"I have to make myself completely elegant on my last evening of this life," I whispered to myself, and the voice of the unknown man agreed with that sentiment. I went into a perfume shop where glass cabinets displayed all different sorts of perfume. Men and women were making their selections, and scents filled the shop. I told the assistant that I would wander around the perfumes to find one that suited me. I thought I must be demanding and have a different temperament, despite the fact that I had only ever bought a few bottles of eau de cologne for shaving. I found a scent that hit me with a new pleasure: "This scent is like a song!" I exclaimed.

The assistant smiled and nodded his head in agreement. After purchasing it, I sprayed my clothes and neck with several squirts of it and left the store. I had gained a new temperament, which made me see the streets growing wider before my eyes, and everything became easy and beautiful.

———

Night descended on Aqaba. The street lights came on, as the lights from the houses chased away the darkness. Pieces of music could be heard through the combined noise of cars and passers-by. Then I saw the sea. The lights from the ships and small boats turned it into a piece of black cloth studded with pearls. I felt tired again, so I sat on a bench on the sidewalk that looked over the sea. The voice of Umm Kulthoum came to me from a car stopped at the edge of the road. It was a gentle sound, which soothed my constant tiredness. But the feeling of calm quickly left me as the night became too oppressive for a man wandering around in the last hours of his life. I could have cured my exhaustion by lying down on the bench, but I had noticed a policeman turn away a shabbily dressed man who was sleeping on another bench.

"It's not right for a man who wants to enjoy the last few hours of his life to stay like a vagrant."

I got into a taxi and asked the driver to take me to a hotel in the town. Then the unexpected happened.

3
Ibrahim

(Final Hours, First Pleasures)

I stood in front of a hotel on the shore for some minutes, looking at something I had never seen before. Posh cars, with men whose faces had never known suffering getting out of them, and elegant, comfortably off women bathed in perfume to flutter the heart, walking seductively and wiggling their bottoms, breasts half exposed. What world have you come to, Ibrahim? A world in which there is nothing for you, and which as far as you know has nothing in it for you that you know anything about. Their pockets swell, while the hole in your own pocket grows wider; it only knows your hand when it is escaping from the cold, or from boredom as you walk in a downtown crowd, at the end of a day in which you have earned a few dinars from readers who still search for the truth in books. What world is this, which violently exposes your ignorance of what is around you and arouses in you the urge to cry for your past life, exactly as if you had slept for a long time and woke to look around you with painful surprise? I said that as I went in, so obviously hesitant that I almost left by the same door to spend my night stretched out on a bench on the corniche or on the sand on the beach. But an overwhelming sense of confusion led me to a revolving door, which in turn brought me into a splendid, spacious hall. I stood meekly in the middle of it, looking all around to examine it in greater detail. I approached a member of staff, who greeted me with a commercial smile, and I hesitantly asked for a room for a single night with a view of the sea. He checked his computer screen and smiled.

"Fortunately, there is a room!"

Did I ask for it to see what place of rest would envelop me, taking with it a totally undistinguished life to relieve it of all its painful monotony? Or was I heeding the voice of a tree that had suffered thirst all those years? The man entered my details into the computer and asked, "Are you here for business or leisure?"

What if I told him the truth, that I had chosen the water as my grave, with the fish, the coral, the seaweed, and the fine sand at the bottom? As my eyes took in these plush surroundings with the eagerness and wonder of a child, I replied, "Business—which will not take long!"

The air conditioning cooled the warm coastal air, bringing with it a mixture of perfumes along with laughs and groans I was not used to. The man gave me an electronic key to my room and said, "Have a nice stay, Mr. Ibrahim!"

His words—"Mr. Ibrahim!"—echoed in my ears as the elevator carried me upward, and they stayed with me as I walked along a quiet carpeted corridor to my room. As soon as I entered, I hurried to the window and opened it. The sea was dark; there was nothing to show where it was except for the sound of the fearful waves racing toward the land, as if the darkness was in a faraway prison, brought by the ship of the night as a hateful cargo to be dumped. I closed the window and threw myself on the bed. Looking around the room, I saw a new world quite unlike the one I had grown up in—a calm atmosphere that evoked a unique sense of peace with its colors, the feel of the things in it, even the whisper that came from the corridors before the doors were opened and then closed. The whispers and laughter gave me the urge to embrace a woman and dissolve in her, but then the wildness of the sea crept into me, stirring in me a vague sadness and fear, with sudden palpitations that I had often suffered and tried to avoid. I picked up the remote and pressed the on button. The wide TV screen lit up and I started to surf the channels. I found some boring news broadcasts and others showing tedious serials. I turned it off and went back to contemplating the silence. The tiredness that had brought me to the hotel abated, and in its place came a feeling that I had made a mistake in coming here. I should have kept wandering around the streets instead of seeing how these people lived. Had I done that, I would have gone to my fate without regretting anything.

"Run away!" I said to myself and drew myself a warm bath, trying to relax and go to sleep so as not to think about anything. I had to clear my head of anything that would disturb the peace of a night I had decided to spend as never before. The bathroom was splendid—quite unlike those we used in my childhood, when baths were viewed as torture. The loofah was hard, and my skin would turn red as my mother—seated on a low wooden chair with a kerosene heater beside it, on top of which was a metal bowl— scrubbed me with all the force of a village woman. She would scoop the water out of the bowl and pour it over my head as I tried to escape the sting of the Naboulsi soap in my eyes and the effect of the loofah on my skin.

I surrendered myself to the warm water for half an hour, then got out and lay in bed. But I could not sleep. I felt bored and fed up; I felt I had made a mistake that would kill me. I was afraid that the creature beside me would wake up and take advantage of my being alone, and that his ugly voice would add a new bitterness to my final hours. I picked up a booklet listing the services provided by the hotel and found that there was a music and dance club attached to it. I looked at the picture, and suddenly the voice came to me as if it been awaiting its opportunity: "Even trains come off the rails!"

I went back, as his laughter rang around the room, got dressed, and quickly went out. Three doors down, I found a club with all sorts of lights. As I stood at the door, I thought the noise of the music would shake the walls from their foundations. The dance floor was full of men and women swaying with the music in a dazed rapture as the colored lights, moving seemingly at random, fell on their bodies in an arousing way. Men and women as well as younger girls and boys were sitting at the tables, with plates of food and bottles of wine in front of them, brought by waitresses wearing dresses that covered only a small part of their soft breasts and tight skirts that reached only just below their navels. I chose a table and sat down at it in some confusion, uncertain what to do on a night like this. The waitress came closer to me so I could hear her through the din of the music and the loud voices of the clubbers, and asked me what food and drink I would like. Her hair smelled of a summer's night in the mountains, and when her cheek brushed my face it felt like the dress of the first bride I saw in the village. I asked her for a small portion of the boiled meat and vegetables that she suggested to me and looked into her playful eyes when she asked me if I would like to order a drink. "Why not?" I thought to myself, "Let it be a wild night!"

Then I recalled a scene with Dr. Valentini from Hemingway's *Farewell to Arms*, where he examines the foot of Lieutenant Frederic Henry and flirts with his lover, Catherine Barkley, promising her a bottle of high-quality whiskey. I read the novel in a mood of extreme depression, for my father paid most of his monthly salary as rent for the house and there was only a little for us to live on. There were only a few customers at the time, and they only glanced at the books and went away. I threw a scarf around my neck to protect it from a cold of forty or so degrees that year, and put a small heater by my feet to avoid the chill of the biting winds that streamed in through holes in the kiosk. A foreign tourist stopped by some old English books and started to leaf through one of them. She had blue eyes and blonde hair, part of which she covered with a red hat. To me, she looked like Catherine Barkley: she had the same kind, feminine temperament and the same full body. I folded the page and looked at her face as I surrendered to a daydream that almost made me go and embrace her—for a reason unconnected either with the poverty that had by then started to drag us into thorny fields or with my need for a woman to sleep with, like any young man at the height of his powers. No, it was a more obscure reason, more like a moment of surrender, a total collapse on the shoulder of a beautiful woman who knows what it means when a man breaks down with such sad generosity. But she just threw me a smile and left. "Whiskey, I'd like a bottle of whiskey!" I replied in a loud voice, so she would hear me through the din filling the hall.

I recalled the tone I had practiced to sound like a man who is used to drinking alcohol, and I laughed. Then, in a moment I don't quite understand, I turned into Frederic Henry, and everything changed to the era of the First World War. The hall was heaving with soldiers wearing military uniforms, dancing with their sweethearts to the strains of the music of the time before going into battle. The waitress came back with the food and whiskey, put them in front of me, took some ice cubes and put them in the glass, then poured a little whiskey over them, smiled at me, and went away. I brought the glass to my lips and took a sip even though I didn't like the smell. It went down inside me sharply. I ate some of my food and followed it with a second sip, then another, until I got used to it and started to feel as if propelled by wings to hover, sing, and dance.

The smell of bodies and the scent of perfume surrounded me on every side as I started to shake with the rhythm of the music, until I found myself between the dancers making involuntary movements and twisting around like a Sufi in ecstasy. The soldiers and their sweethearts stopped dancing and crowded around me as I turned and turned, feeling a new pleasure. On one occasion, the voice of the unknown man burst in, saying, "You must wake up; you are not Frederic Henry getting ready to go to the front. You are Ibrahim the bookseller, the son of successive losses."

I crouched on the ground, looking at how everything was moving around me. I could almost see him. He had a reptilian face and a fluid appearance. I called to him as he moved from one spot to another like a shadow I could not escape from. "In only a few hours I shall be free of you following me around!" His laugh was mocking and contemptuous.

"The people who formed this circle are applauding the failed clown in you as they enjoy a passing amusement to break their monotony. Stop what you are doing; you look like a monkey jumping over a trench full of hot coals in front of people who have spent all the years needed to collect them."

"Your ideas about everything are completely wrong," I shouted at him. "These people are living life as it should be lived."

"Do you know who these people are? Look at them. They aren't like you, and they will never show sympathy with anyone like you, you fool!"

I looked at the faces with the lights in different colors falling on them before hitting the ground, forming a colorful psychedelic mix. He grabbed my neck and shook it hard. "Come on, get up. Look for the electric fuses and turn them off, then go inside, pick up the gas cylinder and light it, then follow it with another and blow the place up!"

I went back to the table feeling exhausted, like a leaf battered by a crazy wind. I started gulping down one glass of whiskey after another in the hope that the voice would disappear. But it was no use. The effect of the alcohol diminished to the point that it was as if I hadn't drunk anything. I paid the bill and left to return to my room, his voice pursuing me wherever I headed: in the bathroom, on the balcony, in bed. Then it disappeared. I buried my head in the cover, willing myself to sleep and hoping to hurry the arrival of morning, but with no success. I started staring at the ceiling again, and it turned into a narrator with a powerful memory who brought

back a series of recollections. I saw my mother and father and my
brother 'Ahid; I retrieved books, and the characters of novels whose
footsteps I had spent days and nights following on paper stuffed
with my memories. I started to wish I could throw a match at him
so he would catch fire. I remembered all the news in the papers
and scenes I had seen on the TV screen. I recalled how dull and
colorless I was, and that I would leave this life with nothing to
show for it! How cruel to suddenly discover that your life is the
creation of others and that you have only ever been a response to
what they thought was right!

<hr>

Lights peeped out, dispersing the darkness of the night, but there
was no noise from outside except for the sound of a lawnmower.
As soon as I got up, I found myself in the middle of a storm so
that I could not even move my hands, a storm in which joy was
mixed with sorrow and with fear of the approaching hour. I went
lazily back to my bed and curled up in the middle of it, fleeing a
fate to which I would go by my own volition. Then I gazed up at
the clear blue sky. After a few minutes I went into the bathroom
and splashed my body with cold water. I made a cup of coffee in
an electric kettle in the hope of relieving my headache. I laughed
at myself for bothering about a pain that would end, like many
others, this morning. From the window of the room I saw the sea
slumbering after a dark night that had tried to steal its blue color
and failed, as it always did. Across the balcony, I could see the
light of the sun, ready to cross the mountains to the east. It had
driven away a little of the darkness. The sand could be clearly seen
as could the surface of the sea, which reminded me of the short
distance between myself and the end. "How can someone like you,"
I wondered, "go on thinking of death, despite the calm pouring
from every direction? What war between you and an unknown

voice is it that raised the banner in the first place? Although you will not find anyone to say he did this, to save himself from a crime for which no one will forgive him."

I will not deny that I felt hesitant and confused in the face of what I was embarking on, especially since life had granted me a little smile when I arrived in this city. I envied it for its closeness to the sea as its blue color became clearer and it began to lift the veil on a new face of life. I dreamed of a home, of a wife and family. I imagined gentle music, during which I saw fine days and heard laughter, cries of pleasure, and bold steps toward life. But the voice came to me again, dispersing a joy that I wished could last longer: "Don't be deceived by your present circumstances, you are living just a temporary condition, after which you will return to your misery and weakness. This is what I want; you can be sure of what I am telling you!"

As I walked toward the edge of the balcony, a shudder crept across my back, as if he was following me.

"Real life comes after some boldness in taking what you want," he said quietly. "Without paying attention to everything that comes into your hand."

"You are making a law to make murder and destruction legal!"

"Destruction only disappears through more destruction!"

I went back to my room, turning around in the hope of finding the source of the voice, grabbing him by the neck, and getting rid of him. Besieged by his voice even more than before, I said, "I will not give in!"

Across the balcony, I saw a wooden bridge leading from the edge of the shore to the water. It looked like a suitable place to throw myself in, as the water would be deep, deep as the death that would stay sticking out its tongue in people's faces without them knowing its secrets. Does death seem beautiful when we undertake it in beautiful places? No, death is death, but we beautify it in order to accept the end. You gave in to your father's fear, Ibrahim, and became a copy of him. You didn't know when you saw him hanging by his neck from the rope he had tied to the kitchen ceiling, that you would have a fate similar to his. The night you left the village, you should have followed the example of Oskar Matzerath, the hero of Günter Grass's novel *The Tin Drum*, who decided not to grow up when he was making his future, for the plan was that he should become a grocer. His shout shattered glass when he stopped growing and decided to stay a child, just like that. But what happened was that your father threw the novel into the oven that winter. Outside, the rain was washing the piled-up dust from the houses of Jabal al-Jawfa and the grime from the car exhausts and factories. Then he started to shake you, as Matzerath used to, when he found you wrapped up in yourself: "You must wake up! You are not Matzerath and I am not Alfred! You went to bed early that day and saw Matzerath in your dreams. You complained to him of your weakness as he sat silent in front of you. When you had finished your ramblings, he patted your head and left. You should have done as he did, Ibrahim!"

I went out quickly with a black cloud enveloping my soul, then headed for the sea along the twisting paths of the hotel courtyard. When I reached the sea, the guests were fast asleep, and the only sounds in the place were those of the seagulls sailing through the air and the noise produced by shoals of small fish fleeing the water together and returning all at once.

As I approached the sea, I was torn between two feelings. One was a happy one, which came from my deep desire to see the sea, and the other was sad, because of the short time I had left to live. It was as if my heart was split in two, one half white and the other black. Here you are, Ibrahim, about to end your own life in something you love—the sea you dreamed about. You would shut your eyes as the heat almost melted everything downtown, turning the kiosk into an oven to bake your fragile body, and you would imagine the sea. You would see its captivating blue color and feel the breeze wafting over your tired soul. You would see a woman throwing her bronzed body into it and then emerge with a layer of water glistening on her smooth skin. You would rush to leap in, and as your body sunk into the water, the cold would make you shout happily. As soon as your head emerged from the water, you would cry out drunkenly. Then you would wake to the voice of a customer wanting a book, and the heat would tighten its grip on you even more.

It didn't occur to me that I would find a woman standing on the edge of the bridge that I was heading for. She seemed so astonished that I lightened my footsteps on the sand until I reached the shore and lay down, tired from a sleepless night and the strange feelings that were assaulting me. I will have to wait, I said, but how can someone wait who has decided to go to his death? I wanted a secret death, unseen by anyone. I would knock on his door with a plea, just like a child who knocks on a door and turns to look behind him in confusion, for fear that a wolf might be pursuing him. The moment of death must come in an obscure manner, like the endings of certain novels that hang in the memory, adding a new secret to the secrets of this life.

I looked at the sea, how it embodied the greatest idea of silence, while the woman continued to say nothing. Only her brown hair moved, spreading over her shoulders as it quickly submitted to the light gusts of wind that had just started up. She was wearing a sky-blue pullover and a white skirt, which quivered in the wind on a shore where only she and I were to be found. I turned my eyes away from her and lay on the sand, filling my lungs with the breeze and savoring the moment. We do not appreciate the taste of things we are used to, or feel their goodness, except when we realize that we shall be leaving them forever.

The sky was clear, and one could see to the edge of infinity. I contemplated how far the sky stretched and how it clung to the end of the sea. Once again, I saw the sky black, full of frightening birds, and from it came a wind that whistled, indicating great sorrow and anger. I coughed and saw no need to hide my voice, which had already disturbed the woman's isolation, when she turned toward me. I raised my hand by way of apologizing to her and she gave me a passing glance before returning to her daydreams. I was swept away by a sudden feeling of calm. I rested my head on my arm as I watched how quietly she stood, as if watching something happening on the open sea. I imagined several things that might lie behind those exceptional moments of hers. I found myself drowning in what I had just seen as if I had viewed a painting of a woman leafing through notebooks with a vague unease. I turned on my mobile and took a picture of her, which I wasn't thinking would accompany my possessions into the water. It wasn't the behavior of a man filling up the last minutes of his life. Then the voice came, as if to make its peace with me: "Sometimes a soldier will remember a rose as he hears the bullets pass, missing his head which is full of the possibilities for destruction. He does that, spurred on by hope."

It was an exceptional sight that I could not ignore. She looked sad, and in a daze, although I could only see her face when she turned. I relaxed more as the moisture of the sand tickled my body, and thought, "These feelings about women are attacking me as though I had been suffering from a chronic disease and then recovered from it." I put my wrist over my eyes then spent some minutes recollecting the details of the scene, as if I were going to an end linked with sudden pleasure. I heard footsteps on the sand gradually approaching me. She was carrying her shoes in her right hand, while her left hand held up her long skirt, showing her light-skinned legs against the blue sea. As she approached me, I got up and apologized. "It seems I disturbed your peace and quiet!"

Her calm, childlike face had a surprised expression and she examined me with her black eyes squinting against the glare of the sun. She put on a smile, which could not hide her surprise, then said, with a sideways look that hid some emotion, "Never mind! Perhaps it is I who disturbed you! No one comes to the sea at this hour except people looking for themselves, or..."

She said no more, and her sentence seemed incomplete. I examined her face for the secret of her confused look but could not find it.

"Please sit down."

She gathered her skirt and sat down, her feet facing in front of her. "I seem to have forgotten my lighter. Do you have one?"

"Sorry, I don't smoke."

"Never mind."

She watched a fisherman who had just returned from the sea. She was still immersed in her daydreams, despite sitting with a man she had just met. The sorrow in her face was too great for her to bother with anything else. To break the silence, I said, "It seems that we come to the sea because it is a keeper of secrets, but we only see its watery face, while in its depths there are many stories unknown to all but the man who rides the wave of adventure!"

She gave me a strange look that I didn't understand. "I used to work as a bookseller in downtown Amman," I said to introduce myself. But she paid no attention. Instead, she went back to looking at the sea with sad eyes, as if abandoned to something faraway that must be tiring her memory. As her eyes continued to gaze upon the sea with a smile, I thought she must have been defeated by some recent memory. Then she reverted to her sad expression, like someone waking from a daydream. I wasn't disturbed by the silence between us, which had given me the pleasure of discovering a more beautiful side of the face of life. I stared at her, sunk in her daydream. She had the face of a little girl, the eyes of a woman able to dispel my old misery, and a mouth that could spread warmth with a sudden kiss. I forgot everything. My eyes were trained on her and I forgot myself, like a shirt hanging on a washing line in front of a woman who brought back the memory of a beautiful night.

"I was walking to the center of town," she said in a relaxed voice, then looked at me with a sudden smile. She looked at me as one looks at someone returning from a long journey, put her chin on her knees, and went back to looking at the sea. "Perhaps," she said, "we come to the sea to retrieve our stolen face!"

I was about to say that I was happy with what the thief had left behind of her face, content with these two hands to treat the wounds, then take me away from my misery so I could rid myself of all my pains, and when I had finished we could carry on walking to our destination. She was so sad I would have liked to put my arm around her neck, cry with her, then collapse. Collapsing in the company of a woman is a confession that hides the heart's wounds, for the female is a broad sky and the sky is a boundless woman, but how can a woman's sadness lead a sad man to her so quickly?

Strands of her hair had been lifted by the wind to reveal a long neck encircled by a golden chain bearing the letter N.

"Although the sea is a departure station rather than an arrivals station, we take refuge in it in the moments of our collapse," I said. Then I began to think of the millions of names that might start with this letter: Nar perhaps, or Nay. I closed my eyes to listen to the sound of a flute that suddenly came upon me, bringing with it a herd of wild stags. She stood in front of me, looking at me with placid eyes that seemed to convey some prearranged signal. "Why did you take a picture of me?"

My body was swept away by a great current of embarrassment that kept me from answering, while her face registered the beginnings of a spontaneous laugh that revealed two beautiful dimples.

"How could you tell?"

"I heard the sound of your mobile; I have the same kind."

I turned on my mobile to delete the picture, but she stretched out her hand to stop me. "Leave it," she said. "I just wanted to know why."

Her hand was warm, soft and inviting, like a poem describing a garden with fountains, roses, and flocks of birds.

"It was the exceptional sight that made me do it!"

She gave a mocking, sorrowful smile. "Exceptional?"

"Yes, especially when one can see sorrow in a beautiful woman gazing at the sea at moments like this."

She put her hands on the sand to support her body and gave a long sigh. Biting her lip with shining white teeth, she turned her head to me and smiled. "How long have you been here?"

"Since yesterday."

I wished she had asked me why I had come. I would have opened my secret notebooks and told her everything. I would confess to things that no one knew about me. I would beg her to stay near me so I could listen to her, to relieve her heart of the sorrow on her face that she was unable to conceal. I would be like her shadow, a faithful guardian until her heart blossomed with joy. Then I would ask her if we could both stay in town and enjoy the sea. But she quickly got up, as if punishing herself for the time she shouldn't have spent with me. She gave me a strange look and then smiled as if trying to hide something—a secret she had almost let out. She looked first left then right, shook my hand, and with a voice that concealed a wish to cry, said, "I have to leave now. Look after yourself."

And with that, she went on her way, carrying her shoes in her right hand while holding up her skirt with the other. "What's your name?" I called after her.

She turned and gave me another smile as the sound of the gulls and the noise of the shoals of fish hitting the water grew louder. "It's not important, believe me, it's not important!"

I stayed watching her until she had gone through the glass door of the hotel. I could no longer see anything moving except for the date palms, quivering like a woman gently swaying to the captivating rhythm of music, while her words rang in my ears, urging me to take care of myself. I was overcome by feelings leading me away from the idea of suicide, but the voice gave a loud laugh and a serious warning that made me hurry my steps toward my anticipated death.

4
Ibrahim

(An Unforgettable Surprise)

I walked toward the bridge with heavy steps. From inside me came the sound of a watch ticking loudly, indicating the approach of a final moment. With every step, my memory contemplated a part of my life, and with every tick of the clock my heart leaped with regret for everything I hadn't done. Then I reached the edge of the bridge, where the woman was standing. The sea was like a mother with a sad face, dissuading me from what I intended to do. I shut my eyes and took a last breath of air before I threw myself into the water. I was carrying the mobile on which I had kept a picture of my family all together, while on my wrist was my father's watch, whose hands would continue turning as my body gradually disappeared into the water. I thought of leaving it and my mobile behind as a last vestige, so I took it off and bent down to the wooden floor of the bridge to put it down there. I saw a thick notebook with a pen and a piece of folded paper inside it. I heard the voice of the unknown man chuckling and making fun of me.

I sat down, opened the notebook, and picked up the piece of paper to read what was on it: "Here you are now, reading this note of mine, while my body had been swallowed by the sea, with its eternal peace. When the light breaks and hits the soft sand I shall be the companion of the fishes of the deep. I do not like the worms of the earth, where darkness and damp give death an extra pain. So I have given my body to the water, the secret of eternal hearing, and the bosom that does not close its arms.

I have not written any will, for I have no bequests for those who failed in their lives, except that they should wish for one of them to tune the discordant string, and I have no advice to give, for I am only a pigeon's feather floating in a breeze that is never still for a moment. I could have alighted on a tree and seen how a pear ripens on its mother's breast or landed on the shoulder of a man on his way to meet a woman he had sworn to love as a bird loves its wings while he trembles as he crosses a road where the pedestrians fight against the crowd. I am just a woman who has been betrayed in her life and has come to the water, thinking of achieving seclusion, like a famous musician at the height of his powers who can sense some weakness inevitably coming to his fingers. I have no advice to give except for these words, so burn this paper and scatter it here so that it may perhaps become a wandering witness to me."

I relaxed where I was and gave in to a strong desire to weep and an overwhelming longing for life while the paper in my hand fluttered in a wind that was driving small waves in the sea. The sun peeped out from behind mountains that stood on the horizon like the backs of old men looking for something on the ground. "So this woman came to the sea to end her life but didn't!" I said, then picked up the notebook and went on reading:

After some events that I thought had refined me, I imagined that I could say the word 'no' in the face of anyone who wanted to put me on a course I didn't want. Before the change that had come over my life, it never occurred to me that I needed to refuse many things, for we do not discover the pleasure of calm until we have suffered the misfortune of noise. I am still a simple woman in everything except in dreams witnessed by the ceiling of my room in our house in Jabal al-Jawfa, which was purchased by my father a long time ago. I have nothing but beautiful, unforgettable memories of my family, which met its end in a horrific traffic accident on the Aqaba road.

Before things began to change at home I would play in the quarter with my sisters and later would go out to meet school friends, accompany my mother to wedding parties held in the quarter, and talk to the neighbors' daughters from the balcony of our house. I would listen to songs in my room, watch serials and plays on TV, read books borrowed from the school library and friends, who made me love reading, and go on school trips with my girlfriends. My take on life was the same as any girl of my kind, based on knowledge of what was right and what was wrong, of what was forbidden and what was allowed. I would wake at dawn and pray with my mother, while my brother would pray with my father.

I grew up in a family made up of myself and my brother in addition to my parents. My mother did not read or write. She spent part of her time on housework and sitting with us and my father, and a small part of her time with the neighbors. She only knew of life what my father knew and what she learned from the neighbors. She was a quiet, obedient woman from whom no one ever heard an angry word. My brother Ramadan, he was wild. His face never showed any sign of happiness except when he imposed his authority on me. My father worked in the Water Authority. A simple man in every way, he left school in the fourth primary grade. He possessed nothing but our house, which consisted of two bedrooms, a sitting room, and another room for guests—where Ramadan slept—with a small bathroom and kitchen.

Like the rest of the residents of the quarter, we were a poor family. We ate chicken once a week and meat once a month, sometimes once every three months, but my father meant a lot to us. We would wait for him to come back carrying whatever he had been able to buy, and we would gather at a low dining table. We were content with what God had decreed for us. As soon as we had finished supper, I would slip onto his lap as he followed the news broadcast, and he would stroke my head until I fell asleep.

Sleeping in his lap with his warm hand on my head meant a lot to me. My mother would put on her glasses, pick up two needles, and start knitting. From time to time she would talk to my father as my brother either watched TV or fiddled with his phone. We stayed living like this (and despite life's hardships there was also some pleasure) until my father's circumstances changed. There was an incident in the quarter when a relationship between a girl and her colleague at the university was exposed. Someone photographed and posted a video on the internet of the girl exchanging kisses with a young man among the trees at the university. The video was widely circulated. When the girl's brother saw it, he killed her. He stabbed her with a knife, severed her limbs, threw them into the street, and then shouted that he had wiped out her disgrace. It was a horrid crime, one that aroused fear among girls and fear of disgrace among the men, and like a snow ball, it continued to grow as people talked about it. We heard many tales and stories about the girl. Facebook users swapped a voice recording of her pleading with her brother before he killed her. It was a frightening recording that made people shake. Some said she deserved it for what she had done; others described her brother as a wild animal without an ounce of mercy in his heart. The recording circulated quickly and drove many people to protest in the street against the personal circumstances laws and the increasing violence against women. Social media became preoccupied with the subject, and there were digital fights between users on opposing sides. We don't know how new recordings of other girls came to light at the time.

My father was disturbed by what had happened and by what was being said in the quarter. Sometimes he would give me an apprehensive look when he saw me on my phone, then turn his face away quickly. His mood changed, and I missed his cheerful smile and his sympathetic touches. He became tense and silent at Ramadan's protests that my clothes were too tight and too revealing of my bodily charms. He would protest if I went out to collect the washing from the roof of the house with my hair showing and shouted angrily whenever he saw me looking at my mobile.

One day, my father came back, his face showing clear signs of displeasure. We had been watching a romantic serial in the living room, after evening prayers. He took his shoes off and sat down, resting his body on the wall, and turned to my mother. "Have you prayed?" he asked, as she followed an enticing scene in the serial.

"We'll pray in a bit."

Then he raised his voice: "This is not right. It's not right."

"No, it's not right!" my mother said and got up, repeating religious phrases as she headed to perform her ablutions. I followed her, intending to pray, but my father unplugged the TV, picked it up, and threw it out the window, cursing the man who made it. The alley echoed with the sound of it hitting the ground. Then he picked up the radio that my mother used to listen to Fairouz's songs and smashed it with a hammer until it was nothing but small pieces. I went to him. He was crawling on his knees, holding the hammer.

"Why did you do all that, father?" I asked. I was stunned by what I had seen.

He looked at me, so angry that his eyes were bloodshot. "These are things that have corrupted morality."

"Who said that?"

"My eyes were blind," he said. Then he took my phone from me and smashed it.

"This is one of those misfortunes that has come to us we know not how. We don't want it, we don't want it!"

He went over to the table, picked up some books I enjoyed reading, and ripped them up. I clutched the books to try to stop him, but he pushed me away and I fell to the ground. He stood there panting, as we both felt the force of the shock, and proceeded to dictate to us his conditions: "From today on: no songs, no music, no soaps, no books. From this day on, you must change your clothes style and stay at home." He was silent for a moment before turning his eyes to me and said in a breathless voice, "And no going to school!"

The man I saw turn against everything wasn't my father. As the days went by, I became imprisoned by silence and loneliness. As for my mother and my brother, they quickly adapted to our new situation. I could not raise my voice with Ramadan, for he watched my movements whenever he was at home. One day, he scolded me for spending a long time in the bathroom. One evening, I was reading a story smuggled in to me by the neighbor's daughter in a loaf of bread—can you imagine something like that?—when there was a knock at the door. When I opened it, Ramadan rushed toward me, tore up the book, and started hitting me. A sudden revolution turned the house into a prison. I could no longer see my girlfriends, stand out on the balcony, read, use my phone, or watch TV. I felt like an inmate awaiting execution. Faced with all this suffering, all I could do was write in a notebook everything I was feeling. I would spend all the time available to me at night writing furiously with my eyes on the door, so no one could come in and see what I was doing. I was forbidden to close the door. And then the disaster happened and my whole family left.

They had gone to Aqaba with my father to attend a wedding reception for one of our relatives. I don't know why my father agreed that I could stay at home on my own on that occasion. Ramadan was very angry and insisted that I go with them, but my father shut him up and embraced me, then whispered in my ear, "Look after yourself, my girl!"

I didn't know that it would be the last time I saw him. A few hours after they left, there was a knock on the door accompanied by an unusual clamor. When I opened the door, I saw my neighbors crying as they hugged me. The bus driver had fallen asleep during the journey and the bus had swerved to the other side of the road and collided with a truck traveling at high speed. Most of the bus passengers died, and I was confronted by something I had never anticipated.

5
Ibrahim

(Introduction to a Story That Hasn't Happened Yet)

When I closed the notebook, the sun had already crossed the mountains and its rays had hit the sea. My eyes raced as far as they could, to where the sea collided with the blue horizon. The gulls were performing their usual exercises. As I threw my body down onto the wooden bridge, the blue of the sky attacked me, as if to wash a deep sorrow from my soul. I realized then that the moment separating life from death is like a hair sticking to the surface of the eye. As soon as it disappears, the vision becomes clearer. Sometimes, there are sudden events that change the perspectives we thought final and irreversible.

"Who are you, woman?" I asked, leaning my head toward the closed windows of the hotel. I shut my eyes and imagined her looking at me through the gaps in the curtains of one of the windows. It seems that people who are similar in sorrow and in their destinies know each other well. I got up, picked up what I had left on the edge of the bridge, and left with the notebook under my arm. There was a voice buried among its words, written in a hasty script that showed nothing but calm in writing sorrow, a voice that made me surrender to the sort of tears that I had all my life wanted in the bosom of my father. The sand still retained the shape of her short footsteps, calm and careless footsteps that did not betray the storm of sorrow I had seen in the sky of a notebook that had made me retreat from my impending death.

My belly swelled, and the voice came back, laughing mockingly at me and my retreat from completing what I had come for. But the voice of the woman, N, was even louder. What was the name that began with this letter, and to what fate would it cast me?

I went back to my room, moving between my bed and the sofa like a caged cat, thinking of a way to reach the woman who had come between me and a strange fate, a woman who was also going to end her own life before drawing back. Several reasons had induced us to embark on death, but a single reason returned us to life.

I went to the hotel restaurant at midday and ordered some food. As I ate, I looked around at the tables and at anyone entering or exiting. I only noticed that some of the patrons had found my careful, scrutinizing glances odd when a woman smiled at me. She had noticed how I turned my face in both directions to see the face of a woman sitting opposite her. She had the same hairstyle as Madame N. Yes, Madame N—this was the name I knew her by before the story grew and what happened happened.

I got up and wandered around the restaurant, looking at every face but without finding her. So I went back to my room, overcome by a new sense of defeat and a powerful insistence on finding Madame N again. I lay down on my bed, unable to ignore that insistence, or even sleep or carry out what I had come for. The sea outside my window was heaving with all its blue might when I found my belly swelling again. Before the voice could come to me, I recalled his fear of water, so I quickly took off my clothes and hurried to the bathroom. How awful for a man to see his belly like the belly of a woman about to give birth! And how harsh the impossibility of anyone believing you even if you plucked up courage and told them what had happened. I stood under the shower with my eyes closed. All I could hear was the voice of Madame N emerging from my memory to speak of the sea. I could see only her eyes as the wind lifted the strands of her hair and then returned them to where they had been, waving around at the ends of her eyebrows and twisting beside her mouth, which seemed to be savoring the taste of the wind as she looked toward the horizon.

Was she just a passing dream? Or was she a woman who shook the dust from the pages of books I was immersed in reading in the bookseller's kiosk, as my eyes snatched a quick glance at the downtown crowd, whenever a line gave me pleasure and I returned to look at it again? I got dressed and left the room and went to the elevator, not knowing where to go. I pressed the button for the reception floor. I said to myself I would ask for her. A ringing laugh came from the voice, which shook the skin of my belly. "Do you know anything about her, apart from the first letter of her name?"

I approached the receptionist, feeling stupid from confusion and the laughter of the unknown man. She looked at me over her glasses and put on a smile, as receptionists always do: "Can I help you?"

"I'd like to ask about a female guest at the hotel."

"What's her name?"

A few moments of silence passed, in which I tried to think of a way to retreat from what I had come for. But the receptionist leaned over to me and gave a laugh. "Have you forgotten her name?"

"I only know the first letter of her name: N!"

The girl looked at her computer, then at me with a good deal of sympathy in her eyes. Then she said quietly, "Unfortunately, sir, there are a number of female guests in the hotel whose names begin with an 'n.'"

"She's a woman in her forties, with brown hair. She was wearing a white skirt and a blue pullover this morning."

The receptionist was silent as she looked at the computer. Then she smiled and said, "There's a lady who finished her booking at the hotel and just left, whose name begins with an 'n.'"

I unleashed a stream of questions, but she excused herself gently, saying, "We keep the details of our guests confidential. Sorry, sir."

I wanted to shout, "You don't know what happened!" but instead I apologized and asked her to extend my stay for another night.

———

Night came, and I had one final try left before returning to Amman. My clue was a single phrase she had uttered: "I was walking to downtown." A final attempt to find her for supper. I went around the tables like a madman, even asking one of the staff about her. I described her, and he swore he hadn't seen a woman of that description in this hotel. I had a little soup and went back to my room. As soon as I had opened the door, the voice returned to me with full force: "You penetrate life from its weakest point. Love is a weakness. I will not submit to it, so that my great power may not be diminished."

I fled to the corner of the room, begging him to leave me, but he was like someone who has been prevented from speaking for a lifetime and was suddenly free to talk.

"Happy you didn't go through with the suicide, but the question that makes me angry is, Why this woman in particular? She was about to embark on death like you, but she drew back. You are both weak and unable to say no. Now here you are on the point of tears for her sake, in spite of the fact that you only saw her for a few minutes, you feeble man!"

I sat on the ground, resting against the wall with my head on my knees as he came closer to my ear, saying, "I was certain your cowardice would bring you back to me, for you to give me a chance to do what you didn't do."

"It was love that brought me back."

I ran to the door and opened it.

"They won't believe you if you tell them about me; they will say you are mad."

I ran to the bathroom and threw my body under the water as his voice resounded. "Your solutions are temporary."

I left the room and took the elevator to a door on the lobby level leading to the sea. I ran like a madman fleeing from some unnamed attacker. I stood on the edge of it. The sea was a cold shadow. The sound of the waves as they collided with the shore made me even more aware of the loneliness I had suffered from all my life, despite all the noise extending around me. It was a moment close to the end. I had prepared myself to terminate all that nonsense, but I felt the touch of a warm hand on my shoulder.

6
The Journalist

(The Loneliness of the Rose)

The hot weather abated, and walking in November became pleasant, the smell of winter in the air. I worked as a journalist and left the office after asking the chief editor's permission. He came with me for a walk from the al-Ra'y Bridge until he grew tired, hailed a taxi, and went on. He was a good man whose one son had gotten an exit permit for Canada ten years ago and had never returned. I walked on a few meters more before stopping under a bus shelter for a few minutes, after which the bus came. I boarded it and sat looking at the people and the buildings, listening to music through headphones connected to my mobile. I was listening to a playlist I had found on YouTube labeled Soothing Music. I had never before thought of working in journalism, but I read an ad from a newspaper needing editors and took an exam, which I passed the first time. The chief editor told me I had excellent skills as a newscaster. I wasn't confident about what he said, I thought what I did was quite ordinary, and if anyone had asked me I would have said that I worked to kill time. I am an unsociable woman, and if I go to an event, I only go when I cannot avoid it. I no longer care about my clothes as I did when I first worked, when I was exposed to many approaches by men. In fact, I became more practical than is right for a woman who loves her femininity. I wore jeans, sneakers, and loose blouses. Perhaps some might judge it a defeat, but I found it more restful for my head, which cannot bear noise, especially noise like that in the streets, and especially the noise pumped out by the crowd as the bus advanced half a meter then stopped in its tracks. I turned up the volume and rested my head against the bus window. I had plenty of time to get home, so I took a notebook out of my bag that I'd found one day. In it the owner had written a story—perhaps it was his—that the doctor had suggested I turn into a serial when I told him about that hobby. He thought that writing might be a cure for depression, so I started to read:

The air was cold in the early hours of November 29, 1947 as it touched the face of Mahmud al-Shamousi. He had his hands behind his back as he walked anxiously with his emaciated body along the wasteland that stretched in front of the tent. Darkness spread solidly in every direction. In Thamad, an area to the east of Madaba, there was a lonely depression from whose painful silence came the barking of dogs and the cries of shepherds as they chased away any possible raids by robbers on a night when hunger and poverty were rampant. Meanwhile, the voice of Amina could be heard from time to time, emitting the painful groans of childbirth. Her screams came from inside, all her resistance having been exhausted. Al-Shamousi sat near the fire pit, whose embers resembled the eyes of mad wolves. Then he quickly got up, with his exhausted body driven on by nervousness, as though his wife were giving birth for the first time. He came back to stand in front of the tent, looking at the desert, then walked away covering his mouth with his head covering and looking up at the sky as he muttered prayers one after the other in a soft voice. He stayed like that until sunrise, when the child screamed for the first time. The frustrated and wilting face of a woman looked over him; she could barely gather together the strength she possessed as she smiled shyly and congratulated him in a feeble voice on the arrival of a son. He walked across the barren earth, sat on a rock, undid his face covering, and looked at the sun, which had appeared over the barren hills like the eyes of a shy child behind its mother. His tears dripped down his skinny face and clung to the hairs of his pointed beard. He cried as he felt sorrow mingled with joy, on a night whose cold went hand in hand with hunger and with the family's nervousness about the two boys, Khazar and Salim, who had been conscripted into the army as the war drums rang out against the Zionist bands in Palestine.

The winter weather should have brought rain two months ago, but it hadn't come as people expected. Only a tiny amount fell. The wells dried up, and the first crop of grass and fields of wheat and barley were barren. The animals that were their sole source of income began to die one by one. The land was exhausted by drought and people reduced to grinding poverty. Later, the state proclaimed it a drought year, for the ground was unproductive, the people were tired, the birds were lazy—only rarely taking to the sky—and the animals had no energy as they walked. Al-Shamousi's family looked after animals for Abu Jaris, one of the landowners of Madaba. They spent a year occupied with grazing the animals, shearing them, milking them, preparing *laban*(yoghurt), cheese, butter, and *saman* in exchange for fifteen sheep or lambs, but the drought threatened all that.

Mahmoud al-Shamousi had five sons and two daughters in addition to Jadallah. Hamoud and Badi lived with Jawazi and Sharifa in the cave in the village because they were at school. Salim and Khazar only came back from military service every two or three months. The eldest one was Ali, who spent his day looking after the animals. He would go out with the other shepherds in the morning and return in the evening in the hope that the sheep would find the remnants of some grass in the desert to eat. Like the others, he was thinly built, with a wilting face and a scrawny belly, which he tied a piece of string around to avoid hunger pangs. Breakfast was a slice of barley bread with a single cup of tea, with no chance of another.

Lunch and dinner were a little lentil soup, or a little crushed wheat cooked in *laban* if the animals had produced any.

A week after Jadallah's birth, al-Shamousi saw Abu Jaris riding toward them around midday. The wind was strong and was making the dust rise. Remnants of dry grass surrounded the horse, which scattered them left and right until reaching the tent, which was also exposed to a mad wind that day. Whenever it was about to give in to the wind, Ali would stagger along, unable to stand up straight to grab the ropes and put more stones on the edges of the tent, while Amina grabbed the pole in the middle in one hand while holding her baby son in the other for fear that it should fall on him.

Abu Jaris, with his tall frame, broad shoulders, and prominent belly, got down from his horse. Ali hurried up reluctantly, under orders from his father, his body shaking in the wind. He tethered his horse and watched Abu Jaris as he went into the narrow opening carrying a wooden box and a sack. Amina was comforting Jadallah, who had not stopped crying from hunger, for her shriveled breast had produced no milk. Ali looked at Fasil through the narrow opening and the women's area where Amina was sitting, then in a low voice, full of passion and anger, said, "If I hadn't been afraid of my father, I would have turned away this miserly man!"

Amina put her finger on her lips and continued to rock her child. "Shh, your father will be very angry, and is it right that we should turn away a guest?"

Ali took some shaky steps outside the house. The wind stirred up the dust, which swept over him and settled in his eyes. He rubbed them again, looking at his mother with one eye and complaining, "Can't he see that there is nothing but cursed dust this year? He didn't bring a single loaf, and on top of that he became angry when he came last week and found that a number of sheep had died. Should we protest at the judgment of god?

Then again, what brought him here on a dreadful day like this?"

"Shut up, boy!" replied Amina, hiding her feelings of anger at the man.

He squatted in front of her and shook the dust out of his thick hair, then took his head between his hands so that the bones in his face stood out more than before. In a voice that was quiet despite his anger, he said, "He usually comes, fills his belly, and leaves."

Inside, Abu Jaris had sat down on the carpet and loosened his head covering so that his red, dusty face could be seen. He turned around him then said, breathing more quickly, "This wind is frightening, Abu Ali. It seems there is no hope of more rain this year. I am very afraid for the fate of my animals!"

Al-Shamousi threw some sticks in the fire pit and the smoke rose up. Abu Jaris coughed and wiped his eyes with the edge of his headdress. He moved his hands in the air in annoyance. His words were clipped because of his cough. "This is a year of drought," he said. "I don't know how my animals will last."

Al-Shamousi gave Abu Jaris a look of reproach. "You're afraid for your animals, and not afraid for us, man?"

"Of course, you are capital, Abu Ali, but you know that these are my livelihood, may God have mercy on us!"

He spoke angrily as he made the sign of the cross on his chest. Jadallah could be heard crying inside, followed by Amina's sad voice as she rocked him. A faint smile spread over his face. "Do you have children?"

He gave the bag to al-Shamousi without waiting for an answer. "This is a bit of tea and sugar, and some Hishi tobacco. Congratulations, it seems you have a son!"

He sat up on the carpet, put the wooden box on his lap, then turned the key. The sudden sound of a man's voice made al-Shamousi ask in surprise, "What's this?"

Abu Jaris laughed. "A radio."

Then he explained to al-Shamousi what a radio was, and how the voices came out of it. When he had finished, he turned it off and put it to one side, relaxing his body on the mat. "The UN General Assembly last week passed a resolution to partition Palestine."

As his eyes widened, al-Shamousi's hand tightened its grip on a stick he was using to put the coals back in their place. "How come?" he said.

"They've given the Jews more than half the area of Palestine."

Al-Shamousi put several coals back into the fire pit. "The 'Reds'—may God curse them—put them in power in Palestine. I heard they were working for that," he said, a look of sorrow mixed with anger in his eyes.

Al-Shamousi noticed the color in Abu Jaris's face, his eyes protruding in anger. "I mean the British, man!" he said, and burst out laughing.

Abu Jaris didn't stay long that day but left as the storm intensified. Ali stood there angrily, hands on hips, as he listened to Jadallah crying and looked at Abu Jaris's horse being battered by the wind. "May God take you and not bring you back, you miserly man!" he whispered. As soon as he saw he had gone, he hurried to where the animals were resting and drew his dagger. Al-Shamousi cried out for him to stop what he was about to do. "These are people's possessions—don't mess with them, my boy!" he said. But Ali slaughtered a sheep anyway and looked at his father proudly. As the blood dripped from the knife, a look of sorrow mixed with pleading appeared in his eyes. "We have the power to resist hunger. But how is Jadallah to live without his mother's milk?" he asked.

Al-Shamousi turned his back and went inside without saying anything, while Ali started to skin the sheep and cut it up. When he had finished, he lit a fire, roasted the meat, and gave some to Amina to eat.

Three men gathered around the fire pit in al-Shamousi's house. It was three months since the birth of Jadallah. The pale light of the lantern shyly revealed one side of their exhausted faces while the other side stayed in darkness, revealing nothing. Outside the house, the night threw the remains of its eternal curtain over the desolate area. The winds whistled, and it was biting cold. One of the men drew closer to the fire and began to shake his thick hair and tattered clothes in the direction of the embers. The others followed, and from time to time the clicking of lice could be heard as they died. Before the drought, they had got rid of them with kerosene, soaking their hair in it and using a comb with a thread attached to the teeth to catch the rest of them. But as their conditions deteriorated, they could no longer afford even a liter of it. It was only a few hours after sunset that they went to sleep, exhausted, and morning was the beginning of a new, difficult day.

The three men were al-Shamousi's relatives: one looked after Abu Mitri's sheep and another looked after Abu Tuma's. They spent the winter in the caves in the village. Every family had a cave. As soon as winter ended, some would take their flocks to the east, while other members of their families would stay in the village. Some of their land was held as security by certain shop owners in Madaba, like Iskandar, who had swallowed up several people's land after the state had distributed it to them, and blood had flowed between the tribes and families on that account. They bought their food on account, to be settled at the end of the season, but the seasons seldom came as people hoped. This year, for example, hunger was so widespread that one of the villagers went out shouting in a sad voice that he wished he could shit. Their food was limited to a bit of barley bread and occasionally some corn. Lentils were the only thing constantly on the table, and their guts had dried up because of it.

Ali came out with a kettle of tea in one hand and some glasses in the other. He squatted in a corner lit up by the lantern and poured the tea, without filling the glasses, then handed it to them. "A month ago, we said 'hani'an, to your health' to anyone drinking a second glass," said one of them with a shallow laugh, which made his shoulders with their prominent bones shake. "It looks like we won't find half that in the days to come."

They could hear Jadallah's crying coming from the women's quarters from time to time. Whenever al-Shamousi heard it, he would close his eyes and shake his body left and right, pained by what was happening. Amina was giving Jadallah her breast to no avail; most days, her breasts were scraggly, and she only gave them to him to stop him from screaming. Since his birth, he had moved between the breasts of several women of al-Farij who lived in neighboring tents. That night, the teats of the ewes only gave a little. Amina milked them at sunset and sat near the milk pail, taking a little from it to suckle her child, while al-Shamousi squatted at the edge of the tent, sheltering from the wind as he tried to light the lamp. Ali arrived after he had finished rounding up the sheep in a pen he had prepared for them, then tripped over the bucket and the milk spilled onto the ground. Amina put her head between her hands and wailed, "Oh my poor child, who has only ever drunk the milk of hunger!"

Al-Shamousi told her off. "Praise God, woman!" he exclaimed, as he hung the lamp on the tent pole. Then he called Ali, who left the tent and sat down near the animals' enclosure, where he burst into tears and cursed the world. Amina got up, picked up Jadallah, and started to rock him quietly.

Al-Shamousi told the men about the incident as Jadallah's crying reached his ears. Then he lay down on his side, resting his head on his hand and fell silent. One of the men got up and went away for a few minutes, then came back with a little milk. The child went to sleep in Amina's lap; she was listening to the men and their quietly told stories. Sometimes they talked of the progress of the drought, sometimes they repeated stories of al-Asmali and al-Hamran, of what they had heard about the defeat of Hitler, or the little news that had reached them of the war in Palestine. She stayed in bed, resisting sleep until the men had gone and al-Shamousi came and lay down beside her, stroking Jadallah's face and looking at him until they all fell asleep.

Winter came to an end. The ground had only received a little rain. Al-Shamousi and his relatives returned to the village and people emerged from the caves onto the face of the earth, which had none of the grass and small plants they usually fed on. The scene of biting hunger was complete, and some people were forced to mortgage their lands with Iskandar or another lender so they could buy berries to eat and wheat for baking bread. On May 15, 1948, al-Shamousi stood looking in sorrow at the hill to the east of the village, where he could see only dust. He thought of Khazar and Salim, who came back home on leave every three months and gave him their salaries, which totaled no more than forty dinars. But this time they had been away on the front for longer. He didn't sleep well that night. His sleep was intermittent, disturbed by nightmares and alarming dreams of soldiers falling on the battle-field. A week later, he woke up thirsty just before dawn, had a drink, and sat on his bed, sad and anxious that his two sons were not there. As soon as the sun had broken through night's curtain, he went down the hill that leads to Madaba, passing shepherds tending their flocks. Then he passed the al-Nawar quarter, where some people had lit a fire and were beating iron after taking it out of the fire red-hot. Al-Shamousi was on his way to Abu Jaris to ask for news of the war.

That day, Abu Jaris sold him a radio and quickly taught him how to use it. In the evening, a number of men gathered in front of the tent, looking at the radio in astonishment at the voice coming from it, until one of them peered around the back, looking for the announcer as he conveyed the news of the Palestinian Nakba. As their voices mingled in confusion, al-Shamousi scolded them ("Listen, let us hear!") and imposed a silence, as they looked at the radio and listened to the announcer read the text of the Security Council resolution demanding a ceasefire. Some men talked about the miracle of the radio and others talked about the war. Al-Shamousi kept silent. Then they left, and sleep left with them. Al-Shamousi stayed awake, sitting in front of the tent and looking at Madaba, which lay on a hill where the lights of the Latin Monastery and King Hussein Mosque could be seen. Just before dawn he felt drowsy, so he said his prayers, asking God in a tearful voice to bring back his two sons safely, then went to sleep.

Al-Shamousi's family lived through weeks of uncertainty before the news came. Al-Shamousi was fast asleep when Amina woke him up and told him there was a soldier outside who wanted to see him. He got up quickly and greeted the guest. As the soldier came in and sat down, al-Shamousi looked anxiously at his face while Amina, inside, dangled Jadallah and paced anxiously as she waited for the soldier to explain his presence. She heard him talking about his friendship with Khazar and the days they had spent together; then he coughed and said, in a rough, hesitant voice: "Khazar was one of the bravest of men—may God have mercy on him!"

Amina's cry of "My son!" was followed by the sound of Jawazi and Sharifa wailing. In a few minutes, the men and women of the village arrived. Amina's lamentations that night made even the dogs sob, and they barked as if they were performing a group elegy. Whenever Jadallah heard his mother's voice break into sobs, he screamed in fear, turning around to where the women were gathered, clothed in black and in the darkness of the night.

———

The year 1949 came and the drought years ended. West of the village, people seemed so tired, as if they were taking their last breaths. The sky turned black that day and dark clouds sailed across it. Men stood in front of the tents, their eyes trained on the sky. Suddenly, lightning flashed in the south, the sound of thunder rang out, and a crazy torrent of rain came down, as if some generous man had poured down everything he had all at once. Voices rang out: men, women, children, sheep, and donkeys, and the horse neighed. The tents were flooded with water, which carried away with it sheep and everything else the people there possessed, though they were able to flee to the caves. The rain continued for seven days and nights, as if a vein had been severed in the sky. The earth uttered a sigh, and life returned, after the "year of the guzzle" had ended. People compared it to what had happened in 1924, when a storm consumed everything that people lived on. In that year, al-Shamousi sowed wheat and barley, and the barren earth turned into fields as tall as men. The harvest season came, and al-Shamousi's family got up just before sunrise and headed for the field. Some carried sickles and some made do with using their hands. Ali made for the ears of corn, singing as if he were harvesting gold.

At noon, al-Shamousi got up, put down his sickle, and went over to the tent that had been set up in the middle of the field, where he had hung a hammock for Jadallah to sleep in. He drank from the waterskin, wiped away the water that had clung to his beard, then took out of his pocket a tin of Hishi tobacco and rolled a cigarette. As he smoked, he looked at the horizon, his eyes sad from Khazar's death. He could hear Amina singing with a voice full of longing as she harvested. Her voice carried him far away and tears poured down his cheeks, but he quickly wiped them away and told her in a hoarse voice to be quiet, as Jadallah had woken up.

The threshing floors were like mountains that year. Ali, Badi, and Hammoud did the threshing, using a metal sheet pulled by donkeys turning around on top of the straw. For several days, they took turns climbing on top of it until they had separated the wheat from the chaff. To preserve their blessings, al-Shamousi and Amina, with their children around them, were silent as the two of them filled the sacks and their children stitched them. The family was pleased with a better yield than they were expecting, and new hope came with it. Al-Shamousi sat on one of the sacks, looking at his sons and daughters as they moved the harvest on the donkeys' backs. He saw Jadallah stumbling toward him, holding a bird in his palm. Jadallah stood by his father, then released the bird from his hand and smiled as it flew into the sky. Al-Shamousi's face flooded with tears as he called out happily, "This is a year of blessing, Amina!"

PART 3

"Unexpressed emotions will never die.
They are buried alive and will come forth later in uglier ways."
—Sigmund Freud

1
Ibrahim

(A Thread of Hope to Cling To)

The sun was inclining toward the center of the sky as the bus screeched across the road, heading north. It was noon in November, when part of the summer heat had abated and the first signs of winter become apparent. I could see the houses racing into the distance, their yellowish color scattered over barren land whose grass had been quickly defeated in the face of the first shout of the sun. I saw pallid, emaciated, sad faces, and others that were laughing. Why should the south be cut off so harshly, like a family sent away from their dwelling alongside the river? I rested my head to sleep, for it was a long way to Amman. Most of the passengers in the bus were sound asleep—even the voice that never stopped annoying me and chiding me was asleep—but I was less fortunate. The driver began to grunt as he struggled to stay awake amid the boredom of the long road and the man beside him, who had been muttering in his sleep since we left Aqaba. He pressed nervously on the radio dial and the voice of Umm Kulthoum could be heard, singing, "Why do you torment me, you, the light of my eyes? What happened in love between you and me, why do you torment me?" The memory of Madam N's sad face appeared, calm, meek, and imploring, but strong at the same time. How, after a whole life devoid of any female, could a woman do to me what this woman had done in a few minutes? I almost cried as Umm Kulthoum went on with her song: "When I loved you and was pining away, I could not sleep, and my heart was preoccupied."

I had gone to the sea, looking for death, but because of that woman, I had given up on the deed when I met her that morning. I almost did it again, but I felt her touching me and stopping me. Was it a fantasy or some strange reality? I switched on my phone and looked at her photo. A woman who had slipped through the gate of a novel steeped in fantasy and pain and had left, avoiding the eye of the writer. At the moment I took the photo, the wind had ruffled her hair, as if the soul of a fisherman had been swallowed by the water only to emerge from the sea to pluck the strings of a *simsimiyya*, shoulder by shoulder with the sadness of a shadowy lady, or to promote a moment of quiet that perhaps had some joy behind it, or other things that it would not be useful to reveal.

A fly was circling around me, adding a sense of repulsion to the feeling engendered by the long journey. I waited until it came near my hands, then swatted it with a movement that made me think of the difference between an accidental death and a planned death. I wiped the fly's blood from my hands and went back to reading what Madame N had written in her notebook, as though a bus was hurrying toward a location I did not know.

The loss of my family induced in me a sorrow that increased as the people of the quarter around me dispersed and went back to resume their lives. I found myself alone in a house that gave me more sorrow than joy—a fact that I admit to myself when I recall how I was just a lump of flesh that everyone had to banish from sight even from a distance. The period of mourning finished and I began to look around me for a way out of my situation. I had to do several things so as not to lose my will to live. The first thing I did, in order to be me, was to change my name. I didn't like my old name, as it reminded me of past pain, like a citizen recalling the legacy of a previous ruler. During the hearing I told the judge to consider my request to change my name, that the old one frightened me. I was a woman for whom the time had come to sleep peacefully. Yes, this was the first thing I did after I found myself alone with no family. The first thing that the residents of the quarter where I lived did was to give me the nickname Malit when they found me going out, unusually, with no headscarf, wearing trousers, a shirt, and light shoes, and sometimes returning home late at night. I didn't care, even when I found out that they had written a letter to my cousin who lived abroad to complain that after the death of my family I had turned into a loose girl. What they didn't know was that I was even changing my address. I rented out my house and changed my place of residence, rented another house, and stayed there for a month without going out or speaking to anyone. I was trying to make whatever it was that was disturbing my memory take a long nap, because I was conscious that nothing can kill the memory except death. I wanted to forget that I was a disgrace. I changed my name, my style of dress, my relations with people, and my perspectives on the world. I raised my level of boldness in embracing what I loved and avoiding what I hated. I chose what I wanted and forgot the girl who had walked with head bowed for fear that some youth might shoot at her with a bullet from his eyes on her way back from school, kept her feet together, and walked slowly, according to the instructions she had been given, for fear of losing her virginity if she slipped on the road or jumped without being careful. I learned to say no when I discovered that this word might help me to avoid a link in the chain that bound my feet, so that I could stick to paths that would lead me to the image I wanted, and not an image they had drawn with their fantastic paints. I adopted a disguise for my memory and those who inhabited it, not because I didn't love them but because I was keen to recover myself after they had sent me the first order.

After a month of isolation in my new home, where I lived on the proceeds of my father's small pension and the rent from our old home, I opened the front door and went out. In reality, I was opening the windows of my soul to the sun to drive out an inner cold that had long prevented me from feeling the benefits of my surroundings. I saw neighbors—Muslims and Christians of different nationalities— living their lives contentedly. The streets were peaceful, tempting me to walk even more than I wanted to. I would smile in people's faces and look at old houses built with stones that would never age, and jasmine that had never wilted. I walked until sunset that day, then went into a restaurant, ate a little grilled chicken, and drank a coffee as I looked at the people and the streets through a wide glass door, thinking what to do in the coming days. I had to find work to help me to live. I thought of completing my education, which had stopped when my father forbade it and ordered me to leave school. I actually consulted the Education Authority and completed the conditions for entering the Secondary Examination. I spent a year with half my time devoted to study, while the other half I wandered around, acquainting myself with the place and with people, with some of whom I became friendly—like Yahya, the owner of the Ghurub café, where I sometimes went to eat a light meal, drink coffee, and read.

Passing the Secondary Certificate gave me a great sense of victory, which made me think of another victory I might achieve by enrolling in university. But that would cost me more money than I could afford. I was overcome by a sorrow I could not get rid of, despite the fact I had promised myself not to leave any openings for sadness to spatter my soul with its painful colors. I left the house, trying to put myself in the way of people, so as to avoid any possibility of succumbing to feelings of that sort. As I walked slowly along the sidewalk, I tried not to think of things that might lead me to despair, even though the rent from the house was barely enough for me. Prices had risen madly, and people were complaining that they could not cope with what was going on. I was sad, despite my efforts to avoid any path that might bring me unhappiness.

I saw a notice in a restaurant window saying that the restaurant management was looking to hire a new waitress. I stood at the door, reread the notice, and thought it would be a suitable opportunity. I got the job. The whole thing took only a few minutes, during which I met the restaurant manager, and he immediately agreed as I lived nearby. It was an unexpected move for me to find myself a waitress in a restaurant most of whose customers were writers, artists, and poets. I put on a short blue skirt, a white top, black shoes, and fastened my hair with a clip, according to the orders of the restaurant managers, who also indicated that I should not engage in conversation with the customers. The first day was marred by some confusion that I could only put right later, and it wasn't easy for me.

I became a university student when my monthly salary and time allowed it. I started work at three in the afternoon and finished at ten in the evening. The customers came at sunset, and I would eavesdrop on their conversations. People sitting at some tables would be discussing politics, while at others, those gathered around would talk culture, and sometimes someone would read some poetry. I got to know the novelist, the poet, the sculptor, and the journalist, but I only talked to the customers about things connected with the service they required. Some customers made flirtatious remarks, but I never showed any reaction apart from what was required by the restaurant regime. There were some regular customers, and others who came more erratically; some came in groups to have supper and stayed drinking and gossiping the whole evening. Some came alone, like the gentleman in his sixties I used to see coming and sitting on his own beside the window. Sometimes he would read a book, and at other times he would fold down the page and retreat into silence. White flecks made his hair and light beard seem attractive. When he came through the restaurant door, he would head for his table more calmly than anyone I had seen, as if he had an appointment with someone only he could see. He would drag his chair back slowly, sit down with his hands folded together, then put his chin on them and stare into the distance. The restaurant staff knew what he wanted to drink and would get him a glass of vodka and a plate of salad. As the days went by, the presence of that man started to give me comfort and drew me to him. Just thinking about him gave me a happiness like no other. He became part of the place, which I couldn't visualize without him. I memorized his expression and way of walking, the movement of his hands as he smoked, and his appearance during his long periods of distraction. I didn't realize I was close to love, and that I was going into a region that would change my life as I had not expected.

2
Ibrahim

(Looking for Madame N)

I was fingering the key in my pocket as I walked up the street toward home, wondering, "Why did I take it when I left?" Was it an indication that I would be coming back? I heard a shout and a scream from Anisa's house, so I walked over toward it, and as I got nearer I saw Anisa wailing and pulling her hair in the courtyard. She looked so miserable, I thought she would kill herself to escape from the pain. A police car came and ordered some people who had gathered around to move away, then they shut the door and didn't let anyone in. I asked a young man who was watching Anisa sadly in silence, and he told me her son had committed suicide, screaming, "The banks have eaten me!" The voice inside me woke up, a harsh voice this time, stressing its words: "How have things reached this point? How many losses can a woman like this bear in the last days of her life?"

He was jumping inside my belly like a cat cooped up in a narrow space. "Your misfortune is in your silence."

I went back home feeling lost, kicking the empty cans and pebbles scattered about the street. From time to time, I was pursued by Anisa's painful wails, from which my frightening companion's voice jumped out sadly: "You have to hang up the bell—take action. The world is hastening toward the chasm with frightening speed. The banks and financial institutions have appropriated a great part of people's salaries. The streets are heaving with cars mortgaged to the banks, and many residential apartments have been bought with loans. Many women have started to sell their bodies. Many people can kill for a few dinars. Look around you. These people are close to taking their last breaths."

As I went on my way, the image of my father's body suspended from the ceiling continued to rip apart my memory, while from behind I could hear Anisa wailing as she cursed the governments and the people who had caused her son's suicide. Her voice had the passionate tone of someone who loathed the world and was close to leaving it. Night had just fallen, making the houses in the quarter even more sorrowful. As I went into the house, expecting to find my father there, I realized he was already on the way to death, but I pretended to forget what had happened to him. (I know how much light this game throws on my secret happiness!) As I stood at the door, sad and afraid, I called him several times, "Father!" But the words came out of my mouth in an imploring tone, smelling of defeat. Only the echo of my voice came from inside. Can we go on loving our homes when the glass in the windows is shattered? Can we love them in the absence of our fathers? As soon as I shut the door behind me, the voice came back again: "I told you before you left that you would come back. You still don't know my great powers!"

I ignored this and opened the doors to the rooms to look around them. I was trying to reconcile myself to what was happening to me. A new order had started to bring me closer to escaping from a darkness that had long enveloped my soul, and from a chill that had not left me since I became conscious of this world.

"I'll stand under the shower in the bathroom."

This time, his voice was mocking, yet with a strange touch of compassion in it. "The water is cold, and you don't like it. So you'll get out in just a few minutes. Have you forgotten how you left that grand hotel with its hot water, comfortable bed, delicious food, and luxury you were living for the first time?"

I hurried to the bathroom and heard his voice, gentle this time: ""Look in the mirror, man, and see how you've changed. New clothes, a smart hairstyle, fresh skin, and now you've fallen in love."

I still recall the echo of my voice as it leaped between the walls. "What do you want me to do? Tell me!"

"I'm certain you won't do anything. It's I who will do it!"

"Who? Who?"

The voice disappeared. Despite being extremely tired, I started to pace around the room, hands behind my back, without thinking of anything—as if our senses were out of action but would inevitably have a moment of sudden awakening. I turned on my computer and checked out some websites before settling on Facebook. A blue screen said everything: "Iyad Nabil urges people to hold out for the country and tells them that the world is passing through a great crisis." In another post, he was standing beside some officials around a table of food at a reception. Behind this picture was a contrasting picture, which drove me to hack into his account that evening and see what I saw.

I woke up at nine o'clock the next morning and stayed in bed for some time, savoring some moments that were seldom granted me. I looked at my belly and found that it was normal. It seemed I would enjoy a day whose peace would not be disturbed by that frightening voice. I shut my eyes and constructed a daydream in which I imagined Madame N floating around the house, humming one of Fairouz's songs. I saw her coming toward me, carrying a cup of coffee with a broad smile on her face. Although I had only seen her face for a few moments, it was etched in my memory as if we had lived a long life together. The sound of a horn from a gas cylinder truck pushed that dream a long way away and I laughed at myself.

I turned on my mobile and went to Facebook's public page. People complaining of the absence of their loved ones, others writing about corrupt people, some singing, others crying. There were people cursing politicians and others praising them. The hubbub emerging from the blue screen made a lot of things seem strangely isolated. I went to 'Imad al-Ahmar's page and was shocked to find that 'Imad al-Ahmar had died. I found several posts lamenting his death and information suggesting he had been found dead in his apartment in suspicious circumstances. What fate was this, that 'Imad al-Ahmar should die on the same day that Anisa's son committed suicide? I found a link on his page saying he had been killed the previous evening and had been found tied to a chair with not a blow or a bruise on his body. I looked at the messages column and there was a message from Dr. Yusuf al-Sammak:

"I know I should not take up your own time with these messages, especially as we do not know each other, but seeing you provoked me, or perhaps I should say, prompted me, to say that they made me think more about what I am engaged with. My friends, it has nothing to do with my living in a tribal society. What I want is not a means to defend, and therefore protect, myself. It is something that comes from the depths of my heart and from my having to endure that empty area in it—the area in which black birds hover. Perhaps you will find this sincerity strange, but it is the truth. The thing that disturbs me most is that nothing I have read and believed about psychology has been able to free me of this nightmare. I know that it is odd for a doctor to consult his patient, but it seems we are sick, my friend, in different degrees. It sometimes seems to me that people need a mental hospital the size of the universe to free them from their misery, but how far can psychology do that, I wonder? After being tossed between books and professors and theories, I have started to doubt everything around me.

"There is a secret in my life that I have to tell you about. I don't believe in that sort of belonging that you yearn for. I don't deny that I long for the village of my birth, but I believe in a society freer than the one we live in. I don't know, perhaps books have muddled my head, as the saying goes."

I dressed and drank a cup of coffee, more quickly than usual, then went out. I had to look for Madame N, like a blind man looking for two hands that rubbed his eyes, restored his sight for a day and then disappeared. The smell of her perfume emerged from my memory, creating inside me a hope that I had to pursue, but where should I look, and how? My only clue was a single expression giving thousands of possible routes: "I was walking down to the center of town."

I looked through the car window as the Roman Theater—like the Antoninus in whose honor it was built—opened its arms to the morning's visitors. On which of your hills, Amman, are you hiding a woman who restored me to life, like a teacher who makes a pupil read a lesson again because he pronounced a word incorrectly? How many wrong words are there in the notebook of life that I have not written yet but others have written about me? And now here is Madame N, making me write it again. On Facebook I wrote:

"Who is this woman who stands on the edge of my confusion, like a note sticking in the mind of a musician defeated by the power of the music when he skims a stone over the lightness of the water and lets his complaint rip through the night to prepare the way for a new explanation of what happened before the trick? Who is this woman who repeats a lesson, meaning a country that breaks the promise of the bonds of her soul and the pledge of a hand to the bolt of the door to her heart, open only to words born in a night made ready for those drunk on dew that settled on the feathers of larks who saw the truth of the dawn when the earth was secretly drunk, and it was almost like silk over a body. The heavens descend from this woman, who now pours for me this brimming cup in a silence mixed with longing for a first tremor on the mouth of a heart that has realized its need for language?"

The taxi deposited me in the middle of town, and I recalled the words of a poem by Borges: "If I could live my life again!" I had spent so many of my years silently in the book kiosk that many people believed I was mute. I read most of the books that came into the kiosk. I thought that a tree had split my head and started to overshadow it; I felt it grow bigger after finishing every reading.

Which house are you in? Which bed do you sleep in? We are like each other in where we went. You left Amman and went to the sea to end your life, with no regrets for all that had gone before, while I did it to let Amman avoid what the creature might do who hides inside me like an evil embryo—Amman, a big sea in which we drown but do not die.

I stood on the sidewalk from where the Al Kalha Stairs lead up to Jabal al-Weibdeh to look at the store that had been erected in place of the Bookseller's Kiosk. The kiosk had been made of old wood, with an old door and window, smelling of books—a smell unknown to anyone who did not know how those pages were written, or that the ink used by the writers came from souls striving for life with the stubbornness of miners digging tunnels. As for the new store, it was built of brightly colored painted metal, with no smell and no memory except for the memories of mobile phones being destroyed in the event of malfunction. Where was Madame N walking to downtown from? What steps did she use? I walked up the Al Kalha Stairs and wandered among the houses, looking at the doors and windows, expecting the miracle of her face looking out at me with a smile. Then I would have shouted something I didn't say to her the morning I saw her, something the Greek lover shouted to his beloved as he implored her to accept his unconditional love (*agape*), which came from the deepest region of his soul. I spent years of my life without even an imaginary woman, and now here was a woman seductively coming and going, leading me back to a man's love for a woman, before whom he strips bare his soul to appear in all his weakness, dreams, and sorrow, weeping on his knees like a spout sobbing over smooth rock.

As the streets of al-Weibdeh led me sometimes up and sometimes down, my eyes remained fixed on the houses. Faces peered out while others hid themselves, but none were Madame N's face. Women came out and others went in, but she was not among them. The sun inclined to the west and afternoon arrived. I felt hungry, so I went into a restaurant and ordered a bowl of *ful*, fava beans, and a glass of tea. There was no one else there in the small restaurant, where only a small glass window separated me from the server. The voice came, telling me off. "You are looking for a needle in a haystack. Years of your life have gone by when you looked only for books. But now you are searching for a dream. You've got nothing to mark you out in this life, Ibrahim!"

The man brought a tray with the bowl of *ful* beans on it, with some slices of onion, a tomato, two loaves of bread, and a glass of tea. He put down the tray, gave me a strange look and went away. He stood at the restaurant door, lit a cigarette, and started to blow smoke into the air with a grunt.

Before I could take a mouthful, the voice came back again. "I know that your money is about to run out, and others are eating things you don't even know about."

I ignored him and ate quickly so I could leave and get rid of him, but he didn't stop talking. "I'll release people like you from this poverty, I have a list to complete."

The mouthful stuck in my throat. I had become sure the "thing" it was about to do was something I couldn't accept. I got up from the table and collided with it, sending everything on it to the floor with a clatter. The waiter hurried over. "Goodness me! Are you all right, sir?"

He looked at me closely, then brought a broom to sweep up the glass on the floor. "I saw you talking to yourself. Calm down— nothing in this life is worth it!"

"Sorry I made a mess!"

The man laughed and gave me a pitiful look. "The place has been a mess for a long time, sir. Don't worry!"

He tossed the pieces of glass in the trash can, dried the floor with a towel, and looked at me with sadness screaming from his tired face. "Nothing can be relied on in this city anymore," he said. "It's started to swallow us up, just like big restaurants swallowing up our small ones. I've been thinking of leaving for a while now."

I sat back down at the table. The man had disappeared inside. He came back with two glasses of tea, put one of them in front of me, and kept the other one, sipping from it constantly. He took out a cigarette and stretched his hand toward me. "Cigarette?"

"I don't smoke."

He gave a mocking laugh. His eyes had a sparkle in them as though he was about to cry. "Are you afraid of dying?"

"No," I replied, sipping my tea. "That's not exactly what I meant, but…"

"But what?"

I didn't know exactly what to say at that moment, so I kept silent and listened as he went on. "I don't know you, and you don't know me, and I don't know why you're making all this conversation between us, but everything around me stirs a feeling of depression and frustration. I spend my days in this restaurant, where I hardly make enough money for the rent and have only a little to spend on my family."

He stared through the restaurant door and gave me a sad look. "Yesterday my wife told me off. 'You haven't made love to me for

more than a month,' she said. 'Is there another woman in your life?'
I exploded in anger and heaped curses on her, then went away for
an hour. When I came back, I apologized to her and told her I no
longer had any desire for anything, even women!"

He lit a new cigarette, which he smoked sadly and quietly.
"Imagine, they've even stolen our pleasure in sex!"

Having said that, he went off to deal with a customer, then
turned to me and said, "Don't pay. I'll count listening to me as
paying your bill!"

3
Leila

(Escaping From the Trap)

The strangest thing that happened to me was my longing for the orphanage, a feeling I tried not to let return to me again. How could I long for a place of which I still retained bad memories? People here are different from how I remember them; they are not all good. There were people who gave me twice the price of a packet of handkerchiefs, and some gave me money for nothing, but I refused that. I was not a beggar. And some would shut their car windows when they found me offering things for sale. I would sit on the sidewalk and look at the cars and their occupants and think, "Perhaps this is my father, a man with yellowish skin and a moustache tinged with white, standing waiting for the crowd to ease and clear a space for him to go on his way. Now he is daydreaming; perhaps he is recollecting the details of a night that hid anyone who wanted to stay hidden, when he met my mother under a tree, behind a wall, or in a room in a house in this city. I can see them, blinded by desire. And when they woke up, they found themselves facing disaster. They would certainly be killed, a good man and woman who did not dare have an abortion, and when the time came for the secret birth, they threw me into the street."

A hubbub of car horns could be heard, so I set off, still looking at the faces—women's faces and men's faces. What would happen, do you suppose, if I stood in the middle of the road, held up the traffic, took off my men's clothes, and shouted, "I want my mother and father!" I looked at a woman who was listening to a song as she looked over the cars. She looked at me with sad eyes; perhaps this woman was my mother, who had been living through the highest degrees of pain since that night when they took me from her hands and threw me in the street to avoid a scandal. She might be looking in people's faces, looking for a clue that would take her to her daughter, but how could she find me when I was wearing men's clothes and had trained myself to imitate men's actions, looks, and ways of flirting to perfection? When I look at myself, I find I have started to turn into a man. A few days ago, Salam asked me why my voice had changed this way. But as soon as I came back from the street, everything reverted to normal: sorrow at our situation, my dream of a family, my dream of a man who would take me in his arms. I stood in front of a fragment of mirror fastened to the wall of the deserted house and felt my short hair and men's clothes—a disguise that had not brought me the security I wanted.

One day I was moving between the cars going up to the Third Circle from downtown. Dark clouds were moving across the sky; it was about to pour, and the beginnings of a wind was bringing a few spots of rain with it. Apparently, a thunderstorm was heading for the region. I was wearing the same clothes: a loose shirt and jeans, but I only noticed that my shirt button had slipped when a man stopped in front of me, smoking furiously and looking at me with bloodshot eyes. I had seen the man spying on me before, but I reckoned it was a coincidence, so I ignored the fears that had started to bother me even previously when sleeping among the orphanage residents. "I want a packet of handkerchiefs," he said in a rough voice. I bent down and discovered that he was staring at my breasts, which he had seen through the opening in my shirt. When I gave him the packet, he stretched out his hand and grabbed my chest. "I knew you were a girl!" he said. I jumped up in terror and threw the bag away as he came closer, his eyes fixed on a man standing near him. "Don't pretend to be good with me. Come on, let's have some fun. I'll give you all the money you want. I like sleeping with women and children all the same. I've had my eye on you for a while, and I'm mad about you!"

The voice of the supervisor the day she violated me struck my ears like the hissing of a snake. I felt her long, thick fingers feeling my body. I wanted to scream for someone to save me from that man, but I found it easier to run away, so I retreated, looking for somewhere to run. I hurried toward the gap that led to the deserted house and ran along the twisting alley, but I turned back for fear that he might discover the building. There I saw the man in front of me at a corner with the horrid smells where the gap led. I cried for help in terror, but the noise of the cars was louder than my voice. As the man gradually drew nearer, undoing his trouser belt and taking out his erect penis, I kept to the wall. "Don't worry! It'll only take a few minutes!" he said, in a hoarse, frightening voice like that of a madman.

I was pressing my body back, as if the wall would respond by clearing me a space to escape. I saw the supervisor beside the man coming toward me. Behind them were a good man and woman, looking at me sadly. Perhaps they were my mother and father. I quickly bent down, picked up a stone, and threw it at the man. As it hit his brow, blood poured out and he fell unconscious on the shit and urine. "Oh my God, I've killed him!" I shouted in terror, as the first of the rain began to pour down. Then I fled, only for something unexpected to happen to me.

4
Ibrahim

(No Home for the Bookseller)

I looked out over Amman at night. The loneliness behind me was great and of several kinds; relieved only by the hands of a clock that I had to smash, it had begun to give me so much pain. Amman was in front of me, but I could not enter it: hotels hosting parties, with food I did not know; club doors manned by personal guards with strapping muscles. Penetrating cities like that required just one thing—money—and I was a man who had known nothing in his life except books, goods that no longer had any value. But was this just the world of Amman? Amman had another world: frustrating, boring, and sad, like a table with three legs.

My footsteps in the house had also started to annoy me, making me even gloomier. Everything was silent; I couldn't even hear the noise from Jabal al-Jawfa that evening. What was I to do? I walked toward the hall, where the books from the kiosk were piled up, and picked up a novel that had fallen from a bundle onto the floor: *Cain,* by José Saramago. I read two pages of it and threw it to one side. I got up and looked for a book that would cheer me up, but I felt a movement in my belly and saw it gradually swelling. I hurried without thinking to the bedroom to look at my body in the mirror, when I heard a warning: "We have to reach an agreement. I will grant you a month's extension. But if you don't do anything within the period of the agreement, I won't regret anything that happens."

I knew he would come back and increase my fear and uncertainty. The phone vibrated in my pocket, scaring me. There was a new message from the same number: "How did what I saw in the kitchen happen?" I stood at the window; my neighbor's balcony door was shut, and I hadn't seen her for days. What if she came out now and invited me into her home again? This time I'd go because of the message—or perhaps just because I wanted to talk to her. I didn't have the slightest curiosity about what lay hidden behind her veil or to check on what was said about her regarding her relations with men. I didn't have any sexual desire for a woman. I just wanted to escape from the thing that was disturbing my sleep and making me unhappy all the time.

The street was empty, and it was almost midnight. Most of the neighbors' apartments were dark, with no signs of movement in them. I went out and crossed the street, looking around me like a robber, went through the front door of the apartment block, then walked up to the second floor. My heart was beating so hard it almost split my chest, as if I was about to commit a crime, and I was breathing so hard from an unexpected nervousness that I could hardly reach the door of her apartment. From inside, I could hear a song about loneliness. I touched the door to knock at it, but what if the woman no longer lived in this apartment? What would I say to whoever opened the door? So I went back to where I had come, blaming myself for a rash step that might have led me I don't know where. As I crossed the street, a man gave me doubtful looks, which followed me until I got home. I lay down in bed and the voice came back, mocking this time: "Why were you scared when you found that man looking at you?" he asked.

"It's not fear, it's caution," I replied, trying to overcome the tension I felt whenever the voice came back to me.

I heard a loud laugh and saw my belly shaking. "Caution is a sort of fear I never know myself," the voice said.

Where had this torment come from? What doctor, policeman, man of religion, or even magician, could get this creature out of me? But how could I go to a magician with the smell of books in my memory rather than their cloud of incense?

My phone played a tune to indicate a message, and I found one from Dr. Yusuf, asking, "How are things?"

"Not good. I am still wrestling with that strange creature."

"We all wrestle with things in our lives, and do not know who will win in the end."

I found this a strange sort of reply coming from a psychologist. I expected him to at least check that I was keeping to the medicine he had prescribed for me. It was a short conversation, and I did not know what lay behind it, but he seemed to need to talk.

———

I woke in the morning to a series of knocks on the door. When I opened it, I found the landlord there. He looked angry; his eyes were almost popping out of his head, his veins were swollen, and his chest was thumping up and down as he breathed rapidly. "I'll not beat about the bush," he said. "You must pay your rent. Isn't it enough that you only pay a tiny sum, when most rents in Amman have gone up so much?"

He said nothing for a moment as he directed a threatening look at me. "There is a family who will pay me twice what you are paying. You must quit the apartment or else … "

He looked around him then resumed his stare. "Or else, I'll send someone who will leave you with a messed-up face," he said, before leaving, dragging his steps on account of his conspicuous obesity.

My neighbor was watching me from her balcony, putting a box out before disappearing inside. I shut the door and sat down against the wall, thinking about what to do. I had only a few dinars left and no one in the quarter to protect me from the people he had threatened me with. There was no way out of this dilemma.

I heard the voice, angry this time. "Do you see how fear exposes you? This cursed fat slob threatened you with the quarter bully and you couldn't even argue with him."

As I went into the lounge, stumbling over the books, my belly was swelling more than before. I stopped at the restroom door to splash myself with water to get rid of him, even if only temporarily.

"The thing you do best in life is run away. Never mind, I will add this man to the list. You no doubt know what I will do."

"What would you have done if you were in my position?"

"I would beat him. The logic of beating can only be countered by beating."

"But beating has no logic to it. If it did, none of the destruction that earthquakes cause would happen."

"You cling to your books to justify your fear."

I couldn't take what he was saying, so I rushed to the bathroom in my clothes, turned on the shower, and let the water rain down on my head. As I cried, I found a strange pleasure in my tears; I cried for fear, and pain, and loss, and for some strange reason that I didn't know, I cried because I hadn't found Madame N, and because I had become a hostage of hers. As on a few previous occasions, I found myself close to surrendering to the voice. As the days went by, the distance between us had started to narrow, and what he said stuck in my memory. At certain moments, I would recollect it, think about it, then suddenly realize the gravity of it. I left the bathroom feeling angry and guilty. I undressed in front of the mirror and took hold of the knife, but he had vanished. I waited for him for a little, but he didn't reappear. My hand was shaking, and sweat was pouring from my forehead and neck. The longer I waited, the more my throat dried up. I threw the knife down, lay on the ground, and burst into tears again, wondering who was to be killed—him or me?

———

The landlord came again. I had returned from a day spent looking for Madame N, like a man afflicted with a cold who needs a coat to bring him warmth and the start of a road to recovery. There was a knock on the door, and I knew who it was. He had brought two youths with him, with tattooed arms and who smelled of drink. They stood on either side of him. "I'll give you until tomorrow noon," he said, in a soft voice that concealed the threat behind the calm. I could see another version of it in the eyes of the two youths. "After that, you will have to bear the responsibility for anything that happens."

My belly stayed the whole night like that of a woman about to give birth, and the voice pursued me wherever I tried to escape. It was a hard night, for he kept inciting me to violence—a thing I was not used to—until I went to sleep and entered a world of so many nightmares that I felt numb in the face of them. I left home in the morning, having decided what I would do. Was it a decision or a defeat that I could not confess to anyone? Is defeat a prior decision we cannot confess to? And what defeat led me to such a painful chain of losses? After all those years, I was left with nothing. The only things linking me to my place of birth were memories that occasionally came back to me, then left me for several years. I had lost the kiosk that for years had given me a haven to compensate me for the oxygen thieves around me. I had lost my mother, father, brother, even my hope of finding Madame N, and now I was losing my home. Losing a home was a disaster, like birds with no protection from a hunter's gun, oblivious to the intentions of a finger egging on the gunpowder to devise a wider form of disaster. From now, then, I shall be Diogenes in a city that has never cared for me, and walk with no compass or direction.

I went to a store that bought used furniture and offered them the few items from my home: my mother and father's bedroom, a sign of contentment in a world full of fear; the bedroom 'Ahid and I used when we were near to collapse; the old set of chairs, smelling of bygone days; the TV used once but more often quiet except for a flicker of light. He bought everything except the books. He wrote something with a stick between his teeth then spat on the floor, saying, "I don't need paper."

At ten in the morning the dealer came with a truck and two people who proceeded to remove the house's contents. I stood at the door holding a case with my computer in it, my father's birth certificate, a picture of the family, my notebook of nightmares, Madame N's notebook, and the Diogenes book. I sold everything for 400 dinars.

Just before they finished emptying the house, I saw one of the pair who were with the landlord checking from a distance that I was complying with their demand to vacate the house. Meanwhile, the neighbors watched what was going on from their windows— just like that female neighbor of mine, who stayed longer on her balcony this time. The truck left the neighborhood, spewing a trail of exhaust fumes through which I could see the truck that carried us from the village that year, and I saw myself as a child, crying silently in sorrow for the place.

The books were lonely in the face of all that silence and emptiness, enough to create an echo. I shut the door and wandered around the house. My shoes clicked with a rhythm like that of strange creatures, producing a sound that leaped around the house. I contemplated the memories that could not be sold and smelled smells whose extent could only be known by those who had been there for the birth of the moment. From the corners of the apartment the voices of my family emerged: friendly voices, loving and warm, as if to compensate me in my moments of loss for what had passed me by. As I wept bitterly, my voice echoed around the walls, which returned it to me laden with an even greater sense of defeat and loss. Then the voice came, full of anger and a mournful tone, reproaching me for what I had done and for my great weakness. "You have only the books now, you cursed bookseller! Take them with you and go!"

As he ranted and raved, I writhed in the face of my sense of uselessness, a feeling that the world was on the horns of a raging bull as it watched from a distance a piece of red cloth and prepared for the decisive moment.

I stood gazing at all the books, creatures recording life with a silence worth its weight in gold. I lay down on the ground and flipped through some of them: the *Kitab* of Sibawayhi, Jahiz's *Epistles*; *Muruj al-Dhahab*; *Ikhwan al-Safa'*; *al-Madina al-Fadila*; along with some collections of poetry, novels, short stories, biographies, books on politics.

I carried the books out of the apartment and put them down in a small area on the side of the street. Some people looked at me, while my neighbor leaned from her balcony in the direction of the passersby. I heard the voice say in a decisive, provocative tone, "You don't need them anymore! They give too much weight to trash!"

Then I felt him pushing me from the front. "Burn them!"

He came closer, and in a voice like a sad song started to recite part of a poem by the American poet Robert Frost: "Some say that the world will end in fire, some say in ice. From what I've tasted of desire, I hold with those who favor fire."

An old man walked past me slowly, stopped and lit a cigarette, then carried on, looking back at me with a mocking smile. I hurried up to him and asked him for a lighter, which he passed to me, and I set fire to the books. As I handed the lighter back to him, he patted my shoulder and went on his way, muttering some unintelligible words from a sad song. I picked up my little bag and went away, the smoke from the books rising into the sky. I had just announced the start of winter.

5
The Journalist

(A Woman Sick of Moving)

I seem to be always moving from one home to another. The Bedouin move throughout the desert, driven by the search for water and pasture. What am I searching for in Amman, a city where I feel more afraid the older I get, but where my strange love for it also grows stronger? A varied city suiting my temperament, which in the last few years has started to toss and turn with a strange rhythm. Downtown suits my sad mood, which requires me to walk alone, with no desire to speak to anyone, and the west of Amman disturbs the temperament of a woman like me, who gets the urge to dance once a year. I change a lot of things: my books, my clothes, my perfumes, even the small number of my friends I have exchanged for solitude. I swapped this house about a month ago and have become an expert in killing the memories of any house or place I leave. Memories pain me and wear me out, like the music I gave up some days ago. I had to empty my inner cabinet of everything in it in order to live. It was a cupboard in which everything of ours had piled up since childhood. We don't know that we can fall down for a simple reason, which is then magnified by our chaos, turning it into a disaster. Recently, I have tried to empty out my possessions in order to enjoy an empty space; if anything crosses it, it will be normal compared with what I have rid myself of. Perhaps the vision will become clearer.

The rain poured down. It was the start of winter, which I liked in the past, and waited for with great patience. I saw the world in a romantic way that no longer has any effect on me. Winter has once again become a strange sort of loneliness for me. It always comes in the shape of a solitary man walking on a rainy night. I picked up a scarf from my cupboard, put it over my shoulders, and sat down on the sofa, looking at the horizon over Jabal Amman, with dark clouds racing above it. I pushed my laptop aside and lay down.

I had finished a journalistic investigation about prostitutes in the city, in which I had often gone looking for them in the streets and alleys, in the places where they stood waiting for clients—sad women, most of whom faked pleasure to gratify the pride of their customers. Some of these men were escaping from wives who were unable to satisfy their men in bed, while others were bachelors with a long road to marriage before them. These desperate women only dreamed of a small, warm house in the company of a man able to heal the wounds that had afflicted them.

It was now raining even harder, and I could smell the scent from a small patch outside, opposite the front door, where a loquat tree and some ornamental plants had been planted. In the past, I had been excited to smell the scent of the earth at the first rain shower, overwhelmed by a burning desire for the love of a man who would make me cry with happiness at being with him. I put my computer in my lap and opened a page to add some ideas I had for a serial I planned to write. In the scenario column I wrote:

"Scene one / outside / night. The camera captures a scene of a man walking in the street on a rainy night. The man is wearing a long coat. He puts his hands on his brow and walks with a sad rhythm. The man seems unconcerned by the rain or the splashes from the car wheels, until he disappears."

I wrote until midnight as scenes from my imagination poured forth in quick succession. Both the easiest and the most difficult writing comes from the depths of what we have lived through. I had to write what had happened in order to escape from the memory, as well as from depression. I turned off the computer and got up to go to bed but I was unable to sleep, despite the pills I had taken to make me feel drowsy. As I looked at the notebook, the man's odor clung to it like a well-made amulet. I picked it up and smelled the paper, then rested my head on the pillow, looking at the pages:

In the summer of 1953, al-Shamousi woke from his sleep. Jadallah wasn't in bed. He looked for him but couldn't find him, so he rushed out of the house and found him on a nearby mound, sitting on the ground with his elbows on his thighs and his hands around his head, looking toward Madaba. That year, al-Shamousi built a house of stone and mud in the village, planted fig trees, pomegranates, and vines around it, dug a well for water, and quit herding animals for other people. He made do with just a few animals, using the money he had saved from Salim and Khazar's wages and from what he had made from the wheat harvests. He was happy with their situation but was worried about Jadallah since discovering that, unlike other boys his age, he wasn't playing or doing what they were doing. He was usually silent, seldom spoke and seldom laughed. Once, when it was raining hard, he saw Jadallah go outside and run under the drainpipes on the house, trying to catch the water; then he climbed the wall and raised his head so that the water fell in his mouth. Al-Shamousi only saw him happy on that one occasion, even when he came back inside and kept looking at the trees in the orchard with the water pouring from them.

Al-Shamousi walked hesitantly toward Jadallah and sat down beside him. Jadallah's eyes stayed on Madaba. It was a morning, when the horizon was bright blue. "What are you thinking about?" asked al-Shamousi, in a tone intended to draw him out.

"Why do people die?"

Al-Shamousi was annoyed. Looking at his son's sad face, he tried to comfort him, saying, "It is what God wants."

Jadallah again became distracted, leaving his father concerned about him. "Father, am I a good person?" he asked.

Al-Shamousi put his arm around Jadallah, close to tears and even more fearful for his son. "Yes, you are," he said.

"I see someone telling me the opposite when I am asleep," he said, his voice betraying signs of fear. He looked his father in the eye and begged him, "Don't leave me!"

Al-Shamousi immediately burst into tears and began reciting verses from the Holy Qur'an, along with other prayers and imprecations. Then he led him by the hand and took him to Amina to tell her what had happened. She put incense over him and hurried to an old woman from the village who made amulets and read fortunes using sand or small pebbles. Greatly afraid, she repeated "Oh my poor boy!" nonstop as they made their way over dry grass and stones. When she arrived, she knocked hard on the door and rushed inside as soon as it began to open. "My boy is in danger," she said, panting.

She then proceeded to describe his behavior and what he had said to his father that morning. The old woman scattered some pebbles of various shapes and colors onto the ground, scrutinizing them until she sighed and pointed to one in front of the rest of the pebbles. "This boy is not yours," she said.

"Will he die?" Amina screamed. She then went up to the old woman, put her hand on her shoulder, pleading with her.

"No, he won't die in this life!"

Amina had taken a piece of Jadallah's tunic with her, which she gave to the old woman. She wrapped the piece of cloth around another piece and stitched it, then brought it near her mouth and muttered a few unintelligible words. When she had finished, she asked her to hang it on his clothes. That year some houses were built in the village, and in the same year Jadallah went to school, joining his brothers Hammoud and Badi, who were two years older than him. Mahmoud al-Shamousi had gone down to the valley, collected all the worn-out old shoes he could find there, left them in a basin of water until they softened, and then made shoes for Jadallah using hammer, chisel, and scissors. He made pants for him from the sacking that held the flour sent to Palestinian refugees, and from the same material produced a school bag with UN written on it. Jadallah got on the back of the donkey behind his father, and the pair went down the western slope of the village and crossed the flat ground with the red soil. It was the beginning of September, and the breeze had taken away some of the heat of the summer, which had been harsh that year, Al-Shamousi took a packet of Hishi tobacco from his pocket, put a bit of it in a small piece of paper, and wrapped it between his fingers. Then he licked the edges and rolled it into a cigarette, lit it with a kerosene lighter, inhaled deeply, and looked into the empty distances stretching around him. "Jadallah, my son," he said, in a quiet, contemplative voice. "Do you remember when you were sick and I carried you to Nicola, the doctor, last year?"

"I remember, father," said Jadallah, one hand wrapped around his father's waist, the other fingering the empty cloth bag hanging from his shoulder. Al-Shamousi puffed on his cigarette, resisting a sudden urge to cry. "I want you to become a *hakim*, a doctor, like Nicola."

There was a short silence, which al-Shamousi broke before his son could speak again. "Do you hear me, son?"

"I hear you, father, and I want to tell you something."

Jadallah sunk into a short silence. "Tell me, what is it you are hiding from me?" asked al-Shamousi.

Jadallah couldn't express what was going through his mind. He was happy that his father no longer worked for anyone. It had pleased him greatly when, the previous year, a man had come to him pleading for him and his family to look after someone's animals, and his father had refused. Al-Shamousi kicked the donkey's belly with his heel and started to sing, his voice tinged with new signs of hope. Jadallah fondled the amulet that his mother had fastened to his shirt and recalled what she had said to him. He looked at the sky, where a bird was hovering, almost stationary in its place, and watched it carefully. Then he snatched the amulet and threw it on the ground. They passed through Hayy al-Nawar and carried on walking to the west past the police station until they reached the school.

The school consisted of three rooms built of a yellowish stone: one for the headmaster and two teachers, and the other two for the pupils. It stood on a slightly elevated area that looked out over the eastern plains of Madaba, which stretched out uninterrupted. Al-Shamousi stopped and glanced at them briefly, then at his village and his house standing on top of the hill while Jadallah looked at the school in astonishment, hiding his fear. It was the pupils' first day. Some had come from the villages, some from the city. Their faces were different: those from the city tended to be red mixed with white, and the darker among them had pure skin and full faces. Most of their clothes and shoes were new and brightly colored. The village children had tired, thin faces and thick hair, and some of their clothes were patched and worn out. Their eyes had a surprised and yet a blank look, unable to comprehend what was happening around them. These children moved quickly, suddenly turning around as if anticipating a threat. Al-Shamousi walked toward a man wearing an olive-colored safari jacket. He had a smooth red pate and protruding eyes behind thick glasses. In his hand he held an oleander branch of medium length. As soon as he saw al-Shamousi, he went to him and embraced him warmly. "Greetings, Abu Ali!"

Jadallah took refuge behind his father's tall frame and looked at the man suspiciously. Al-Shamousi turned to his son and said, "This is *khatib* Awwad."

They called the schoolteacher *khatib*, honored him with the best seat they had, and held him in the greatest esteem. The pupils revered him, as did even those who had never been to school.

"This is my boy, Jadallah. I told him I want him to become a *hakim*, a doctor, like Nicola."

Awwad laughed and frowned. He looked at Jadallah. "Go with your brothers, he said. "God be with you, Abu Ali; we will keep Jadallah in our sight."

Al-Shamousi looked at Jadallah fondly as he watched him join his brothers, who were sitting on the edge of a low wall in the school playground. Then he said decisively, "*Khatib* Awwad, the bones are ours, but the skin is yours if he is lazy."

This was al-Shamousi's way of asking the teacher to be stern so that Jadallah should not neglect his studies. If he didn't pass by the children, he might let them think the schoolmasters' stick was no harsher than poverty and the harshness of life. Jadallah sat on his school chair that day, looking at Badi and Hammoud in the other room, their shaved heads marking them out from the others, while the teacher distributed books to the pupils. When he had done that, the lesson began. "Abjd, hwz, hty klmn ..." said the teacher, who then told the pupils to repeat it. Their voices were all different from one another: some vigorous, some shy and fearful, like Jadallah's, who chanted with the others without understanding anything. In the second class, the teacher walked between the desks, stick in hand, and asked, in a slightly threatening tone, "Have you brought notebooks and pencils with you?"

Several pupils replied all at once, in different tones, and took out their notebooks and pencils from their bags. The teacher looked at those who had said nothing and then went up to Jadallah, who suddenly found it difficult to breathe, looked into his embarrassed eyes, and said, "I want to see notebooks and pencils with you tomorrow."

Some pupils nodded, while others gave the teacher a silent look from which nothing in particular could be understood. The classes went on until break time arrived, which lasted for two hours. The schoolyard was empty, except for Jadallah, Badi, Hammoud, and a few village children. The three of them sat on the edge of the wall, looking into one another's faces. Jadallah felt a great hatred for the school and wanted to leave, but he was scared of his father's reaction if he did. "Where have the others gone?" he asked in a low voice, afraid that someone might overhear him.

"They've gone to have lunch at home," replied Badi, scratching his head as he looked at the village; their house looked tiny from this distance.

"What are they eating?"

Hammoud noticed how his toe was poking out from a crack in his shoe and chuckled. "I heard them say they were eating *maqlouba* once."

"What is this *maqlouba*?" asked Badi, sighing.

"I don't know."

Jadallah was silent for a moment as he looked at the village. "Why don't we go home to eat?"

"You'd only find bread and tea there," replied Hammoud in a lazy voice.

The pupils returned and crowded into the schoolyard. Jadallah stood to one side and looked into their faces one by one before crossing over to the classroom with the others after the bell had rung. Only Hammoud was left in the yard, standing like a statue, and when Badi waved to him to go in, he remained glued to the spot. Jadallah watched what was happening in amazement. When Badi asked from a distance why he was standing there, Hammoud pointed to something under his foot, looked around in every direction, and picked something up. Then he quickly went in, sat down panting, and said to Badi in a whisper, "I found a *qirsh* (coin)!"

Hammoud was extremely happy as they returned from school, clutching his *qirsh* and keeping it away from Badi, who wanted to hold it. Jadallah looked at them, sometimes with a smile, and sometimes with a puzzled look, until they reached al-Dawwaj's shop, where they used the *qirsh* to buy more than a kilo of dates. By the time they reached the edge of the orchard, with the well that al-Shamousi had dug there, the dates were all finished. Hammoud looked at Badi, hands over his stomach, laughing and pointing at Badi's face, which had turned red. Meanwhile, Jadallah sat on the edge of a stone water basin watching them laughing and then picking up a bucket of water and drinking from it greedily before spraying each other with the rest of the water.

Hammoud and Badi didn't ask about food that day, as they usually did, although they knew they would only find lentil soup or corn broth. Instead, they went straight to the animal enclosures. As the sun disappeared behind the village hills, the animals returned, making a great noise as they made their way into their pens to attack the water basins while Hammoud and Badi grumbled at the goats they were running behind to herd them into the enclosures. Whenever al-Shamousi looked at them, they hid their anger and went on with their work in silence, preparing the animals for milking, having tied most of them up with rope. Then Amina and her two daughters, Sharifa and Jawazi, sat down to milk them while al-Shamousi hovered over them, giving orders in a hoarse voice. Night descended, and pale lamps were lit in some of the tents along with one in al-Shamousi's house—two rooms built of stone and mud. The family gathered around a plate of corn broth cooked with *laban*, and when they had finished eating, everyone except for al-Shamousi and Amina went to bed. From the edge of the village came the sound of dogs barking and women calling to one another, interrupted by the continual coughing of an old man in one of the nearby tents. Hammoud, Badi, and Jadallah lay in a single bed.

Hammoud and Badi chatted for a few minutes until they fell asleep, while Jadallah stayed awake thinking about his first day at school, the teacher's voice never leaving his ears as he told him to bring notebooks and pencils. Several times he got up and went to his father, standing at the door of the room that looked over the veranda as the moon peeked out, lighting up the village. "The *khatib* asked me to bring notebooks and pencils," he said.

Al-Shamousi looked at Jadallah and spread out his arms with a smile. Jadallah walked toward him, relaxed his skinny body for him, and al-Shamousi whispered in his ear, "Tomorrow I'll go to Madaba and find the money to get you what you want."

When Amina noticed that the amulet wasn't in its place, she asked about it, but he said he didn't know what had happened to it. She spent some time searching the house for it but eventually she gave up the hope of finding it and went to bed, with a plan to go to the old woman and have her make another one.

Next morning, Jadallah woke up to the sound of his father's voice calling out, "Sleep is for women, and the animals for men!" He rubbed his eyes with the back of his hand, followed his brothers to a barrel filled with water, splashed some on his face, and dried it with his shirt. Meanwhile, the cock had been crowing nonstop, standing on the back of the coop as he announced the start of morning. He looked at his sister Jawazi, who had fastened a kerchief around her waist and was busy distributing water and straw to the animals. He thought of what his father had said, and about how desperate men and women were linked together, and he was not happy. He went up to her and kissed her, then put on his shoes and sat near the stove his mother had lit on the veranda, putting a tea kettle and coffee pot on top of it. He poured a glass of tea for himself and drank it, looking at his sister Sharifa, who had just finished preparing bread. Jadallah knew that family members were not allowed to drink milk more than once a week.

Amina's stern regime, to avoid famine—which had been harsher in the past—was to make *jameed* (dried yoghurt) and clarified butter from the milk to sell in the market. So she gave everyone a fixed portion of food and hid her supplies in a box that she kept locked with a key that hung around her neck. She mended clothes when they had been torn and even made Badi and Hammoud rub out what they had written in their notebooks so they could be used again. Jadallah ate half a loaf with some tea and walked his frail body along with his two older brothers, in fear of the teacher's stick. In this, he was just like Badi and Hammoud, who knew the sort of punishment they could expect. It was just as they anticipated: the teacher separated out the pupils who had brought notebooks from those who hadn't. Jadallah scowled as he watched the teacher bring the stick down on the pupils' hands. When his turn came, he refused to hold out his hand. The teacher looked at him angrily and contemptuously, bringing the stick down on his hand in a threatening manner. "Hold out your hand," he said, and when Jadallah refused to comply, he looked him in the eye and said in a threatening tone, "I told you to hold out your hand!"

"My father is going to get some exercise books for me today," said Jadallah, quaking with fear. "Tomorrow I'll bring them with me."

And when this didn't spare him the punishment, he picked up his bag and walked out of the room, paying no attention to the teacher, who called him back with a threat.

A Nightmare

I knock on the door to the apartment, put on a mask, and pick up a revolver. The door opens and 'Imad al-Ahmar suddenly looks out. I kick him and point the revolver at him; he shakes violently and I hit him on the back of his head and he loses consciousness. I put him on a chair, tie him up with a rope, gag him with a piece of cloth, put a chair in front of him, spray perfume near his nose so he wakes up, and tries to scream. I expose to him all his filth, the payments he agreed to in exchange for bribes, the sums he embezzled. I show him the obscene pictures he exchanges with his lovers. I show him the records he keeps of women he exploits for money. As his attempts to scream and plead grow more intense, I take a knife from my pocket and tell him I will cut off his fingers and chop off his penis. I take off his pants, then his underpants, clutch his penis, and bring the knife toward him. He tries even harder to scream, and then he dies of fright.

PART 4

"Violence produces only something resembling justice, but it distances people from the possibility of living justly, without violence."
—Leo Tolstoy, *War and Peace*

1
Ibrahim

(What Happened Under the Bridge)

That day, I became homeless, just like a bird whose nest has been destroyed by the wind and cast out alone into the open air. The rain poured down, more frightening than I had ever known. I was like someone walking naked, unable to cover their private parts, and I recalled what my father said to me a year after my mother's death: "I feel I am in a freezing cold desert."

I walked the whole way from Jabal al-Jawfa to downtown, where I wandered until nightfall. The bitter cold spread everywhere, racing through the alleys and slipping along the streets. Death seemed to me like some fantastical bird planting its claws into my soul, which was always thirsty to be propped up by someone when it was close to collapse—like a river that would not be a river were it not for the contours of the valley and its two banks. I looked at every face hoping to see Madame N, although I was sure she had become something I had lost before I ever gained it. Her face was suspended like the pendulum of a clock before my eyes, never leaving me. I sat in a small restaurant, ate a plate of beans, and drank a glass of tea. Apart from me, the only other person was a man in his fifties who looked like a tramp. He ate quickly and then left, coughing and blowing into his small hands. There was a tatty picture of the sea hanging on the restaurant wall, with a fisherman in the middle casting his net. I turned on my phone to look at the picture of Madame N. I wished I could tear up that picture and go back to that moment and reconstitute it. I wrote on Facebook:

"When does the heart become a house? When the homeland neglects us and concerns itself with the ins and outs of politics, and with politicians falling into the pit of error of their own free will; when the sky is cruel, opening its doors wide to the frost and creating a new meaning for the open air. Your heart is my home, I was certain of that from those first rays that shattered the wall of my darkness that morning, raising my hand aloft, stirring my feet that were clinging to the ground, and enticing me to fly. When love happens in war, it ignores the shadows, bringing relief from the smell of death and distracting us from the destruction that has occurred. When love happens in sorrow, it extracts from the heart's mouth a ball of thorns mistakenly slipped in by time, which refuses to acknowledge the error. When love happens at a time of grief, it prompts us to sing, like a father pushing a daughter with amputated feet to dance on the ground of the imagination. It happens that you spend all those years, and I love you in a fleeting moment like a bullet that misses its target and rattles in the peace of the air."

The stores shut their doors, and the number of cars and pedestrians gradually decreased until there were only cats, police patrols, and a few drunks in the streets. Rain seems friendly when we see it through a window, with music behind us making things pleasant and different, but now I was seeing its wilder face, for cities in the rain are a terrifying desert. My feet were tired, so I sat under a public bus shelter on King Hussein Street, tightened the collar of my jacket around my neck, and contemplated the empty space. All the gates were shut in the heart of the city except for the one letting the icy cold air in. Everything was silent, even my phone, which no longer rang with calls from people asking for a book. I looked at the screen, but no one had called. I tapped on the Facebook icon and found a picture that had just been published of Iyad Nabil sitting in front of a splendid stone fireplace. A misleading caption had been added to the picture, as if he was sending a message to someone: "In the company of friends." But he had forgotten that there was a woman's hair clip on the edge of the fireplace. It was his secret house, which I learned about when I hacked his account.

The bus stopped in front of me, opened its door, and I boarded. Where it would take me wasn't important, for nothing had any value anymore. I no longer had that secret view of the wheel of time or of how it moved forward. I was like a dry leaf on a tree, like the one I had seen through the bus window floating on a stream of water flowing toward downtown. I ignored my feeling of remorse that I was going where that leaf was going—into the city sewers. A strange feeble-mindedness made me not even think of finding a refuge for myself as the bitter cold intensified. I took a quick glance around me. Half the seats in the bus were empty. Some faces were silent and full of tiredness, while others contemplated a winter that had come to cleanse the night, empty the city of its pedestrians, and spare the tramps, some of whom were hiding in the alleys. Through the bus window, the city of Amman resembled a silent film, increasing my sense of loss. I opened my bag and resorted to reading a book about Diogenes, who mocked everything and roamed the streets naked, leaning on his stick and carrying a lamp in broad daylight, with no home except for a wooden barrel. I whispered to myself: I will teach myself to walk in his path from tonight onward. Nothing has any value; lies have become a great cloak to cover this city's body. I will not hate anything or love anything except my freedom.

My phone buzzed, signaling a message from Dr. Yusuf al-Sammak:

"Dear Ibrahim, In spite of your suffering from the voice that dominates you, you are stronger than me. You have thrown caution to the winds, with no regrets over the house you were evicted from. A great faith in yourself—this is what can help you avoid my situation, despite the hard times you are living through."

I thought this message odd; in fact, I was stunned by it.

"How did you know that I had left my apartment?"

"You wrote to me?"

My God! How had this happened? I studied the list of messages and discovered that I really had written him several messages. Now a new message came from him:

"In my previous message, I told you there was something I was hiding from you. Do you know that the thing that can ruin us most in this life is our inability to reveal what our memory is hiding? Imagine that you see your father in front of you and do not dare approach him; imagine that he will laugh at you if you call him 'Father.' 'Get out of my sight, you idiot!' he will say. Imagine looking at your personal ID and finding your name linked to another man's name. It's the most confusing area. This is what happened to me, to the extent that I don't dare conceive children, as I know that I will not be able to play the role of father properly when I have never lived it, never felt it, and have never had the chance to acquire those characteristics that might make me a head of family."

I turned off the phone without finding any explanation for messages I had written to Dr. Yusuf without being aware of it. How and when had I written them? And why had I forgotten them? Had my brain stopped functioning? Despite the fright it had given me, I forgot the matter and plunged into the book, but I don't know how long I spent reading. Did I go to sleep or lose consciousness? Did I get off the bus and board another one? Something of the sort happened to me, which I can vaguely recall. What I do remember is that the bus dropped me off when I was the only person left on it. I stood on the sidewalk, looking at unfamiliar streets: splendid buildings surrounded by high walls, posh cars, and windows with no one behind them. The sky opened in a torrent of rain, which hid everything from my sight, like smoke rising from the streets. Lightning started to flash on the horizon, and the noise of thunder rang out like a sudden air raid in a peaceful city.

Scenes from the World War flashed through my mind. I took
shelter under the awnings of a shop, but the rain was stronger than
anything. I ran I knew not where, sometimes up and sometimes
down, until I reached some shrubs on a hill and walked down it.
The slope was slippery; I fell, got up, and found myself under the
edge of an enormous bridge whose ends rested on two hills, with
rows of bright lights along the sides. "Now I've got something over
my head," I said, panting as I looked around at where I had ended
up. A cold wind blew madly under the bridge, and a few cars passed
on the road that had been built underneath it. I rested against the
wall as I looked down at the street from above. How had the days
stumbled over one another until I reached a place like this? What
series of mistakes had unfolded in such a disturbing way?

The fog began to gather in every direction. Sometimes it looked
white, other times I thought it black, accompanied by wailing sounds
and shrieks of laughter coming from a wide, empty place.

"You friend with the lamp didn't complain; he took pleasure
in wandering. If you are serious, you should respect your situation."

I was startled by the voice speaking into my ear. My head hit
the wall, and I felt warm blood dripping onto my brow, mixing
with the remains of cold water on my face. It was a superficial
wound, which I bandaged with a handkerchief.

"Live part of what you have read in the hope of hanging the
bell!" it said, in a frightening, gloating tone.

I fled from him away from the bridge and stood in the rain,
and he left. Then I went back to my cramped position down below
and sat thinking about my situation. Two feelings were competing
for my attention. One was Diogenes urging me to accept what was
happening; the other came from the idea of Gaston Bachelard
about the warm house, with its memories and childhood secrets.
My body was overwhelmed by cold and my limbs started to shiver.
Whenever a flash of lightning appeared over the buildings, it lit up

part of the place. I rubbed my hands together, blew in them, and rubbed my feet continuously, but with no effect, for the cold was too intense to drive away. I checked how much money I had and started looking for a cheap hotel on my mobile.

I had to escape from the bitter cold. I noticed a flicker of light from one of the bridge's enormous pillars, and a few seconds later I heard a cough echo around the place. Perhaps it's the sound of a pedestrian, I said to myself. But would there be anyone else walking around on a rainy night in this city? Would there be anyone else without shelter? The light grew brighter, still reflected on the walls and pillars of the bridge. I heard another cough and smelled fire so I got up and walked a little. I spotted someone in a corner a little larger than the one I had taken shelter in, near a fire pit. His head was on his knees and he didn't see me at first, but as soon as I moved a few feet away from him to ask to share the warmth, he looked at me and crawled away in a manner that suggested extreme fear. He coughed again, then made a few moaning sounds. "Don't be afraid," I said, trying to reassure him. "I only want a bit or warmth, like you."

He said nothing but crouched in the corner with his hands pressed to his temples. I moved a little bit backward and sat down, leaning on the wall. I didn't want to move any closer to the fire, despite the cold, which worsened as it made its way under the bridge. He crawled nearer to the fire and held out his hands toward it. Another flash of lightning lit up the place for a moment and I saw him more clearly. He was a thin young man in his twenties. He looked at me and rubbed his hands and shoulders. Noticing that I was staring at him, he retreated again and took a stick from under something that looked like a bed and held it, looking at me with discomfort and doubt.

The cold had got to me, numbing my body. What if I were to go toward the fire pit and just ignore the young man? I could no longer bear any more cold, which I thought must be punishing Amman for some obscure reason. For a few difficult seconds, I envied the young man for being so close to the fire in a corner much like the one where I was crouching like a lame monkey. Two hours went by, the rain becoming even heavier and the cold more intense. I curled up tighter and rested my head on my knees, sometimes thinking of my situation and sometimes about this youth. We seemed to be in the same boat, heading for a strange fate. When I heard him cough, I looked at him and he waved to me. I got up and approached him cautiously so he would not be startled and greeted him hesitantly, "Good evening."

As I said it, I sat down near the fire, so near that I was almost touching it—because the cold had penetrated the pores of my body. I could hear a rattle in his chest; he seemed to have a cold, which had affected his airways. I told myself that I wouldn't speak to him now but would leave him alone so he would become more comfortable with me. The steam was rising from my damp clothes in front of the flames, which had risen after he had thrown two pieces of wood into the pit. The heat shyly began to touch my body, awakening the pains in my muscles from my long hours of walking. I raised my head and looked at him but he turned his head away from me. Behind him were some pieces of cardboard he was using as a bed, a bag with a few loaves of bread in it, and a bottle of water. I could smell tuna and saw an empty can.

"I haven't come here to disturb you," I said.

He turned his face away from me again, the sound of the rattle in his chest still apparent as he stifled a cough. "Like you, I have nowhere to stay. I came here by chance to escape the cold, so please don't be afraid."

I was silent for a little as I looked at the fire and then back at him. The glow of the fire showed part of his face and I saw that he was quite good looking.

"We are scared—that is why we are here. You can sleep; I can see that you have a bed."

His cough worsened and he put his hand over his chest as he coughed several times, a whistling noise emanating from his lungs. He seemed close to exhausting his remaining strength. The wave of coughing gripped him even harder until he suddenly was unable to breathe; his head started to shake and his body gradually became limp. I went to him and put one hand on his back and the other on his chest to help him regain his breath, and I discovered that I was touching not a young man but a girl—and that my hands were on her breasts. She started up and pushed me away, afraid and disturbed, then moved away and looked at me doubtfully, her body trembling as she continued to cough. She was seized by a wave of fear that made her start to cry and moan intermittently. The best thing I could do at that moment was to say nothing so that she wouldn't run away and have something terrible happen to her. I looked at the fire and said nothing, and when she saw that I did not pose a danger to her, her agitation started to recede. As she lay worn out on her bed, I fed the fire with wood and thought about what I could do on a night like this to help a sick, homeless girl with pleurisy—a disease my brother 'Ahid had suffered from for several years, during which I had become familiar with the medicine to alleviate it.

"Do you have any medicine?"

She put her arms over her eyes as she shook her head. I checked my pocket, and the money I had gotten for the sale of the furniture in my apartment was still there. She patted down her short hair, which was styled like a man's.

"Don't worry. I'm going to get you some medicine."

Before I could leave my place under the roof of the bridge, I heard the voice say sadly, "You are both afraid."

I carried on walking, trying to ignore him, falling and getting up, but the voice came again, this time shouting angrily. "But you are both cowards!"

A stream of water was flowing down the edge of the hill, and I was hardly able to walk. I fell several times until I reached the place where I had come in. The rain hadn't stopped; indeed it was even heavier. As I climbed the slope, my feet stuck in the mud and became heavy until I reached the street and freed myself from the clumps of mud that had stuck to my shoes. I had to go some distance to find a pharmacy and, as I ran, I looked behind me to check the direction I had come from so as not to get lost. I felt tired and was panting when I stopped. I looked in every direction for a pharmacy, but I couldn't find one. I hurried back along the same route and found one still open. It was a miracle I hadn't expected to happen on a night like this. When the pharmacist saw me coming through the door spattered with mud, he gave me a curious look and gestured for me to stay by the door. I explained what the girl was suffering from and asked him for the same medicine my brother 'Ahid used. He came over and handed me what I wanted. "What's the name of this district?" I asked as I was about to go the door.

He gave me a pitying look. "Abdoun."

"Would you know somewhere near here that sells a hot drink?"

The pharmacist came up to me, obviously sympathetic but at the same time afraid of causing complications for himself if he asked me about my own situation. He pointed to a store with a light shining at the door. "That's a store selling hot drinks."

I went in and bought two cups of tea and left. The fog was becoming thicker, like smoke from a massive fire somewhere in the city. I almost got lost on the way back, but I saw the lights shining on the bridge and found my way. So my refuge tonight is a bridge, the top of which several sad people have leaped from to end their lives. What sort of fate is this, Ibrahim? With the cold, and with a sick girl you know nothing about, except for the sorrow that drowned your soul in secret tears. I stood under the edge of the bridge, thinking, "What if I went with the girl to a hotel, or anywhere that could shield us from the cold?" But this solution immediately seemed doomed to fail, with an exhausted girl and money that would only last us for a few days. When I got back, I sat down beside her and put a bit more wood on the fire. "I've bought you an inhaler that will help you to breathe," I said, "as well as some other medicines that will relieve your illness.

She rested her body and seemed fairly comfortable when I handed her the medicine. Then I helped her to use the inhaler. "Thank you," she said in a feeble voice.

I removed the lid from the cup of tea and put the cup in her hands. She sipped it and looked at me. I saw that her eyes were glistening with tears. "What if you hadn't come? What would have happened to me on this dreadful night?"

I patted her shoulder. "You just need to sleep. Some of the symptoms will disappear in an hour," I said. The cold made any possibility of sleep remote, but it was night, and it had to pass. The girl lay curled up on a bed made of several layers of cardboard. I took off my jacket and put it over her, then put some more wood on the fire. She was a tall, elegant girl wearing men's clothes—what could have brought her to a place like this? I looked at the street under the bridge, part of which was hidden in the thick fog. It is the first night, Ibrahim; how many lamps will I need to carry with me as I walk the streets of this city, which deserts its disciple so quickly? How many steps will bring me to a village that is no longer a village, where there is no one left whose door I can knock on, for the ugly hand of death has snatched them all away? A village where my father sold his house, and sold a childhood that so recently held its memories within it?

I woke at dawn, surprised to have slept despite the bitter cold. My sleep was full of nightmares and hallucinations. I found that my jacket was over my shoulders while the girl sat near the fire, which she had fed with wood left over from the construction site on the bridge. Faced with cold that had awakened in us our selfishness in matters of warmth, she had favored me over herself. As she looked at me, her eyes smiling despite her tiredness, I saw that she was about to say something, but she stopped herself. I took the jacket off and went to her and wrapped it around her. "You are ill—you need it more than me."

"I feel warmer than I've ever felt before," she said, trying to get her words out between repeated coughs.

I moved a piece of wood that had fallen from the bottom of the fire and looked at her face, which she had started to warm with her small hands. "What is this warmth?"

"I lived several years in a house where I was cold despite the heaters in it, and now here I am under a bridge on a cold night, feeling warm just because you hurried to bring me some medicine."

The wind had calmed, although a harsh, cold breeze was still blowing under the bridge. It was bitterly cold, but we were partly protected by some nearby shrubs.

"Believe me, I wasn't bothered by the cold, but I was afraid of the dark and of something happening to me."

"I can understand that."

Despite her exhaustion, the girl seemed to be slightly improved, and some of the rattling in her chest had abated. She put her hands close to the fire and shyly asked, "What brought you here?"

"I lost a lot of things, the last one being my home."

She suddenly brought her legs together; she had forgotten

herself and relaxed. She felt a fear, which she quickly hid when she found me looking at her sideways.

"Has disguising yourself in men's clothes anything to do with why you are here?"

She seemed hesitant about answering and busied herself with the fire, moving some embers with a stick and putting them back in their place. She wiped her nose with the hem of her jacket. "Yes, it has."

She threw the stick on the embers and it flared up, lighting up part of her face. As she looked at the light of the dawn, which could be seen over the buildings of Amman as the fog cleared, she seemed less pale. "I disguised myself to escape from men, but it didn't save me. Someone assaulted me and tried to rape me," she said, and began to shake. Then she lay on her side on her bed of cardboard and quickly went to sleep, like a cat that finds a friendly person and stretches out next to them. What chance was it that had brought me together with a girl who had suffered the same fate as I had? I turned on my mobile, which still had some power left, and looked at the picture of Madame N. The sea in front of her was a universal ear listening to her innermost secrets. To banish the hand of loneliness from my neck, I wrote on Facebook:

"In the cold, a lonely man's dreams fail, except for the image of the warm bosom. Warmth drives moisture from things through evaporation, and dryness is victorious. The cold brings birds' hopes for more straw to preserve their nests. Here I am now face to face with the sharp knives of the open air; I am not sad, I am not afraid, but I need you very much."

I spent the rest of the time throwing wood on the fire, which seemed tired of its task, until the bridge became more clearly visible and the city started to become recognizable again. The girl woke up and said "good morning" to me in a voice that sounded better than before. She then took a packet of cheese out of a bag and made two sandwiches, which she heated on the embers. She gave me one and ate hers while watching me carefully. Day had come, making everything visible. Her face was dark and full, with a mole on her right cheek and wide eyes with pupils that moved quickly, as if anticipating some sudden occurrence. She had a beauty that neither her tiredness nor her disguise could hide.

"If I had met you in the day, your clothing wouldn't have fooled me."

She moved a little farther away and gave me a sideways glance. "What do you mean?"

"I mean that you wouldn't have succeeded in hiding the girl underneath these men's clothes."

There was a short silence between us, after which I stood up to look outside our hiding place. It had stopped raining. The girl seemed to be experiencing some fear, as if she believed I was behaving toward her as men do when they approach a girl in a secluded place.

"Do you sleep here every day?" I asked, looking at the buildings and the streets that had just been heaving with cars. "No, this is the only night I have slept here," I heard her say sadly from behind me.

I turned to her. "It looks as if the low-pressure front is coming back. There are a lot of black clouds on the horizon. Won't you leave?"

She seemed afraid and confused, looking first at me and then beyond the bridge. I picked up my bag and slung it on my shoulder. "If you stay here another night, you will die of cold."

"Where will you go?" she asked in a shy, pleading voice.

There were still some embers in the fire pit. I sat down beside her, not knowing how to reply to her or to myself. "I don't know. Yesterday I left a home that was full of memories for me, some painful, some happy. I think I am still alive because of them, but now

I am taking shelter beneath a bridge where some misfits have come to end their lives." The girl was listening attentively. "Go on," she said.

"Go on how? Shall I tell you that yesterday I decided to be Diogenes? But I didn't become like him, and didn't stay Ibrahim either."

"Who is that?" Her wide eyes narrowed as she tried to suppress a laugh.

"A man who spent his life searching for a human being he didn't find. I will go, but I don't know where."

She wiped the dust from the seat of her pants with a succession of smacks. "There is a deserted house we can shelter in until you sort yourself out."

She looked at the part of the horizon visible to her, sadness lining her face, her fear evident through her tiredness.

"But..."

"But what?" She was about to say something but stopped herself.

"You are right, it seems there is a storm coming."

She smiled, despite the cold she was suffering. "What's your name?"

"Ibrahim. They called me Ibrahim the bookseller. And you, what's your name?"

"Leila. But Leila what? I don't know, even though on my identity card they added a father's name to my name, and mother's and grandfather's names, and a national number with a lot of zeros."

2
Ibrahim

(The Deserted House)

"I'm like you, Ibrahim, with no family, but you are lucky, for you know who your family are and you have many memories, whereas I have nothing," Leila said as we left the Abdoun Bridge behind us. The bridge rested on two hills and was supported by enormous concrete pillars designed to look like people raising their arms, like mourners carrying a large coffin. "Our melancholy temperaments create imaginary meanings for us, but the symbols of cities are obscure, hinting at things that perhaps we only understand later. How many symbols? How many signs have you seen in your life, Ibrahim?"

I would have liked to go a different way than Leila but I was afraid of meeting the sound of that thing again. Being with her was a sort of escape, for if I were on my own, it would get on top of me and mix everything up inside me. Leila said nothing. She had seen that I was distracted and walked a few paces ahead of me with her hands in the pockets of her pants. She was small, and in spite of being tired, she kept jumping onto the sidewalk and jumping off, laughing as she looked at me. Then the expression on her face changed, as if she had remembered some danger pursuing her. I didn't ask her anything or try to find out more about her, despite my curiosity. She struck me as the sort of person who is best left to speak spontaneously.

We passed the Fourth Circle and headed for the Third Circle. I didn't ask her where the house we were making for was located. Time was of no importance to me; the only thing annoying me was the biting cold, so strong that it made walking seem easy. She turned to me and spoke, as though reading my mind:

"I was an orphan; they found me lying at the door of a mosque in Amman and took me to the orphanage—or so they told me when I was thirteen and starting to think of my father and mother, my family, and the world outside the orphanage walls. I had actually thought about it from a young age, but only asked about it later. It was fear, fear that made me do that."

Hunger began to steal my remaining strength. I told her I had enough money to allow us to eat. She nodded her head and carried on walking, looking straight ahead, as though remembering something:

"The male and female supervisors weren't fathers or mothers to us. They were just employees who played the part of jailers to keep their jobs. It was obvious to us that they hated the work, as they constantly complained about it and about their lives with foundlings and bastards. We only knew a little about life outside the orphanage, from what we saw when we went to school, but what we did know was even harder than what we lived through. From day one, the other pupils refused to mix with us. When I went up to one of them, she said, 'My family won't let me play with you because you are a bastard!' When I was thirteen, they kept us away from boys and I didn't understand why. I remember one night when I cried in my bed until dawn because I could no longer be near Said, who had changed in a painful way over time into a 'wild man' they locked up in a dark room with no food."

She looked at me with tears in her eyes. "Whenever they found a 'wild man' among us, they would beat him relentlessly, and when he heard them describe us as bastards, he would become wild. They made the girls hate the boys and vice versa. If they saw a boy joking with a girl, they would beat him violently. There was a boy among us who had thalassaemia, but he couldn't go to hospital to have his blood changed. The bus wouldn't take him because the manager was using it for personal purposes. Then his health deteriorated and they were forced to take him to hospital. None of the supervisors went with him or visited him. Then his health collapsed and he died, but only one supervisor and his friends from the orphanage attended his funeral."

The wind was getting up, and it looked as if a stronger storm was on its way. Leila's nose was becoming red from the cold and she was getting tired. The rattle from her chest was becoming louder. We stood under a bus shelter and I helped her use the inhaler, then we walked on. Suddenly she stopped, deep in thought. Her face was covered in fear and she was obviously disturbed. "I want to go back to the bridge," she said. "I am afraid."

Seeing my puzzled look, she smiled and said, "No, it's all right—let's go on!"

She laughed as she looked around, then at me. "This world is new to me. I don't know the people or the places. I heard one of the supervisors once describe me as a cat with closed eyes. It's only now that I understand what it means to have eyes and still not see with them."

We walked on until we had passed the Fourth Circle, then we took a street leading downtown. We went into a restaurant where we were the only customers, sat down, and ordered food. The waiters eyed us suspiciously, for we looked like vagrants. Our clothes were dirty, our shoes covered in mud, our faces black, and our eyes wilting from lack of sleep. When the waiter came, I showed him the money I had, and he was satisfied. Leila held her head in her hands and looked at me, as if she was wondering who this man was who had befriended her overnight. As she dragged herself to the restroom, the voice came back to me, saying, "Your solutions are temporary, Ibrahim!"

"I haven't found a solution to anything; I am just going on my way."

"You are going through an endless tunnel. You will fall before you reach the light you think of as a beacon of hope."

I left the table in confusion to look for the restroom, battered by the voice and its calm but angry words.

"Leila is right, you're just like each other, but she is stronger than you are, and you will find this out."

"I have never claimed to be strong in the way you claim to be strong and boast about it."

"That is my true nature, which I will not hide. But you hide a great weakness behind your phony calm."

Just then, Leila emerged from the ladies' restroom and stood at the door, looking at me in surprise. "Are you OK?"

I turned toward her and stopped for a moment, not knowing what was happening, until I came around and asked her for the men's room. She pointed to it without understanding what was wrong with me. I went in quickly, still suffering the torment of the voice, and stayed some minutes there, splashing my face with water before returning to the table. I pretended to be calm and charged my mobile and laptop. Leila gave me a sideways look as I checked the Facebook pages. "What's up?" she asked in a concerned voice when she saw my shocked expression.

"Iyad Nabil was found poisoned in suspicious circumstances in a second home belonging to him, in the company of a woman. He's the man in whose interests the Bookseller's Kiosk was removed."

"Are you happy about that?"

"I don't know," I replied, as the waiter put the food on the table.

We ate hungrily, feeling even more tired, then drank tea as we watched the rain, which had started again, through the restaurant window. Leila said nothing; she was thinking about something and shaking her foot. "What if you found out I killed someone?" she asked.

I didn't like what I had heard. She sounded as if she was about to cry. I asked her to tell me what had happened, and she told me that a man had harassed her and that she had hit him on the head with a stone and he had fallen to the ground.

I searched on Google and Facebook for any mention of an incident near the Fourth Circle but found nothing. I reassured her that perhaps he had just lost consciousness because of the blow, nothing more, and that the matter was at an end, especially as she did not know where he lived. The rain stopped as we left the restaurant and walked along a street where the water was flowing as if someone had turned on a hose at the top of it. We passed the Income Tax Department. I didn't know where Leila was taking me, but her mood had improved after she had told me what had happened to her.

There was a hole in a wall on the right side of the street, which Leila crossed cautiously, then waved her hand to invite me to follow her. She led me to a small room with no ceiling, smelling of urine, with rubbish and rocks piled up in it. I was surprised she would go into a place like this, but I followed her. From one corner, a twisting passage full of rubbish led off—though it would be difficult for anyone to know that it led inside until they had passed the corner. I followed Leila down the passage until we reached an old, deserted house built of stone. It had a high front door with an arch over it that was decorated in the same way as the windows, which had been beautifully built to architectural perfection. It was surrounded by a low wall enclosing a small area from which an old cypress tree emerged, with some other shrubs that had dried out so that only their stumps remained. Leila pushed the iron door of the house and went in. I followed, feeling my steps in the darkness, which was punctuated by a faint light coming in through the window and some holes in the walls. I went on, stumbling over the rocks and pieces of wood and rubbish until we reached an out-of-the-way room with one window, barred with iron and secured with chains. There were a few old blankets in the room, and some worn-out clothes lying on the floor; the place stank of urine, damp, and mold.

Leila sat on a blanket and rested against the wall. Her breathing became louder from the inflammation in her lungs, but she used the inhaler and became calmer. As the cold crept in on us, she got up and lit a fire with the wood scattered around and the remains of some furniture that had perhaps belonged to the house or else come from outside. The sound of the rain and thunder made the place seem even stranger. A young man came in as we hovered around the fire; he was short, with a full, round face—this was all I could tell at the time in the darkness, in the middle of which the flames from the fire occasionally leaped up while at other times it gave out a smoke that made our eyes water and our noses run. "Adi?" the youth asked suspiciously.

"It's Leila, Nur."

The youth rushed over to her, asking her anxiously where she had been and where she had spent the previous night. Had anything dreadful happened to her? Before he could receive a reply, he pointed toward me. "Who's this?"

"Ibrahim."

She briefly told him how we had met, and he came over and shook my hand to show his gratitude.

"Thank you, Ustadh Ibrahim!"

I suppressed a laugh as I thought about what he had said. How could I be an "Ustadh" when I was a vagrant like them, with no home and no family? She told him what had happened with the man who had harassed her, and after she had described him, he recognized him. He said that the police had arrested him, for he had previous convictions and was wanted by them.

———

Two girls arrived just before sunset, followed by two youths. It was obvious they had sneaked in, for I only became aware of them when they were standing in front of us, complaining of feeling cold,

rubbing their hands, and stamping their feet on the ground. Nur
put a piece of wood by the side of the wall and gave it a kick. When
the wood broke, he threw it on the fire, and the resulting flare revealed the contours of the room. I saw two girls of about nineteen
and two youths in their twenties whose clothes were dripping with
water. They quickly moved toward the fire, and when they saw
Leila, they all at once asked, "Where were you?" Then one of them
asked about me. Leila introduced them to me and briefly told them
how we had met. There was a girl scratching her head and rubbing
her neck; she had long hair, which she had tied with a piece of cloth
so that it hung down behind her. She looked at me with tired eyes
and said in a lifeless voice, "We are foundlings with no family so
we've taken shelter in this house. What brought you here?"

"Salam," said Leila sharply, to stop her from speaking. But I
interrupted her. "I'm like you, I no longer have a home or family.
That's all there is to it. I just came to bring Leila here."

I got up and picked up my bag. Leila stood up and one of the
youths came up to me. "Ustadh Ibrahim, this house is deserted, as
you can see; it doesn't belong to us, and it is our last resort, so none
of us has the right to turn you out, or even make you stay here. But
it seems you are older than us. I like having you here, but I don't
know about the others."

"Ra'id is speaking the truth," said Leila. She asked me to sit
down and then pointed to the door, through which the sound
of thunder could be heard again. She then came up to me and
whispered in a pleading tone, "Please stay!" She said nothing more
as she awaited my reply, while the others gathered around the fire,
even though the smoke had no way of escape except the door.

"I'll come back!"

I had no use for my remaining money except for us to eat. I
hadn't seen any of the young people carrying food with them when
they came back to the house, so I went out. The sky looked as though

it wanted to relieve itself of any water it still retained, all at once, and as soon as night fell a powerful storm arrived. From the street came the noise of rain and thunder, together with the sound of a few cars passing by from time to time. Before I could start to walk through the alley, my belly grew larger and I retreated in panic.

"They live in a deserted house near a street in a quarter of a city that never sleeps. While you live between your wandering philosopher and Ibrahim, and you're neither one nor the other."

I fled from him to the alley, but he threatened me again, hiding a great anger behind him.

"The respite has still not finished. There is a list of people's names and places. I will inform you of it soon. You should know that I have no right to act before the end of the respite."

I was near the street when he let out a sarcastic laugh. "Go on, Diogenes!"

How could this be happening to me? Some creature inside me was forcing me to do things I didn't want. Both of us knew the shape of destruction, and both of us had a way of looking at it. I had gone to the sea to frustrate what this fantastical creature was doing, but fate pitched me in the path of a woman and I had clutched at the weakest thread in the hope of finding her—a hope that still shone before my eyes on every street I trod. Do you suppose I had chosen this wandering to find Madame N? Or had I done it because I had arrived at a point where I couldn't say no? How many people would I find like Leila on this road, a road whose end point I didn't know?

I was completely soaked when the man standing at the table in the fast food restaurant repeated his call, "You, can't you hear, man?"

"Sorry!"

The man laughed and figured I was absent-minded. I told him what food I wanted, paid for it, and started watching how the fire was roasting the meat and chicken on a night full of frost. There was a cat there, but as soon as it approached the restaurant, an employee glowered and shouted at it as he worked—though the only thing I could gather from his repeated words was that he was moaning about the bad state the city was passing through. Then the cat came back, slipping inside this time, so he ran after it, slipped, and fell on the floor, eliciting hearty laughs from many of the people waiting for their food. The man glared at them and asked angrily what was so funny. Then, as most of them fell silent, he got up and limped off until he reached the restaurant door, where he nervously lit a cigarette and started to puff the smoke into the air, where it mingled with his breath. He raised his head to the sky and cried, "What have I done, Lord, that you punish me like this? Even the winter is mean in this city! How long do I have to work like a bull to achieve the little that my family wants?"

He threw his cigarette in the air and went back to work, asking God to forgive him "I'm not a cat hater!" he said.

I picked up the food I had ordered and went back, but as soon as I had entered the alley the voice caught me and took possession of me, so I walked faster. "Deserted houses will not show you anything but the past, so you are a loser!" The sight of the books consumed by the fire in front of the house had never left my imagination since my departure, but this time it gripped me even harder and started to hurt me, as if a fire was burning in my head. Leila took the bags of food from my hand and asked anxiously, "Has something happened? I see that you are not yourself!"

"Don't worry, I'm fine."

Some of them had gone to sleep by the fire on worn-out blankets, while others simply sat silently. In the corner of the room, a youth had his nose in a brown paper bag . "What is he doing?" I asked. "He's sniffing glue," replied Leila. I didn't understand at the time what she meant but I became annoyed. As we hovered around the food, Leila tried to put an end to my annoyance as everyone ate greedily. My eye was on the youth who had dropped the packet of glue, the smell of which spread as he lay down, seemingly un-conscious. I couldn't finish my food, so I stood up to stand by a chink in the door looking out over the alley, where nothing could be seen except darkness. "Everything in this house induces sadness and despair," I thought to myself. "I am in a dilemma, and in a place I cannot leave. What will happen in the days to come? My money will run out, and I shall be less able to endure living like a tramp."

I turned around as a hand touched me. Leila had some food in her hand. "You must eat," she said. There was a ruined sofa by the door, which I sat on to eat. As she sat beside me, eating slowly, I asked her, "Why do you bother about me?"

She replied softly, sobbing a little, "And why did you bother with me yesterday?"

"How could I not help you on a night like that?"

I left the food on one side. "While we were under the bridge, and although you were extremely fearful, some of the loneliness left me. Would you believe that that was my most precious gain?"

She came closer and I could hear her labored breathing. She seemed on the verge of tears. "That is exactly what makes me care about you."

She burst into tears before continuing in a slightly confused tone. "Ever since I became conscious of myself in the orphanage, I have been trying to form an image of my father and mother, but my imagination failed. This was something that caused me even more pain. When you came back with the medicine I could see your face despite the darkness around us. I felt you were the father I was looking for at that moment. Believe me, people like me with so much cruelty in their lives just want a good father like you in the face of their desolation."

She put her head on my shoulder and let the rest of her tears pour out, as I wondered how pain could make a girl of this age see all this reality.

"Do you know something?" she asked, as though getting ready to sleep. "We bear the sins of our fathers and mothers. Bastards, in the eyes of all who see us, seem to have something in our faces that marks us out from the rest of mankind. A policeman stopped me once when I was wearing men's clothes and asked for my ID. He thought at first that I was a boy, and he laughed when he read my identity card and discovered I was a girl. The color of his face changed as he read my national number marked by zeros. He asked me where I was from and where my family was, and he forced me to tell him that I was an orphanage graduate, a foundling, a bastard. We are in a world that gives rise to fear. We cannot even work if we carry an ID marked with several zeros, as if to tell anyone who sees it that we are nothing."

She raised her head from my shoulder and pointed to the people sleeping in the deserted house. "Do you believe that any of them could marry, even if they found work in a society like this, which praises principles? Adi, the young man you saw who is addicted to sniffing glue, still suffers psychological trauma because of the death of his friend in the orphanage who suffered from thalassaemia, and died because they only sent him to have his blood changed occasionally. Can you imagine how that could happen?"

As it got colder, we lit a fire near the door so the smoke could get out through the hole. Everyone was sound asleep, despite the cold and the thunder and wind, which kept up their madness all night. Leila carried on telling me stories of the people in the deserted house until she fell asleep on the ruined sofa, wrapped in an old blanket. I searched the house for leftover wood, and whenever the fire died down I built it up again. I looked at the photo of Madame N as I searched for some heat that would relieve my soul of the growing cold inside it. How could I get her to turn to me and speak to me? How could one movement picked up by the camera in less than a second become my world, which had disappeared from sight and appeared at the strangest moment of my life?

3
Ibrahim

(Intersecting Destinies)

The early morning sun shone on me in the deserted house, as rays of its light crept through the chinks in the walls. Particles of dust and small creatures danced around. I had a headache, and my limbs felt numb from the cold and from sleeping on several pieces of cardboard. I shut my eyes as I thought back to my time in my apartment in Jabal al-Jawfa. As I dozed off again, I had even worse nightmares, but I woke to the sound of the door as Nur opened it and left, followed by Ra'id and Salam. That left only Leila and me, with Adi and a girl still asleep. I didn't know where they were going or how they would spend their day. More light crept in through the door and through gaps in some of the windows. I could now clearly see the place, which would even disgust animals if they were put here. Adi leaned back against the wall, which was extremely damp and moldy, and picked at one of his nostrils absentmindedly while Leila curled up in her bed, looking at me through a hole in a worn-out blanket. There was a cold silence, broken only by the girl snoring and groaning from time to time.

From house to house, Ibrahim, as though it is your destiny not to enjoy complete affection or security. In the village, when by chance you saw your father making love to your mother one night, you hid in a corner of the room the following day, trying to understand what you had seen. And when you saw your first dead woman, and the first bride crying as the women bade her farewell with a sad song, you did the same thing. Whenever you wanted to understand something or reflect on something, or take pleasure in recalling an incident, you would hurry into the corners of the house. You felt a confidence whose value you only appreciated when the truck carried you away and you plunged into the raucous world of the city. You put your hands over your eyes as the din and car horns of Amman assailed your ears. You tried to comprehend that new rhythm, but at the same time you recalled the shouting of your friends in the village as you ran toward the traps you had set for the birds, happy with your catch. You were the only one to free a bird from the trap and release it into the air, until you gave that up when the birds hurt you as your friends' hands tore their heads from their bodies. When your mother died, you understood the enormity of your loss in your first house. You understood what it means for a man to live nine months in his mother's womb—their home, to which they continue to think of returning, even though that is impossible. That was how you thought when faced with Amman, an enormous secret in the face of which you simply gave up, contenting yourself with your route from your home in Al Jawfa to the kiosk. And now you are in a deserted house. What memories, what dreams, what life have the people living between the walls of this house had? Houses related to one another like a string of beads, so that if you join them with a thread, you will see a big house.

I walked down the alley toward the street—the alley leading to the deserted house, hidden by the high wall that perhaps belonged to a factory or a commercial building like the other buildings in this area. The rain had stopped, and there were only a few dark clouds in the sky, racing toward the east. The traffic and pedestrians in the street were as usual, but the air was cold and sharp, gnawing at my bones. I emerged from the alley and walked along a sidewalk leading up toward the Third Circle, looking for a shop selling coffee. I was afraid people might notice my dirty clothes, but I didn't advertise my fear.

Cities had become used to their miserable inhabitants and had even begun to exploit their wretchedness, to relate their painful stories and turn them into icons in the hope of lightening their darkness.

"No one has noticed me, and no one will!" I thought, as I guffawed to myself thinking of how I would manage after my money ran out and what scrapes I might fall into, like a bird falling from a great height. Was this all I had left in life, a deserted house in the company of people rejected by society? My reflection in the shop windows as I dragged myself along sometimes seemed funny and at other times sad. My eyes were tired. I was unshaven, my hair was uncombed, clothes dirty, shoes soaked and spattered with mud. How could I walk on embers and not feel the heat? Books and papers followed one another in my imagination like a wheel that would settle on a particular lucky number. I heard the voice of Madame N talking about the sea, mingling with the sound of gulls. I stood at a window in which I could see my reflection more clearly than before, and then came the mocking voice. "Your wandering friend rose above everything. If you want to be an image of him, you should know that you have a long time ahead of you, but remember—when the respite ends, you will not enjoy what I'll be doing."

"I will not let you defeat me," I shouted angrily, my mouth looking larger in the window.

He gave a mocking laugh: "Do you think I am going to wait for you to agree to obey me, you idiot? What are you defending? A country whose body has been eaten away by the corrupt?"

"Why me? Go to someone else!"

"Because you have read. Because you know!"

"And because I know, I reject all you say."

A security guard emerged from inside. "For God's sake, get away from here, man," he said. I could feel his stare as I went on my way. I looked behind me and I was in front of a bank. The man already thought I was mad, so how would it be if I told him

I talked to someone who lived inside me? It would merely make him more convinced that I wasn't sane. The hardest thing that can happen to someone is to be unable to find any way to convince a person of a truth that cannot be proved.

I saw a store opposite the coffee shop selling household goods, some of them displayed at the door: woolen bedcovers, pillows, and bedroom furniture. I longed for a quiet moment of sleep to banish the effects of that extra-cold night. I crossed the street and went into the store and bought some blankets and padded mattresses. When I came out again, carrying my purchases on my head, people looked at me oddly. If anyone had asked me, I would have replied that I had purchased some temporary warmth in a cold city.

"This is what I managed to buy," I told Leila when I returned and set my purchases down. I saw a smile on her face, followed by two tears that ran down her tired cheeks. After saying I'd be back, I went out, followed by her grateful voice asking where I was going. It isn't easy for me to see someone crying: it feels like a moment of defeat after which everything will disappear. And it wasn't easy seeing Leila cry when she had started to pick up the threads of a lost fatherhood whose ends were with me. I bought coats for everyone in the house that day, as well as a quantity of canned food and some other essentials. We spent half the day clearing the room of its filth and stones, and set aside the wood to use for heating, storing it in a metal container I had found in the alley. The people who had been out came back that evening, and their expressions changed when they saw the change in the place. Mattresses, coats, food, candles to light the place, and a metal container with embers in it to spread heat around the room. "How did you do all this?" Nur asked, confused and surprised, his voice like that of a child.

Salam picked up a coat thrown over her bedding and looked at Leila, who smiled in turn. "Yes, this is for you."

Then she turned toward the others, some of whom were

crouching in front of the fire and others standing. "This is what Ibrahim has been able to do."

"This is the money I had left from the house furniture I sold," I said, warming my hands near the fire. "I don't have any home now except for the one I am sharing with you so I have no need of money, if you need it. Believe me, it's not a question of generosity, or pity—you can say that it is simply inexplicable behavior."

They looked at me in amazement. "I am not sociable; I am a solitary man like you, ignorant of this city and its residents."

Meanwhile, Leila had finished preparing the food. As they stared at me, I ate and said, "This food is for us all."

We took our supper and talked for a little, then everyone sat on their beds, expecting me to break my silence. They were too young to bear what had happened to them, when life was showing them its other face. That evening, I got to know them one by one. There were beggars among them, people who sold simple things at traffic lights, and some who were simply unemployed. What they earned was not enough to feed two people, but they behaved as though they were members of one family, shunned by everyone so they had come closer to one another.

I lay down on my bed after they had gone to sleep. There was a candle beside me, the light from which disturbed the air coming in through the cracks in the walls, creating weird shadows on the walls and ceiling. It looked like a silent shadow play, and it had quite a story to tell. I opened my bag and took out Madame N's notebook. It had a smell that hadn't gone away. This wasn't the scent of perfume but the smell of something hidden, like whatever it was had propelled me toward her so crazily. I opened the notebook at the page I had folded over:

As the days went by, I started to know the times when the white-haired man would come to the restaurant and the times when he would leave. I never served him; my colleague did that, in silence except for a few clipped words. It turned out that she didn't know anything about him and that he had no connection with any of the restaurant's regulars. He came in without saying anything and left the same way. A vague feeling linked me to the man; the explanation seemed to lie in his appearance, his calm, his sadness, and his isolation—all of which he seemed to accept—as well as the mystery that surrounded him from the first moment I saw him. I thought the reason for it lay in a hidden sense, like the desire for a warm bosom on a cold night, though I knew that a man can hide great sadness behind his calm and needs the bosom more than a woman like me, who lived alone in a house unvisited by anything except the rays of the sun and the chirping of the neighbors' birds.

Winter set in early that year. After working in the restaurant for some months, I was surprised to find he had disappeared. I asked my colleague about him but she didn't know. I asked the restaurant manager, on the pretext that no one was sitting at his table, but he didn't give me an answer. A strange feeling came over me, a mixture of unease and a sense of loss. I thought of how I might find out where he lived, but nothing would free me of the anxiety that stopped me sleeping or paying attention to my university studies, even though I blamed myself for irresponsible feelings like that.

But he came back. I was preparing an order for a customer when he came through the restaurant door holding an umbrella, which he folded as soon as he entered. He undid his woolen scarf and walked slowly toward the table, where he took off his black coat and hung it on a hanger beside the wall. After setting down a thick notebook, a lighter, and a pack of cigarettes, he seated himself at his table, took out a cigarette, lit it, and proceeded to smoke. I went to him, my heart racing wildly. He was looking out the window as I put a glass of vodka in front of him. "Sorry, I'd like a coffee this time," he said in a quiet voice.

I didn't know what to say to him, despite all the usual things we say to be polite to our customers. As I brought the cup of coffee to him, I decided to say something to him that I had never said to a customer before. As I bent down to put the cup on the table, my nose was hit by the smell of his cologne mixed with that of his cigarettes. How I would have liked to sit by him and put my head on his shoulder at that moment! "Coffee in winter is a faithful companion," I said, summoning all my reserves of self-control.

He picked up his cup, looked at a tree fighting the winds that had just gotten stirred up, and said, "It is the mistress of every time, my dear!"

There was a silence between us, from which I was saved by my colleague, who called out, "Enjoy your coffee, sir!"

"Your name is beautiful!"

He drank from his cup of coffee, opened his notebook, and started to write. My eye tried to follow the pen to see what he was writing. From that day, he came in regularly. I tried to destroy the wall that seemed to stand between us with a few words, but he preferred to be alone with his writing. After a bit, I saw him working furiously, lighting one cigarette after another, looking at his notebook as if he was pursuing something. Then I saw him drying tears that had flowed down his swarthy cheeks. I would have liked to rush over to him at that moment, but my colleague dissuaded me. He shut the notebook and began to smoke absentmindedly before getting up, putting on his coat, collecting his umbrella, and leaving. Somehow he forgot his notebook on the table, so I picked it up and left the restaurant, running along the street, but I could find no sign of him. It was raining nonstop. How could things happen like this, and how do wishes come true?

I shut the door behind me when I came back home, as if I was closing it on myself, together with the man whose shoulders I had clung to and never let go of. I was in such a state. I changed my clothes quickly, then made a cup of coffee, sat by the heater, and passed through the door of a man full of sorrow and secrets.

4
Ibrahim

(An Apparently Unplanned Incident)

I spent two weeks in the deserted house, after which everything became tiresome and oppressive. Two weeks during which I didn't take a single step outside the house, as if I were waiting for someone to take me out of this world and deposit me on an uninhabited island, an island that would free me from everything and give me a chance to recast my life. Things had become even more difficult as my money had run out and it had become colder. None of the young people went out, as Ra'id had been arrested raiding a shop and Nur had given up begging, for fear that he would be arrested as well. Even Salam, who sold paper handkerchiefs, didn't leave the house, as she had a bad cold. Forgotten people, whom no one bothered about, as if they were bird droppings that had fallen on the shoulder of someone wearing a smart suit and been quickly wiped off in disgust. As I walked slowly toward the door to look through a hole at what was visible of the city, I heard Leila behind me, stifling a groan from an ache in her stomach. Like all of us, she had known no food for several days. Salam got up, put two loaves of dry bread on a plate, and poured some water over them, so that they softened. She sat by Leila's bed and fed her. I wandered around the house, or to be more accurate, turned around and around in a daze. I could hear dance music outside, punctuated by the noise of a car engine of the sort bought by youths attracted by racing cars. There was a short silence, broken by the whistle of wind coming through a hole in the wall. I opened the door and left with no clear intention of where I would go. In the alley, the wind was blowing leaves, plastic bags, and earth around, then scattering them all at once, while the sky was threatening a new low front. It was a winter more severe than we were used to, and an odd savagery strutted in every direction. I had not yet reached the end of the alley when my belly swelled and the voice came to me with a warning. "The respite will end soon!"

He seemed to be on the point of creating some chaos, so I hurried into the street to escape from him, but I slipped and fell in a small pool of water. When I got up, my clothes were soaking wet and spattered with mud. There was a man standing on the main street; I didn't know he was watching me as I waved my hand in the air, as the voice pursued me like a swarm of flies. "Your weakness is the secret of your tragedy, Ibrahim!" This time, he clung to me like a shadow as I walked along the sidewalk, trying to ignore him, so no one would see me talking to myself and think me mad. His voice was like an awl piercing my skull: "Weak, and afraid!" I almost went back to the house, but I was afraid the young people would notice something about me I didn't want them to see. Instead, I walked on, looking for a crowd, to avoid a voice I could not escape. I stopped at a small toy shop to talk to the owner, for any reason. When the man saw me looking at the goods hanging by the door, he asked me to guard the place for little so that he could go to another store to pee, then hurried off.

As I looked at the toys, I heard the voice again. This time, it was sad. "Haven't you noticed that when you were young you were no good at games? Look at this toy revolver. Look how nice and well-made it is!"

"You used to make your toys yourself," he went on with a mocking laugh. "You would use two pieces of wood for a revolver and a sardine can tied up with string you'd call a car."

He said nothing for a moment and then spoke in a provocative tone. "Look to your left. Do you see this bank, where you checked how you looked in the window? Look how happy the people are as they come out—because of the money they've made."

I pictured him clinging to me, his voice even closer. "You are inhabited by Mehran, the hero of Naguib Mahfouz's novel *The Thief and the Dogs*, who has now woken from his sleep. You thought you had killed him to make room for another character from a novel who had lodged in your subconscious. Mahfouz's words created a picture of him in your imagination, and his narrative skill made you penetrate inside him to see his sorrows and hopes, and why he became a thief. You never told anyone that you sympathized with him, while your family looked at you, finding it odd how you took on the features of particular characters. The country had just awoken at the time to the news of an important man who had embezzled a large sum of money then fled. Said Mehran took you over, and your family were unable to stop you when they saw someone else who was not their son walking around the house. Your father was unsure about which doctor he should consult to talk about your strange passion for dressing up."

The voice seemed to be wrapping itself around me, speaking quietly but stressing the words.

"Now here you are, Said, coming out of prison after four years of punishment for a theft you carried out, on your way to your wife, Nabawiyya, whom you left on account of your friend, Ilish Sidra. Your heart was on fire, like a field of wheat just before harvest, and you were at your wits' end to hold back your tears, for you didn't want your breakdown to be visible to anyone. You would ask to see your daughter Sana', but they wouldn't agree, so you would be angry and sad, frustrated as you heard mountains collapsing inside you in anger. You would take a lot of books and leave home, having decided to kill them both."

I felt him close to my face. "Come on, Said, you have to leave behind the good Ibrahim and move on."

Said Mehran's face began to appear from the sky of my memory, a moment of concentration that came over me after every novel character I fell in love with. My facial muscles began to twitch, and my bones prepared themselves to look like someone different from myself. Said Mehran's voice came, revealing his great sadness and anger.

The voice became louder, and its movements almost ripped my belly apart. "Take this revolver, Said!"

His hands began to push me forward with a force I could not resist, so I picked up the revolver. Before I could move off, he pointed me to a mask hanging there. "Put on this mask; you will need it. Come on, hurry to the bank. The security man doesn't seem to be at the door."

The voice continued to propel me toward the bank. I passed through the door, Nabawiyya's voice echoing in my ears, egging me on as she flirted with Ilish Sidra and laughed seductively, making me cry in a way I only do when I sense defeat. I raced across a waiting room with a few customers in it, the voice exploding in my ear. "Jump, Said, get over the counter!"

Nabawiyya was sitting at the counter. My heart had been transfixed by her beauty ever since I had gotten to know her as a servant in the Turkish lady's house. With every step I took toward her, I would either recall our wedding day or else imagine her in Ilish Sidra's embrace—when a powerful shriek of grief would explode. I would kick inside so as not to seem weak in the face of the treachery they had perpetrated against me in full view of people who had climbed on people's shoulders to power. In the bank, I could smell their rotten smell clinging to the banknotes and the walls, exactly like the smell of the air in the working-class quarters, where they make fun of the people there using expressions of contempt that no longer serve any purpose.

A woman waiting her turn cried out. It was Nur, the "girl of the night" I had stayed with for some friendly evenings in her house near the graveyards, and who loved me as no woman had loved me before. The words were shackled to her mouth as she begged me, "Please don't do it, Said!" Two men got ready to flee as I pointed the revolver at Nabawiyya's head, who was arranging a large sum of money. At the same time, the other employees put their hands up.

"If anyone moves from his place, I will kill Nabawiyya and anyone else who runs or tries anything. I'll kill her as the evildoers killed you."

As a security guard emerged from inside, revolver on hip, Ilish Sidra ordered him not to point his revolver at me. He wasn't angry but smiling. He looked at Ilish and laughed.

"'Who said anything about pointing this revolver at anyone? If I draw my revolver I will fire a bullet in the air for fun because he has come at last. I have spent the years working in this bank and thinking of what the masked men did, but I didn't dare. The smell of money here makes me cry. It reminds me of my impotence and my poverty, which I cannot escape from. It reminds me of the people who have mocked us."

I heard the voice say in a decisive tone, "Let Nabawiyya put the money in a bag."

Nur had her hand over her mouth to hide her sobs, her body shaking with fear. I told her to be quiet, then tried to calm her by saying, "Do you recall what you used to say to me during our nice nights together? 'I will put you in my eye and put kohl on you!'"

Nur smiled. "I will put you in my eye and put kohl on you!" she said in a whisper of pleasure that was stronger than her fear.

Nur's body was trembling as she put all the money she had in a linen bag and put it on the counter. I looked in her eyes, then in Ilish's eyes, who had put his hands up.

"Couldn't you find anyone apart from this dog to betray a lion like me with? Aren't you one of the people the dogs have bitten?"

Without a word she sat down, unable to control herself. Through the bank window I could see the street, which had become more crowded. It was a good opportunity to flee safely, so I picked up my bag and hurried toward the door, everyone watching me in silence as I pointed the revolver at them. I turned my back to the security camera at the door and quickly took off my mask, then hid the revolver in my pocket and rushed through the door, followed by the voice: "Walk calmly, Said, so that no one suspects you."

The crowd moved back as I walked in. I was almost running, but the voice spoke again: "Go in calmly so you don't arouse suspicion."

I didn't turn around but went in calmly and quickly covered the distance of the alley until I reached the door of the house, collecting my breath and talking to myself deliriously. "What have you done, what have you done, Ibrahim?"

The sound of police sirens rang out in the street as well as the sound of a commotion, which I could hear echoing through the buildings.

"What you have done will make me conclude a new agreement with you."

I heard the voice in the alley but no one was following me. The entrance to the alley was narrow; few people would notice it. I felt the weight of the bag as I stood confused outside the door. How was I supposed to behave when I had such a large sum of money on me? "Creep into the house," ordered the voice, "then head for the side room with the piled-up rubbish, stones, and wood from the remains of the old furniture."

When I hesitated a little, he shouted at me. I cautiously opened the door, crept into the room, and looked around me. I moved a pile of mud in the corner and stumbled over a tile that moved. I lifted it and dug underneath it until it became wide enough for the bag. The voice was dictating every step I took so I could no longer say no to him: "Take a small sum, leave the revolver and the mask, put the bag in the hole, and go inside. Behave as if nothing has happened. And don't go out for a week."

Several people were asleep when I went in, while from the street I could hear the sound of police cars moving away and then coming back. "What's the matter with you? Has something happened to you?" asked Leila, as I rested against the wall, saying nothing and staring into the half-light of the house.

"No, nothing."

I lay down on the bed and covered my head with the blanket. What new crisis had I put myself into? It felt as though I would be arrested any minute, for they must be going back to the security cameras now. The voice reassured me. "Don't worry! They'll find a man wearing a red mask, but even if he takes it off, they'll find Said Mehran and not Ibrahim."

"How have I turned into a thief so quickly?"

"You are an honorable thief."

The voice had started to invade me even when I was among people. I was angry at what I had done; I felt ashamed and regretful.

"There is no honor in theft."

"At this stage you must relax. In the coming days, I will prove to you that there is an honorable thief inside you, and I will tell you what you should do."

"Do you think that I will remain under your instructions?"

"Yes," the voice replied decisively. "You will remain until you fulfill our new agreement, which I will tell you about shortly."

Salam removed the blanket from my face. "Are you all right? Why are you talking to yourself?"

I got up from the bed as I tried to disguise what was going on. "I must have been dreaming."

Some of them looked at me feebly because they were beginning to lose strength. They had not eaten in days. How could I bear to stay in this house for a week when everyone here was hungry and I had all this money? I felt like a father does toward his sons, but going out was an adventure whose consequences could not be calculated. The police must have been spread out in every street around the bank, stopping people and checking their ID.

We spent two days without food. I had to do something, although I knew how dangerous it would be to leave the house. I might be arrested at any moment. I wasn't a professional thief; it was something that just happened suddenly, driven on by that cursed voice. I stood by the door before going out, listening carefully for any sound coming from the alley. Then I closed the door and slowly walked out.

"As you have gone out, walk calmly and do not turn around. Get away from this quarter, go into a small shop, buy something, and leave."

How did the voice acquire all this prudence and precision? What if it were left to do what it wanted? What destruction would ensue! I bought a bottle of water from a small store; the man gave me my change back and went on talking to a customer who had bought a pack of cigarettes. "It's the first time I've heard of a bank robbery happening here," he said. "I thought they just happened in films."

The customer opened the cigarette pack, took a cigarette out, lit it, and left. "There will be more than that happening if the situation goes on as it is."

I took a gulp from the water bottle and turned off downtown to get away from the place and avoid any danger. I stood on the edge of the street and flagged down a taxi. The driver nodded when I told him where I wanted to go. A radio station was broadcasting news of the bank robbery. Oh God, I had done something so wrong! And I had been so reckless to go out into the street! The driver looked at me with a smile as the announcer relayed details of the incident.

"Everyone is talking about the news of the masked man," he said. "Including the press. He got away with a large sum of money." The driver let out a loud laugh and then fell silent, an expression of sadness and anger on his face. "I hope they arrest him!"

The man continued talking as I looked at him stupidly until we reached downtown. I left the taxi at the al-Hussein mosque and cut through a packed crowd, thinking, "How did all those books not help me avoid all of this?" They had built for me a world in which I believed it was impossible for me to fall, but as soon as I lost my home, I fell. I went into a clothes shop, bought some new clothes and put them on, then threw away the old ones in a trash can. There was a bank branch next to the store with a security guard standing behind the façade, turning first left then right with an expression of annoyance and anger on his face. "Look at this bank. Although it is situated on a main street, you can raid it quite easily. It must have only a few clients, for it's a long way from the residential areas. The front window is covered with paper ads, and when you run away there will be a crowd in front of it, allowing you to enter this alley, which will certainly hide you from your pursuers."

The voice was directing me to a new theft with a strength that I could no longer refuse. I looked at the bank and its surroundings more than once then went on my way and walked into the city center. I bought a small kerosene heater, some meat, bread, fruit, and vegetables, as well as medicine for Salam. I went back, and they looked at me in astonishment as I put my purchases on the floor. Nur was talking quietly to Leila and they looked at me suspiciously. Leila asked for us to talk privately, so we moved away a little. "Where have you got the money to buy all these things?" she asked in a whisper.

I told her I had borrowed some money from a friend, then I told the others in the house that I had done it for them and that a day would come when I would pay back my debts. Their reactions varied. Some thanked me, some rejected the idea of me taking a loan, and others said nothing. We prepared supper, everyone with a task of their own, and ate. Life crept into the house. We moved the mattresses nearer the fire and talked until everyone fell asleep. I stayed awake, thinking of the days to come. I heard a movement of feet near the window of the room we were in, the sound of someone walking cautiously. The sound came closer to the door, and I realized that I had almost reached the end.

5
The Journalist

(Escape Toward Memory)

A shaft of light came through the window of the third floor of the newspaper building and settled on the table where I was sitting. A delightful silence permeated the place in the final hours of work. One colleague was away, another had left, and the rest were busy in other departments. I loved the peace and quiet of that day, which was a little warm, making Amman seem peaceful and submissive. As I rested my chin on my hands, which were flat on the table, I looked at the city, and a gentle noise came in from the streets. I was thinking about what to do after work. Perhaps I would go to a café, drink a cup of coffee, and take in the faces of the customers. Perhaps I would walk through the streets or wander around a shopping mall. My mood wasn't quite clear; most likely I would stay at home. A young man climbed up to the roof of a nearby building; it looked as though he was repairing a satellite dish set up there. I thought how I needed a man to come into my life and put an end to this monotonous rhythm. Then I shook my head, rejecting the idea. I had avoided men since my first experience, like a diver who has gone to the bottom of the sea and almost drowned, then come back feeling frustrated having forgotten something he could not go back for. After work, I walked slowly as usual.

I was convinced that walking might relieve my inner store of chaos. I didn't know how true or false my conviction was. I walked until I reached the Dakhiliyya Circle, which was crowded with people and cars. The sun was about to set, and people's shadows, and those of the cars and buildings, were gradually lengthening. I continued walking past the Parliament building, in front of which some people had gathered to protest against rising prices. I passed the crowd without hearing anything. I could see their mouths opening and shutting, and their hands waving in the air. A silent scene, through which I saw a sad man walking on a rainy day with his hands in his coat pockets. I shook my head from side to side, as if to shake him from my mind, then hailed a taxi and boarded it for al-Weibdeh.

The duduk music playing in the taxi began to intrude on me, making me want to cry. I looked out the window to escape from it and spotted the man still walking on the sidewalk in the rain. Trying not to cry, I told the driver, "Please, turn off the recorder!"

He looked at me in the mirror and said, "It's broken, madam."

I cried in silence, like those who hurry into the dark to hide their sorrow as the music surrounded my soul. The man kept walking along the sidewalk, looking at a fixed spot on the horizon. At the Paris roundabout the taxi stopped, and the driver bowed his head in silence. I dried my eyes, but burst into tears again. In a croaking voice, the driver turned to me and said, "Madam, I once heard something in a film which said that there were many reasons for crying, but if we give in to them, they will take us to places from which we won't be able to come back. Believe me, that statement helped me a lot."

He was a polite young man, still in his youth, and he appeared to be one of those people who had had jobs shut in their faces. When he saw that I couldn't stop crying, he touched my hand, which was clutching the armrest like the hand of a drowning person. Then suddenly he apologized for what he had done. "Don't worry," I said. "Thank you!" I gave him his fare and headed toward the café, where I sat at a table facing the street. Some people were walking on the sidewalk around the Paris roundabout and I saw him again among them, walking absentmindedly. The sound of the duduk struck my heart with its intense sadness, pushing me to the edge of a chasm of tears. I recalled what the doctor had said: "You have to write to escape your condition. As you prefer to write drama, you must see what has happened to you as a serial on the TV screen."

I took the notebook out of my bag and returned to the painful revelations in it:

Jadallah didn't like Ustadh Awwad from the very first day at school. In his early years, he spent most of his time in a grumpy mood, and his school grades were average until the teacher died one day after collapsing in the schoolyard. A pupil ran to tell another teacher what had happened. Jadallah watched from a distance as the pupils stood over Awwad's body. They carried it inside and covered his face with a blanket. "Where will he go?" Jadallah asked the teacher when he came out. The teacher, looking sad, found his question strange and didn't say anything, but he recalled a strange situation in a geography lesson when he was explaining the proofs that the Earth was round. Jadallah interrupted the teacher and said, "You are speaking to us as though you had actually seen that it was round."

"I haven't seen it. But the scientists said so."

Jadallah laughed, which was unusual for him, saying, "I don't like absolute opinions!"

The teacher was surprised at Jadallah's response. He watched him during break time and followed him as he went into the library, chose a book, and read it. After the death of Ustadh Awwad, Jadallah excelled at school, but he continued asking questions about death and life and human behavior. His school years passed over him like a barefoot man in a field of thorns. Badi had left school when grief over the death of his brother Hammoud got the better of him. Before Hammoud's death, they had not been able to overcome the effect that poverty had had on them, and they had kept away from everything students usually aspire to. They realized that school was a gateway to escape from all the suffering they were living through, but they pictured it in a different way from the general picture of the school and city that was taking shape just then. Jadallah realized during those years what he had to do, especially once he showed a remarkable ability with regard to reading. He would spend most of his free time after school reading novels, poetry collections, and biographies in the shade of an olive tree, feeling a strange detachment from his surroundings. In winter, he would sit in a corner of the courtyard in the house and read continuously. He needed a space to give him personal privacy and chose a small, neglected room attached to the house, where he set up a bed of remnants of wood and tree stumps, covered with a woolen rug. He spent part of the night pursuing his studies and reading books and newspapers. In those days, the Left was active in the country, especially in Madaba, and by chance Jadallah became a communist, recruited by a colleague at school who invited him to his house and talked about communism and the Soviet Union. He listened carefully, with the image of his father in his mind's eye. His father had spent years working as a hired laborer for a feudal lord who gave him little. The image was interrupted only by the distant memory of the death of his brother Hammoud.

It was pouring rain that day. They had taken a path leading down from their house to the valley and from there to Madaba. Hammoud was wearing a military uniform that had once belonged to his soldier brother Khazar. It was too big for him and he looked like a bird in a pile of straw in it. Badi wore a military shirt and boots that were not his size. They followed Jadallah, despite being older than him, and he showed them paths where they needed to avoid slipping, and mud that they had to remove every few meters as it weighed down their steps. It started raining even harder. The rush of water in the valley separating the village from Madaba was loud and it scared them. When they reached the water, they found that it was sweeping rocks along with it, along with mud and tree trunks, one of which became stuck so it could be used as a bridge to the opposite bank. Jadallah held Badi's hands and encouraged him keep his balance as he walked over the tree trunk until he had crossed the torrent. He turned to Hammoud, who was frightened, and realized he had to make a great effort to persuade him to walk carefully over the tree trunk. He held his shoulders and pulled away some strands of long hair that covered his one of eyes. "Spread your arms to control your movement," he said. "Don't look down, look forward, and when you move your foot, put it on the trunk gently. Think of the bank, not of the current." He repeated what he had said to him more than once, for he realized that Hammoud was simple and his movements were slow. The current was still roaring when Hammoud set his foot on the tree trunk, looking at Badi on the other bank in fear and confusion. He took his first step and was about to follow it with another, while Jadallah watched him tensely and nervously from behind. When he saw him wobble, he called out in a loud voice, "Spread your arms!" Hammoud quickly lifted his arms, but a few paces before the bank his foot slipped and he fell and was carried away by the current. On the other side, Badi began to shout and jump around while Jadallah ran beside the torrent, shouting and calling to Hammoud, who had disappeared in the muddy water. Then he squatted on the ground, beating his head in grief at the loss of his good brother.

―――

Jadallah left his friend's house carrying forbidden books and newspapers and thinking of what he had said. He passed through the al-Nur quarter, the memory of his father's voice ringing in his ears when he asked him that year to be a doctor like Doctor Nicola. On the last day of school, Ali and Salim married. The wedding went on for seven days, during which he heard more than one person call him *hakim*. They wanted him to be a doctor. "Listen, son!" said an elderly man, stretching his legs out and putting his stick between them then clutching it. "You know that people among us got sick and died without our knowing why. Herbs are no longer any use, so your family in the village are expecting you to be a doctor."

The man looked at other people dancing the *dahiyya* and then at Jadallah. "You are the only one in the village who has stuck it out at school. Some boys will be called up into the army, and we don't know what the others will do."

The men were repeating the refrain of the *dahiyya* in hoarse voices ("*al-Dahiyya, al-Dahiyya, al-Dahiyya*"). I followed him as he left the tent and made for his room to look at the books of philosophy that he loved, the man's voice still following him, saying, "We want you as a *hakim*." He lay down on his bed and, taking a chance on how much fuel was left in the lamp, opened a book about Confucius and immersed himself in it. He could hear the men's stirring voices coming to him from the tent, interrupted by the voices of women singing songs about the bridegroom, the buttons of whose uniform shone like stars in the sky, until he fell asleep and was assailed by nightmares he told no one about.

Jadallah passed the General Secondary Certificate that year. He had spent most of the year devoted to his studies. As soon as he got back from school he would take his books outside He had marked out a path to the east of the village where he would walk back and forth carrying a book and reading aloud. At night, when there was no electricity to keep the darkness from the village, and no lamps that would let it stay awake, he would go to the outskirts of Madaba, to a street lit by an electric light, which he would sit under, holding a book and reading until midnight. A week after successfully finishing school, he was called by his party colleague, who whispered in his ear,

"We've arranged a scholarship in Moscow for you!"

This news was like seeing a broad smile on the horizon, pointing to his days to come. He hurried back home that day and looked for his father and found him digging by the trunk root of an olive tree. As soon as he saw his father, he thought he must be bringing good news. They sat on the ground as the sun inclined to the west, throwing the shadows of the trees over the ground in the orchard. Al-Shamousi looked carefully in Jadallah's face and said, "What's up, son?"

"I've got a scholarship to study in Moscow."

"Misca?" al-Shamousi replied, pronouncing the name incorrectly as he struggled to keep the tears in his eyes from flowing.

"Moscow, father."

"Is that far away?" asked al-Shamousi, in a voice wracked with sobs. When he received no reply from Jadallah he looked at the horizon, where the hills of the village were gradually hiding the sun, and began to rake the ground with his finger as a tearful gasp escaped from his chest. In the morning al-Shamousi went with Ali to Iskandar, who had just arrived at his shop on King Hussein Mosque Street and was looking around for someone to help him lift the iron door. He asked more than one passerby, but they paid him no attention. When Ali showed pity and wondered why they were so reluctant, al-Shamousi just laughed. Then he asked Ali to help Iskandar, who was leaping all around with his short, plump body. Iskandar noticed al-Shamousi, who was standing near him, and greeted him as usual with quick, jumbled words and went into the shop to buy some straw brushes, plastic buckets, and things he hung outside on the shop wall to sell, grumbling all the while about how people hated him. When he had finished, he sat at a wooden table looking at al-Shamousi and said, "Hello, Abu Ali!"

"Hello, Iskandar!"

Al-Shamousi took out his tin of tobacco, prepared a cigarette, and lit it as Iskandar looked on, waiting for the reason why he had come. Al-Shamousi did not conceal it for long. "I've come because I need some money from you. Jadallah is going abroad to study."

Iskandar looked around, suggesting a lack of interest in what al-Shamousi was saying. He repeated his request, in a slightly pleading tone. "Didn't you hear me, Iskandar?"

"Yes, I heard you. It seems your son has won a scholarship and what they've awarded isn't enough for him. Studying abroad will take years, Abu Ali, and you won't just be coming this time to ask for money. You'll be coming to me a lot, and in that case you will have to mortgage your land as a guarantee for whatever I pay you."

Ali looked at his father in a state of shock and stood up angrily, but al-Shamousi ordered him to sit down. "I agree," he said.

Iskandar smiled happily, then took a piece of paper from a box behind him and spent some time writing. When he finished, he moved an ink bottle closer to al-Shamousi and said, "Fingerprint!"

Rather hesitantly, Al-Shamousi put his finger on the paper and pressed it, gritting his teeth in silent defeat. Ali got up and started to pace in front of the shop until al-Shamousi went out, fingering the dinars in his pocket.

"What else could I have done? But don't worry, we will settle this sum and take the paper."

Two weeks later, Jadallah traveled. The evening before, the guest room was full of people saying goodbye. He was the first person in the village to go abroad. Al-Shamousi went around the men, cigarette never extinguished, his smile hiding his pain about the imminent departure of his favorite son. Before they left, the well-wishers had plenty of advice to offer. The plane was scheduled for midnight. Jadallah got dressed and scanned the room, its walls covered in newspapers he was reading, books piled up around the sides. He got his bag ready, took out some political pamphlets from under the bed, and burned them. He went out and hugged his mother, brothers and sisters, and well-wishers. He wanted to cry but hid his feelings, although the others were crying openly. He then got into a car that took him away with his father and brothers, Salim and Badi. He said farewell warmly at the airport and burst into tears when his father hugged him, emphasizing his words as he gave him his orders. "We will expect you back as a doctor!"

6
Ibrahim

(Characters of Paper)

A week after I had taken refuge in the deserted house, a new morning's sun shone. I remembered the fear I had felt that night when I heard a strange movement by the door—a fear that had stopped all thought except of one possibility—that I might be arrested. I hadn't the patience to stay where I was that night so as not to give myself away; I looked through the crack in the door and saw a dog searching the rubbish for food. Fear is a strange artist—it draws things we do not expect on the paper of our fantasies.

Everyone went out except Leila, who was fast asleep, and me. The cold had retreated, and in its place came a little warmth. I turned over in my bed and sunk my head in the blanket, thinking that if someone suspected me and knew my route, they would have detained me the same day. I got up, lit the heater, and made a cup of coffee. Then I walked over to the door and looked out the window. I would have liked to have gone out for a little just then, but I was afraid someone might see me. I went back, thinking that the bank's CCTV must have a record of me and they must have constructed a rough image of me, despite my mask.

Leila got out of bed and came over lazily. "It's true that this house is deserted and no one comes," she said quietly, "but I've been uneasy ever since I came here; perhaps the owners will return at any moment and accuse us of wrecking it."

She stood beside me and I saw her eyes close up; they were shouting innocence and sadness.

"It's painful for someone to dream of a house and not find it. This world is more cruel than I expected." She fingered her hair and rested her head on my shoulder.

"It's true that this world is cruel, Leila, but you see the light coming through an opening in this rusty door. It is hope."

"There is a lady who works in a charity that Salam went to one day looking for work. Some days ago, she suggested to Salam that she go to live with an elderly woman and look after her in exchange for payment. They don't want a nurse, but rather a girl who loves her job and belongs to the house, and they thought that someone of unknown parentage might be better for the task. Salam told her about me and thought I would be better at it than she would."

"OK, if it's a good family," I said, without knowing if I was right or not. She was a young girl who knew nothing about life. After Leila had left, the mocking voice returned. "And what do you know about life except for reading books? They have all deserted you: Descartes, Confucius, Avicenna, Gregor. In the end, you are just carrying a book about a loser like yourself."

The voice stopped for a moment then came back with an order: "The house is empty now. Come on, check the money you have."

After I checked that the door was shut and no one was coming toward the house, I lifted the lump of mud and the tile and took out the bag. I put the revolver and mask to one side, counted out the money, and found it was 1,900 dinars.

"My God, did I steal all this money?"

I got up in terror, slipped on the stones, and fell. "Ssh. I told you you would be an honorable thief, and now I shall tell you about our new agreement."

I turned around and then looked back at the money. The voice, clearly confident that I would no longer be capable of refusing, said, "You have to double this sum!"

I put the money back in its hiding place and made my way inside, the voice still close to my ear. "I have made a list of the people I will take revenge on. Aren't you pleased about that? OK, I will abandon this list on one condition, namely that you double the sum of money until you reach a stage where you can build a house for these vagrants and make a plan for them to live by."

I sat on the floor, unable to summon the strength to resist. At the same time, I liked the idea of homeless people having a house to retreat to. "OK, what do you want me to do?" I asked submissively.

"You need to retrieve Quasimodo from the hiding place in your memory where you hid him. Have you forgotten him? The hero of *The Hunchback of Notre Dame*—how you loved him! And how many times did you read the novel for his sake? You deserted Ibrahim for him, as you always do, and spent time skillfully playing his part until your mother forbade you, in case you really became a hunchback. Go downtown, buy some used clothes like his from the clothes shop, and let Quasimodo raid that bank."

———

As soon as I entered Italy Street and stood by the door of a store there, I smelled the odor of second-hand clothes. My memory opened its door upon the day when we went with my father to the Madaba market. Outside a shop there was a powerful smell, which grew stronger once we entered. My father started turning over a pile of shirts and pants to choose something that suited us—red, yellow, and blue shirts and pants. On the way back, I clutched my bag of clothes the way 'Ahid carried his. As my father walked along with his hands behind his back, I asked him, "Why do these clothes smell different from other clothes?"

"That's what things belonging to the poor smell like," he replied, with a touch of annoyance.

He smiled at me and, as if going back on something he had

said that I hadn't understood, said, "The smell is something they put among clothes so insects won't hide in them."

We went past the market and reached the outskirts of the village. My hands were sweating as I happily clutched the bag of clothes, thinking about the "smell of things belonging to the poor." At home, I smelled the pillows and mattresses and the kitchen equipment, and didn't detect that smell. My father was sitting at the door, looking at Madaba. "Are we poor?" I asked him.

He didn't reply but continued gazing at Madaba absent-mindedly. Purple clouds were hanging over it, pierced by the rays of the sun, which had inclined to the west, making way for the return of night.

I woke to the sound of a man saying, "Please, what do you want to buy?" I bought whatever I could find that seemed like something Quasimodo would wear. The shop assistant offered to show me more, but I told him I had what I needed and would come back again. After I paid for my purchase, I entered an alleyway, put on the clothes, and contrived a fake hunch, repeating, "This is madness itself, Ibrahim!"

The voice burst out in protest. "You are Quasimodo, heading for the dreaded Claude Frollo."

As I emerged from Italy Street, I heard someone call out to me, laughing, "Quasimodo!" I didn't like this name, which had been given to me by the judge Claude Frollo when he imprisoned my father and mother out of a desire to cleanse Paris of gypsies. "Half complete" is what the dreaded Claude Frollo meant by the name Quasimodo. As I walked along King Hussein Street, people avoided me: some looked at me baffled, while others covered their eyes with their hands in fear of my appearance. A girl took her mobile out of her bag and took a quick picture of me, then went on her way after giving me an odd look. She had a face like Esmerelda's—wow, Esmerelda! I wish I could find her now in the Amman crowd so I could kneel at her feet and tell her of the great love for her that still consumed my heart—just like the love she must have felt herself. My heart was almost torn from my chest when she saved me the night I came down from the tower of Notre Dame to the Festival of Fools, to see for the first time people who thought I was disguised as an ugly man when they saw me. When Frollo discovered who I was, he was angry that I had disobeyed his order to remain a prisoner in the tower at Notre Dame. I could only observe people from there. My God, how I would have been beaten that day! How many painful ropes would they have used to tie me up if Esmerelda hadn't freed me and captured me in her eternal love.

I continued on King Hussein Street toward the bank where I would no doubt find Claude Frollo and defeat him, just as he was defeated by the soldiers of the judge Phoebus the night he attacked the square of wonders to punish the gypsies and marry Esmerelda. A man walked past me laughing, not repulsed by my appearance like most people. "I'll tell Napoleon about you," he said mockingly. "He must be reading books now under the trees of Amman, which are blessed with the strangely behaved."

The Amman sky had given people a rest that morning from the rain and intense cold for several hours. The streets were crowded, heaving with local residents as well as casual visitors. I stopped to rest briefly and look at the kiosk that had replaced the Bookseller's Kiosk and sold mobile phones rather than books. I wish mobiles had been invented then; I would have told Esmerelda every night what was in my heart, and I would have told the citizens of Paris about the evil intentions of Claude Frollo.

At the bank door, people gaped at my hunched back, and the ugliness of my face aroused such disgust that they turned their faces away. I hesitated a little, but the voice pushed me inside. "Come on,

Quasimodo!" There was an electronic device for booking one's place. With gloved hands, I pressed the button and sat as though awaiting my turn as the clerks looked at me with pity and amazement. Claude Frollo was sitting at the counter, his eyes full of anger, at a window above which "Number 1" was written, while two women sat behind the other windows. I murmured to myself, "Claude Frollo, you wretched man, your hatred of the gypsies made you burn half of Paris, and your sick passion for Esmeralda drove you to imprison half the gypsies and burn down many houses in your search for her.

I looked at the dimensions of the place and the number of people in it. There were only a man and woman in the customers' hall, and they were about to leave. The voice spoke, egging me on to zero hour. "Get ready, Quasimodo!" The man left, followed by the woman, who stared at me nervously, exactly like Frollo and the employee who was also looking at me. The recorded voice of a woman called out my number; a glass screen separated me from Claude Frollo. On the left side of the hall was an open door, from which I saw an employee come out into the hall and then walk back to where Claude Frollo was sitting, while another employee was busy working on a computer. As I moved toward the door, I recalled that the cameras could take a picture of my eyes, so I put on a mask and went through the door quickly. As soon as I was inside, I grabbed Frollo by the neck and pointed the revolver at his head. Straight to his face, which was screaming with fear, I said, "Frollo, you miserable man, you were the cause of my mother and father being imprisoned. When you found me alone, you had pity on me and imprisoned me in the tower of Notre Dame. This is the fake pity of people like you."

I turned to the security guard and ordered him to shut the door and throw away his weapon. I warned him that if he made any movement I would kill Frollo. The guard walked toward me and threw down his revolver in the trash can as I had asked him to. Then I ordered the bank clerk, who had wet herself, to put all the money she had in a plastic bag. When she didn't move quickly enough, I shouted at her, "I'll kill him, then I'll kill you."

She hurried up and emptied the metal drawer and handed me the plastic bag. I picked it up and moved back, with Frollo in front of me. Meanwhile, a woman had come in, and when she saw me point the revolver at Frollo's head she screamed and tried to flee. But I threatened her, and she moved away from the door and sat on the floor. I released Frollo at the door, pushed it open, and started to flee, but I collided with a young man who looked at me in consternation. I pushed him and he fell to the ground, and I took off running.

I ran as fast as I could along an alley by the side of the bank. I had taken off the mask and hidden it with the revolver in a bag. I pulled off my coat and threw it to one side, along with the piece of cloth I had used to make the hump. I stood in the middle of the road, took off the pants I had put on over my other pants, and got rid of them. After a few meters, the alley took me in a northerly direction. I stopped for a little, put the stolen goods in another bag, and threw away the bag I had come out of the bank with. Then I took off the gloves and ran back, accompanied by the voice spurring me on. "Run, Ibrahim—don't go back!"

The alley became darker. I didn't know where I was, but after a distance I saw that it would take me into the street. The voice returned, to alert me as to my next move. "As you emerge into the street, you must adopt the character of Prince Lev Nikolayevich Myshkin. You surely haven't forgotten the novel *The Idiot*, and its author, Dostoevsky. You are now Myshkin, with his simplicity and a facial expression indicating extreme goodness. He is a unique expression of idiocy. Put the picture you painted of him when you read the novel at the forefront of your mind's eye now; look at it carefully and your face will take on the same features as his.

I emerged onto the crowded street as if I had just alighted from the train back from Switzerland to St. Petersburg, to meet my only relative from his family, the general's wife Lizaveta Prokofyevna. I walked on slowly, thinking of the beautiful Aglaya Ivanovna, daughter of General Epanchin, whom I often thought about on those fine evenings. The public bus stopped and I boarded it slowly—unlike other people, who crowded into it—and sat down with two images alternating in my mind. One was Aglaya, and the other Madame N. The bus stopped and a young man got on and sat down beside me. I saw that he was following a live broadcast of a bank raid on his mobile phone. He noticed that I was looking at his phone surreptitiously and said, "They say a quarter of a million dinars has been stolen." He then went back to looking at the broadcast, sometimes smiling, sometimes with a serious expression on his face. "I swear it's a man!"

He turned off his phone and gave me a sideways glance. "He's the masked one—he raided a bank near the Third Circle about a month ago and they found no trace of him."

I smiled naively as I looked at General Epanchin, then stood up in preparation for leaving the bus, which was on its way to the Third Circle. I picked up the bag and pressed the button a few meters before the opening that leads to the alley. I got off the bus and the voice urged me to walk faster. "Come on, Ibrahim!" There was no one on the street to notice me going in through the hole in the wall, and no pedestrians on the sidewalk, so I entered calmly and hurried along the alley. I opened the door to the house quietly and checked that no one was there, then quickly moved the lump of mud to hide the money under the tile.

"Stop! You must prepare to leave this place tomorrow after leaving the money here. You now have roughly half a million, stolen from two banks in two locations near to each other. You must leave and look for an apartment far from here. You will stay there, and I will tell you the second half of what you have to do. No more bank raids now!"

I hid the money after taking 20,000 dinars and hiding it in my bag. Then I lay down on the bed and took a deep breath. The sounds coming from outside were ordinary noises, and the temperature was moderate enough to have gotten rid of some of the humidity in the house. Ibrahim the bookseller, then Diogenes, and now you are Robin Hood—three people but you cannot be any one of them completely. Where are you going? What will the end be? Sleep seemed like the best way to drive away the anxiety that had come over me, so I slept.

———

Despite not sleeping well because of a fierce attack of nightmares, I woke up early. I drove from my imagination several fantastical scenes and cleared my throat of an old bitterness. Yesterday I had raided a bank and managed to flee. How could I, a bookseller whose head is stuffed with books, allow myself to do what I had done? I closed my eyes and saw myself as a child in the village, walking toward the sun's disk and dreaming of holding it. The farther I walked, the farther away it was, and the farther away it was, the farther it sank until night fell, and I lost any sense of direction.

The girls and boys were still asleep when I lifted the blanket from my face. What I saw looked like a scene from a film I had seen of people sleeping in an airport when the plane's take-off had been delayed. What were they waiting for? What plane did they expect to take them away from this deserted house?

The voice was eavesdropping on what I was thinking. "What you do for them is the plane that will take them away from this desolation."

I got out of bed, splashed my face with a little water, dried it with the sleeve of my shirt, then looked out through the hole in the door at what I could see of a world that couldn't easily give you what you wanted. The weather was still warm, so I went out and bought some papers. I would have liked to sit in a nearby café, redolent of the smell of coffee, with the voice of Fairouz singing to the morning, but the voice stopped me. Security would doubtless be searching for me everywhere. I went back and lit the stove, made tea, and sat flicking through the papers. I found the news about a masked robber in the middle of the front page, as well as some editorials devoted to the incident. Leila woke up, poured herself a glass of tea, and sat beside me with a blanket wrapped around her shoulders. "Today I'll be going to the house I'll be working in, but I'm happy to be living with an old woman."

She became distracted and stopped talking, then started telling me how she had been raped by a female supervisor in the orphanage called Rinad Mahmoud. She told me this as if she were trying to get past her fear of people resulting from that incident before she started her new job. As she spoke, her lips trembled and her hands clasped the glass of tea with evident tension. "The face of that woman pursues me in my dreams and when I am awake. Her hands crawl over my body, which I have hated since that time," she said, then wept in pain. She looked at me as if hoping I could help free her from the effects of what had happened. Then she picked up a bag and went into a room that was full of rocks and dirt where no one went. After a few minutes, she came back wearing her women's clothes, saying, "It makes no sense to go disguised in men's clothes."

Feigning a pale smile, she went to look for her shoes, found them, and started to put them on, sitting beside me. "I'll visit you all on my day off to check on you."

Nur was looking at Leila from under the blanket. "Will they let you visit tramps like us?" he asked, his voice strangled by sobs so loud that they woke up the others.

"Even if they don't allow it, I will visit you anyway."

She knelt down by Nur's bed and they said goodbye, weeping with a bitterness I had never seen before. She embraced the rest of them, one by one, then she came to me, wiping away tears. "Although you are silent most of the time, I have felt your fatherhood, which I was yearning for all those years in the orphanage. I won't stop coming to see you, whatever happens."

She embraced me and left in tears. I lay on the bed, searching the newspapers for an ad for furnished apartments. I found one for a building near the Seventh Circle. "I'm going to visit a friend, then I'll be back," I told them. As I looked at the faces I could see through the darkness, I wondered what would happen if they knew there was a lot of money in this house. How could I tell them I was leaving when they had found in me a refuge from their many sorrows? Should I give them some money? The voice protested against this line of thought and warned me that it was a mistake that could reveal my crime. I couldn't say anything, so I picked up my bag and left. Nur caught up with me at the door while the others looked at me sadly and silently. "Even you are leaving us?"

I stroked his head as I looked at his tearful eyes. "Believe me, I will come back."

A Nightmare

I hack into Iyad Nabil's mobile, read a list of the food he ordered, check the time when his order will arrive, reread his Facebook messages to one of his lovers, reach the house before the arrival of the delivery man who will bring him his order, make him think that I am employed by Mr. Iyad, pay the man, pick up the food, check the man has left, put the poison in the food, and bang on the door. A woman opens it and tells me to put what I have in the kitchen. I take the money from her and I leave. I wait near the house and hear the woman laughing. When her voice disappears, I break the door down. Iyad Nabil is lying on the floor with the woman beside him, both dead. I look for the device to which the security cameras are linked, delete the recording in which I appear, and leave.

PART 5

"What a heavy price man pays for the truth of himself and the truth of things to become clear to him."
—Tayeb Saleh

1
The Journalist

(A Love From Which There Is No Escape)

I was staring through the bus window as if I were looking for something to light a fire in the fields of the dejection that had raided my inner space. Amman has moments that make you fall in love with it, however many reasons there are that make you feel dejected, like the crowds of people in the morning, the people, the cars, the buses—a morning that arouses a sort of pleasure in you and gives you a bit of balance. I took a picture of people in the street on my phone, posted it on Facebook, and captioned it, "Crowd." I checked a public page and found several accounts talking about the masked robber. He had caught my attention for reasons I didn't understand. In fact, it made me knock on the door of the chief editor that same day and ask him if I could write a series of articles about this man, and he agreed. A feeling something like admiration had drawn me to him, as if I needed a man like this. How odd it would seem if I were to tell any of my colleagues about it! What strange desires lay hidden in the soul, that well full of secrets! I sat down at my table looking at the Facebook pages again. An artist had drawn a strange portrait of the masked robber: a man in old clothes wearing a bright red mask with "Shanfara" written above it. This became a principal image for hundreds of users' accounts who applauded him and praised him and sympathized with him. But how could people praise a thief? And where had they got all these stories detailing his biography and his robberies? And how did I find myself feeling a strange desire for a man who might perhaps be imaginary? Someone wrote about him,

"A quick-footed man who jumps at night from buildings with the agility of a desert fox, visits the houses of the poor, and brings them joy."

This man preoccupied me and dominated my thoughts—a fine state of affairs if it really was as told, and perhaps even finer than people knew. In the evening I searched the internet for books about the personalities of robbers. How do they think? Why do they steal? Then I read about Shanfara. I spent that night looking through any books I could find for any information to help me understand what was happening. I went to bed at eleven o'clock, as an image of the robber and the mask on his face came to me out of the room's partial darkness. "I wish I could remove this mask to see who you are!" I said to myself when I noticed I was waving my arm in the air. I turned over in bed trying to sleep but couldn't. From some secret place I heard the sound of the duduk and saw the man walking along the street on a rainy evening, heading for somewhere unknown, a man who had left me and shut the door on me. I lay in bed, assailed by an image of a masked man walking side by side with the man on the rainy evening, as if it was part of a series I was working on. I turned on the light and grabbed my laptop, and went on writing the scene as if afraid of losing it. Although I had spent hours writing, sleep still eluded me. I shut the computer and picked up my notebook from a table near the bed to read what the man had wanted to say.

On the evening of June 5, 1967, Jadallah was climbing the stairs of the building where Tamarka Ivanovich lived. He had loved this girl since the first time he met her in the courtyard at Lomonosov University. He was sitting on a chair in the outer courtyard, soaking up the rays of the sun, engrossed in translating some information from a book in Russian by Nikolai Strakhov. Across from him sat a girl of medium height with curly, fair hair that hung down over her blue eyes. She had crossed her legs and was flicking through the pages of a book, smiling at what she was reading. She put the book aside, took a pack of cigarettes out of her bag and lit one, then blew smoke into the air. She noticed that the man opposite her was looking at her with a smile. She nodded her head to return the smile and went back to her book, but with every page she stole a glance at Jadallah, whose concentration disappeared when he suddenly found her eyes noticing he was staring at her.

"Are you an Arab?" she asked in a soft voice. Struggling to contain the flow of warm blood to his face, he closed the book and replied, "Yes, from Jordan."

Tamarka looked at the swarthy youth with dark eyes and black hair tucked behind his ears. He seemed confused to her as he rubbed his thin mustache.

"What are you studying?"

"Philosophy."

His father's voice, as he said farewell at the airport that year and told him to come back as a skilled doctor—better than Nicola—had never left Jadallah's imagination. But despite that, he had studied philosophy, which he had loved since the first book he had read at school. He didn't see himself as a doctor when he lay in the village on the bed he had made; he saw himself as a philosopher, having fallen in love with books that influenced him in those years, keeping him company and illuminating new paths for him. He struggled in his first days at the university learning Russian, but he settled on philosophy, despite being aware of the needs of the villagers who called the doctor *hakim*. They seldom went to him, for the desert was their constant pharmacy: wild medicinal herbs such as *shih*, *qaisum*, *ba'itharan* for stomach aches, *halilawan* (seasonal dog excrement) for ophthalmia; *jadha* to treat the joints, and flour, eggs, and cloth as means to set broken bones. But they could not do without Nicola, who treated diseases they could not cure. Despite people's need for it in those days, Jadallah didn't want to pursue medicine. He didn't tell anyone what he was studying. Instead he contented himself with sending them photos and letters in which he replied to his father's and brothers' questions.

From the day he got to know Tamarka and started to call her Tammy, he became stronger inside. It was a strength that drove out his weakness—the sense of shame he felt for having not fulfilled his father's wishes—and made him stronger in the face of the nightmares and strange feelings that tormented him. Tammy loved him; she loved his gentleness, his seriousness, his politeness, his enthusiasm for life, and she loved his deep love for her. She was studying art at the same university he attended. Every day he would go to her college, plant a kiss on her cheek, and give her a rose. She would laugh and say: "The university will run out of roses if you pick one for me every day." In the evening they would meet at her apartment in Bolshaya Nikitskaya Street and he would leave at midnight.

Jadallah hung onto Tammy, as he didn't have a lot of friends. He had a touchy personality, which made him lose a lot of people he had gotten to know. So he made do with a few of them while remaining afraid that they would leave him. But his relationship with Tammy made him more contented, as if through her he was craving more stability than before. In one meeting, he told her that he wanted her closer to him—he wanted her with him always. They traveled together to Uzhhorod, a city in western Ukraine, on the border with Slovakia near the Hungarian border where Tammy's family lived. He spent a week with her family, and her father liked him; he liked his culture, his open-mindedness, and his deep philosophical vision. And Jadallah found things in her father that attracted him. He wrote a letter to his own father, explaining how he had gotten to know her and fallen in love with her. He told him about her father and mother and siblings, and asked his permission to marry her. With the letter, he enclosed some pictures of him and Tammy and her family. The reply came some weeks later. "The horseman must have a horse."

Jadallah laughed uproariously, delighted with this reply despite the lump in his throat—how could he go back with no medical degree?

It was June 5 when Jadallah reached the final step on the staircase and knocked on the door. Tammy, who was engrossed in a TV report on the battle of 1967, came out. He dropped a newspaper and some books, then sat on the sofa watching TV as an announcer relayed news of the battle. Tammy stood nearby, stirring some food she was cooking.

The announcer had just finished reading the news bulletin. Tammy was stroking his hair. He switched on the radio and just managed to pick up the Voice of the Arabs station, where the voice of Ahmad Said ordered the fish in the sea to feed on the corpses of the enemy. He listened for a moment then switched it back off, saying, "It looks as if the Arab world will be entering an extremely difficult period after this heroic enterprise!"

His friends came after a few hours: a Cuban guy called Battista Manuel, who was studying art, Na'il, a Palestinian studying medicine, and Khalida, an Iraqi girl studying chemistry. They brought a bottle of vodka and some fruit and vegetables with them. Over dinner, they embarked on a conversation about the war. Jadallah was afraid of its consequences and thought that the Arabs were ill prepared for a war like this. The voices of his guests grew louder as they called him a "defeatist" and said he was spreading an idea being repeated by foreign agents.

Six days later, Jadallah was leaving the university on his way to meet Tammy so they could go home together. His colleague had given him a newspaper with a supplement with many pictures in it. One photo showed an Egyptian military plane brought down in Sinai, with some Israeli soldiers standing beside it. There was one of an Egyptian Mig-21 fighter destroyed on the ground at an airfield, one of Israeli parachutists near the Wailing Wall after the fall of East Jerusalem, one of Syrian fortifications in the Golan after the troops had quit, and one of captured Arab soldiers with bound hands in front of an Israeli soldier's gun barrel. He read the headline and burst into tears, even though he had expected the result in advance. "So we lost the war," he said.

Jadallah went back home that day on his own. He couldn't bear the scenes he was seeing on the TV screen so he turned it off and sat drinking vodka. When Tammy came back, he was asleep and hallucinating. He woke at midnight to the sound of his friends, who spent the night chatting about what had happened. Jadallah said nothing, but just drank and smoked. After they left, he slept soundly with Tammy beside him. She woke up whenever she heard him talking in his sleep. In the morning she went out and brought some things for the apartment as well as a letter from Jordan, which plunged Jadallah into tears when he read it, for his brother Salim had been martyred.

From that day on, he felt wounded inside. He became depressed and wore a permanent frown on his face. He rarely went out, spending most of his time reading for his university specialty and immersing himself in books on philosophy and politics. He became isolated but retained his love for Tammy, who knew a lot about his life in Jordan and was preparing to move to live there with him after she had finished studying. But everything changed when Jadallah returned from meeting with some Arab students, who stayed up till midnight talking about literature and politics. When he reached the apartment, he found his Cuban friend Battista Manuel sitting by the door. His face was sad. Jadallah had never seen him like that when he had been chatting about drawing and art. "What happened?" he asked, moving closer to him.

But Battista stayed silent, shoulders shaking as he cried silently. "What happened?" Jadallah shouted, his voice echoing around the walls.

"Tammy is dead."

"What? How?" Jadallah shouted, kneeling down and clasping Battista's hands.

"She was crossing the road and was hit by a car; she died instantly."

That night, Jadallah had a new defeat to add to his existing defeats: Tamarka, whom he had loved as a tree loves a nearby river, had died. He cried silently in his apartment, refused to go to the university, and only responded to his friends' knocking on the door after a week. When he finally opened the door, he had a thick beard; his eyes were sunken and his body wasted. He couldn't control himself and fell down in a faint.

———

Jadallah didn't go back to Jordan during his vacation: he was grieving for Tamarka, as well as avoiding his father's eyes, which pursued him even in his sleep as he awaited his return as a doctor. His psychological state deteriorated, and he became more reclusive. He became a silent person, someone who found no pleasure in anything and spent most of his time reading until he graduated in the summer of 1971. But he didn't leave for Jordan; instead, he was arrested. It happened one May evening that year when he was with several Arab and Soviet students in the university café talking about the 1967 defeat. Jadallah became agitated and loudly cursed the Soviet Union and Brezhnev. Addressing one of his Soviet colleagues, he cried, "You abandoned us; you deceived us when you sent Egypt information in which you declared there were Israeli military reinforcements on the border with Syria. You drove us to war although you knew our capacity."

Battista clamped his hand over Jadallah's mouth to try to stop him speaking, but Jadallah pushed his hand away and exploded in anger. "By doing that, you expressed your wish for Israel to deal us a blow."

Jadallah got up and walked a few paces and then turned back to the table, where everyone stared at him in stunned silence. "We believed in you, but you abandoned us!"

That evening, there was a loud knock on the apartment door. As soon as he opened it, a man hit him in the face and knocked him to the ground. Other men tied him up, led him away blindfolded, threw him in a vehicle, and whisked him away. He found himself in a dark prison cell with one small window high up. He tried to comprehend what had happened and who these men were who had arrested him, but after a few hours the walls seemed to be creeping in on him; the time and the darkness he had been plunged into weighed heavily on him. He recalled his life, from the hard times of his childhood to his schooldays and his time at university. He felt his strength ebbing from him and was overcome by a bout of hysteria. He started banging on the door and shouting, cursing the people who had taken him to this prison, refusing him water or food or even a vessel to pee in and forcing him to do his business in the corner. After three days they took him out and brought him to a dark room with a single lamp on a table. They sat him down opposite a man who put to him a direct question: "What is your source for what you said about the information sent to Egypt?"

Jadallah realized that he was in the company of Soviet intelligence. "Just an analysis," he said emphatically.

The officer laughed, concealing his annoyance. "This is not an analysis, it's information."

"That's all I can say."

They dragged him to a wall, tied him up, and rained blows on him, but they didn't get the answer they wanted. They tried several varieties of torture until they found that his mental state had deteriorated. Jadallah had started talking to himself, sometimes laughing and sometimes crying, so they took him back to the cell. Some weeks later, they subjected him to a lie-detector test, which showed he was telling the truth, and after a few months they released him. He was remembering his first meeting with Tamarka, conscious of a new wound in his soul and without knowing what to expect.

.

2
Ibrahim

(A New Disappearance)

Over the last few weeks, the deserted house has carved out a place for itself in my memory. I have grown used to its cracks, its holes, its damp smell, and even its cold. When familiarity follows hardship, it leads to a longing of the sort that leads to pain. Halfway along the alley, my steps were interrupted by the voice. I had believed him when he told me what he wanted and said he would not come back for days.

"You must go to a shopping mall and buy some new clothes like those of Doctor Zhivago, the hero of the novel you were afraid to talk to your father about, because Boris Pasternak mounted a strong attack on the Communist regime at the time, which did not conform to your father's thinking. You'll still recall the expression on Doctor Zhivago's face, his way of thinking, and even the way he walked—so much so that when you read the novel in the bookseller's kiosk, completely untroubled by the downtown din, you would repeat: "How great you are, Pasternak!" Do you remember how you cried when Lara came in and found him in a winding sheet?"

I rested against the wall and put the bag down on the ground with a vague sense of sorrow. "I remember well."

"Then come on, Zhivago!"

On the way, the driver let me charge my phone on the taxi's charger, and I turned it on and found Ranad Mahmoud's page. A woman in her forties with many female friends, she wrote nothing on her page, just published songs and a few pictures, most of them in the company of women, usually young, who traveled more than once a year. In her information column, she had written that she was divorced and did not wish to receive messages, especially from men seeking women. She said she didn't want to get married. In an old post, she wrote, "I am the happiest when I am alone." As I turned the phone off, I realized that the driver had been talking the whole way without my listening to him. Remembering my father's voice—"Be careful of taxi drivers, many of them are informers"—all I said to him was the name of the mall in Abdoun.

When we reached the mall, I was uncertain where to go in such a large building. I also had a headache, which had come on suddenly, and I stood still for a few minutes, looking at so many unfamiliar faces. I pulled myself together and walked around in a confused way until I came across a store selling posh clothes. I told the sales person I wanted some classic style clothes, and she showed me several designs, from which I chose a long-necked jersey, a suit, a coat, and leather shoes. I put them on in the changing room and went out. I found a barbershop and described to the proprietor the shape of Zhivago's hairstyle, and he cut my hair accordingly. I went into a store and bought a pair of sunglasses then slipped into a perfume store, bought an expensive perfume and went out. People were constantly on the move, going into stores and restaurants, and making a noise that never deserted the walls. I took a long look at myself and wondered what was I doing here and why I was wearing these clothes. The voice came with an order.

"In order to escape, you must hide in Zhivago's character—you can no longer go back. You have committed two bank robberies, and the police are looking for you in the neighborhood, so you must do what I ask you to do—carefully."

"The police will be looking for Quasimodo and Said Mehran."

"We must rule out any possibility, however small."

I shut my eyes and saw the pages of *Doctor Zhivago* move quickly. His image gradually took shape in my imagination until I had gone as far as I could to disguise myself and heard the voice ordering me to leave. "Come on, go and meet Lara!"

Taxi drivers in Amman usually talk to their passengers, but unusually the sixty-year-old driver that day just gave me a quick greeting and some fleeting glances before listening to the news. From a distant place in my memory, I heard the echo of the announcer's voice giving the news of the revolution in Russia in 1905, which I knew would be a prelude to the 1917 revolution. But they were unfair to Pasternak when he wrote me in his story. They said he was opposed to the revolution without realizing that he was not a Stalinist. The taxi continued to snake its way between the buildings until we reached the building whose address was in a newspaper I had given to the driver. I leaned out of the window looking for a balcony with a woman standing on it. In which apartment do you suppose Larisa Feodorovna would be waiting for me, now that she has fallen in love with me despite her earlier love for Pavlovich? The driver looked at the number of the building, then at the newspaper and pointed to a number hanging over the main door. The he started to read aloud a large headline on the first page of the paper: "Masked robber forces banks to change security systems."

He laughed as he took the fare from me then gave a deep sigh, saying, "Perhaps you're not concerned; you look as if you're well off."

I looked at him without saying anything and he laughed again: "In the old days, when people died of hunger, women wouldn't accept a man in marriage unless he had raided and stolen."

The smile disappeared from his face and in its place came a sadness that drained him of much of his energy. He looked at me with eyes that were plainly listless. "I'll have passed sixty soon, and there is no hope on the horizon except for more debts piling up nonstop," he said, as we approached my stop.

"I told my children that the masked man is a thief and that they shouldn't help him, but believe me, I'm secretly pleased with what he did."

I stood by the door of the building not knowing where I should go to rent an apartment, but I saw a young man coming out of the building's underground garage and hurrying toward me. "How can I help you, sir?" he asked.

"I want to find an apartment to rent," I replied, in a humble tone that concealed a certain pride.

The man smiled. "You'll find a lot of apartments. Don't worry, demand isn't as high as before."

He asked me with exaggerated courtesy to follow him and we went up to the seventh floor, where he opened the door to an apartment and we went inside. It was a luxury apartment, with two bedrooms, a sitting room, a guest room, two restrooms, and posh furniture. Here Lara and I could vanish from the eyes of those who were pursuing us and accusing us of opposing the revolution, and I would write the first drafts of the poems going around in my head. I only realized that the man was speaking to me when he reminded me; I apologized, gave him twenty dinars, and asked for a contract to sign. He left, saying he would be back soon and calling me "Sir" a lot. I wandered around the apartment and went into the bedroom, where there was a comfortable bed opposite a wide mirror, from which I found Doctor Zhivago spying on me. The same expression, the same movements. How could someone take on the appearance and consciousness of someone else? What madness happens to the brain at moments like this?

The man returned carrying the contract. I wrote my name and signed it. He looked at the piece of paper and exclaimed in astonishment, "Your name is Yuri Andreyevich Zhivago?"

He was silent for a moment and then exclaimed, "But you speak Arabic!"

Like someone who has suddenly awakened, I found myself unable to answer the man. I snatched the paper from his hand and ripped it up, saying, "Sorry, the pressures of living have begun to confuse us." Then I signed a new, renewable contract for two months and gave him the rent in advance—after selecting bank notes that did not have the same serial numbers, mostly ones that I received back as change after paying for things I bought at several places. He gave me back the contract and said, "This is my mobile number. Contact me if you need anything, sir."

"Your mobile?"

He took a phone from his pocket and lifted it up so I could see. "Yes, yes," I said, correcting myself. "But I lost my mobile; where can I buy a new one?"

"There are several stores, and there is a mall nearby where you will find what you want."

As soon as he left, I shut the door and heard the voice. "You must remain Doctor Zhivago to everyone you meet."

I lay down on a soft sofa in front of a widescreen TV in the hall. The smell of the perfume I had sprinkled on my clothes gave me a little of the peace I was seeking. I recalled the deserted house and its residents. "So here you are now a thief masquerading as Zhivago."

I feared the return of the voice so I stood at the window. Part of Amman was visible, with its multi-storied buildings, its villas, fancy cars, and beautiful women, but I only wanted Madame N. I loved her—like any man who loves a woman. But I had not found her—like anyone separated from the object of his desire by bad fortune. I wandered around the apartment, which was devoid of anything to eat or drink. I wondered if I should go out again and was answered by a new silence with a rhythm unlike the one I knew: the silence of my village punctuated by birdsong, the bleating of goats, and shepherds calling. This was the silence of al-Jawfa, punctuated by the voices of children playing in the alley and the voice of a woman calling to her neighbor across the nearby balcony. The silence of west Amman had other sounds I was not used to: the sound of speeding cars; strange, loud songs that could be heard from time to time; the sounds of ambulances and police cars.

I checked the messages on my phone and satisfied myself that I hadn't written anything to Dr. Yusuf, but I found one from him: "Apologies for the delay in replying to you."

I checked my messages again and found nothing, so I wrote back, "I didn't send you anything."

He replied with a copy of a message he had received from my number. How could that happen? It seemed I was on the way to going mad.

"I will reply to you. My father got to know my mother a long time ago when they were both young. She loved him a lot and he loved her, but when she was pregnant with me, he left her and disappeared. By pure chance, I found out that my father was not dead as had been rumored; my father was another man, a famous man of the sort we see on our TV screens, rich, handsome, smart, with a definite charisma. But between him and me there was a distance that could not be bridged. Although I knew the problem, I went to him and knocked on the door of his palace. I sat in the hall waiting for him and told him the story from the beginning. I reminded him of the moment he got to know my mother and of the moment he left her. The thing that pained me most was that he got up and said, in a mocking tone, 'I've no time for all this rubbish.' I hated him. In fact, I harbored such a great loathing for him that it spared me the idea of wanting to belong to him and his great family."

———

At the door, as I was getting ready to go out, the voice cautioned me, like a father reminding his son of what he had to do: "Don't forget that you are Zhivago; you have to avoid any possibility of being exposed." I didn't forget. I walked along the corridor toward the elevator as if I were Zhivago going to meet Lara Antipova. I was back in 1917, when Zhivago got to know her as a nurse at the time of the struggle between the Bolsheviks and the Imperial Russian Army. As I stood at the door of the building, the man asked, "Do you need a taxi, sir?" I nodded. He made a call on his mobile, and a few minutes later a taxi came and took me to a mall near where I lived. It was a new world that I knew nothing about. Elegant women shopping for pleasure, girls and boys wandering between stores selling goods I didn't know, the smell of perfumes, interwoven sounds of music. I went into a mobile phone store where a girl was smiling despite looking tired. "I'd like the latest phone you have," I said to her as I calmly looked around.

The voice whispered to me, laughing beside my ear. "You are excellent at dealing with people, Zhivago."

The girl brought out a phone, pressed a button to activate it, and explained to me how to use it. Then she scrutinized my face with the smile of a girl who wants to approach a silent man. "You're like someone I saw in a film, but I can't remember the name of the film or the name of the character."

"Perhaps."

She gave me the phone in a neat plastic bag, and I repeated what I had said: "Perhaps."

It was almost four in the afternoon when I bought a new laptop to go with the phone, as well as enough food for a month, and went back.

My first evening in the new place arrived and allied itself with the silence against me. I tried to rid myself of my irritation by cooking a little meat and preparing some vegetable soup, which I ate. I could hear voices from the staircase from time to time, breaking the monotony of my isolation. I lay down in front of the TV, moving between stations without listening while scenes from the life of the village invaded my imagination, together with the voices of my father, my brother 'Ahid , and my mother. I felt disturbed, conscious that I was making a mistake. Where had the stain of this voice come from, to involve me in something I did not believe in? I heard the voice reproach me. "There is no need for these ideas or this remorse."

I swiped my finger over the screen of my new phone and pressed the Facebook icon. The first thing I read was news of the death of an orphanage manager, Ranad Mahmoud. Her page was heaving with condolences and expressions of regret. I Googled her name and found details of the incident: "The manager of an orphanage has been found drowned in the swimming pool at her apartment." I went back to Facebook and found an illustrated account by an activist, inviting sympathy with the case of this divorced woman and relating details of the incident. Ranad Mahmoud, who had caused psychological damage to Leila when she assaulted her in the orphanage, was now dead. I wasn't happy at the news, but I still felt a little sadness—and some fear.

I spent two hours looking through Facebook pages and finding posts praising the masked robber. I drowned in a flood of comments and replies that puzzled me. The picture they painted was not mine, creating events I had not been involved in. They did all that and believed it.

I couldn't sleep that night. I tossed and turned in the bed as Madame N appeared to me from the darkness and peace of the room, lovingly lying beside me, clasping my head to her breast, and whispering to me that I should keep calm. Behind her shoulders, gulls flew and then descended. Music grew louder then softer. Shooting stars and comets raced down in a summer night sky. I spread my arms to embrace her but only found air.

I turned on the light and looked around me but found only silence. Her notebook was lying on the bedside table like a single exit from a dark cellar. As soon as I opened it, I found that she had completed the story for me:

His words took me to what no one knew about him. That is what I felt when I had finished reading the notebook, which had become more than a bundle of piled up pieces of paper, but a life full of pain and joy and many losses. So here you are, a man hiding a history steeped in grief in a calm and leisurely walk, in eyes that never cease their contemplation. Do you have a homeland to go back to, lonely one, where you could recover some of the health of your spirit stolen by broken dreams?"

I hid the notebook carefully in my bag as if hiding a world of chaos that might become a substitute for an imaginary calmness it claimed to be the world. The man disappeared for a week, which passed as slowly as time passes for a prisoner in solitary confinement. It was a sudden sort of attachment, with no causes to explain it or excuses to confirm the logic of what was happening. I sat at the counter looking at the customers, with eyes that saw nothing but jelly enveloping everything except his place, which remained empty as it had been. A musical lament spread through the place, just like the grief of a woman like me, for a man about whom I knew nothing except what he had written in a notebook where he hid behind the story. At first, I disguised my passion for him, but some days after he had disappeared, there was no longer any point in it. I repeatedly asked my female colleague whether he had come back, though I didn't receive any reply to quench the fire that burned inside me, turning me into a woman unlike the one I had been.

Some days later, I saw him come slowly through the restaurant. I almost shouted for joy. I looked at his face, which had become familiar to me through what he had written in pages whose paths

I had spent a whole night walking, like someone discovering a new city. I hurried to him and asked in a panting voice, as if I had just finished a walk of several hours, "Are you OK?"

He looked at me and began to undo the buttons of his long woolen coat. Then he took a deep breath and let out a long sigh. "Yes, fine, my dear."

He said, "My dear!" I shouted to myself in surprise as I followed him to his table.

"Your place is vacant!"

He looked at me with a smile on his face that gently touched my spirit. "So my papers are okay."

I didn't know how to respond, but he saved me by saying, with a warm confidence, "I was sure they were in your possession. So I wasn't afraid for them."

"In fact…"

I wanted to apologize for what I had done, but he forestalled me, as if returning an apology for which there was no need. "I'd like a cup of coffee."

I quickly brought him he wanted with a pleasure that only women know. I set the cup down and left to attend to the other tables. He snatched a glance at me that made me go back to him and inform him about his notebook. "I have your notebook, but it is at home."

After work, I found him waiting for me outside the restaurant, leaning on a wall and watching the passersby. As I hurried toward him he said, "I won't detain you. I'll just take the notebook and leave." The weather had become warmer, which added a nice rhythm to the calm of the streets and made walking more pleasurable. He looked at his watch and said, as if to break the silence, "It's ten in the evening."

"It's still early," I replied, looking at the way he lit his cigarette and gazing at his dark face—a chin on which black mingled with white, and gentle eyes, which widened when he smiled. "Excuse me," he said. "This is one of my bad habits."

"Never mind."

I wished he would tell me about all of his habits all at once. How eager I was to penetrate the world of a man like this! Like those cultured men from classical times who came out of books. We were some way from the restaurant when a youth passed close by us riding a new-style motorbike. The noise made me jump, but it didn't affect him. "It seems Amman is changing, don't you think?" I said, trying to make him speak so I could listen to him.

He made for a trash can and threw the stub of his cigarette in it, then said, "The whole world has changed."

"Will we be OK?"

He looked at me as if he found my question odd. "It seems we are walking toward the edge. There are many wild beasts, and their victims are many as well," he said, laughing quietly. "But afterwards we will emerge and we will be OK. That's life; it only gives you in exchange."

At the apartment door, he looked around and said quietly, "I'll wait here for you to bring me the notebook."

He was like a polite child not wanting to cause problems. As I turned the key in the lock, I said, "Do you think I'm so mean as to let you leave without even a cup of coffee? Don't worry, I live alone."

Once inside the apartment, he looked around and walked slowly toward the living room then sat looking at the pictures hanging on the walls. He seemed shy despite his fine self-confidence and pride. "You have a quiet house," he said, and lit a cigarette to hide his confusion about what he would say. I gave him his notebook and he quickly put on his glasses and started to read. I saw him through the kitchen door, which opened on to the sitting room, turning over the pages of the notebook as if finally in possession of something he had been waiting for a long time. He didn't hear me when I came to him with his coffee—he was so absorbed in reading—so I spoke again. He apologized for being so absentminded, unaware that finding him as a reality before my eyes was the best moment of my life.

He didn't say much about himself, except that he lived alone in a small house not very far from my apartment, and that he was retired and didn't know what to call what he was writing—was it a novel or a memoir? He said he had discovered that the only thing that helped him relax was writing. I was embarrassed to ask him what it was that tired him out, for it wasn't right to ask a man about his secrets such a short time after meeting him. He was skilled in directing questions and in listening when I talked about myself. Perhaps I summarized too much to keep from boring him, though I was prepared to tell him everything. From that day, we started meeting constantly. He would wait for me until I had finished work, then we would leave together. We spent a lot of time walking in the streets of al-Weibdeh, and when he was tired we would sit in a café and he would talk about books he had read, as if there was nothing else in his life. Once I asked him, "Aren't you married?"

"I was."

He carried on talking to me in his slow manner as if he was a professor carefully explaining an important lesson to his students. I fell in love with him. I had to confess this to myself at the time, to put him in the appropriate place in my life. He knew I was finishing my university studies, so we stopped meeting. He said he didn't want to cause me to fail, but what happened was that I wasn't able to study as I ought to. One night I knocked on his door late in the evening. There was surprise on his face when he looked out from the door of his house and saw me. It wasn't a suitable house for a man like him; it was just a room with a small kitchen and bathroom, a damp place that never saw the sun, and its walls were moldy from the excessive damp. It had a bed, with a chair in front of it, a table with books on it, and a box containing some medicines. He seemed embarrassed by the surprise visit. For the first time I saw sadness take the form of a laugh in a man when he asked me, "How did you come?" Then he got up, as though running away from a conversation he had expected, and said in a confused voice, "I'll get us some coffee." His clothes were hanging on a peg on the wall, covered with a plastic bag, under which he had placed his shiny shoes. The smell of his cologne competed with the musty smell in the place, and there was a small tape recorder playing a song in a language I didn't know. It was a sad song, inviting reflection followed by a quiet sort of weeping.

He put the cups of coffee on a small table between us and lit a cigarette. "Welcome!" he said, in a voice that seemed to be reproving me for something. That night he told me his story in full, as if I had come at just the moment when he was psychologically ready to unveil what it was that kept him awake. He spoke to me as if he was dominated by a feeling of retreat to the past. I cried, smiled, then I stared at him until he cried. When I put his head on my chest, he came close to sleep, and then he slept. When he awoke, I cuddled his head and looked into his sad eyes. "Do you know how much I love you?"

"I know," he said with a smile. That night, I slept in his embrace, my head on his naked chest, listening to his heartbeat, his breathing like that of a child resting and at peace.

3
Leila

(The Secrets of Madame Emily)

I looked at the piece of paper Salam had given me, made sure I would pronounce what was written on it correctly, and told the driver, with feigned confidence, "To al-Rabiya." Before setting off, he asked for specific directions so I just handed him the piece of paper. Hope was giving my heart a little of the happiness I was waiting for, even though I was a young woman heading for the house of an old woman at the end of her life. It didn't matter; this was a house where I would find a warm bed and hot food. Even more important, it was a place that would let me believe I was a girl with a proper family. In short, I would try to live outside the truth. When I was in the orphanage, I thought of the other residents as my siblings. I felt they were a family, compensating me for a great lack of one of my own. For all those years, there was a good-hearted supervisor among us who had no children and who devoted most of her time to us, making life beautiful in our eyes, until she died. One morning she was found dead from a heart attack, and after her death we went back to suffering as before.

In al-Rabiya, I stopped at the door of a villa built of white stone, surrounded by a wall, in front of which roses and ornamental trees were growing. I checked the piece of paper to make sure I had the number of the building right. (Elderly women are goodhearted —no doubt I will find with her what I had missed all my life.) Before ringing the doorbell, I told myself I knew nothing about it. I didn't have to wait long, for the door was opened and I was greeted by the woman Salam had told me about. She waved me inside with a smile that faded slightly after she had looked at my tatty clothes. She shut the door, with her hands below her large breasts, then said with a cheerfulness that had a little impatience about it, "Your duties are not difficult. I'll explain them to you, but first you must shower and put on these clothes."

She walked over to a chair in a sitting room with posh chairs in it and pictures on the walls. From the ceiling hung chandeliers in the shape of bunches of grapes. She picked up a small bag and gave it to me, then showed me to the restroom, saying, "It's there; I'll wait for you."

As I showered I thought about the woman's unfathomable expression, which somehow made her seem off-putting, but I ignored all that, showered quickly, and put on the new clothes. There was a change of underclothes, jeans that fit me, I don't know how, a red blouse so small that my chest seemed to spill out of it, and light shoes that were also too small.

"You look nicer now," said the woman as she led me toward a staircase. Then she continued. "From now on you will be responsible for an elderly woman who suffers from several illnesses, the least of which are high blood pressure and diabetes. There are set times for medicines that you must follow. As for your other duties, you have to help her with things like going to the toilet."

She stood at the end of the stairs and put her hands on her hips. "You know that it is hard for a woman of this age to go to the toilet."

I nodded to show I understood and then followed her up the stairs and along a carpeted corridor from which I could hear music that grew louder the closer we got. "You will have a list showing the food she is allowed."

The woman stopped near a door at the end of the corridor and quickly turned to me, as if she had remembered something. "Can you cook?"

"Yes, madam, they taught us that in the orphanage."

"Good. There is another thing—there is a man who brings things for the house every week. The woman's condition will not allow you to leave her."

She was about to go in, but then she added, "You will receive 400 dinars a month."

"Good, madam."

She gently opened the door, and the sound of music became louder. I saw a lady in her mid-sixties sitting in a wheelchair, looking through a wide window at a balcony with several roses on it along with some ornamental plants. The window looked out over a willow tree with swaying branches. She had a white woolen shawl with round holes over her shoulder. Her soft white hair was tied back, and her small hands rested on the arms of the chair, completely still. The woman took a few steps and stood beside the old lady, then looked at me and said quietly, "She hasn't left this room for years."

The bedroom was spacious and extremely elegant in every respect: the furniture, the color of the walls, and its peaceful atmosphere. At first I felt slightly afraid, but my fear quickly vanished, to be replaced by a sense of calm that I normally lacked. The woman pointed to a modern-style tape recorder that was playing a piece of music: "This music will carry on playing by itself. Don't stop it, except at the lady's bedtime. If it stops, her condition will deteriorate."

She looked at me with a smile. "The Blue Danube, that's the name of the piece."

The woman picked up the remote control and showed me how to turn the recorder on and off and then left. I didn't learn her name or who she was, even after she had told me some essential details she hadn't mentioned before and showed me a room opposite Madame Emily's room, which from that moment became my own room. "A nice room. We chose it for you so you could be close to the lady," she said. She gave me a piece of paper with the times for her medicine and food written on it, as well as the times when Madame Emily woke and went to sleep and gave me a phone that she said had internet access and had her number on it for use in case of an emergency. Emily is a nice name, I thought, as I climbed the stairs, stopping halfway to look at the hall. I was in an elegant house but it was so quiet it made me feel afraid from time to time. I thought to myself that it wouldn't be difficult to work with a woman who certainly wouldn't be demanding. I checked the piece of paper; there was still some time before her lunch and medicine, after which she would sleep until five. I knocked on the door, went in, and found Madame Emily still looking at the willow tree, like a doll. The only thing one could notice was the movement of her chest as she breathed. Wasn't she aware of my presence? I was about to go out, but I had another thought. I stood beside her and said, "My name's Leila."

I awaited her reply, but she continued to stare in the same direction. I crouched down so that my face was opposite hers. "Can you hear me, Emily?"

She looked at me in her strange silence. She had eyes whose beauty was unaffected by age, a round mouth with prominent cheekbones, and a raised nose. Her face had a profound calm to it, as if she was recollecting an event that made her happy. I went down to the kitchen to prepare the lady's lunch, after scrutinizing the details more than once and checking that all the ingredients were there so that I wouldn't be late in preparing the food in the future. I gave her a meal of vegetables that day, helped her drink a cup of fresh juice, and gave her her medicine. She said nothing; her eyes were fixed on the same point even when I lifted her frail body and put her on the bed. Her face kept the same smile, her gaze fixed on something unknown.

4
Ibrahim

(An Honorable Thief)

A month of isolation went by, and the conversations on Facebook about the masked robber died down. A lot of gossip had been fabricated about me, and so many images of me had been painted that I almost believed what people had been saying.

"A man who raids banks with exceptional bravery and skill, like mercury, he is difficult to catch. A man with no castles, no posh cars, and no bank accounts, with a heart that is pained by the poor. It's said that at night he runs from one quarter to the next like a wolf, tosses people's things into an envelope and leaves."

As I lay on the sofa looking at the ceiling, a repeated warm sensation came over me for the first time. "Now you've become free!"

The voice came from the ceiling. I was on the point of springing up, but it ordered me to stay where I was.

"No one can do what you do. They must know your value and extraordinary powers and know that your silence, which lasted for years, was only the calm before the storm. They saw you, because you are bigger than the buildings that have started to mushroom recently."

I got up and made a cup of coffee. As he continued to follow me, I said, "You are mistaken. You invented this word to corrupt the meaning of power. You must know that my obedience to you is temporary."

"It is not temporary. What you have achieved is just a stage that will lead to other stages in which you will need assistants."

I was thinking of going out, but he came back at midday and forced me back.

"You've certainly found out a lot about your devotees on Facebook. Did you see that rich man who boasts of his photos every day? Did you look at his photos as a traveler in Europe and regret that you only crossed the boundaries of East Amman after about forty years? Did you see how splendid his house is? Did you ask yourself why you were searching for it on Google and found a map of the location? Go back to your computer now and write down what you find; it may help you to succeed in your task."

I went to the rich man's page, pencil and paper at the ready. The voice was speaking to me as if he was standing behind my shoulder as I looked at the screen:

"This man is uneducated and uncultured. His style of writing doesn't suggest that he has a B.A. in management as is listed in his information column. His style of expression is naïve and stupid. It seems he paid for this qualification. Look carefully at this video, in which he defends a minister against whom a campaign has recently been launched. Look how his eyes go left and right, and how he moistens his lips all the time, scratches his nose and the back of his head. It's obvious he's lying, that he's a chancer, not a regular guy, and that he has many characteristics of a daredevil. He owns a company that doesn't have a good reputation, which shows that he is probably someone who has set up a company to hide its dubious activities. It's clear that he frequents nightclubs. Look at this comment with a link to a video, how he showers money on a dancing girl who climbed onto his table. It's obvious from this that he keeps a large sum of money at home. Look at this post, in which he makes up to his wife in order to cover up his behavior. Come, let's go back to his latest post: several photos with his location in Europe on holiday with the family. So he's not in Jordan now. This time, you will raid that house, and you will certainly find either money or jewelry."

I spent many hours that day looking through the man's Facebook page. I read everything, studied all his pictures and illustrated posts. I stopped to take in everything I found, even his friends' comments on what he was posting. I collected a certain amount of information about the house and its dimensions. From his wife's page, which I thought was more boastful, I found out some of his and his family's habits. I also collected some additional information, leaving the rest to supposition. The following day, I surveyed the house. How had I dared do everything I had done and what I was about to do?

The taxi driver hummed a sad song as he drove me along, and I reviewed the dimensions of the house. It was two stories high, built of stone, with a sloping, tiled roof. In front was a garden surrounded by a low wall with a metal gate in the middle of it. There were no security cameras on the front side, and there was no security. The windows and doors of the houses around it and opposite it were closed, as if no one was there.

I looked at his pictures and started to envision the moment when I would go in. The voice was indicating every step I should take; everything I did was at his suggestion, everything I did came from the obscure place in which he lived. I knew how women become pregnant, but I didn't know how this creature had come into existence in me. Who had slept with my soul to burden me with a strange creature who drove me to do what I did not want?

As soon as I had entered my apartment, I nervously took off the mask from my soul. "I am Ibrahim the bookseller and not Zhivago." As if he had beaten me to the apartment and waited for me behind the door, the voice said, "So that you will not be exposed, you are Zhivago now, and will be someone else in the coming stages. You have to be a thousand people to live in this life. When you put your head on the pillow, be yourself, because you are in a space where you won't need anyone but you."

I took off my suit and tie and lay down on the sofa, then sat at the table and rested my head in my hands. "Please, that's enough, I am tired."

I felt him press on my neck and whisper, "We have an agreement that you must keep, otherwise I will do something with the list that I still keep."

He was silent for a short time, and then it seemed like he was pacing around the room. "You must review all the information you collected about the rich man's house. Think carefully about your route to it and do what we agreed tonight."

It was almost twelve noon. I ate a sandwich and slept until six in the evening. I woke up with a bad headache, made a cup of coffee, and sat looking at the lights of Amman, thinking of what I was about to do.

Suddenly, I heard the voice say, "Do you know in which character you will disguise yourself this time?"

I imagined him squatting in front of me, with his hands fingering my chin. "Mustafa Sa'eed, the hero of the novel *Season of Migration to the North*."

At two o'clock in the morning, I alighted from the taxi. The driver looked curiously at my appearance. Hadn't he seen a Sudanese before? When I spent two years in London, I learned that the only thing the English know about the Arabs is that they have dark skin, ride camels, and lust after women. It was a sort of game to try to reverse that picture. How could I change a picture the executioner had painted of his victim? I completed the remaining distance to the rich man's house on foot, wearing an English-style suit and shoes, and a classic watch on a silver chain. I recalled the first meeting with Ann Hammond, and how I spent hours teaching her the correct pronunciation of my name, Mustafa Sa'eed.

I became agitated, but the voice put an end to my confusion with commanding words. The street appeared to be deserted, and no one could be seen in the houses around it, so I jumped over the wall and followed a path between the shrubs in the garden, and came to a large wooden door, which was difficult to open. What if someone sees you who knew you from the evenings of cultural clashes in the cafes of London, Mustafa? Would they believe that you were now about to raid this house? I walked to the rear portion of the house, where there was another door made of aluminum. I stood there for a moment surveying the place; no sounds or lights came from the house ("So no servants inside!"). I hid behind a table near the swimming pool for a few minutes, checking my assumptions about this venture. Then I approached the door. My hand was shaking as I grasped the handle, wearing gloves, and putting the mask on my face, but the voice reprimanded me:

"Fear will paint pictures for you of things that do not exist. Go in as if this is your house and you suspect there may be a thief in it, Mustafa."

The door was locked. I tried using a screwdriver and, as I'd learned through the internet, shifted the bolt of the door from its position. A strange sort of pride came over me at that moment as the voice praised what I had done. The gate led into a sitting room with wide glass windows looking out over a swimming pool, exactly as I had seen in the pictures on Facebook. There was nothing in the house but the whisper of emptiness. I found the staircase leading upward, and as expected, it led me to the upper story. There were a number of rooms, which I entered one after the other until I reached the man's bedroom. My breathing grew louder from fear, which the voice continued to chase from me. I took a quick glance at the room and then opened the cupboard. Searching it cautiously, I found a box containing a fair quantity of expensive jewelry and about 2,000 dinars. I looked at the jewelry; this necklace would suit Ann Hammond's white neck, hanging down to the parting of her small breasts. She would be delighted and whisper in my ear, "I love you, my dark horse."

I searched the rest of the room and went out, looking for the study I had seen in the man's photo, and I found it. It was a spacious room with elegant furniture and a library containing a small number of books that looked new. There were no papers on the table to suggest that the owner of the study was engaged in anything in particular. All I found was a pack of expensive cigarettes and some pens with an international trademark. As I flipped through some of the books, the words of a poem by Ford Madox Ford from the World War echoed inside me:

> These are the women of Flanders.
> They await the lost.
> They await the lost that shall never leave the dock;
> They await the lost that shall never again come by the train
> To the embraces of all these women with dead faces;
> They await the lost who lie dead in trench and barrier and foss,
> In the dark of the night.

I opened the desk drawer and found an envelope with 20,000 dinars in it, an expensive watch, and a gold chain. I put all my spoils in a bag and left as carefully and cautiously as before. The street was empty. If I had walked along it, I would certainly have encountered a police patrol, which would be my end. How would I say to them "I am Mustafa Sa'eed, who has just returned from London and done this?" I hid behind a tree, thinking of what to do. No place in that neighborhood would protect me. The only thing I could do was go back to the house I had raided. It was almost three in the morning. I told myself that I had two hours to get out, for it would be almost sunrise. What comedy was this, which was pushing me to return to a house I had hurried to escape from for fear that I would be exposed? I went in through the back door in some confusion. Where would I be safe in this house if someone came in and surprised me? I was still standing in the middle of the hallway with the mask over my face. I would have taken it off, but the voice forbade it. I sat on a rocking chair opposite a rear garden with the swimming pool in the middle, clutching the bag, leaning backward, and looking at what was visible through the darkness.

I was surrounded by a profound silence coming from every part of that spacious but deserted house. I looked at the furniture I could see, and everything that my eyes could make out in the darkness. Our house in the village was just two rooms with another small room we used as a kitchen. Small houses are at least warm and comfortable.

Only a little of my tension remained, and I felt at ease. There was no one in the house and no one would come. I felt a little hungry, so I went into the spacious kitchen. There was a large refrigerator, where I found lots of fruit and other food. But how could I eat from a house I had raided? I shut the refrigerator door. It seemed I wasn't a proper thief, or perhaps it was that thieves were really honorable people driven on by a particular event to act dishonorably. Or maybe they were they like me, with someone inside them driving them to become a bank robber and then a house thief, not knowing where they might be taken.

I went back to the chair and found myself gripped by a cold that I had not properly prepared for. There was a woman's woolen shawl lying on a sofa near me, which I put on my shoulders for a little warmth. The smell of a woman's perfume clinging to the shawl aroused warm feelings in me and I shut my eyes. In my mind, I saw a woman I sometimes thought was Ann Hammond and sometimes Madame N. I opened the door and she walked toward me slowly. I stopped suddenly and she stretched out her arms and hugged me to her chest. Her hair covered the right side of my face, and there was a ring in her ear that rubbed on my neck as she whispered, "Why are you sitting in the dark?" As her perfume encircled me, she grasped my hand and led me toward a piano in a large hall and started to play. I saw myself running over a vast cloud, weightless. The earth beneath me appeared sometimes green and sometimes gray; the cloud was fresh, the air was fresh, and my spirit was soaring with a lightness I'd never experienced before until my foot fell into a space with no cloud in it, and I fell and woke up.

It was six o'clock. How had I slept so easily? I tried to get a grip on myself and drive away the tension that had overtaken me. There was no movement in the street, though the light had begun to emerge from the darkness. I took off the mask, took a path between the shrubs, and jumped over the wall away from the house, crossing the street to reach another street. As I moved away from the quarter, movement crept into the place; there were cars, a few pedestrians, and some shops that were opening their doors. I would have gone back to the apartment, but the voice told me to go to the deserted house.

They were asleep when I crept in and put the money I had taken into the hole. "What madness is this, Ibrahim?" I said to myself as I sat on the large lump of mud, which I carefully put back in its place. I would have liked to stay with them just for one day, but the voice forbade me from anything like that, having taken all the possibilities into account. I walked on tiptoe and left some money beside Salam's bed. I intended to leave, but the voice admonished me. "Don't go out, Ibrahim—it is Zhivago who has permission to leave!"

5
Ibrahim

(Who Is Madame N?)

A week after my raid on the house, fresh news began to be published again about the masked robber. Video recordings and photos of me circulated on Facebook. It seemed the house was equipped with cameras that recorded my movements, and the man had published them. I was stunned. Fear crept into me from every direction, even though my face never appeared in the recordings. Perhaps I had left behind a clue or someone suspected me. But what I saw in the recording was Mustafa Sa'eed wearing a mask. I lay down on the sofa then got up and walked about in a confused state. "I must not go out to avoid any possibility of being arrested."

"Yes, you mustn't go out, but not for long, for perhaps your isolation will become a cause for suspicion."

I made a cup of tea, threw a slice of lemon in it, and went back to Facebook. My news dominated it. People were talking about a noble thief who stole for the poor; they had even drawn a strange caricature of me. I was disturbed by a post on one page:

"Masked man, they see you as a wolf running through the city night, dressing up and stealing, then entering the houses of the poor and throwing them their share of what they need. They see you as a scalpel lancing the boils that are paining their souls, a sickle harvesting the thorns beneath their bare feet. That is how they see you, so are you an illusion or are you real?"

I clicked on a link that took me to a page displaying the cover of the book *The Unbearable Lightness of Being,* and included a series of personal pictures with some identified with the letter "N." As I looked through the pictures, I eventually found myself looking at Madame N. Narda—her name was Narda. What a coincidence, bookseller! The picture had been taken at someone's birthday party; people were laughing loudly, and she was the only one smiling, although behind that smile was a sadness that I had noticed that day when she stood gazing out at the sea. Narda! My God, how can this be happening? A woman I searched for like a convict searching for the single proof that he is worthy of life, and now I find her here in an electronic box!

I went to the messages box, extremely happy, and wrote: "I asked as I looked for you even in the stones of the houses I passed."

She read the message and after two minutes she replied: "Who are you?"

"I am the person who found your notebook and left his lamp, and since that time has been looking for you."

"My notebook? Do you mean my diary?"

"Yes."

"It's a miracle it's been found."

"It found me!"

"Please. Please. You don't know what these pages mean to me."

"And you don't know what they mean to me as well."

I received a Friend request from her, which I accepted at once, and it was only a few moments before she contacted me via Messenger. I was on the verge of replying, and though I was more in need than anyone on this planet to hear her voice, some obscure impulse made me hesitate. She contacted me again more than once, but I didn't reply.

"You don't know what you did for me with that message!"

I read the message and said nothing, for a feverish ranting had come over me as I looked at her photo. Everything was valueless, and she was somewhere else. Should I explain to her who I was?

I gathered together all the possibilities of the universe as creatures from outer space see a man. I could not bear to lose her, so I had to be careful in what I said. Could a man who has loved so madly be careful?

It was shortly after eleven in the evening. I lay in bed thinking about how I would approach a woman who had brought back life to me again. I thought of what I had done: I had raided two banks and a house. I had turned into a robber between night and morning. It was almost as if I had done that on account of an irrational certainty that Narda was a dream I had seen for a moment and then disappeared. My belly swelled and I heard the voice, more angry this time. "It seems that a new change will make you tear up our agreement."

"I love her, this woman who stopped me from killing us, you and I." I said this sitting on the edge of the bed looking at my belly, which had swollen even more.

"I don't object to your loving, but you love with a weakness, of which you have a lot."

I jumped off the bed and headed for the restroom. He followed me. "You don't need to shower to get rid of me. Finish what I asked of you, and I will leave you alone to do as you please."

A Nightmare

I shave my beard well, powder my face, put on a wig and woman's clothes. I check my appearance in the mirror to ensure it corresponds to the picture I sent to Ranad Mahmoud, as a lesbian. I slip out, board a taxi, and reach Ranad Mahmoud's house. I look at the clock, check that I have arrived at the right time, and do my best to play the part of a woman. I knock on the door. She receives me warmly, puts her arm around my waist, and I go with her into the hall. She gives me a glass of beer, lights a cigarette, and sits by me. I ask her to fill the bathtub with warm water. She takes off her clothes, and gets into the tub now filled with water. I push her to the bottom, she tries to escape and dies.

PART 6

They'll catch me, hang me high
in blessed earth I shall lie,
and poisonous grass will start
to grow on my beautiful heart.
—Attila Jozséf

1
Narda

(Another Love)

Night fell, the hubbub grew quieter, and silence stole into the house. I sat opposite the window, looking out at the houses as the lights were lit inside them, announcing a new part of what remained of the day. I was overcome by a feeling of uselessness. Everything had changed in me. I no longer saw the night in a calm way, bringing contentment. Rather, I had started to see it as arousing gloom, as a door to pains that might emerge even from holes in the walls. I am a woman with nothing. How hard it is for someone to become an empty thing after being full of hope? A simple mistake in a game of chess can defeat you, and a simple move can return to you the hope of victory.

The masked robber occupied my thoughts throughout the last few months. This man is not just a passing thief; he is like those people who emerge from pain and return to their tree to uproot it. A dreamer who doesn't know that the roots of that tree are sunk firmly in the ground since Cain killed his brother, Abel. I saw him walking across the white of the page as I wrote about him and tried to find a path that would lead me to his secret vaults. He walks with the mask over his face as if he doesn't want the world to see his ancient sorrow and his embarrassment at what he is doing. I wrote several essays, so many that some people regarded me as a specialist on his actions. But the security services issued an order that I had to refrain from that. An officer contacted me and told me in a peremptory tone, "Madam, you are making a story out

of a thief and encouraging people to adopt his ways of burglary."
That day, the chief editor received a handwritten order to stop me
writing about it, and on the same day they issued another order
banning social media users from praising him. Was I relieved,
or did I ignore my inability to empty my inner cupboard of its
contents by siding with the masked man? Or had some obscure
interaction between my situation and his led me to that?

I turned on the TV and watched for a few minutes, then turned
it off. It seems I had lost my appetite for anything and nothing had
any flavor anymore. I picked up my laptop, lay on the bed, and
looked at my Facebook messages. There was one from Diogenes:

"I don't know how feelings are born and become like grass
growing over a neglected rock. Or how they hasten to one person in
particular with that sort of delicious pillaging. As if the directions
have disappeared, and all that remains is one direction to which
the compass looks. From that day, when I became aware of myself,
I have been certain, as I searched for you with a strange burning
desire, that I had fallen in love, a love for which I am not suited,
and which does not suit a miserable wretch like me. I didn't like
novels that are full of passion until one day I found that they were
a means of removing a hardness that was filling my heart. I chose
novels that many readers had liked and published excerpts from
on their Facebook pages: *Jane Eyre*; *Anna Karenina*; *The Story of a
Magian Love*; *Under the Linden Trees*. When I read them, I wrote
on my Facebook page, "The only situation in which you won't blame
yourself for weakness is love." From that day, I started to avoid my
colleagues' advice about novels or books of that sort, although I
realized that the fault was mine. It was a state of submission to a
defect in feelings I thought there was no escape from.

"How can one understand the love of a man for a woman
when he does not even know her name? Feelings that I said at first
were caused by illness, but I could not shake them off. It is like a

sick man waiting for the moment of death who suddenly realizes there has been a mistake and so clings to life again."

Who is this person who found my papers and did not respond when I begged him to return them? He writes to me constantly; he tells me about a unique form of love that I think it unlikely the earth still sees after everything that has happened to it. As the days went by, his letters underwent a surprising change: I would open up my messages to read what he had written to me, about love, philosophy, pain, loss, and hope. I saw him carrying a lamp, walking barefoot in broad daylight in Amman on a rainy day, walking side by side with a man wearing a coat with his hands in his pockets. From the direction of the door, I heard the noise of the duduk, sad and hurtful, and rushed toward it to turn it off without noticing that it was blocked off. I was surrounded by the wailing of the duduk, chasing me from the music that in recent days had begun to drown me in sorrow and melt me like a lump of mud dissolving under a water tap. I turned off the computer and sunk my head to sleep, but it was a sort of digging in air.

The doctor told me to treat my depression by writing. I recalled that as I lay on the sofa, looking at a scene of the masked robber to be added to the scenes of the series I had written. The producer, to whom I had told part of the story, said, "It will be a great series if you write it faithfully." But he didn't know that nothing makes us more faithful in writing than pain. A flash of lightning lit up the sky, followed by thunder. Then the rain poured down. I stood looking at the trees, how they surrendered to the water, and behind the wall I spotted the man walking with his hands in his coat pockets. I heard the wailing of the duduk surrounding my spirit. I escaped to my room, begging for sleep to transport me to worlds with no sorrow, but to no avail. I told myself that running away from sorrow was an opportunity for him to reinforce his attack as he slid behind me. So I had to run toward him, even if I collided with him. I opened the man's notebook to see if it could free me from a sorrow he had injected in my veins:

Electricity hadn't reached the village yet when Jadallah came back one evening in the summer of 1971. He hadn't told anyone that he was coming to the village. He expected to be arrested for engaging in political activities during his years in Moscow. All that happened was that an officer interrogated him for half an hour at Marka Airport. After that, he went on his way to Madaba. The taxi took him to his house, where nothing had changed except for two rooms that had been built while he was away. He looked around—the horse was in its place, the donkey in its stall, the sheep in their pen, and the chickens in their coops. The dog barked several times and then approached the taxi. Jadallah got down on his knees and patted its head lovingly. From behind the wall came the voice of al-Shamousi, followed by a commotion from inside.

"Who is it?"

"Jadallah."

It was almost eleven in the evening. The sharp silence of the village was broken only by the noise of some night crickets. The only lights to stand in the face of the darkness were some feeble glows from a few lanterns in some tents and a small number of stone houses built while Jadallah was away. Al-Shamousi came down a few shallow steps from the veranda, and Jadallah hurried toward him to kiss his hand and embrace him as they both dissolved in tears. The family woke up: his mother, his brothers Badi and Ali, and his sisters Jawazi and Sharifa. There were loud shrieks of joy, and Badi fired some shots in the air from sheer happiness and repeated, "Welcome to the *hakim*!"

It was only a few minutes before the residents of the village gathered in al-Shamousi's guest room. Al-Shamousi wandered among them, a great smile of pride on his face, while Jadallah sat on two woolen blankets in the middle of the guest room. All eyes were on him, scrutinizing his appearance as if there was something new about him.

"Haven't you married a European, *hakim?*" asked an elderly man, as he stretched out one thin, smooth leg, folding the other beneath him as his hands rested on a stick with several bends in it. Tamarka's voice rang in his ears when she told him one night, as he told her about the customs of the village, that she would go into the men's guest room and greet them all one by one. He remembered her laugh with a short burst of happiness, followed by a shooting star of grief that descended in the dark sky of his soul.

"I married, but she died."

"A man can marry again, four times."

From the corner of the guest room a man stuck his head out from behind the head of a stout man and said in a weak voice, "But we heard that she was a Christian."

"No. Neither Christian nor Muslim. It's said they have no religion," came another voice, almost hoarse.

Al-Shamousi sat himself down steadily on the covering and said in a commanding voice, "Praise God! We are all human beings!"

Then he looked at the man with the hoarse voice and smiling eyes. "When the *hakim* gets to work he will treat the hoarseness in your voice, so your children don't get your voice mixed up with that of your sick sheep!"

Everyone laughed, and then they left, one by one, until the place was empty except for Jadallah and his father. His father came close to him to see the expression on his face more clearly. "I know you are grieving for your wife. I was hoping she would come with you, but it is God's command, my son."

Al-Shamousi didn't know that the wound caused by the death of Tamarka was only one of the wounds that had overtaken his son's soul and that he was no longer the man he had known before.

That night, Jadallah was swept by a whole host of sorrows, the biggest of which was how to tell his father the truth. He tossed and turned in his bed, then got up and went out of the house. He saw Ali sitting by his father on the threshold of the courtyard, speaking angrily. "If Iskandar does that, I will kill him."

As soon as they saw him approaching, they fell silent. Al-Shamousi thought that something like this had to remain secret from Jadallah. Pale lights marked out Madaba in the darkness all around them. The three of them sat on the threshold of the courtyard and looked at it in silence. Jadallah clasped his hands together and looked at the sky, which was empty of stars, and said, "Did you mortgage land to Iskandar?"

Al-Shamousi lit a cigarette and seemed uncertain of what to say. Jadallah looked at him and said, "Father, you spent years as a shepherd for Abu Jaris, who lived in a house in winter while we lived in caves. In the summer you spent your days running behind the herds while he was resting at home, throwing you only a little. I was very happy when we acquired a house and animals and trees—and a life that Abu Jaris had nothing to do with, so how can you gamble away the only thing we possess?"

Al-Shamousi said nothing. His eyes stayed fixed on the darkness that had poured from the hill between Madba and the village. Ali, unable to hide his anger, started to breathe faster. "We did it for you, *hakim!*"

Jadallah looked at Ali in surprise, following him with his eyes when he got up and walked into the darkness. When he came back, his anger stopped him from settling in his place. "Didn't you ever think about where we got the money we sent you all through your years of study? When you told us that your scholarship allowance was not enough?"

Al-Shamousi told him off and ordered him to stay silent. "None of that is important, my son," he said, trying to make light of what had happened. "The important thing is that you've come back as a *hakim*. I'll sort out Iskandar, don't worry!"

Jadallah felt extremely upset. Not just because he hadn't come home as a doctor but because he had realized that he hadn't been thinking of his family during the last few years. He thought that what his family earned from farming and their livestock, as well as the monthly allowance provided by the state after his brother Khazar was martyred, had been sufficient for them to deduct a sum and send it to him each month. He felt pained by his miscalculation and feared that his extreme selfishness would make them lose their home. He felt the air drain from his lungs and that he was close to fainting. As he burst into tears, his father embraced him and calmed him down until eventually he became silent. Al-Shamousi took Jadallah's face and said, "Listen to me—even if I lost the house, that would not be any loss compared with the fact you have become a doctor at a time when people need you. A lot of people are dying, and we do not know why. The only medicine people know is some herbs and other prescriptions that only rarely cure the sick."

Jadallah didn't sleep that night. He knew that if his father found out that he hadn't been studying medicine, he would lose him.

2
Ibrahim

(A Final Struggle)

I woke at sunset dripping with sweat. My head felt heavy, and I was extremely thirsty. I drank two glasses of water, made a cup of coffee, and sat on the sofa, surrounded by silence. It was hot, as though summer had arrived to pester the winter, the intense cold of which had only passed with difficulty. I turned on the air conditioning and lay on the sofa. I imagined the walls of the room creeping toward me, with a kind of loneliness that creates a feeling that nothing in this world has any value and drains one of any desire to do anything. I checked my phone messages and found a message from the same unknown number that I had saved with the name "neighbor." ("I wish I hadn't seen what happened in the kitchen.") I looked at the message more than once and then read another message from the same number that gave me extra pain and threw me into great confusion. What was the purpose of those messages, and what was I supposed to do, as I was incapable of ignoring them?

I got up to go to the restroom and peed while watching my face in the mirror. Untidy hair with puffy lids from too much sleep, an unshaven chin, and a dumb expression. How had I changed into this surreal appearance? I stole from several rich people's houses, and would hide away for a month and devote myself to a careful plan for a theft, relying on the internet, which gave me details of the houses and particulars of the residents. It was all I had to do to become the personality I was disguising myself as. Whenever I raided a house, there was more talk about the masked man; even robberies I had nothing to do with were attributed to me.

My mobile played a tune indicating a new message. No one wrote to me except for Narda, and in the last month her insistence on demanding her notebook had slowed. Yet we conversed daily. At first she urged me to return her notebook, but as time passed she began to speak to me like a close friend, in exchange for my runaway love for her, developments that gave me much pleasure. She would tell me the details of her day, from leaving the house where she lived alone to going to the newspaper where she worked and her return just before sunset to spend what remained of the day reading and writing. She read novels like an addict and couldn't spend a day without reading at least fifty pages. She said the best thing that novels did was to kill her loneliness and help forge relationships with people who could not harm her. Narda didn't trust people, especially men, many of whom had tried to seduce her. She knew that all the courtesies and kind words they spoke would end up with her in a bed not of her choice. So her colleagues at work had nicknamed her "Mistress of the Long Silence." I checked my phone and found a message from her:

"When you told me my notebook was in your possession, I went mad, and my purpose in writing to you for months was to get it. For some obscure reason that I no longer wish to discover, you refused. I will tell you something: Your daily exchanges with me broke a loneliness that was enveloping me. Reading had lately become incapable of it, since I started to wake up with a consciousness I could not classify, though it classified itself by itself. It was the familiarity that happens to us with someone else. Diogenes, I shall continue to call you by this name even though I have discovered your real name. You forgot yourself when you wrote to me and ditched the character of Diogenes, so I found a man who loved me as I had never dreamed, a man who made me grumble if his messages were late. At first, I didn't care about anything you talked about, but lately I discovered that I would be missing something if you stopped writing to me for a single day. Was it getting used to your daily presence? A presence that gave me comfort during the past months with an extreme lightness, or was I in love with you in the surreal way that has come over our relationship? Believe me, I don't know!"

I read the message more than once and then wrote to her.

"You have an answer and know how much I await it."

She didn't read the message. I thought she must have turned off her computer so she could read before going to sleep, as she told me she always did. I turned on my computer and selected a piece of music to help me to relax. I lay on the sofa watching TV, which was showing silent scenes of youths protesting rising price rises in the country. Meanwhile, I heard the voice say, "You've waited a reasonable time to avoid any suspicion; we need to prepare for the next goal."

I sat on the edge of the sofa, clasping my head between my hands.

"I know that you are preoccupied with Narda, and I recognize your need for a love that will drive out from inside you the cold and darkness you have been suffering since you left the village."

I got up, feeling that he was following me and breathing close to my ear, so I suddenly turned around. "Haven't we done enough?"

His voice was tinged with anger. "No, it's not enough. We need a theft or two for you to have an opportunity to save the residents of the deserted house. Then I will let you go from me."

"But you turned me into a thief."

"There is a thief hidden in everyone's mind."

"But you brought it out into the open," I said, as I walked toward the restroom to splash some water on my face. "I wasn't the one who did all that—it wasn't me!"

"I only came on account of the wounds and scars and weakness that had affected your spirit. This world needs a wild beast that comes out at night to hunt its prey, then during the day it shows people what a humble lamb there is inside it."

The voice continued to hover around me, talking in a hypnotic way. I searched Facebook for a page with an fake name that I'd seen a few days ago. I started to collect information about the house where I had seen her, through which I discovered her address and started to prepare for a new robbery. As I read news about the communications revolution, I considered the idea that the world has become a single village. When I immersed myself in the online world and began to grasp it, I realized how much we had become exposed, how secrets had disappeared, and how we could no longer hide anything. Yes, the world had become one village with no secrets. Everything in it would change into something electronic, superficial, easy to control, slavery in a new form, neat but terrifying.

I received a message from Dr. Yusuf, which I was nervous about reading. Should I ask him if I had written him a message or not?

"When longing turns into the hardness of hatred, it is certain that destruction has taken over, and it is no longer possible to stop it. Certainly, when I contemplate it, I am seized by a great sorrow, a struggle that destroys me. I stopped watching TV or reading the newspapers so as not to see his face and stop experiencing the nightmares that have never ceased disturbing my sleep. Yesterday, I saw him in a dream coming near me and embracing me. I cried a lot and embraced him hard. I woke to find only my wife beside me. That night, I would have liked to speak to my mother about my suffering."

"Can you send me the last thing I wrote to you?"

I was certain I had done that but was shocked when I read the message: "Dear Dr. Yusuf, it seems we have to kill our fathers..."

He wrote to me again.

"Yesterday I saw myself in a dream killing my father. I woke up in a sweat panting, and when I thought about what I had seen I found that I had a hidden desire for it, not just because of the great suffering he had inflicted on me but also because of what he did to my mother. Since the time I met him in his house I have harbored a great hatred for all forms of fatherhood, but the question that never ceases to plague me is, will we find peace and put an end to our illnesses if we kill our fathers? It seems we are burdened with fatherhood. Perhaps my saying this will seem sick, but this is what I have come to believe at this moment. Yesterday my wife was following the news broadcast and I saw him talking about the homeland in words that made it difficult to discover the falsehoods that were hiding behind them. How can a man believe in a homeland that he has not granted to his son?"

I lay on my bed wondering how many people have such difficulty sleeping as I do? Hands intertwined on my chest, I tried to embrace myself, thinking, "Loneliness is a thorn in the pupil of the eye; the tighter I close my eyes, the more it hurts. Loneliness is a breathing space before the bitterness of bereavement. How near you are, Narda, and how far you are! This silence pains me in your absence. Life is a feather hanging on the minute hand of a wall clock whose color pales as time moves on. I turned on the light and reached for the notebook. Before opening it, I whispered, "So your name is Narda." I saw her face look out at me sadly as she told me the story:

It wasn't easy to persuade him to move into my house. He propped himself up against the wall with a lighted cigarette in his hand, the ash suspended at the tip on the verge of falling. He was thinking absentmindedly of something when I took the cigarette from between his fingers and threw it in the ashtray. "Before I knew you I was comfortable with my loneliness," I said to him, "but now it is a sort of delusion to try to do that. I want us to live together, and it's OK if I stay with you here."

As we left his room, we took only his books and papers and clothes. He stood at the door and turned around sadly. "Don't blame me; places are dear to me. If these walls could speak, they would tell you why I am casting a farewell glance at them."

Our move to my house was a new step that I hadn't expected to be taking, a step that brought a sun inside me and gave me a warmth I had needed since childhood. We married. One night he told me that he wanted me to be his wife. He got down on his knees, took a ring from his pocket, and put it on my finger. I cried because I hadn't expected to marry one day. The following day we went to the court and registered our marriage. From that day, I embarked on a new life. My love for this man grew stronger with each day that passed, for he possessed me with a strange, captivating love. I would wake up in the morning and make coffee, and we would drink it on the balcony and talk about books and music, and about his childhood and youth. It was as if by belonging to his past, he was resisting a new time that was threatening him. After a time, he started talking about politics. He viewed what was happening in a different way from most people and was afraid of what was coming. He once saw an elderly lady carrying some bags of vegetables and other food. He put down the cup and started to look at her, repeating in a soft voice: "Ah, mom…" He said she was like his mother in pain. He relaxed, propping his head up with his hand and looking at the sky, which looked clear that morning. Then, as though speaking to someone else, he said, "The world moves on in a mad, frightening way. But a moment will come when everything in it will collapse, and things afterward will seem like a rose growing among the rubble, scattering seeds that will turn the ground around it into a field."

He turned to me and touched my face with his warm hand and said, as if apologizing for the obscure nature of what he had said, "Do you see this tiredness that shows on everyone's face?"

I nodded. "I feel it paining me also."

"This rain will lead to a new time."

As usual, he lay down on the sofa that day, put on his glasses, and got ready to read before I left for university. I was the happiest of people to enjoy the love of a man like this. In the morning we would sit for an hour, and when I came back from the university we would spend another hour. In the evening we would either go out or spend our time talking or watching a film. Three months went by in a way that might have continued to crown me with any remaining happiness in the universe. But suddenly things changed. I started to wake to the sound of his voice prattling in his sleep and shouting because of nightmares. These incidents showed me how much this man was hiding from me and I became more sorry for him. I wanted to talk to him about his nightmares, but I waited for a suitable opportunity. Things didn't stop there but became even worse; his temper began to change. Sometimes he was silent and calm, but at other times he seemed tense. What made me especially uneasy was his habit of hitting me as we lay together in bed. At first, it was an acceptable sort of beating in passionate moments, but as time went on it became savage, turning him into a raging bull when he made love to me. Even stranger was that as soon as he became drunk, he would dissolve in tears, as would I when he turned into a defeated child in my hands. I asked him why this happened to him, but he didn't reply, just said, with exaggerated sadness, "My memory is like a needle moving in my guts. If I am hungry, it hurts, and if I am full, it hurts more."

After some months, something happened that could not have been predicted. We had finished eating supper after I had come back from work and were watching a news broadcast. The presenter of the program was hosting two people who were arguing loudly about the fate of the world after every vision of how to manage it had failed. I said that there was no way except for absolute freedom for us to avoid the destruction that the world was anticipating. He looked at me, the anger plain in his eyes, then went back to watching the program.

"Yes, absolute freedom," I repeated.

He took off his glasses as his face exploded in anger. "These are poisonous suggestions. What freedom, when the world is going to ruin? Freedom is a delusion and a lie which they made appear to you."

I argued with him, and he slapped me, so I left him and took refuge in my room. He knocked on the door repeatedly until he grew bored. I kept silent the whole night, thinking about what had happened. In the morning, he apologized profusely, weeping bitterly and expressing surprise at how he had behaved. I forgave him, for I knew how free he was, but I didn't understand why he said what he had said. And why had he hit me? Despite that, he didn't stop hitting me; his behavior had changed, and I started to hear him dreaming during his sleep and talking about days gone by and about the days to come. I didn't tell him that his voice woke me up and that I stayed awake listening to him talk in his sleep. It didn't make me love him less, but I was becoming afraid for this man and for myself—until what happened happened.

———

On the balcony overlooking the mountains of Amman, he sat in his chair, letting his gaze wander over the distance. The morning had welcomed several flocks of pigeons as well as paper airplanes hovering in the air. He made no movement except to move his shaking hand toward the ashtray and let the ash from his cigarette drop into it. His eyes were fixed on space, having lost his desire to watch things in the morning hours like this. Anyone who saw him would think that he took pleasure in what he was looking at, when he was really searching his memory like someone flipping through a notebook whose pages had wilted and turned yellow. He put out his cigarettes, stroked his white beard, and then, lazily, hands trembling, picked up his cup of coffee and took a sip. Returning it to the saucer, it produced a clicking sound, like every one of his attempts to put things back in their place. He lit a new cigarette and resumed his daydreams. As I crossed the corridor that leads to the sitting room, I tried to hide the clatter of my shoes so as not to break the silence. "Good morning," I said, trying unsuccessfully to disguise my tone of pity.

He didn't look at me, the thread of smoke from his cigarette poised in midair, but he returned the greeting in a quiet voice with the hint of a rattle and a hidden nervousness: "Good morning to you!"

He heard my footsteps move away toward the door and turned around, saying, in a slightly louder voice, in which I detected a tension he was unable to hide: "Where are you going?"

I was wearing black jeans and a white shirt with black patterns that day, and I had tied my hair with a piece of white cloth that hung down behind my back. "To the doctor," I replied, looking at him with tired eyes beneath which a sudden black patch had appeared. He put out his cigarette with a movement that betrayed a nervousness that could no longer be endured. "Haven't you noticed that you're going out and not telling me?" he asked, turning toward me.

I was about to reply, but he raised his finger to his lips. His expression suggested the first signs of an explosion. "Ssh—I'm not just something neglected in this house. I'm not something ordinary in this wretched world. You know who I am."

I put down my bag at the edge of the sofa and slowly walked toward him. With a forced smile on my face, I touched his face and stroked the hair on his chin with the palm of my hand: "My love, please don't leave room for a new quarrel between us. I know who you are, and I know your importance. Yesterday we ignored what happened and agreed that we would open a new page."

A smile formed on his face, then his eyes wilted and sorrow shone in them. Then came louder breaths as his chest rose and fell. I moved closer to him and placed my palm on his face. "My love, I am tired. I have been having some strange health issues, and I must go see a doctor I visited last week. I didn't want to upset you."

He pushed my hand away, his sympathetic expression now gone. "No, you no longer see me as you used to."

I stepped away from him, but he took hold of my hair and lifted his hand, intending to hit me. I grabbed it and pushed it back at him. "That's enough," I said. " You destroyed all your history when you let your jailers silence you and started to punish me for what they had done to you."

I pulled my shirt off, shaking with rage and sorrow, so he could see the effects of his blows on my body. "Look—is this what a cultured man like you does to a woman like me, who loves you as honorable people love their homelands?"

I took off my jeans and started to turn around and approach him, pointing to the remaining effects of his brutalization of me. "You inflict torture on me through which you justify your hidden weakness. You are sick, sick—you have killed a love in me that can no longer return. Countries are not just destroyed by their occupiers; they are destroyed by their lovers as well."

I got dressed quickly and tensely as he remained silent and confused in his place. I closed the door behind me and stood catching my breath, the sound of his weeping coming to me from inside the house, more painful than it should have been.

3
Leila

(The Lady Emerges From Her Silence)

Despite the silence that filled Madame Emily's house, I began to grow accustomed to it and felt secure whenever I anticipated it. Every week a man would come with Madame's medicine and the food supplies needed by the house. I spent part of the time in the kitchen, a bit of time following TV and Facebook, and the rest of the time with Madame in her room, giving her her medicine and her food and then sitting with her as she stares at the willow tree while the Blue Danube waltz plays on the tape recorder. I often tried to get her to speak, but none of my efforts met with success. I wanted to break the cycle of boredom and feeling of loneliness and isolation that had begun to creep into me, making me aware of how little I knew about this lady, about this large empty house, or why no one ever visited her. I was silent as I looked at the tree, immersing myself in the music, through which I could see men and women dancing completely happily. My daily routine continued like this until things suddenly took a different twist. I had helped her take her food and was sitting with her looking at the tree and listening to the music when I heard someone speak. "The memory has scars that are visible to the eye."

I whirled around in terror to look for the source of the voice. Madame was in her usual state: silent and still—even her eyes were unblinking. I went into the corridor and from there to my room and downstairs, but I didn't find anyone. Was I dreaming? I ignored it and went back to my chair.

"I got to know him in 1970."

I heard the sound again and turned to the lady. Her eyes were still fixed on the tree, but there was a new brightness in them.

"It was one of the most beautiful nights in Vienna."

My God, it was Emily who was speaking! I went to her and touched her hands, which had slipped down over her thin thighs.

"I'm listening to you, madame, please go on."

"I had been studying medicine in Vienna for two years. As a student, I had received a lot of advice, most of it focused on preserving one's virtue. The first year passed, with my life confined to the path stretching between the university and the students' residence where I lived. I knew nothing about people or places except what I could see through the bus window and what I picked up from short conversations with Austrian students and others of different nationalities. But as the year went on, I became more adventurous and wanted to discover everything in a city I had fallen in love with, so much so that I wrote more about it in my letters to Amman than I did about myself. When I found myself free from the pressures of studying, I would go out on my own to the cinema and libraries and to public parks, and I would return with a great feeling of pleasure—until something happened I had not expected."

Madame Emily resumed her silence as she contemplated the willow tree and settled back into the music. I left to get her food ready before her afternoon nap, wondering what could have happened to this woman, who took refuge in so much silence. When I saw her for the first time, she seemed like an elderly woman weighed down by illness, but now she struck me more as a woman weighed down and pained by her memories. She woke just before sunset, and I picked her up and put her in her chair, which I moved to its usual place. I switched on the tape recorder and sat looking at her eyes as they focused on something in the distance. I touched the back of her hands tenderly. "Carry on, madame, with what you were speaking about during the day."

She didn't say anything, just continued looking at the same spot. I resumed my usual silence in her company, but suddenly she started speaking again:

"I met a Jordanian youth five years older than me; I met him in the Danube Island Park. I was sitting on a bench opposite the river. The sky above it was blue and clear, intersecting with its color, and I was enjoying moments in which the heart of a young girl like me is content, with nothing to hurt it, enjoying the richness of nature, which stirred in me songs coming from my soul, which was longing for life as never before. It was a moment of contemplation, interrupted by a young man passing in front of me. He stumbled and fell to the ground, then got up and looked at me as I dissolved in spontaneous laughter. He looked at me, angry at my reaction, then tidied himself up. I apologized to him in my slightly weak German and he replied in stronger German, his handsome eyes sparkling with words he was unable to speak: "It's not right for you to laugh!"

"Sorry, I couldn't help laughing."

"You're not from this country," he said, a smile like a ray of spring sunshine covering his face, as if he had just woken up to something.

"I'm from Jordan."

"Jordan, I know why I stumbled, and I'm no longer embarrassed," he said in Arabic, turning his shoulders left and right, and singing a song whose words he enjoyed. I stood up, and something in me drove me toward him when I saw him brush his long hair from his eyes as his mouth gave out a fresh smile. I corrected myself and went back to the bench, watching his pleading look after he had picked up from the ground his books and notebooks that had fallen.

"What's the connection between my being Jordanian and you slipping over?"

"There are seeds that only grow in certain ground, even if they have all the water they need."

I was moved by his description; in fact my body shook in a way that needed a warm coat for it to pass. It was a moment when I saw that I was in front of a man who might be a permanent warm coat for me. I don't know what courage that day exploded in me. I made room for him on my seat and invited him to sit down. "Come on, then, sit beside me."

He seemed shy despite his initial courage. He looked at me out of the corner of his eyes, then gazed at the horizon and fingered a book he had put on his thighs.

"Do you suppose my being beside you now, beside the Danube, in a silent song guarding these handsome eyes is by chance?"

"Nothing happens by chance."

That day he introduced himself to me as if he had been waiting for me for ages. He was a student doing a master's in engineering after completing a BA in that country which he seemed to love a lot. We spent hours wandering around the park, talking as though we had been friends for ages, until evening came and I went home and slept, certain he was the only choice. A love I had waited for since I knew the pleasure of songs and the scenes of love in the romantic stories I read during my school days. The next day we met and he took my hand and led me to a café looking over the romantic Vienna night. As though he was singing, he started talking to me about everything: music, drawing, engineering, love. My eyes never left his face, gathering his words, arranging them in a thread, and hanging them on my soul. The thing that greeted me most obviously in love was his virginal looks, exactly like a farmer exalting in ecstasy as he planted a tree and thought of its future fruit.

The days went by and he became a light that could not be dispensed with. We went out together and came back together. Each of us harbored a love for the other that we only revealed during an evening when a musical concert had been arranged to celebrate fifty years since the death of Strauss, and the Blue Danube waltz was played. He knew my passion for music, and so bought two tickets for us and we agreed we would meet in the evening. I dressed up smartly that evening and waited for him on the corner of the street, as I lived through the loveliest moments of waiting. When he got down from the bus, he was like a violin bow that knew how to touch my strings, so that my hidden melody fled in my heart, which I had stopped surrounding with the constraints on an oriental woman who should keep away from men. He took my hand and led me on a path toward the evening. "Every day, you look prettier," he said and gave me a look as if he was seeing me for the first time. Then he started to talk, with indications in his eyes that he was thinking of something else. I wanted him to stop halfway and speak the words I was waiting for, but he hid his confusion until we arrived at a hall that was heaving with people, and the evening began. His hand in mine was warm, his breathing erratic, and I almost threw myself into his arms. I found the music to be just birds fluttering around me. The Danube changed course and flowed into my heart when he looked at me with his gentle eyes and confessed his love to me. He said it sincerely and I could find nothing like it, so I confessed to him a love that I had felt since the first day I saw him, a love that had made me aware of my femininity and enabled me to think as a woman about her beauty.

Madame Emily returned to her silence again, looking at the willow tree as the Blue Danube waltz echoed around the room. It had a nice rhythm on my heart. Before sleeping, I read up on it on the internet and also about Johann Strauss as I tried to form a picture of the man with whom Emily had fallen in love.

A week went by without Emily saying anything. The fact is, I didn't know what had induced her to emerge from her silence that day. I did everything I had done before, in the hope she might tell me the rest of her story. I put on the same clothes and sat in the same place, but she maintained her usual silence. One morning, a Sunday, she spoke to me again. I had washed her, changed her clothes, given her her breakfast, and sat down opposite her, looking at her with a new feeling that sprang from a sense of her being a mother to me, that I was at home and belonged to this unique woman. For the first time since I came to this house, Emily looked straight at me, with the trace of a sympathetic word in her eyes that moved me to put my head on her knees. It was a look full of peace, which increased when she put her hand on my head and her fingers rubbed my hair. I cried quietly at that moment because of how my earlier years had affected me and what she had begun to tell me:

"One evening, we were coming back from a restaurant where we had spent several hours. He was telling me about the days that would unite us in one house. I was dreaming of becoming a doctor. I could find no value in anything at that time in his absence. He had taken me over, and I had become a pawn in his hands. I told him that as we stood opposite the building where he had his apartment in the Innere Stadt, and he invited me in for a cup of coffee. I didn't know that what would happen that night would change everything."

The lady was silent for a short time, and when I raised my head she was staring sadly at the willow tree.

"I don't know how he drew me into his arms. I was propelled by so much love. When I woke to find myself naked in his arms, I remembered the warnings of some of my family members who had opposed the idea of sending me to a faraway country. When he saw me crying he embraced me and said, "Don't worry, we'll get married" to reassure me. But that didn't happen. Our relationship faded and lost its sparkle over time, as my belly gradually swelled and I no longer had the energy even for my studies, which I lied about to my family. The man disappeared, as though he had never been. I inquired about him and was told that he had gone back to Jordan. I wrote a letter, telling him what had happened, and gave him two options: either I come back, and we find a solution to my problem; or else I stay in Vienna permanently.

"I came back, having abandoned my dream of being a doctor. Over a period of several months, my father wrote many letters to the man without receiving any reply. I learned from one of my colleagues at the university that he traveled to America for a doctorate. All my family did was marry me to a man with whom they had agreed that he would divorce me after a week so that we would avoid what people might say. Despite that, many stories were circulated about me, which made my father move house. I isolated myself for years in the house, as my son grew up with no father. When he asked me, I told him, "Your father died." But he heard my mother, who had not forgiven me for what had happened, shout at my father and accuse him of dishonorable behavior, blaming him for what had happened to me, so I told him that Iyad Nabil was his father."

When I heard that name, I recalled what I had read about an important man called Iyad Nabil who had been found dead in a second home of his. I thought that Madame Emily didn't know about what had happened.

"Before my father died, he distributed his possessions to me and my brother, and some months after his death I moved to a new house and worked in business until I had made a considerable sum of money. I owned a company and through its activities I was made to meet Iyad Nabil. In those days I had come to terms with part of what had happened to me. As soon as I saw him walk into my office, time took me back, dragging me to pain, and however much I begged him to reveal his paternity to Yusuf, he lit a cigarette and looked at me with different eyes from those I had seen in the Blue Danube Park. "How do I know that he's my son?" he asked haughtily.

"I threw a heavy ashtray at him that cracked his skull, as a result of which I was put in prison for two months. After that, he made war on my work activities until I was forced to declare bankruptcy."

That night, Madame Emily told me about Yusuf and how he had grown up in difficult psychological circumstances. The thing that kept him awake most was his feeling that he was a bastard and didn't belong to a family. She told me sadly that she had never seen Yusuf laugh except when he was a child, that he had no friends, and that he had studied psychology and excelled at it.

4
Ibrahim

(Narda and Diogenes)

I wiped the steam off the bathroom mirror and looked at my face; isolation had left its marks on me. Isolation is a voluntary prison where our souls wilt, and we become like trees irrigated with salt water. As I left the room, I felt the walls shift in their places, and everything was tottering—the TV, the computer, the coffee cup, the glass of water, even Narda's notebook. I felt an odd sort of choking come over me, which I could not stand, so I got dressed and went out, free of all the characters whose disguises I had adopted. "I am Ibrahim, no one else!" I said to myself as I passed the Seventh Circle on the sidewalk, not knowing where I was headed. When the taxi driver asked me where I was going, he found my confusion odd, and laughed.

"Don't you know where you're going?" he asked.

I told him "downtown," then fell silent as I recalled what Narda had said in her last message. I pondered her words with pleasure, imploring them to bring me out of my present state, and wrote her a message: "Hasn't the time come for us to meet?" Her reply came quickly: "I've left work and don't want to go back home." It was a hint that we should meet, so we chose downtown. "I'll wait for you at the Bookseller's Kiosk," she said, then corrected herself. "I mean, at the place where the Bookseller's Kiosk used to be."

All at once, things took on a new meaning, and it became possible to see more clearly. What miracles could love accomplish? What life could it impart to a body that was going to the end without sorrow? Would she remember me? That man, impotent as a wingless bird standing on the seashore, thinking of the last scene his mind would record before he took refuge in nothingness. Then suddenly, and without life giving him any sign, he falls in love, kicks the fox of death, and pursues her, searching for her with the appetite of a blind man who has regained his sight. And if she remembers me, what word will she be repeating to herself, or have on her dark lips? I was going to tell her we should meet away from the kiosk, for some memories are knives to sever the neck of the moment, especially for someone like me, who for many years always preferred to run away—though this time, I didn't, for I was afraid of losing my best chance of doing something just because I wanted to.

I got out of the taxi at the start of King Hussein Street. It was a nicer evening than any I had seen in all the years I spent in the kiosk—a night that would lead to a fresh happiness, to embrace my heart as generously as knights returning from a successful battle. I stood on the opposite sidewalk, looking at the store that had replaced the Bookseller's Kiosk. It was like dozens of others that had spread through Amman. I had heard that it belonged to Iyad Nabil, which puzzled me, for why would a man with so many investments need stores like that?

Narda arrived in a taxi. She was wearing jeans and a white shirt, and her hair was shorter than before. She walked calmly and elegantly, as if she was walking on a string in my heart, which played a tune as my eyes stayed fixed on her. When she reached the site of the kiosk, she looked around and crossed the street quickly. She came toward me like a prisoner of war who reaches the shore and jumps off the boat and into the water in order to reach dry land more quickly.

"Narda."

As soon as she heard me say her name, in a happier and more breathless tone than was proper, she looked at me astonished.

It was the same expression she'd had when we encountered each other for the first time. She took a step back with her hand over her quivering mouth, trying to disguise her reaction. Hesitantly, she held out her hand to me and we shook hands. "It's you?"

"Diogenes, yes, Diogenes," I stammered, looking at the store and then at the street, which was heaving with people and vehicles.

"How is this happening?" she asked, doubtfully.

I made a gesture indicating that we should walk on. The touch of her shoulder against mine in the crowd of pedestrians was warm. She stopped to speak to me over the shoulders of the crowd, in a voice so strangulated it was verging on sobs. "Is this chance, or fate, or something you have arranged?"

I didn't understand what she meant, but I said nothing. All I wanted at that moment was not to lose the biggest opportunity I had ever had. "There's a café near here," I said, in a pleading tone.

"Sorry," she said, almost crying. "I want to leave." Then, moving her hand between her brow and her mouth, she turned away.

I believed Narda was so upset because I had hidden under the name Diogenes, so I tried to explain why I had done it but things only got worse. I begged her to sit together just for a few minutes, and eventually she agreed. I was so happy, but sad at the same time! How could the loaf of happiness arrive chewed like this? We sat near the window on the second floor of a café that looked out over the street. She ordered a cup of coffee and started to smoke, shaking her foot in a strangely tense way as I began telling the story of my journey to suicide. I told her everything from the beginning—though it was nothing compared with my beginning with her. Gradually, she became calmer, her expression turned thoughtful and sympathetic as she looked at me, as though comparing the image of Diogenes she had formed in her mind with the person sitting in front of her. Whenever she joined in the conversation, her eyes would relax and acquire a compassionate look. I almost confessed to her what had happened to me after my return from Aqaba, but the voice angrily intruded, alerting me to the seriousness of what I was about to do. I stopped myself and remained silent, like someone waiting for an acquittal from a judge after passionately defending myself. She smiled, and then, eyes fixed on the street, asked, "Where is my notebook?"

"I will bring it for you next time."

"Next time?"

She said it with a quiet laugh that assured me that the distance between us was shrinking, then became distracted for a few moments.

"So now you know everything about me."

"I know what you wrote," I replied, trying to clear any hidden obstacles from my path to her.

"I was hoping to find the intimacy that you showed in your last messages to me."

She lit another cigarette and ordered another cup of coffee, as if trying to find the right words to express what was going on in her mind. "I am like a traveler who finds herself at a crossroads," she said.

I talked to her about books that evening. I was trying to get her to spend as much time with me as possible. I told her about my ability to imitate people and to adopt their personalities and said that I was incapable of adopting the personality of someone I didn't like. She laughed as she rested her chin on her hand. She was more beautiful than I'd ever seen her look before.

"Let me see this gift of yours!"

What made her say that? Was she testing my love for her, or was it mere curiosity? I stood by the table looking at her until the muscles in my face started to twitch and my face began to resemble hers, and I started to walk like her. She stood up and gave a shriek, which attracted the attention of the customers in the café, some of whom were quite taken aback by what they saw. She picked up her bag and left, but I quickly caught to her and walked behind her until we reached the street. She said nothing as I walked beside her. The evening crowd downtown had dispersed, and it was quieter. Suddenly she stopped and turned to me. "How did you do that?"

"It's a gift I can't explain."

"This is madness," she said, with an amazed laugh.

Then she checked her watch and held out her hand, saying, "I must go. It's getting late."

I stayed watching her until she had disappeared, at a loss to explain her reaction of surprise or why she had seemed so hardhearted.

PART 7

"I am so puzzled at the gap between what I want and what I can do."
—Naguib Mahfouz

1
Narda

(New Confessions)

It was a week of mixed emotions. I found myself in the midst of a storm of different feelings. How had Ibrahim come into my life? His words had ambushed me and returned me to a place that I still feared. At first, I thought he would free my heart from the pain caused by the absence of a man I could love with total devotion, but when we met, I found myself confronted by a sterile love. I could not tell him the truth, but he was relentless and never stopped writing to me, as if through words he could defeat any possibility of losing me. His face as he imitated me stayed with me even in my dreams. A strange hobby, which made me feel both amazed and confused. Whenever I wrote to him, I would delete part of what I wrote. My mental state reached a crisis point; I was in a trap, from which I had to escape. I told the doctor I was suffering from the sight of the man who walked on rainy nights, and that of the masked man with him as they both headed off, destination unknown. Once again, the sight of Ibrahim had been a part of it.

I almost told him the secret that had returned me to the abyss of despair, but I drew back. Perhaps I should have come out with it maybe he would have shown me how to escape. After checking that I was still taking my medicine, he asked about my writing and suggested that I add Ibrahim to the characters of the series I am writing. I sat at my desk that day and wrote until dawn, for the director had agreed to take the series after I sent him a summary, and told me he would await further installments.

I couldn't sleep that night, not with them staring at me through the window. I buried my head in the blankets, but they crept in, destroying the slightest possibility of living without sadness. I got out of bed and wandered around the house. When sadness becomes overwhelming, our memories escape to the first phase of our lives. We construct a daydream, as if to persuade ourselves that we are returning to the beginning of the road, to avoid all the mistakes that have occurred. His notebook was lying on the table like a wilted rose between two book covers. I made a cup of coffee, then picked up the notebook and returned to his world:

Some days after Jadallah's return from Moscow, al-Shamousi decided to throw a banquet. He invited the people of the village and the Madaba notables, put up tents, and slaughtered half his animals. At midday, he put on new clothes and sat awaiting his guests, wearing a black cloak to match his moustache, which he had dyed black. Once the guests began to arrive, he ordered Jadallah to stand by him and greet them. The tent was full of men, and Jadallah's party comrades had come. "How will you tell him the truth?" one of them whispered to him. Jadallah didn't reply, but walked among the men ruminating on the desperate situation he was in. After the meal, one of the Madaba notables approached Jadallah. Stroking his reddish moustache, he asked him point-blank, "Is the medicine course in Moscow five years?" Al-Shamousi heard the man question his son and sensed that Jadallah was hiding something from him. When everyone had left, he and Jadallah walked from the house and sat by the same olive tree where they had sat by before he left the village. "Tell me, son—what's up?"

Jadallah told him everything that day, talking and sobbing at the same time, while al-Shamousi stared silently into space, his face devoid of expression. After hearing the truth, he simply got up, walked unsteadily into the guestroom, and shut the door behind him. Meanwhile, Jadallah sat under the tree, whose shadow spread toward the east. The sun's rays fell on his face as he watched a bird whose wing had caught in some threads. More than once, the bird tried to fly away but it failed, caught in the tree's intertwined branches with a pleading look in its eyes as it desperately tried to escape. As Jadallah watched it struggle, he thought of the pain it must be feeling, so far from the sky. He got up and carefully began to undo the threads until the bird was free and soared into the air.

At that very moment, a bullet fired from al-Shamousi's gun, whose barrel protruded from one of the house's windows, struck Jadallah's shoulder, and he fell to the ground. Feeling the warmth of his blood pouring onto the earth, Jadallah kept his eyes on the path of the bird until his vision blurred and he lost consciousness.

He woke up in a hospital bed with several people standing over him. He didn't recognize them at first, for his vision was still blurry, but when the doctor asked him who they were, he was able to identify them as his brothers and some of his relatives. Ali leaned in close and whispered in Jadallah's ear in a sad, pleading voice. "Tell the police, 'My brother Ali was cleaning the rifle and the bullet went off by mistake.'"

"Where's my father?"

"At home—he's sad about what he did," replied Ali, stroking Jadallah's hair to comfort him.

"Tell him that if he finds the rifle relieves him of his feelings of disappointment, he can point it at my head next time!"

The news quickly spread through the village. Some people came to comfort al-Shamousi, who showed no remorse for the incident. He remained composed until Jadallah returned home, when he wept, paying no attention to the villagers who had hurried to congratulate Jadallah on his recovery. The same day, al-Shamousi received a communication requiring him to appear in court, for Iskandar had brought a case against him, in which he claimed ownership of the house and land. Al-Shamousi walked into the orchard, took hold of a tree branch, and looked into the distance. He was thinking of the losses he had incurred: he had lost two sons in the war, lost his dream that another son would return as a doctor, and now he was close to losing his home. He stayed sitting under the tree until sunset; when night fell, he went to bed early to escape the feeling of impotence in the face of all that had happened. In the morning, the family woke to the sound of Amina wailing. She had just watched as two policemen arrested Ali, whom they charged with attempting to murder Iskandar.

Seeing his father miserable, Ali had left the house just before sunset and waited until Iskandar closed up the shop. Ali followed him down the street and into an alley, where he stabbed him with his dagger and then fled, unaware that Iskandar was not dead—and that he had recognized his attacker.

That year, Ali was jailed for the attack; Sharifa married, two years after Jawazi; and Badi found work as a civilian employee in the army. It was a difficult year, and both the family's situation and that of al-Shamousi changed drastically: al-Shamousi no longer spoke much, and spent most of his time in silence, but he approached a number of his friends to act as mediators for him, and Iskandar agreed to be paid back the debt he was owed in installments, for which Badi acted as guarantor.

As time went on, no one spoke about what Jadallah had done. Even al-Shamousi appeared to have forgotten the affair, despite the agony in his heart. But people continued to call Jadallah *hakim* and consulted him on all sorts of things, including if someone was ill. They trusted him and loved him more than before, even though he had begun to alienate people with whom he had differences. He would spend his days in Madaba with his friends and political colleagues, planning party activities in extreme secrecy. In the evening, he would retreat to the same room where he had spent his last school year and spend time reading and writing. Two years after his return, Jadallah was appointed a schoolmaster. He and Badi paid most of the wages they received to Iskandar until they had cleared the debt.

Jadallah saw how the village had begun to change during this period. A number of new houses had been built, some with TV aerials on their roofs, and there were now shops. Some villagers had been appointed to government positions, and there were fewer people farming. Jadallah encouraged them to cultivate fruit and various crops that grow in the red soil around Madaba, and he urged the few remaining shepherds or herders for the cattle owners not to accept low wages. He met with every one of them individually and spoke to them in a way that seemed casual and without condescension. The schoolchildren loved to hear him talk about the country where he had studied and tell stories about people's lives there. When he had finished teaching them their lessons, he would talk to them about the books he had read. One day, a pupil asked him, "Why did you study philosophy, although you traveled to study medicine?"

He leaned on the table, looking as though he was preoccupied with faraway things, and said, "A man will not be able to make his life unless he uses his mind to understand everything around him. That is why I studied philosophy."

As he looked at the pupils' faces, he realized they hadn't understood what he had just said to them, so he walked between their chairs and continued. "When people looked at the distant stars a long time ago, they were afraid of them, so they worshipped them—because they didn't know what they were. Whenever they didn't understand something, they worshipped it." Then, with a smile, he added, "A man has nothing except his mind with which to understand life."

He looked at them, then said with a smile: "A man has nothing except his mind with which to understand life."

That day, he told his students what was right and what was wrong with people's lives in the village. Once he saw that they were listening carefully, his manner of speaking became more bold.

One evening, al-Shamousi came into Jadallah's room and sat down beside the bed, where his son was reading. He set down the book and showed him great respect, but his father' silence made him nervous, for he knew that he must have something to say. Finally, Al-Shamousi looked at him and said, "How long are you going to stay as you are, my son? We need to find you a wife."

Jadallah didn't argue; he had been expecting to have to fulfill a request from his father, in the hope that it might help him forget the sorrow he had brought him. So al-Shamousi built two rooms for him, and Jadallah married Maryam al-Shamousi, a relative, even though Tamarka had never stopped visiting him in his sleep. Even when he was reading, he would see her swinging between the lines, sticking her tongue out at him in fun, as she used to in their apartment in Moscow.

———

On their wedding night, Maryam sat on the edge of the bed, eyes cast down, rubbing her hands together, and breathing erratically from fear. Jadallah stood in front of her, thinking of what to say to a woman who knew nothing about him except that he was her relative. He sat down beside her and took her hand.

"I know you are expecting me to beat you as men do in this village. I know you are frightened of the violence you've heard about when some men take a woman's virginity, but I am not like that. Would you expect me to accept anyone hurting me? Of course not. So you must understand that there is no difference between you and me."

Maryam looked at him doubtfully, and in a quiet, shy voice said, "No, we are not the same, I am a woman and you are a man."

"In time, you will understand what I mean. Change your clothes and come nearer so we can talk."

Maryam got up and shyly changed into new clothes as Jadallah looked to one side. That night he told her about women in Moscow, and she listened to him without even blinking an eye. He didn't tell her how she ought to be, but left her to see another image of herself she didn't know. As dawn broke, he told her he wouldn't take her virginity until she had stopped being afraid, but as soon as they lay down together in bed, she came nearer to him and embraced him, and they experienced a joy she knew nothing about as he drove Tamarka from his mind.

As the days went by, Jadallah made his peace with the idea of Tamarka's death and started to focus on the loving relationship he had with Maryam—and enjoy it. His respect for her grew, but he couldn't escape bouts of depression. As soon as they struck, he would stay to himself or leave the house. He often thought of confessing his unhappiness to someone, but he concealed the strange emotions that pained him and drove him to isolation.

Maryam hadn't been to school as a child, but he talked with her about the stories and novels he had read, and she was a good listener. She remembered everything he said, then passed it on to her neighbors with her own additions. Maryam told them that he stayed up all night reading and writing, that he saw no difference between men and women, and that he believed some people understood their religion wrongly. She also admitted, "He even told me once that if I wanted to walk down the street without a head covering, that would make him happy." The following day, Maryam overheard some of the women saying bad things about Jadallah.

"They say you're a Commie!" she said, confronting him as he sat at the table, reading. "They say you've become an unbeliever, like the people you spent all those years with, who don't believe in God and even sleep with their sisters!"

He looked at her with a shocked expression, and then, without a word, Jadallah got up and walked outside. He sat in front of the house, smoking and looking at the village, which was sleeping silently in the darkness. That night he thought about the reasons for what had happened. Eventually, he decided to refrain from saying anything to Maryam and to confine himself to talking to her about ordinary things.

Maryam had a son, whom his grandfather called Ibrahim; a year later she gave birth to 'Ahid. The village changed: electricity arrived, roads were cut through it, and a mosque was built. The image of the *hakim* Jadallah also changed: people no longer consulted him or trusted his opinion. He became someone who was avoided by the faithful at gatherings, and whispered about among others. Jadallah's family noticed that he had started spending a lot of time away from home, but they didn't know what he was busy with. He would often meet his comrades and go out secretly, for arrests had become more frequent the year when Anwar al-Sadat visited Israel. Jadallah joined the demonstrators and spent the hours of the night reading and editing materials for the party newspaper. He was angry at what was happening; his mental state deteriorated and he seemed to anyone who saw him like a defeated man.

One evening he went out carrying an announcement to give to a colleague to distribute in Madaba that same night. Jadallah usually varied his route, but that night he wasn't as careful as he should have been and he was arrested in an alley leading to his friend's house. A security guard had recognized him. He tried to escape when he saw the patrol approaching him, but one of them hit him in the head and he fell down, unconscious. On the way to the police station they beat him in a way that reminded him of the beating he had received in Moscow. It was only a few minutes before a man came and began to interrogate Jadallah, to find out who he was with, but he didn't say anything, appearing stubborn and unconcerned. The soldiers took him, ordered him to take off his shoes, and took turns beating him until the blood ran from his feet. Then another officer came and started to interrogate him again, but they had no success. He endured many beatings and much abuse that night; it was only when they believed he was about to die that they threw him into a cell, moaning and hallucinating, sometimes in Russian and sometimes in Arabic.

In the morning, they put him in the dark rear compartment of a military truck. He thought they must be taking him to Amman, and then he realized what awaited him. As soon as they arrived, two men led him away, beat him, then threw him into a dark cell. The darkness seemed more painful than the bruises left by the kicks and sticks of the two men. Melancholy thoughts came into his mind: he was torn between feeling he must resist and other vague feelings mingled with fear. After a few hours, they took him to an office, where a smiling investigator stood up and shook hands with Jadallah.

"What are you doing with these suspicious activities, man? You are from a respected family."

The investigator pointed to a chair, and Jadallah sat down. A few seconds later, someone else came in and set down a cup of coffee in front of him. The investigator looked at him and ordered, "Drink your coffee, *ustadh!*"

After a moment of silence, he went on, with exaggerated politeness. "*Ustadh* Jadallah, you have a family. It would be advisable for you to consider them. You have a job, and if you concentrate on it, you will become someone of standing. All you have to do is issue a retraction."

Jadallah said nothing. He didn't even look at the investigator's face, even as the man repeated his offer—this time with a hidden frivolity.

"*Ustadh* Jadallah, what do you think?"

"About what?"

"About your retraction?"

"No."

The investigator used a variety of carrot-and-stick techniques but got nowhere with Jadallah, so they returned him to the cell and beat him hard again. After a week, they tried with him again, but he maintained his position, so he was referred to a military court and sentenced to three years. They moved him to Al Mahatta prison and put him in a cell, where he stayed until eleven in the evening; then they took him to the prison gate, where there were trucks and soldiers bristling with weapons. He saw several of his comrades getting into the trucks and followed them with his swollen feet; then one of the soldiers ordered him to get in as well, and he was taken to the Al Jafr desert prison.

That was the second time that Jadallah had been detained, even though he had never been summoned for investigation before. The truck arrived at four in the morning. After they had been let out into a large yard, the soldiers ordered them to squat, and that was when he started to think of his family, his wife, and his two small sons. He again recalled the day when he was arrested by Soviet intelligence, as well as many other things in his life. He was not afraid, he was merely depressed. He had spent years of his party life careful to remain in the shadows, and had remained cautious of any activity hat might give him away. He didn't know how he had been exposed. He didn't integrate with the other detainees, some of whom he knew, but stayed apart, taking no part in conversations or in any activity they undertook. As soon as his feet stepped on the prison ground, he felt a sudden weakness that he could not explain, despite the fervor he had continually demonstrated before his arrest. He was in constant need of silence and seclusion. All he did was read whatever books were available.

Some of the prisoners tried to draw him out of himself, but they didn't succeed. In 1980, he was summoned with some other prisoners to Amman and shown into an office where two men were sitting: one was a foreigner and the other a Jordanian, who translated what the other one was saying.

"Do not imagine that your long silence can disguise your importance in the party!"

Jadallah looked at the foreigner but said nothing.

"We know the importance of your ideas and the nature of the role you are playing."

The foreigner got up and walked around the large room. The clicking of his boots sounded like the rhythm of a prearranged threat. He came closer to Jadallah and then spoke in English as the other man translated what he said:

"You were talking to the extremists in a language they understood, to the Bedouin in a way that could turn them into Communists, and to women using words appropriate for them. We know the intention behind your conversations with students and everyone you meet. You thought you were concealed, but you have been visible to us for some time. Even the resolutions and investigations published in your newspaper—we knew you were behind many of them. The language of philosophy is evident in what you say, and in this role you are more important than people who act on impulse."

The man paused in the middle of the room, then said, in a gentle tone, "You can leave this office, return home, and go back to your work, where you will hold important positions."

The man sat back down at the table. "That is, in exchange for your retraction and providing certain information."

In the course of the day, Jadallah received numerous threats as well as promises of a better future. For a while he remained silent, until he announced that he had left the party, divulged some secrets, and left under the terms they had promised, feeling disappointed and conscious that a new hurt had been added to his existing ones.

2
Ibrahim

(Before the Deception)

I woke early and checked my Facebook messages, but there was nothing from Narda. I had contacted her more than once recently, but she had not replied. However, there was a message from Dr. Yusuf.

"Iyad Nabil has begun to give me nightmares. Do you remember the day you came to me, wanting me to help you commit a crime of murder? Now I am writing to you to see if you can help me escape from my father's nightmares. My life has started to go toward the chasm with laughable speed. I cannot even meet my mother Emily when she is living in this disgraceful state. She reminds me of him, sitting silently, contemplating the white pages of his black book."

What do you suppose I had written to Dr. Yusuf for him to speak like that? I ate my breakfast without appetite and turned on the TV. I found a program on a satellite channel about the most talked-about subjects on Facebook. The presenter of the program started talking about the masked robber, quoting things that users had said about him. People had drawn a contrary picture of me. "This isn't me," I said, as I threw the coffee cup at the screen. Then I stood up and started pacing around, repeating: "This isn't me." My belly swelled up and the voice came back, angry and reprimanding. "No, this *is* you!"

"No, it isn't me!"

He seemed like a father lecturing his son.

"People draw pictures of what they want."

I stood at the mirror, my face full of sorrow.

"How can people want a thief?"

The voice became a little calmer. "A thirsty man in the desert sees a mirage as water, and you know that people are thirsty."

"Enough, enough. I won't carry out any more burglaries from now on."

I felt an intense pain in my belly and ran terrified from room to room, with a ringing in my ears. I fell down panting as the voice lodged in my head, threatening and frightening. "In light of your intransigence, I will do what I have told you."

The pain grew worse as my belly swelled up more. "OK, let it be the last one!" I cried frantically.

I don't know if I lost consciousness or if I simply fell fast asleep on the ground after those terrible moments. When I woke at noon, my belly was normal and the voice was gone. I took a shower and then lay back down, staring at the ceiling and thinking of Narda. I needed her to put a stop to a pendulum swinging in my head, but she no longer replied to my messages or my attempts to contact her. For some obscure reason, she had disappeared like a mirage that had enticed me to catch up to her all that way, then left me a victim of illusion. Could a shattered heart find love? Perhaps she had found in me a place to escape from her memories, medicine for her many pains. I opened her notebook to finish the remaining pages:

Before I reached the doctor's office, I looked at my face in the mirror and removed all traces of my crying. After taking a deep breath, I knocked on the door and went in. I was trying to escape from my feeling of chaos. The doctor examined me as I sat there, feeling sad despite my forced smile. He looked at a file, closed it, then folded his hands over his chest. "I purposely listened to you at the previous session without saying anything."

I gave him the impression that I was in control, despite the
sudden disturbance in my chest, nodding my head as I realized I
was so confused I would not be able to speak. He got up from his
chair and sat in front of me: "You are suffering from depression."

A strange feeling of calm came over me, as if he had told me
that I had the flu and would recover in a few days. He found my
composure odd, having seen me as someone distracted by something of no value.

"You must cooperate with me to get over this illness."

"I'll try," I said, in the tone of someone entering a house to
check how much furniture is left in it.

The doctor went back to his desk, where he studied a file and
then wrote on a prescription pad: "Continue to take the medicine."

He took a sip of water and then said in a concerned voice, "I
know your family has left the area, but I would like to meet a friend
of yours, of either sex."

"I don't have any friends," I replied, and left quietly, the hospital's long corridor walls echoing with the clicking of my shoes.
On the way back, I looked gloomily through the taxi window,
thinking of nothing at all. I viewed the faces of the passersby on
the sidewalk, and every one conveyed a different expression: there
were calm faces, sad faces, happy faces, and neutral faces. I could
hear nothing, despite the noise of the cars as they moved along
at varying speeds, as if all I could see had changed into a silent
scene. A woman was pushing a pram with a baby girl sitting in
it, watching the people with wide eyes sparkling with childhood,
her astonishment punctuated with a silent laugh that spread over
her pale, round face. As I rested my head on the seat and looked at
the baby, it was as though I was peeking at something I shouldn't
be looking at. I saw myself, and in my memory I heard rumblings
from the distant past, separated from my present self by many
years, during which I had not enjoyed enough of the happiness that

should last and turn into happy memories. I carried on looking at the child and at how she waved her hands at the pedestrians until she disappeared at a bend in the road.

I left the taxi and stayed looking at my front door for a few minutes, thinking how it would bring me to a new time. I climbed the steps calmly and went in, then walked past him and went into my room; as usual, his mind was on other things. I lay down on the bed, calmly contemplating the ceiling, and thought about my real illness—how I had caught it, and when it began. I stood at the mirror, undressed, and checked my body, searching for traces of bruises caused by a man I still loved despite his violence toward me. I put on my pajamas, locked the door, and slept for twelve straight hours. I woke to the sound of his loud knocks on the door. I didn't respond to his shouts or his questions about why I had slept so long. I simply left the room, made a cup of coffee, and sat in front of the TV, which was showing a video in which women were dancing around a youth and singing about life. He got up from his chair and sat down beside me, stinking of cigarettes. He seemed hesitant about what to say and started to stroke my hair with shaking hands, which made me jump as if an electric current had just coursed through my body. He moved a little away from me, a look of surprise on his face.

"What's up?" he said, moving closer again and breathing faster, as though he had just returned from a long walk. Without replying, I went back to watching the TV. He got up, went back to his chair, and sat there without saying anything.

"I have something to ask of you," I said, staring into space.

"Ask me whatever you like," he said, as he turned to me, in an almost apologetic tone.

"Divorce me."

He said nothing as he took in my words, then went inside for a few minutes and came back, carrying a bag. "You are divorced," he said, trying to retain his forced smile. When he reached the door, he turned back to me, and his smile had vanished, replaced by a sadness I had never seen before; then he left. I was on the verge of running after him to dissuade him from leaving, but I was of two minds. There are stages in life that have to end for us to preserve the bright side of the picture—and that depends on the memory of joy to fight the sorrow we have been given. That step of mine had taken me along a path I thought would be hard to abandon, for I had been overtaken by depression, and this had begun to ruin all my attempts to live away from a man I had begun to see wherever I looked. He was walking sadly on a rainy day—a scene that pained me a lot, and one I was sure I could not escape in the shadow of a cruel loneliness leading to an abject sense of defeat. The cruelest stages of the illness are those that appear when you are tottering alone and can find no one to support you. The doctor prescribed more drugs for me, which numbed me and turned me into a body with no energy. Just as I had abandoned my university studies, I abandoned my job, and soon after losing it I became unable to express what I was suffering from. A single visit to a psychiatrist was enough to convince many people that I had gone mad; then the distance between us would increase and my condition would become even more impossible. On my first day at work after a long holiday, the chief editor saw something in my face that I was trying to hide and asked me to come and see him in his office. When I showed up, he shut the door, sat down opposite me, and smiled to encourage me to open up. "What's up?"

"Nothing, just a bit tired, it will pass."

"No, I can see it's more than that."

When I said nothing in response, he could see I was reluctant to tell him anything. After a moment of silence, he looked left and right, as if he had realized what was wrong with me.

"You're on leave for two weeks. I want you to come back after that as you used to."

Perhaps the chief editor had touched on what grief had done to me since I left the restaurant and found work on the paper, like someone taking the first steps to escape from the love of a man who gives a rose with one hand and burning embers with the other. As I left work that day, the chief editor gave me a wave. I didn't know how to escape my sorrow or the clutches of depression in a city where I had turned into an impotent woman, changing my places, my possessions, and my friends—everything in order to rid myself of a stern man.

I didn't go back home; instead, my steps led me to Jabal al-Jaw-fa, seeking the image I had of myself—which I hoped would relieve me of my depression—and looking for a man. When he told me he lived in the same quarter I was born in, I had cried out in surprise at the years when I hadn't known him and at how I had never met him, even by chance. I told the lady who was renting the family home that nostalgia had led me to this house. Then I cried so much it made the lady cry, too, and she hugged me, unaware of what lay behind all that nostalgia. Sorrows are pages in the hearts of men; they need a light breeze of regret to turn them over again. That is something I learned a long time ago when I went with my mother to a funeral where women were crying and lamenting nonstop. On the way back home, my mother told me about the wounds of many of the women there, some of whom had lost a son, or a husband, or a motherland.

On the day I returned to Jabal al-Jawfa, the lady made space for me to wander around the house on my own as I tried to recover years past, unable to stop crying—especially in the room that had witnessed all my shattered dreams, before a life I'd imagined would be easy and would respond to everything I wanted. I don't know why I asked her for news about the quarter; perhaps it was to complete my attempt to recover my early life, despite the pain it held. I wish I hadn't asked, for she began to give me all the local news: who had died, who had been born, who had married, who had moved away, and who had been put in prison. Then she started telling me about the man whose great love had worn me down—as if relating a story she had found in a book.

Then she said, "He ended his life by committing suicide at home."

As soon as I heard her say that, I went straight to the door and ran out onto the street, pursued by feelings of guilt and disaster that propelled me toward his house. I could still remember it as he described it, along with many other things impossible to forget. I knocked angrily on the door, as if I was expecting him to come out to me from inside, so I could dissuade him from doing what he had done. A young man opened the door and was taken aback to find me shouting and astonished when I tried to push past him, but then I fainted. When I came around, there was a veiled woman beside me who lived in the building opposite. She told me the young man had sought her help because he was alone in the building. With that, the woman apologized to the young man and escorted me outside. When I asked her what had happened, she at first denied any knowledge of the incident; then, as I was about to be on my way, she admitted that she had heard what had happened. She looked at me oddly, then asked me about my relationship to the man, but I didn't tell her anything. She went home and stood on the balcony, watching me as the street swallowed me up—just as the sadness had swallowed me, with no hope of escape. I couldn't stay in the house for more than a few minutes. His voice surrounded me from every direction, and I had a deadly feeling of guilt and loss. Had I unconsciously killed him? I wish I could have shielded him from his sorrows more than I did. I had completely lost my ability that helped me to stay by myself. So I wrote a message to a friend who lived with her husband in Aqaba and told her I was coming.

The road to Aqaba was as long as the mountains of sorrow, the sand yellow as grief, and the songs on the bus's tape recorder made me start sobbing again whenever I was about to stop. Wherever I looked I would see him, sometimes among the bus passengers, sometimes beside me. Even if I looked out of the window, I would see him going along the same road, which had begun to overwhelm me since he left, never to return. I shut my eyes as the hand of the universe pressed on my chest, starving me of air. The same scene overwhelmed me, as if inviting me to join my husband through a single gate, the gate of death.

Before I reached Aqaba, my friend called me. She didn't sound happy. I felt there was something troubling her, perhaps connected with her husband, with whom she had been arguing a lot recently. She responded that she was expecting me, so I wrote back to tell her I had reserved a room at a hotel and would call her. But I didn't. How could a worn-out person lean on a wall that was still solid after being rocked by earthquakes? I spent the first night within the hotel's walls, feeling upset and afraid, with obscure emotions that the drugs could no longer do anything about. I finally threw them in the toilet. Everything was black, as far as I was concerned, even the light. I felt useless, and unable to banish the image and voice of that man as he committed suicide out of grief as a protest from my memory. I lay awake until morning, having made up my mind to put an end to my life.

I put the notebook to one side and sat at the computer looking at the page of the man who posted information and images that could lead me to my new goal. The voice led me to the details with perfect skill, and whenever I found myself wondering what I should do, it whispered in my ear and pushed me on to proceed with my strange action. I studied all the details: How many people lived in the house? When did they go out? When did they return? How was it divided internally? I learned about its location and got to know its entrances and type of doors—from Google I discovered how I could get through them. I collected as much data as possible, then made a drawing, in which I plugged the gaps of missing information and chose a night to carry out the last of my robberies. I turned off the computer and sat silently, struggling against my overwhelming exhaustion I heard the voice laughing. "This time, you have to adopt the persona of Ahmad Abd al-Jawad, the hero of Mahfouz's *Trilogy*."

I liked the personality of Ahmad Abd al-Jawad, despite its objectionable duplicity: a man who was pious and stern at home, but strong-willed in his secret worlds. One time, my father saw me with a skullcap on my head, wearing a *jilbab*, and behaving in the house like Si al-Sayyid. He lowered his voice so no one could overhear him, and said angrily, "If these sort of men gain ground, they will become a thorn in the throat of freedom. Women will remain prisoners of repression, and there will be nothing but more injustice." He urged me to stop dressing up, and even asked me shyly to stop reading novels. I was going to ask him whether someone like him should be afraid—afraid of being what he wanted. I could have said it, but I said nothing, hoping not to make his symptoms of depression any worse.

By the time I had finished acquiring clothes like those of Ahmad Abd al-Jawad, the afternoon sun was still spread over the downtown buildings and casting shadows over the pedestrians. In an effort to add a bit of stability to my temperament, I made sure to look very elegant. This requirement took me to the café where I had met Narda. I ordered a cup of coffee and sat by the window, looking at the store that had taken the place of the Bookseller's Kiosk. I realized that for all those years I hadn't looked around me much: I hadn't seen the people or the shops properly; I hadn't even seen this place, which I discovered was like a microcosm of life. I was so immersed in books, it was as if I had undertaken a silent sort of flight through years that changed me into a black-and-white picture.

I wrote to Narda. "What is happening to me with you seems like an expression with a bracket at the start of it, while the ending is open. Despite that, I will not put a comma, or even a full stop; I will leave the expression without any punctuation."

She seemed to have read the message. "I haven't slept since that day," she wrote.

"I am in the same café, sitting at the same table."

"Wait for me, I am coming."

As soon as I saw her response, I kept my eyes glued to the street. It was one of the nicer forms of waiting. A hand reached out to my memory, deleting painful images, voices, and scenes. I was still searching for her in the crowd when she walked through the café door, her shoes clicking on the ground like a metronome preparing me for an exceptional dance.

"You look as if you are reading faces, glowering like that!"

"I was waiting for you."

She was wearing a purple dress and had let her hair down. She was beautiful: a long, unblemished neck, with a necklace around it bearing the first letter of her name, and eyes in which her dark pupils seemed even darker against the white background. She seemed happy; her face had lost the sadness that made me fall in love with her.

"Even I haven't been sleeping properly," I said, gazing at the street and then back at her, again noting how her pupils expanded and contracted. "I love you."

She bit her lip then gave a long sigh, as if trying to hold back tears.

"I'll tell you something, which I know will hurt me more than it hurts you."

I took her hand, shut my eyes, and kissed her. In my heart, birds were flying away and music was playing. I saw two tears drop onto her cheeks.

"Your way to me is closed," she said.

"I will dig it with my own hand," I said, moving my chair toward her. The distance between our two faces had become as close as it could be to a spontaneous kiss. She looked at the ceiling then out at the Amman crowd, unable to speak the word caught in her throat.

3
Leila

(Similar Outcomes)

Ever since Madame Emily resumed her silence, I had continued to spend my days sitting beside her, gazing at the willow as she did, and waiting for her to speak again. The Blue Danube only increased my sense of gloom. I would have liked someone to talk to, someone to look at me and prove that he could hear me.

I prepared supper and ate despite my lack of appetite, then I helped Madame to take her food and medicine. Later, I wandered all around the house, which was quite spacious, but every day it made me feel lonely. I sat on the staircase, looking at the door and the spacious lounge, and wept. From isolation to isolation, and from desert to desert, I wanted a father, a mother, brothers. I wanted someone to wipe that phrase from my forehead that marked me as a bastard. I went back to Madame Emily and knelt down in front of her:

"Speak, please—or even just look at me!"

She sank into a painful silence, so I sat on the floor and put my head on her knees.

"It's not my fault that I am the product of a moment of forbidden madness. 'You bastard!' is a phrase people say daily, but I have never been able to feel comfortable with it. Aren't they fathers? Aren't they mothers? How can a man be a beast and a docile lamb at the same time? Whenever I recall how Ranad Mahmoud violated me, I remember how my heart was torn in two and I suffered a torment worse even than the one I suffered when I found myself with nothing in the street."

I lifted my head from her knees. Her eyes were still fixed on the willow, or perhaps on a point far beyond it. I don't know, perhaps she was looking at something I couldn't see. I carried her to her bed and went back to my room, afraid, extremely lonely, hurt, and bored. I watched an episode of a series then turned to Facebook. Several items about the masked robber, others about rising prices and the tough times many people were going through. I didn't expect life outside the orphanage would be so hard.

It was almost eleven in the evening when I went to bed, with no desire to sleep, but it was a way of killing time. Madame Emily was fast asleep and would wake at six in the morning. I wished she could wake up and keep me company. Once I closed my eyes, I heard the sound of footsteps in the corridor and then a door being opened. I listened more carefully, but the noise stopped.

"Perhaps the silence in the house makes me imagine I'm hearing things," I said to myself. I put my head on the pillow but felt frightened and wondered: "What if a man found out I was in a house, alone with a woman unable to move?" I sat in the middle of the bed, hunching myself up and feeling extremely afraid. My fear only increased when I heard footsteps coming from outside Madame Emily's son's room. As I tried to calm myself, thousands of possibilities ran though my imagination, one of them being that Emily had gotten out of bed and was moving around the house. How could such a thing happen to a woman who was unable to move?

I remembered the woman who had met me on my first day in the house, who had given me a number to contact in situations like this. I called her, but there was no reply, so I wrote a message to explain the situation and prepared myself to leave this house. I had to do it. I was afraid for Emily more than for myself. As soon as I had opened the door and hurried out, I collided with a man wearing a loose *jilbab* with a mask over his face. I screamed in terror but he stood rooted to the spot, staring at me. I was so scared that for some reason I was induced to pull the mask off him. At first I was confronted by a man I didn't recognize, but after a few moments I could see that it was Ibrahim. "Oh my God, how could this be happening?" I cried, stunned again and in utter disbelief that someone like Ibrahim had become a thief.

I wondered about that first expression on his face and about his mask and strange clothes, but I didn't understand any of what I was seeing. Then I recalled what I had read on Facebook and realized I was standing face to face with the masked robber. He fled, and I followed after him as he ran down the staircase and through the kitchen door. I was greatly distressed: How could this be the same man who had given me fatherhood as no one else had? I almost caught up to him, but at that very moment, the lady I had contacted arrived. As she climbed the stairs to the second floor, she said, "I have informed the police—don't worry, the house has security cameras."

I followed her as she went into Madame's room, and when she found her sleeping and left, I locked the door. Then she searched a number of rooms on the second floor. In the corridor, panting, she asked if I had seen the intruder, and I told her the identity of the robber without revealing my connection with him.

"So this is the masked robber," she said, on her way back downstairs, where a police car was waiting just outside the front door. I went into my room, sad at what I had done. There must be some mistake. Ibrahim was not an evil man, and he could not be a thief. How could he set aside the love I had seen in his heart that night and steal? Why had I told the woman about him? But the person I had seen was Ibrahim. When I removed the mask, he had features I didn't recognize, but suddenly, as if in a dream, the features changed, and I was face to face with the man who protected me the night I was wandering under the bridge. It seems I had made a big mistake. I shouldn't acknowledge Ibrahim, but should leave it to them. What would happen to him because of me and the way he had acted? Had I wronged a man who had shown me the right way? And now I was identifying him to them, so that he could follow the road to prison. There was a knock at the door—it was the woman: "The officer wants to ask you some questions."

I would have liked to stay in my room or run away or retract my statements, but what had happened had happened. I stood in front of the officer, unable to stop from shaking.

"Tell me what you saw," he said.

"I saw a man wearing a *jilbab*, which looked Egyptian, with a turban on his head and a mask over his face. I don't know how I dared, but I ripped the mask from his face. It was an extremely scary moment."

"Go on," said the officer.

"The strange thing, officer, is that when I removed the mask, I found that his face looked different from the one it quickly changed into."

"How?" asked the officer in surprise.

"At first, I didn't recognize the man, but suddenly I did."

"Who is it?

"Ibrahim the bookseller."

4
Ibrahim

(A Shocking Reality)

The night turned into a torn cloak, unable to hide me from what I had done. I was consumed by fear and full of regret. What chance was this that had brought me face to face with Leila? I had lost the picture that she had hung for me on the wall of her heart and which had given her great pleasure. I took a side road, took off the *jilbab* under which I had put on jeans and a shirt, and walked on, not knowing where I was going. I could almost feel someone watching me and pointing at me from behind every house window. I could hear a collective voice coming from the houses, streets, and alleys: "Thief, thief, thief!" In the meantime, the voice began to quiet the sound of my footsteps and calm my nerves, urging me to walk slowly so as not to attract attention. I wished I could kill him to free myself from what I had done. I wished I had thrown my body in the water that time when I went to the sea, driven by fear of and for myself.

I stopped walking, feeling completely lost. Should I go back to the apartment? Should I roam the streets aimlessly? Should I go to the deserted house, or to Jabal al-Jawfa? I had been swept away and lost my sense of equilibrium, so I was no longer Ibrahim or Doctor Zhivago or Ahmad Abd al-Jawad. I was just something of no value. I had lost my ability to speak or understand. But then came a call from Narda that made all choices irrelevant. The phone rang several times as I sat looking at the screen, totally mesmerized; I took a deep breath, pressed the "receive" key, and heard her voice like a distant echo.

"Awake?"

There was plenty of pity and fear in that word, but not much of the love I had dreamed of.

"And I'm feeling bored."

She laughed, like someone comforting a child who has dropped a paper airplane, and asked, "What do you say to a cup of coffee at my place?" She seemed to be trying to rescue me from a field of dry grass that has caught fire in a moment of inattention.

She sent me a link to her home site and ended the conversation, her words ringing in my ears. I crossed the side street, hailed the first taxi I saw, and hurried to the apartment, where I changed my clothes. I picked up her notebook and set off. I forget what happened to me, but I kept telling the driver to hurry up, driven on by my desire to meet a woman who had brought me back from within a hair breadth of the mouth of death, and now she was saving me from a harsh desert.

She was looking at me through the window when I went through a low gate to her apartment on the first floor of the building. I didn't even have a chance to knock on the door before she opened it and greeted me with a smile. I tried to hide my considerable agitation as I entered, and occupied myself by looking at the pictures of her on the walls as well as the antiques scattered in several places around the small apartment.

As we made our way to the kitchen, she took a long look at me, trying to read my expression. "I'll make coffee," she said.

There was a desk with a computer and some books on it, and I flipped through one of them—a book about the psychological motives of thieves who commit burglaries.

"I bought it because I was interested as a journalist in the masked robber," she said from inside.

She came in, carrying a tray with two cups on it, and sat down, stealing glances at me. I left the book and sat down beside her to drink my coffee, observing how calm she appeared. What if she knew that the masked robber was sitting beside her right now? And that he had been discovered! A bookseller becomes a thief, that's the easiest thing to say; all the stories that had been woven around me would collapse, and the lines people had devoted to me would become just a poetic event and nothing more. She moved a strand of hair from her eye and said:

"When I was a child, our house was broken into. I saw the robber wandering around the house in a mask when everyone was asleep. My memory has retained a frightening image of robbers. I imagine them with a wild look, like the one my mother told us about on rainy nights, to get us to sleep. As this image grew uglier, my fear grew that one of them might break into my house after all these years, but the masked robber put an end to those fears; he is an honorable thief who steals for others' sake. I thought about him a lot, until I dreamed of him!" she added with a laugh.

I almost told her the truth, but the voice warned me of the error I would be committing. She talked a lot about the masked man, and I sat looking at her as she spoke, a woman I knew things about that others didn't—for the word is a window into our inner homes, for us to see what life has hidden.

"I haven't found any better gift than to return your notebook to you."

Her face flickered with conflicting emotions as I extended my hand toward her, holding the notebook. At first, she seemed close to tears, then I saw that she was smiling as if she no longer cared about those pages. She flipped through the notebook, then turned to look at a picture on the wall.

"I read you carefully," I said.

"Why were you going to commit suicide?" she asked, in a voice full of sadness, yet mingled with a hesitant happiness. I couldn't tell her the whole truth; I could only reveal half of my motives to her.

"The hardest sort of pain is for someone to discover that his life has taken a shape in which he has had no part in creating. I was pure stony earth, which my father irrigated with the water of fear. To this day, I don't know why he was so afraid of everything. Eventually, I reached a stage when darkness filled my soul, and death became an opportunity to go toward the light."

She disappeared inside and came back with a notebook, which she placed in front of me. She was silent, as though unsure of what to say.

"This is your father's notebook. You will find the answer there."

"My father's notebook?" What had my father to do with Narda, I asked myself.

"Yes, your father's notebook."

She let out a long sigh. "The man you read about in my notebook was Jadallah al-Shamousi, Jadallah the bookseller. When we met on the beach, I recognized you but I didn't tell you. He had pictures of you all in his wallet, which he showed me. He spoke about you often in the year he spent with me; then he left after a big celebration of pain. Your father was my husband."

How had I fallen in love with a woman my father had loved? What path had led me to this fantastical spot? What fate had brought me together with this woman, on the pinnacle of whose soul rests a cloud filled with sadness, which my father hewed from his soul and released in the sky? He made me afraid and he made her miserable. I recalled everything I had read in her notebook in a flash.

"So my father lived in a shabby room on the outskirts of Jabal al-Weibdeh!"

She came nearer to me, her eyes full of a mother's fear and compassion.

"One day, he heard you talking angrily in your sleep about the fear he had instilled in you. So he left home, on the excuse of working away. He wanted to free himself of his fear and let you live away from him. He felt very guilty about you."

She came nearer and grasped my hand. "He would come at night while you were asleep, see you, then leave."

I got up to go. I wanted to read what he had written on my own. I could not have known my father as I should. But she stood between me and the door, crying.

"I won't let you leave in such a miserable state."

She made up a bed for me in the sitting room, then disappeared into her own room. I started to read what he had written, pausing at every word, his image never leaving my mind. He was reading to me what he had written in an unaccustomed voice, the voice of a man who had been born on a bed of thorns and returned to the same bed. How close, and good, and loving he was! He was just as I had dreamed he might be. I shut the notebook, seized by a bitter lamentation. My belly swelled, and the voice came, more repulsive than I had ever known it. "Don't forget that he is one of your executioners!"

I waved my hand in the air in anger as I tried to find him. "No," I shouted. "We execute ourselves without being conscious of it, and we do it with those we love."

I got out of bed, his voice close to my ear, like a bee pursuing someone who has disturbed its hive.

"You are sorry for what you have done."

"Yes, sorry."

"You had a final step to take, but let us pass over that and do something that will make you forget your regrets."

I was startled by Narda clutching me and shaking me. "Ibrahim, Ibrahim!"

As if I had been momentarily unconscious, I found myself looking into her terrified face. She was shaking, unable to make sense of what she was seeing. Her lips were moving as if trying to speak, but she was unable to get out a single word. She led me to the restroom and put my head under the tap. I didn't notice her silent sobs until she took me to bed; I asked her why she crying, and she replied in a strangled voice, "Please, all you have to do is calm down."

She guided me to the bed, sat beside me, and stayed stroking my head until I fell asleep. It only lasted half an hour, and Narda went to sleep herself. It seems they were looking for me in several places; I imagined my situation had become widely known. I checked Facebook and found that the truth was out. On the verge of throwing up, I threw the phone on the bed and rushed to the restroom, and when I returned, Narda was looking at my phone.

I left Narda's apartment that night knowing I had to go to the deserted house, but she stood between me and the door.

"They'll arrest you," she said. "I know." Then, despite the sadness and fear for me that was plainly visible on her face, she smiled. She was still standing in the doorway when I picked up my pace and took a side road away from her apartment.

I walked along a dark road adjacent to a lighted street. Everything was superimposed: people, cars, buildings, lights. What farcical destiny was this that I had been granted? I had no family to break this miserable branch of my tree, no house whose door could stand between me and a cold wind whose whistle invited a deadly loneliness; and when I fell in love, I fell in love with my father's divorced wife. What sort of fate was this—what an unheard-of outcome! As if I was a worn-out rag, ruined by the sun, which would disintegrate just as soon as it was touched. How much life did I have left for me to take a correct step, to cancel the mistaken ones? There were hands in Amman that would encircle my neck. How many people were there like you, Ibrahim, with the oxygen draining gradually from their chests?

I left the dark road and walked along the street, not at all concerned about the possibility of being arrested.

"You are violating the final stage," I heard the voice say, sternly and in great anger, as it forbade me to go out among people.

"It is you that violated the stage I was comfortable with by your evil ideas."

"You complained silently. All I did was to explode this silence of yours, and you had to destroy what remained of it."

There were only a few taxis and pedestrians in the streets. Silence had descended on everything. The city was sleeping, as though its everyday bustle was a short-lived quarrel that would not return. Everyone had taken a rest from their actions, which were not like their faces. In the day, we can be beasts in human form, but when sleep takes us over, we revert to the first image of the face, which looks out over life from the womb. I wandered aimlessly with no feeling except for the uselessness of everything. There was no compass to point me in a direction; even my memory was no longer of any use to me at all.

I asked the taxi driver to take me to Abdoun. When he asked for the exact address of where I wanted to go, I told him to take me to the bridge. It seems there was no stopping point left to me except the one that would help me escape from myself. A year ago, I had gone to Aqaba one morning to escape life through death, when a woman appeared, who brought hope with her, which then disappeared, never to return. Now I was heading for the Abdoun Bridge, with nothing behind me and nothing in front of me, to join people who had seized the pleasure of the moment in renouncing this life, in protest at what was happening in it and to it; suicide is an extreme moment of impotence, but it at least offers one the pleasure of having made the final decision.

There were lights on both sides of the bridge. They seemed more welcoming than before, as if they were obeying the souls that lived beside them and ordered them to celebrate a newcomer. But the night kept pouring in from every direction. If I decided to die, I would only be passing through the door by which I had entered. My father told me that his mother had given birth to him at daybreak, and fate had decreed that I should be born at the same time. So the morning was my appointment with that imminent moment.

I walked down the slope beside the bridge and went on until I reached the place where I had met Leila. There were some signs of people having been there, but what would induce poor people to seek shelter by a bridge in an area different from their own? Was it a coincidence that some people should flee an everyday death to a bridge, from the top of which some had chosen to end their lives?

I lay down, thinking of my brother 'Ahid, and Narda, and Leila, and the residents of the deserted house. I felt exhausted; but the voice dispersed my tiredness, arriving loaded with an echo, as if to leap over the bridge walls: "You make the prospect of suicide seem attractive, to hide your old feeling of impotence, Ibrahim!"

"I am not impotent—I am in fetters," I replied, as I angrily propped myself up.

"Chains are weakness; you seek oblivion because you are too weak to attack the things that constrain you."

"Even granted that what you say is correct, I have to tell you there is nothing worth rebelling for."

"But remember that you stole to revive those outcasts. You hung the bell, but now you are silencing it."

"I did what I could."

"Today you have adopted the persona of the Hungarian poet Attila József. You spent several months reading his poems, then you spent a few days looking at his image until you finally sat down at your desk and began write. But when you studied the episode of his suicide under the wheels of a train, you cried so much that it made your father curse you for what you were doing. But you didn't try to conquer your fear as Attila did. You fled from yourself by adopting the personas of characters you had come across in books. And whenever you had finished with one, you went on to another."

I got up and took a few steps away from the bridge, then went back. There was a shout inside me, ready to explode. The voice had stopped when I started to recite out loud something from a poem by Attila József:

> I know as children know
> That the happy man is the one who knows how to play
> There are many games I know
> For the truth may wilt
> And appearance remain.

I woke in the morning to the noise of cars and the echo of their horns. I looked around at the place and wondered how I had come to end up there. What had happened? I couldn't remember a thing. My throat was dry and my limbs ached. Once I realized that I was under the Abdoun Bridge, I began to recall the events of the previous night. I checked Facebook, and there were more posts about me, one leading to another. I was surprised to see that heroism was a central theme of what many people had written.

"I have made a hero of you."

The voice sounded angry, then it began to shout at me. "But heroism is a complete act; you have to complete it to win the medal!"

"You made a thief of me," I replied, my voice echoing around the walls of the bridge as the cars raced under it.

"The world moves on in a way I can do nothing about."

"Because you are useless, but you will see what I can do."

As the voice disappeared, I was struck with terror, for he would no doubt do something momentous, for which I would never forgive myself. I recalled the moment when Attila József decided to commit suicide. As I closed my eyes, his image gradually took shape in my mind's eye, and the words of his poems came from a distance in a quiet voice that grew louder and louder until it overwhelmed me. I walked slowly away from the bridge, up a slope, until I reached the edge which was crowded with traffic. A single step, then, separated me from release. I threw a quick glance around me as the soul of Attila József hovered in the sky of Ibrahim's soul—a clear space from which came the sounds of weeping and laughter, songs and poems. I took my phone from my pocket and wrote on Facebook:

"The criminal may be a victim, and your imaginations may make a hero of a victim." I took a picture of myself and posted it with what I had written. But I was surprised to find a new item circulating about the imminent demolition of a deserted house near the Third Circle.

———

It was nine in the morning when I left the taxi near the Third Circle and ran until I reached the house. The wall that had once stood in front of it had been demolished to expose the house. A large crowd had gathered to watch the bulldozer lift its giant hammer over the roof, the noise of the machine mingling with the clamor of people and cars and the sounds from other streets.

How could I tell them I had hidden things in this house that would make its residents something in this world? How could I tell them that I had devised a family for them, weddings, and a new life? Would they be convinced if I shouted. "All we want is something to heat the house. The frost is in its way; if we remain afraid, we will freeze, and our bodies will be drained of blood."

I saw Salam running and shouting as she made her way through the crowd, shouting "There are people inside the house—don't demolish it!" My belly swelled up more than ever before, and as it got bigger the skin gradually tore until I saw a child with the same features as mine emerge. It raced through the crowd, still attached to my belly by its umbilical cord, and then it started jumping on people's shoulders and heads until it reached the top of the bulldozer and screamed, in a voice that echoed all over the city, "Don't demolish the house!" But the hammer had already come down on the roof; the house collapsed, and thick dust flew into the air. As the bulldozer stopped, the driver turned off the engine, and the noise subsided, a strange silence filling the city as I looked at my belly, at Salam, Leila, and Narda, and a lot of people with silent faces.

I stood rooted to the spot, open-mouthed and looking in every direction, until someone took hold of me and quickly put me in handcuffs. I looked behind me and saw several policemen who were arresting me. One man pointed a TV camera at me, while another one spoke into a microphone as he described to the camera how the masked robber had been apprehended.

5
Ibrahim

(A Thread Linking Fantasy and Reality)

They took me to an officer's room, where a soldier sitting beside him examined my face carefully, as if to verify that the person in front of him was indeed the masked robber who had preoccupied so many people, or someone else.

"Mr. Ibrahim," he said, clasping his hands together, "you are charged with robbing two banks and a number of houses. The video recording of yesterday's incident confirms this, in addition to previous recordings in which your face did not appear,"

"Yes, I confess to those robberies."

The officer ordered the soldier to record my confession. Then he gave me a look to encourage me to make a new confession. "Mr. Ibrahim, you are also charged with the murders of your father, Jadallah al-Shamousi, 'Imad al-Ahmar, Iyad Nabil, and Ranad Mahmoud."

He took a notebook from a desk drawer and held it up so I could see it. "We searched your apartment yesterday and found this notebook, in which you have recorded the details of all the crimes you have committed—you call nightmares. Then your neighbor informed us she had seen you on the night when your father attempted suicide, and described how you pushed the chair and were the cause of his death."

Meanwhile, I had seen the child who had come out of my belly stand at the window outside. His face looked miserable, angry, and frustrated, with an expression I didn't understand. He looked at me with bloodshot eyes, then leaped into the air and through the window. Splinters of glass were scattered all over the place.

"You didn't kill them!" he shouted, standing on the officer's desk.

He was silent for a little as he began to breathe faster, then he started to leap around the room from side to side, extremely angry and tense. He was stubborn as someone with nothing to lose. My limbs started to shake, my throat went dry, and I felt the same headache. I didn't know what he was going to do, so I felt more afraid than ever as my sobs and my shouting mingled with his. It was a difficult and ambiguous moment, which made me feel some compassion for him—or perhaps it was another emotion, like sympathy with a being like him who had kept me company for several years. I got up and walked toward him; I would have liked to hug him to calm him, but his voice burst out loud, mingling with all the other voices, then changed into a dreadful ringing sound that put me into something almost like a faint, through which I saw the shadows of hands handcuffing me and preventing me from moving at all. I heard collections of voices urging me to be calm, in the midst of which was a voice calling a doctor urgently.

———

A silent wall clock was showing five in the morning, but no nurse had come yet to give me the daily injection in my backside that would knock me out and sedate me. My memory had lost many things as a result of the shock treatment they had treated me with for a month in the hospital for nervous diseases; but the early morning hours gave me a unique clarity and powerful opportunity to recall what the electricity had knocked out of my head, and what I had heard from Narda and Leila. So now I am opening a final page of the notebook:

"I write despite my conviction that my writing will not let me escape from the place I have arrived although I am certain that it will repair my dark abyss so I can find peace. I have poured out everything on the white pages of a notebook I have found to be the best present Narda has given me. She comes twice a week to visit me, and sits with me for two hours, talking to me about everything. She even told me that the store that has taken the place of the Bookseller's Kiosk is selling drugs, like the other stores belonging to Iyad Nabil. Narda, who gave up the idea of suicide that year when she saw a boat out at sea returning alone to dry land, realized then that loss is not to be confronted with death but with life. Today is her visiting day; I will give her this notebook, as I gave her the other notebooks. But I am not sure I am persuaded to give her the notebook in which I recorded the nightmares in which I saw my father pushing himself off the chair, or Anisa's son killing 'Imad al-Ahmar, or Yusuf al-Sammak killing Iyad Nabil, or Leila killing Ranad Mahmoud. I won't do that because we must keep quiet when fantasy is mingled with reality."